WE'LL ALWAYS HAVE VENICE

LEONIE MACK

Boldwood

First published in Great Britain in 2022 by Boldwood Books Ltd.

Cover Design: Alice Moore Design

Cover Photography: Shutterstock

A CIP catalogue record for this book is available from the British Library.

Paperback ISBN 978-1-80162-395-7

Large Print ISBN 978-1-80162-394-0

Hardback ISBN 978-1-80162-393-3

Ebook ISBN 978-1-80162-396-4

Kindle ISBN 978-1-80162-397-1

Audio CD ISBN 978-1-80162-388-9

MP3 CD ISBN 978-1-80162-389-6

Digital audio download ISBN 978-1-80162-391-9

Boldwood Books Ltd
23 Bowerdean Street
London SW6 3TN
www.boldwoodbooks.com

For Sam, the original and best 'friends to lovers' romance of mine

'...the last few eventful years, fraught with change to the face of the whole earth, have been more fatal in their influence on Venice than the five hundred that preceded them...'

— JOHN RUSKIN, THE STONES OF VENICE,
VOLUME II, CH. I, SEC. II

AUTHOR'S NOTE:

Readers may notice a deviation from the usual Italian spelling in many words used throughout the book. I have taken pains to reflect the language spoken in Venice by the people who call the city their ancestral home. The Veneto dialect (or dialects, as they vary by area within Veneto) retains elements from the time before Venice was conquered by the Hapsburgs in the late eighteenth century and was its own Republic, covering parts of Italy and Croatia. What used to be a distinct language has now changed and mixed with standard Italian over time. It is not taught in schools and there is no official spelling, but it remains a source of regional pride. In case readers do wonder at the strange spelling, the explanation is that I wanted to bring you some words with the distinct flavour of Venice.

PROLOGUE

'Saffron, will you marry me?'

Norah froze. This wasn't happening in reality, right? A relative stranger asking her mother to marry him. On Christmas Day, during the gift giving. No way.

She must have been back in the hospital, on a cocktail of medications, imagining the middle-aged man on his knee in her sister's living room. A twinge of pain shot down her bad leg on cue.

'Neal, I – I'm so happy! I'd love to marry you!'

Unfortunately, the passionate smooch Saffron smacked on Neal's lips, complete with kissy noises, was not a hallucination.

Norah met her sister's equally horrified gaze over the tops of their bobbing heads. If Didi was seeing this too, it had to be real. With a whump, the feelings hit her all at once: doubt, fear, annoyance and, worst of all, jealousy.

Saffron, who'd rarely kept a boyfriend for longer than a phone contract, was slipping a diamond onto her finger, while Norah had committed everything to Andrej and all she had left was the taste of disappointment, still sour after six months.

Should she be happy for Saffron? Could she fake it? Was she a terrible daughter for doubting Neal would last, despite the diamond? She dreaded the prospect of attending a wedding. She hadn't been formally engaged to Andrej, but they'd both pictured it in their futures – until she'd faced the challenge of learning to walk again.

He'd been gone before she'd even woken up from surgery. Maybe Saffron and Neal did have a chance. What did Norah know?

But who the heck was Neal and how well did Saffron know him after a whirlwind romance on a cruise? He was mild-mannered and polite, and he'd bought an enormous rock for a woman who'd previously only worn amber and crystals. And he apparently did public displays of affection. Ew.

Her sister looked green. Didi was the sister who'd always had everything together. She had a good job she loved and owned her own flat in London, while Norah had half a PhD in Marine Biology and a pair of titanium rods screwed into her spine. But even Didi looked shaken by this Christmas development in their lives.

The lovers finally pulled apart and Saffron turned to wink at Didi. *Oh, God, no.* Norah cringed, but Saffron had another unwelcome wink for her younger daughter. 'I think I'm just about ready for marriage, at sixty-three!' she said gleefully.

'Congratulations, Mum,' Didi managed, her voice gravelly.

Saffron patted her on the knee. 'Someone needs to show you how it's done, sweetheart,' she said.

Norah choked, watching Didi's pallor change from green to white. She knew Didi hated the hints about getting a boyfriend and Saffron had no right to judge, after the example she'd set her daughters. It was one of the reasons Norah had been so happy with Andrej: she'd pictured them together forever, in contrast to her mother's revolving door of boyfriends.

She stood, her brain whirring into gear as she grabbed her cane. She'd drag Didi into the kitchen on the pretext of doing the dishes.

Then she remembered that Didi had been slaving away all afternoon in the kitchen.

She glanced at Didi's guest – an Italian artist called Piero, who appeared to have invited himself. Whatever the weird vibes between him and Didi, he could at least make himself useful.

'I'm going to do the dishes,' Norah announced. She caught Piero's eye and tipped her head in Didi's direction.

He caught on quickly. 'I have a... long walk back to my hotel. I... got a little lost on the way. Perhaps you can show me back to the main road, Didi?'

Norah reached the relative safety of the kitchen and released her breath as slowly as she could. She set her cane against the wall and rolled up her sleeves. She didn't want to deal with the soap opera in the living room today.

She was sick of the shocks, the loneliness and the helplessness. She needed to step out on her own and work out how to deal with her new life, without her mother's drama and even without the safety net of her sister's care. She needed to accept that the old Norah, the one who was going to marry Andrej and share a glittering career of rational scientific inquiry, was gone. She would try to get to know the new Norah.

For that, she needed a change of scenery. She just had to find somewhere to go.

1

FIVE MONTHS LATER...

It was the first day of the rest of her life and she was going to a bloody wedding.

Norah stood in her finery – the only dress she'd brought in her luggage for her internship – and waited for her new boss. She was here to bury herself in work, to study the unique ecosystem of the Venice lagoon and to forget about the disaster of her personal life, but even here, in the long foyer, the 'portego' of a Venetian palazzo, the past year haunted her.

The eyes of a maiden in a tapestry on the wall – yes, there was an actual mediaeval tapestry on the wall – followed her as she wandered the tiled portego, clutching her cane. The Greek marble bust seemed to look through her with his sightless eyes. The cherubs in the corners of an enormous tarnished mirror were whispering behind their hands about her and wiggling their little bottoms. They hung from the frame precariously, as though, any minute now, she'd hear a crack and a little figure would fall onto the black-and-white tiles.

A grand but worn marble staircase led to the upper floors,

including Norah's tiny studio apartment underneath the aging beams of the roof – her home for the summer. The apartment was cramped and the ceiling was low, but at least it didn't have creepy décor that appeared to watch her every move.

Worst of all was the damn bird.

It was a bas-relief phoenix in an elaborate marble portico over the door. A phoenix. Of course there was a bloody phoenix. And she knew it would haunt her for the next ten weeks, making her think that she might still make something of her life, that Norah York could rise from the ashes of hurt and failure and face her future. Norah Phoenix York, to copy precisely from her birth certificate.

She'd always thought Saffron must have been high when she'd filled out the forms registering her birth. Now it felt as though her mother had planned all of this, giving her a ridiculous middle name in a conspiracy to make her believe there would always be hope for the future.

She wasn't ready for hope. Bitterness had been her good friend this past year. And this 'new start' was a poorly paid internship at an environmental NGO, not the prestigious PhD programme she'd left behind. But at least she was out of London, out of the clutches of her loved-up sister and her mother, the bridezilla.

Instead, she stood in a Venetian palazzo, the ancestral home of Emanuela Delfini, world-renowned biologist, philanthropist and sustainability campaigner – who obviously struggled with interior decorating.

She scowled at the phoenix. Its beak and the tips of its wings looked as though they'd once been gilded, but there was only a patina remaining, a ghost of gold. Perhaps this phoenix was approaching five hundred years old and was about to go up in a puff of smoke. Good luck to it in its next life.

A dark portrait of a menacing-looking woman with a stiff lace collar was watching her, now, as though she were whispering, 'For the crime of being young and naïve and thinking you are in love, you are cursed to attend weddings endlessly! Mwahaha.' At least she was now only one of those three things – although she certainly felt older than her twenty-five years after the past twelve months of pain and heartache.

'Buongiorno, cara.' Her host Emanuela – or 'Manu', as she'd told Norah to call her – swept into the portego. She clasped Norah's shoulders and kissed her on both cheeks, which seemed a little familiar after less than a day, especially in combination with the 'cara', which she thought meant 'dear' or something that sounded similarly patronising to Norah's English ears. But at least Manu was friendlier than her house.

Manu had neat dark hair clipped back at the nape of her neck with a tortoiseshell clasp. She was as elegant as her aristocratic background and her forty-something years and just looking at her made Norah stand up straighter. She wore a flowing dress, simple, but stylish with an asymmetrical neckline and three-quarter sleeves.

Norah patted her hair, rolled up as neatly as she could in some kind of chignon. She'd never had the patience for her long hair, but Andrej had liked it – a feminine touch, he'd said. Hindsight made her wonder if he'd meant that she was too much of a tomboy, but she reminded herself crossly that wondering wasn't doing her any favours now.

She smoothed the A-line of her frock. Manu had said nothing about a wedding in the stack of materials she'd emailed in preparation for Norah's stay.

'You look perfect,' Manu assured her. 'Although...' She glanced critically at Norah's shoes. Norah had put on the pretty slingbacks she'd inherited from Didi even though the low heel made her feel wobbly. Looking at Manu's fabric slippers made from thick embroidered silk, she wished she'd stuck with her comfy espadrilles.

'Oh, it'll be all right,' said Manu with a dismissive wave. 'Come. Let's go catch our boat.'

'What kind of wedding is it, anyway?' Norah asked as they made their way down the stone steps to the ground floor. Manu had assured her she was invited, but had said little else. Norah hoped there would at least be decent food.

'You'll see,' she said with a twinkle in her eye.

Manu swung the door open and Norah jumped. She couldn't be certain whether it was because of the suddenness of the movement or the creepy bronze door knocker that looked like an angry demigod in mid-yawn.

They stepped out into the cool, shaded alley at the back of the house. There was bright sunshine somewhere high above them, but it didn't penetrate the alley at this time of the morning. Manu set a brisk pace through the labyrinth of Santa Croce, past mask workshops, under an archway bearing a skull and crossbones and around so many blind corners, they would have collided with at least six tourists if the hour had been any later.

Before Norah realised how far they'd come, they'd reached the Rialto Bridge. Manu steered to the right, avoiding the little stands selling all manner of tat, and they walked along the stone balustrade and over the Grand Canal.

The air was still fresh with dawn, although the sun came up early in mid-May. The canal shone golden in the long rays, sending glittering ripples over the palazzi along the canal. The buildings were red and pink and terracotta, with white detailing and awnings in bright red or green. Boats bobbed gently, although there was little breeze.

Norah was struck by the immensity of the sky. Cottony clouds hung lazily over the city, but it was otherwise wide and blue and stretched in all directions, as though Venice sat on clouds, rather than sandbanks and ancient tree-trunks.

It was a stunning setting for a wedding. The thought made Norah scowl.

From the Rialto Bridge, it didn't take long to reach the heart of the city, the Piazza San Marco. Norah's steps faltered when she walked out from under the arches into the famous square, but it had nothing to do with her cane or her damaged nerves. It was the sudden shock of being here, in *Venice*.

She'd tried to tell herself she was excited about her work: the lagoon, the unique geographical and environmental challenges. But it was impossible to think about algae when she was confronted with the overpowering golden grandeur of the Basilica di San Marco and the countless arches, hewn from bright white stone.

She could stare at it all day, watching the figures and creatures on the façade come to life.

'Are you coming, Norah? The basilica won't leave without you, but our boat might.'

She shook herself and hurried to catch up, feeling sluggish in comparison to her lively hostess. They bustled through the smaller square, the piazzetta, past the pale façade of the Doge's Palace, to where a crowd was gathered at the edge of the lagoon. But the crowd was nothing in comparison to the flotilla of boats dotted across the basin. There were hundreds of them, from tiny two-man craft to larger vessels with rowing crews of twenty or more, all wearing matching striped shirts and holding their long oars. Aside from the sound of jovial voices, the basin was silent. No motors, only hundreds of oarsmen.

A gilded barge was docked in front of the crowd, decked with long, thin flags in red and gold, and in the bow stood a band in mediaeval costumes of red velvet, holding bugles.

Norah recovered from her confusion quickly enough to snap a few pictures. She didn't often regret deleting all of her social media accounts after the accident, but she would have enjoyed posting pictures of this event. Was this maritime fanfare normal for a Venetian wedding?

A priest in a black cassock and a purple silk stole greeted Manu with kisses on the cheek, as did a man in a grey suit and a sash in the colours of the Italian flag. He looked a little old to be the groom, but what did Norah know?

'Where's the bride?' Norah asked when Manu returned to her side. Manu gave her a smile that suggested she was enjoying a joke at Norah's expense, which didn't help Norah's mood.

She trailed Manu to another barge moored nearby, with no gilding, no trumpeters and no red velvet. It had the shape of a gondola, with a raised prong on either end, one of them bearing a viciously jagged metal comb, but it was much larger. Four wooden dining chairs stood at the stern, looking rickety and out of place behind the team of rowers. The boat bobbed and tipped in the waves, but the rowers stood in place, their feet planted.

Manu stepped on gracefully and took her seat while Norah shuffled closer with a deep breath. It could have been worse for her first time in a boat since the accident. They would be slowly bobbing across the canal, not roaring off. She could swallow her nerves in front of her boss. The phoenix was right: she had no choice but to face her fears.

Norah stepped out – only for the boat to rock at precisely that moment, and her foot slipped. Stuck with one foot in the boat and the other on the pier, she threw her hands out for anything that would stop her falling. The nearest object was a rower.

She grabbed fistfuls of his shirt and hung on as the boat tipped and swayed. For a second, she hung out over the water, staring into the murky turquoise of the lagoon.

She dimly heard Manu's cry of alarm, but it was an indication of Norah's mental state that all she could muster at the prospect of a drenching in the lagoon was a cynical groan. She hated weddings and it seemed the feeling was mutual.

2

The rower Norah was holding on to was surprisingly solid. He staggered, but remained upright so she could claw her way up until she had both feet on the deck. She let go of his shirt hesitantly and plonked her backside into the seat.

That was when she remembered her cane. She cursed and glanced around for it, expecting to see it sinking into the lagoon, but, small mercies, the thing could float. It bobbed innocuously a foot or two away from the boat.

She reached for it instinctively, but a hand closed around her wrist and a sharp voice reached her ears, although she couldn't understand the words. She glanced up at the rower and her mind blanked.

Even if he'd been speaking English, she wouldn't have understood a word. She could only stare. He was beautiful. There was no other word for those warm brown eyes, thick lashes and sculpted features.

Norah swallowed.

'I'm sorry, what?' she murmured.

He switched to English. 'I'll get it.' He turned away before she could thank him, lifting his long oar to fetch her cane. In comparison to the sleek polished wood of his oar, her medical-issue aluminium cane looked stumpy and cumbersome, but she sighed with relief when she held it in her hand again.

'Thank you, grasie,' she said, trying not to stare at his cheekbones.

'Gnente,' he said with an easy smile.

'Buongiorno, Gianluca,' Manu said, rising from her chair.

His smile tightened and he hesitated before turning to her. 'Ciao, Manu.' He kissed both of her cheeks.

'I didn't know you'd be part of our company today,' she said, but his only response was half a shrug. 'This is Norah,' Manu continued. His gaze flickered over her again, taking in her dress and heels.

She held out her hand, 'Ciao, come xeła?' she said carefully. She'd asked her sister's boyfriend – the Italian artist who'd witnessed the debacle at Christmas – to teach her a few phrases in Venetian dialect and, when the rower's smile widened, she was glad she had.

'Stago ben,' he said, inclining his head. He took her hand and shook it once. It was long enough for Norah to notice he had calluses. And very nice hands. 'I'm Gianluca.'

'Norah is my student, the one you'll be taking around the lagoon in your sanpierota.'

He froze, staring at Manu. Norah looked between them in confusion. The weird vibes were impossible to miss. Given her temporary boss's poise and beauty, Norah wouldn't have been surprised to hear that Manu had had a gorgeous, younger lover, who was apparently Norah's tour guide for her sampling trips around the lagoon – but he didn't look too happy about it.

'That booking was from you?'

'I thought you realised,' Manu said with a careful smile.

'It was under the name "Signora Scienza". You could have just booked under "Delfini" if you wanted me to know.'

Manu shrugged, but Norah thought she looked a little sheepish. 'Who else would make a booking for "Madame Science"?' she said lightly. Norah snorted.

'I thought it was a joke. You're lucky I didn't delete the email.'

'You should take payment at the time of booking,' she chided him. 'One day your calendar will be full.'

'One day,' he said with a huff.

A shout went up over the lagoon and the sound of drumming made Norah jump. Gianluca's hand landed heavily on her shoulder. 'I'm not going to fall off,' she insisted and he glanced at her cane. 'Truly. I'm capable of sitting in a seat on a boat,' she said tightly.

'Scuxa,' he said, those eyes much too warm. He was hospitable and polite *and* beautiful. It only served to remind Norah how grumpy and bitter she still was, nearly a year after the accident.

He turned and settled his oar into the bracket on the side of the boat near him, then called out to the crew, who followed suit. And with another shout, the boat pushed off into the basin, oars cutting through the water.

The wind whipped up immediately and Norah had to force herself to stop clutching the seat. A blue jet ski emblazoned with the word 'Polizia' zoomed past and she flinched, the roar of the motor taking her back to the day of her accident. She released a slow, measured breath.

'Are you all right?' Manu asked and Norah nodded stiffly. 'I didn't realise you walked with a cane. If you need help with anything...'

'I'm fine,' Norah insisted, because that was what the doctors had told her. She jumped again when the bugle players started up. 'Is this a typical Venetian wedding, then?' she asked, squinting at the fleet of boats, flags flapping in the breeze or trailing their soggy tips in the water.

Gianluca glanced back, one thick eyebrow raised as he looked at Manu. She blushed. 'When I said this was a wedding... it's not a wedding like you're thinking. You'll see.'

They followed the golden barge in the direction of the Lido di Venezia, one of the narrow islands that separated the lagoon from the Adriatic Sea. The crew rowed in rhythm and Norah tilted her head to study them as they pushed on their oars from a standing position. Norah felt as though she should be draped in silks and furs and gold, to have a matching crew of oarsmen hauling her through the lagoon on a giant gondola. Although, they weren't all oars*men*. She counted three women among the crew.

Their pace was modest and the boats crawled through the lagoon as the May sunshine gathered strength, making Norah wish she'd brought her sunglasses.

When the boats approached the Lido, they bunched together, bobbing haphazardly. A crowd was gathered on the shore, cheering and applauding the approach of the gilded vessel, but they weren't dressed for a wedding. No one appeared to be dressed for a wedding – except Norah.

Voices in Italian – or Venetian dialect, she wasn't sure – sounded from a speaker and, with a sudden lurch, the rowers lifted their oars out of the water and held them vertically. Norah gripped her seat, staring at the water dripping onto Gianluca as he held up his oar in a Venetian salute, his back straight. He had shoulders for miles. Nice one, Manu. Being single and in her forties sounded pretty good if there was a guy like that in Norah's future.

'If that's the groom, where's the bride?' Norah asked Manu.

'The groom is the sindaco, the mayor, on his official boat, La Serenissima, which is built to look like the Doge's bucintoro from history. The bride...' said Manu, pausing dramatically, 'is the sea.'

Norah blinked and then burst into laughter. She clapped a hand over her mouth when she noticed how the sound rang out over the solemn occasion she was witnessing on the breezy lagoon. A female rower shot her a look over her shoulder. But really, someone was marrying the sea? In a fancy gilded boat, with a bunch of buglers in tunics? Why was she the only one laughing?

She squinted to watch the mayor take a small object from a velvet cushion and toss it into the sea. It landed with a subdued plop, dragging its waving ribbon under the water after it. 'The wedding ring?' she guessed, with a snort of laughter.

'Exactly,' said Manu. 'It's called the sposalizio del mare, the marriage to the sea. It's been performed in Venice for over a thousand years, off and on, around Ascension Day – the Festa della Sensa. And afterwards we celebrate with regattas and mass.'

As Norah imagined the ring slowly sinking through the cloudy water, pulling its ribbon, she could almost believe there would be a ghostly face tracking its progress with longing eyes: the spirit of the lagoon, wishing she could take human form and consummate her love for the city. Norah had to stifle another laugh.

Up went the oars again and Norah ducked instinctively. Those things were more like lances than oars, long and sleek and made of solid wood. She almost expected the boats to line up facing each other and perform a weird aquatic tournament where they tried to knock each other out. It would be a fitting celebration for a wacky wedding ceremony between an imaginary sea naiad and an allegorical city.

The trumpets started up again, and the sound of drums echoed around the lagoon, whipped up in the wind. Manu stood and Norah followed suit, gripping her cane. She applauded as best she could, but the lurching of the boat was proving that she'd lost her sea legs in nearly a year on land.

She glanced up to find Gianluca watching her, but he looked

away quickly. She sighed. She must look like a complete liability. If she'd been given the task of ferrying herself around the lagoon, she wouldn't be looking forward to it, either.

But she was here to collect samples and further Manu's research, not to wallow in self-pity and certainly not to check out handsome men. She would do her job, no matter how much her body and mind conspired against her.

* * *

Gianluca stood on the pontoon with his hands behind his back an hour or two later, as a choir sang in front of the brick church of San Nicolò on the Lido. Winning the Regata della Sensa with his crew had been good for his pride, which always seemed to suffer when he conversed with Manu, but it had also resulted in his awkward position, facing the crowd, while they all waited for the song to finally finish.

The breeze pricked him. In mid-May, it wasn't warm enough to be standing in the Adriatic winds, soaked in sweat. He needed to change and then he'd have to get back into the gondola and row Manu back to the old city – Manu and her new wide-eyed intern.

Manu was holding court near the mayor, the intern standing awkwardly by in her flirty dress, her long hair slowly coming out of its knot. She looked too young to be a graduate intern, and kind of insubstantial.

He'd have to check she could swim. It wasn't any of his business why she walked with a cane, but if she couldn't swim, she'd have to wear a life jacket. The lagoon wasn't deep, but he couldn't afford to take those risks when his second business hadn't even got off the ground.

He eyed Manu. Why had she booked *him*? She could have hired anyone. She must have known he needed the money, but that almost made it worse.

The choir fell silent and the crowd cheered the end of the song resoundingly. With unnecessary fanfare, the mayor presented Gianluca, his best friend, Pino, and the rest of their four-man rowing crew with the winners' flags. He grinned at his friend Chiara in the crowd as she whistled and cheered. She'd won the women's event, as she always did, and then screamed her lungs out for the crew from their rowing club.

They posed for photos in their striped shirts and then he was free to leap off the pontoon and join the crowd for a rousing chorus of 'Viva Venezia', which sounded more like a football chant from his rowing club friends than the folky chorus sung by the grey-haired gondoliers for the benefit of the mayor.

The intern – Norah was her name – was taking photos of the ritual with a baffled smile. He could imagine it all looked strange to an outsider: the boater hats, the white embroidered robes of the priests, the mandolin and the bunch of sweaty rowing hooligans crooning in the background.

After the crowd dispersed, heading either for the market or into the church for mass, he took his bag from Chiara and fished out a fresh shirt, peeling off the sweaty one with one arm. He was about to tug the clean shirt over his head, when he caught sight of Norah, staring at him. She stood frozen, her phone up as though she'd been in the middle of taking a photo – when he'd stripped off.

Ah. This could be a problem.

He pulled his shirt over his head and shoved his arms into the sleeves. She hadn't looked away, yet. His skin prickled and it wasn't from the wind.

He caught her eye deliberately, keeping his brow low. He didn't want to embarrass her, but he also didn't want her to make assumptions about him. He was used to being watched and looked at and judged by a crowd of tourists who thought his home was a theme park and his job just for show, but he couldn't handle the assumptions that, because he was single, he would know how to show a visitor a good time, no strings attached. He had strings. Big ones.

But when she met his gaze, she didn't look embarrassed. She looked... annoyed, as though it were his fault she'd been staring at him. How strange.

He approached and finally a tinge of pink touched her cheeks, but he didn't speak to her. Instead, he touched Manu's arm lightly to get her attention. She turned to him with a smile that he always imagined looked a little pained.

'What time would you like to go back? I'll be in the market with the others,' he said in dialect. Manu preferred to speak standard Italian, but he was stubborn like that.

Manu grasped his hand and he stared with misgiving at the unexpected gesture. 'Gianluca, won't you take Norah with you? She'll be so bored in mass.' Norah looked warily between them.

'Okay,' he said, switching to English, as Manu had done. He jerked his head in the direction of the stalls stretching along the waterfront. 'Come.' Norah's expression suggested he'd been unnecessarily abrupt, but he was wary of Manu's motives for involving him.

'Ciao, bella! Who's this?' Pino asked with a grin when Gianluca approached. 'New friend?'

'This is Norah. She's working for Manu for... how long?'

She shook hands with Pino. 'Ten weeks,' she said. 'I didn't realise Italians actually said "ciao, bella" for real.'

'Ciao, bella, that's amore, la dolce vita, capisci? Welcome to Venezia, Norah. I'm Pino. You want to ride on a gondola, you come to me, okay?'

'You're a real gondolier?' she asked. 'Not that I imagine there are any fake ones.'

'Only in Las Vegas,' Pino quipped. 'But the gondoliers are much better looking in Venice.'

Gianluca couldn't quite muster a smile. He was curiously unwilling to join in with the habitual banter. If Norah was Manu's protégé, then she wouldn't fit in with his old friends. But there was something about her droll smile that he liked, despite his reservations.

'Chiara is a gondoliera, too,' Gianluca explained.

'But they won't let me work as one officially and I'm not as good-looking as Pino,' Chiara said with a dry look for her friend. 'So he's right: you want a gondola, you pick him.'

'Got it,' Norah said. 'But I thought... I thought Gianluca was going to be taking me out into the lagoon.'

'Ái brava, yes. If you want to go out into the lagoon, then Lulu's your man,' Pino said. He pinched Gianluca on the biceps, making him yelp and scowl at his friend.

'Lulu? Is that really your nickname?' Norah asked.

'Gianluca is fine,' he said flatly.

Her eyes were bright with amusement. 'Aye, aye, Captain... Lulu,' she snorted. He couldn't help it. He smiled back.

Pino laughed. 'We'll keep you.' He slung an arm over her shoulder and steered her in the direction of the market. Gianluca shook his head and followed slowly. She was in Venice for the summer and then she would leave. He understood better than most the importance of keeping his distance.

3

'Mum?' Norah paused on the last step of the scuffed marble staircase, holding her phone to her ear. Manu had invited her for aperitivo, drinks and antipasti, after a busy week getting to know the lab on the mainland, and preparing equipment for her first sampling expedition the next day. After a week of eating mainly Pot Noodle either in the lab or her apartment in the palazzo, she couldn't wait for some proper food. Although, to be honest, she'd loved the fact that no one was there to tell her off for her student habits. She'd felt a bit more like her old self – except she didn't, because her old self came as a pair with Andrej and was gone for good.

'Sweetheart!' Saffron's exclamation would have echoed embarrassingly around the walls of the palazzo, if it hadn't been on the end of a phone call. 'I'm glad I caught you.'

'I'm likely to be free on a Friday night,' she muttered.

'No handsome gondolier sweeping you off your feet, yet?' Saffron asked.

'I did meet a gondolier, actually,' Norah said, glad her mother couldn't see her poor attempt to keep a straight face. Pino, with his hipster beard and poor-taste jokes, wasn't exactly a romantic hero, and besides, he'd been open about his homosexuality, but Saffron didn't need to know that. 'A lovely guy called Pino.' She took the last step and approached the enormous wooden door that led into the portego. One leaf stood open, but the other was bolted shut, looking creepy in the insufficient light with its dips and pockmarked carvings.

'Marvellous!' Saffron's voice lifted a further notch. 'You'll have someone to bring to the wedding, perhaps!'

Norah nearly choked. She leaned heavily on the door. 'Have you set a date? Is it that soon?'

'Oh, no, sweetheart! Next year, I think. But I do worry about you, coming to your mother's wedding alone.'

That was her fate, wasn't it? *Coming to her mother's wedding alone.* But once that was done, she could happily focus on her research career and be single and elegant like Manu – or as best she could without the inherited wealth.

'But I understand,' Saffron continued, although Norah was pretty sure she never would. 'You're not ready for another long-term relationship.' Saffron wasn't given to understatement, but she achieved it then in spades. 'Just a fling, then, with your gondolier?'

'Something like that.'

'So, sweetheart, I wanted to give you a quick call about something important. You know how much trouble I've been having deciding on a theme for the wedding,' Saffron continued and Norah breathed out. Nothing important, then. 'Well, your photos from last weekend, combined with everything Didi has told me, have convinced me that I simply *must* get married in Venice.'

Norah blinked. 'Get married in Venice?' she parroted. 'Is that even legal? What about expense?'

'Don't worry about that. Neal is... quite well off, you know. He's completely supportive of celebrating in style and we both loved the city when we visited in January – our first mini-honeymoon together. We'll book out one of those charming palazzos and everyone can arrive by gondola.'

'Mum, I'm not sure you understand just how expensive that would be. Booking out a whole palazzo?'

Saffron hesitated. '*You* might not understand just how... rich Neal is,' she said carefully. Her tone was unusually sober.

'He'd have to be a multimillionaire at least to be able to afford what you're thinking,' Norah pointed out.

'At least,' Saffron murmured.

Norah's jaw dropped. 'Neal is a *millionaire*?' She'd never met one before – Manu probably excluded – so she couldn't have been expected to know they could look like ordinary balding men who wore loud bow ties. 'I had no idea. I've never even heard his last name.'

'It's Brunswick. Do you think I should change mine? I thought I'd been Saffron York for too many years to manage changing it, but Neal and Saffron Brunswick does have a certain ring to it.'

'Neal and Saffron Brunswick,' Norah repeated dumbly, letting her forehead drop to the rough wood of the door. None of this felt real.

'This is where you come in, sweetheart.' *Oh, no.* Norah was regretting this already and she hadn't agreed to anything yet. 'I know you're busy with your work, but if you could go to a few wedding venues, talk to them, get a feel for the place and recommend five or six to me, that would be wonderful, darling. Then when I come to visit, I won't have to start from scratch. There must be so many lovely palazzos.'

'You want me to... visit wedding venues for you,' Norah repeated, her voice weak and her blood rushing in her ears. Had Saffron realised that was pretty much her worst nightmare? Did she think it was funny to send poor Norah on a wedding-related errand? Or did she think it would be character-building, a chance to remind herself that she'd been wrong about Andrej?

'Just think of the fun it will be! You get to picture all these different weddings and report back!'

No, Saffron hadn't realised. Norah couldn't speak for a moment, she was so frustrated. She stepped through the door into the portego, her mind racing. 'Mum, I just don't think I'll have t—'

She froze, her gaze flitting between the two figures standing underneath the grim portrait of the woman with the stiff lace collar.

When Manu spoke, she said the last thing Norah expected. 'I can help you draw up a list of venues for your mother.' Norah opened her mouth to reply but she couldn't begin to think of what to say. 'And you're most certainly welcome to take the time out to do this.' Beside her stood Gianluca, still as the marble bust and just as sculpted, watching warily.

'Seriously, you don't have to say—' Remembering the phone call, she cut herself off. 'Sorry, Mum, I'm talking to my boss.'

'Oh, your boss! I'm sorry, sweetheart. I can talk to you about this later.'

'I mean it, Norah. I'd be happy to help... plan a wedding,' Manu said. The tilt of Gianluca's brow at that statement was eloquent, but Norah couldn't interpret it.

'It's highly unprofessional,' Norah murmured.

'Don't worry about that. You're a guest as well. I'll help you gather some ideas.'

'Er, thank you?' Norah said, her voice high.

'I'll go now,' Saffron said over the line. 'Keep me posted on the gondolier.'

Norah couldn't stop her eyes from swerving to Gianluca. His hair hung over his forehead in a dark wave and those cheekbones looked divine in the shadowy light of the glass chandelier. Manu clutched a hand to his forearm in an odd gesture that Norah interpreted as proprietary. He pulled his arm back in discomfort. Saffron had hung onto some of her boyfriends like that – and some of them had been nearly as young as Gianluca. Urgh.

Norah disconnected the call with a rushed farewell. 'I'm so sorry about that,' she blurted out. 'You don't have to help. I'll just tell my mother I can't, I'm too busy. I'm here to work, after all.'

'No!' Manu insisted, a little too strongly. 'I'm not paying you enough for you to ignore your mother's wishes. And tell her she's welcome to stay here if she comes to visit. Space is something I have a lot of.'

Gianluca shifted uncomfortably. He clutched the handle of a shopping trolley bag and Norah wondered why he was there. Perhaps Manu had invited him to dinner?

'I'll put together a list of venues for you to start with,' Manu said with a firm nod. 'But for now, Gianluca needs to know what you are taking tomorrow.'

Right. Tomorrow. Her day out on a boat with a hot man. A day full of *sampling*, she reminded herself. That was why she was here. 'I packed up the sampling array downstairs.'

'I noticed that. It should fit.'

'*Should* fit?' she said in alarm. 'I can't do my job without that equipment.'

'Then perhaps Manu should have hired a motorboat,' Gianluca said firmly, but not unkindly.

'It's not a motorboat?' she asked. 'How's it powered?' She pictured a high-tech craft with solar panels and an electric motor.

'It's not. Powered,' he explained. He glanced at Manu. 'You wanted an eco-friendly mode of transport. Manu booked... me.' Norah's gaze slid to his muscular arms. 'If you want to get all the way out to Torcello tomorrow, I'll have to get the boat to Murano tonight.'

'We're... *rowing* to Torcello?'

'*I'm* rowing *you* to Torcello. You can't get into the salt marshes in a larger vessel anyway.'

She thought guiltily of her sampling array – a plastic crate filled with tubes and stoppers and scrapers and anything she might need to bring her algae into the lab – and the essential, but heavy vacuum pump. She was making him transport it with nothing more than sweat and muscle.

'We'll have to leave early for the colma de aqua, the high tide, then the magra de aqua, the low tide, will be just after lunch. I'll meet you here at five-thirty and we'll take the vaporetto to Murano to collect the boat.'

'Five-thirty?' she cried.

His only response was a measured nod. 'Can you swim?'

'Of course I can,' she insisted – not very well, any more, between the stiffness in her back and her dodgy leg, but she could keep her head up.

'Good. I only needed to know... for safety. Is there anything else I should take now that we can't bring on the vaporetto tomorrow?'

She shook her head. 'Just the sampling equipment. I'll bring the vacuum pump and chamber with me.' She couldn't leave Manu's expensive equipment out on a boat overnight.

'Se vedemo, I'll see you tomorrow, then.' He gave Norah a polite smile and turned to kiss Manu's cheeks.

Manu clutched his upper arm. 'Won't you stay for aperitivo? There's plenty of light to get out to Murano.'

He shook his head, making Norah wonder again if she was interrupting something important between them. 'After I get back from Murano, I have to go to see Nòna. I usually take her shopping on a Saturday, so...'

Norah smiled, imagining this tall, gorgeous man standing solicitously with his stooping grey-haired grandmother and carrying her purchases. Add a kitten and he'd go viral in a heartbeat.

'Oh,' Manu said, her voice hollow. 'Pass on my greetings.'

'I will,' he said. Norah wasn't imagining the stiffness between the two of them. Had they recently broken up? That could explain the vibes. It was probably best that Norah didn't ask, as curious as she was about Manu's life. Gianluca turned back to Norah, his expression faintly grim. 'Until tomorrow.' She nodded. 'Wear a hat. And sun cream. It's not summer, yet, but the sun can still be strong.'

'Of course,' she responded. Was he making assumptions about her because of one wobble on the boat a week ago? Or because of her cane? Or was she being oversensitive?

She inwardly sighed as she watched him go. What did it matter what he thought of her? She should have learned a year ago that other people's opinions of her were completely out of her control. She'd do her job and prove she was capable. He didn't need to be her friend.

* * *

Norah didn't think of herself as particularly chatty, but the silence of the city at five-thirty on a Saturday morning got to her. Gianluca said only a few words in hushed tones as he led her through the warren of cool alleyways. The seagulls were making more noise than they were. Even the stalls on the Rialto Bridge were firmly shut.

Norah yawned, muttering, 'Sorry,' when she realised even that had broken the silence. Her stomach growled and Gianluca glanced at her with one of his mild looks that she couldn't interpret. What on earth were they going to talk about all day? Her algae would be better company – although he was unarguably better-looking.

Norah would never have been able to find her way back the way they'd come. She followed him blindly as well as dumbly and there was no straight line connecting anything in this city. She couldn't tell one smoky green canal from another, but at least she was too busy glancing at him to take note of the bizarre stone creatures and deformed bronze faces adorning the buildings.

When they spilled out onto a wider footpath that ran along the lagoon, it felt as though they were about to step off the edge of the world. The sun was below the wispy clouds on the horizon, hovering over a distant island and sending a fiery haze over the lagoon. Norah took a deep breath of salt-scented air and stared at the distant towers and narrow cypress trees on the near islands and the wooden pilings, aged to silver, dotted about the lagoon by the old city. Clouds piled over the mainland, but old Venice, with its pink and terracotta buildings, was bathed in sunlight.

'Do you have your ticket?' Gianluca asked, breaking the spell. She pulled out the card Manu had given her and held it to the reader, as Gianluca instructed her.

He took her elbow as they stepped onto the pontoon housing the vaporetto stop. 'I'm wearing more sensible shoes today, so I'm not going to fall off,' she said quietly.

He peered out at the lagoon with a smile. 'It wasn't kind of Manu to make you think it was a wedding.'

'Oh, I was glad it wasn't a real wedding in the end,' she murmured.

'Pino and Chiara say hello, by the way.'

'I say hello back.'

Silence fell again, broken only when the vaporetto puttered into view with a rush of water. At least she was hopeful about the project as she stepped onto the water bus and took a seat. She wasn't sure she'd ever be able to dive again, her PhD was firmly sunk under the weight of history and blame, office politics and an insurance nightmare. But she could do this.

She would get to know this lagoon and she suspected Manu had hired the best guide, even though he was quiet enough to make her own thoughts echo.

'Do you row out here often?' she asked.

He nodded. 'But not usually so far in the sanpierota – that's the boat we'll take.'

'Are you a professional rower? Like a gondolier on steroids?'

Even that didn't earn her much of a smile. 'I'm not a rower or a gondolier at all. I'm a remèr – an oarmaker – by trade.' He rubbed his hands together, and now that she knew his profession, it was clear they were hands that were used for making things. 'I have a workshop in Cannaregio.'

'Is that like a carpenter?'

'A remèr is like a carpenter if you think Venice is like London,' he said lightly.

'"Oarmaker" does sound more like a tourist attraction than a profession.' He gave an indignant huff, which only encouraged her. 'You basically hang out in your workshop looking buff and the tourists take photos of you?'

'I hang out in my workshop completing my *orders* the best that I can,' he countered. 'Handmade Venetian boats require handmade Venetian oars.'

'Of course!' she agreed with mock fervour that made his eye tic.

'Take a look next time you pass a gondola and you'll see. A well-made oar minimises hydrodynamic drag. It is eco-friendly and looks beautiful as well. And I don't just make oars. I make oarlocks, too – fórcole.'

Wow. She had got him talking and he was suddenly going on about hydrodynamic drag. Did he read *Classical Mechanics* at bedtime? It was kind of hot. 'What is that? A fórcole?'

'Fórcola is the singular. I'll show you on *Dafne*.'

'*Dafne*?' she repeated.

'That's the name of my boat. We'll be there soon.'

She ignored his proffered hand when the vaporetto pulled up to the small port in Murano, and stood, slinging her heavy backpack over one shoulder. He took the backpack from her.

'I can carry it,' she insisted. He hesitated, studying her face. 'Why don't you just ask me about the cane?' she prompted, sounding belligerent even to her own ears, but she was already sick of the chivalrous routine and those wary looks. She just wanted to get the awkward part done so they could get out on the lagoon and do her job.

'It's none of my business,' he muttered as they turned for the exit. 'As long as there's no safety issues – and you tell me if you do need help.'

She gave him a small smile, but said nothing to reassure him. She was done accepting help. She wanted to make it on her own. 'I appreciate the sentiment. I was in a boating accident a year ago and I was pretty badly injured, but I am theoretically fully recovered.' She glanced at her cane. 'Fully recovered' looked a little different from how she'd expected.

'Are you going to be okay on the water?' he asked in an even tone. He sounded unflappable – a trait she could appreciate, although it also made her wonder if he ever... flapped.

She nodded. 'The sound of a motor makes me jumpy, but I should be fine with a rowboat. I'm a marine biologist and I'm here to get back into a boat. And I need to be able to carry a vacuum pump myself,' she explained, taking the backpack before turning away to end the subject.

She snapped a few pictures as they walked along the fondamenta in the direction of 'Dafne' the boat. Norah would come back to Murano when she had more time and, in the meantime, she'd send pictures to Didi and make her guess where they'd been taken.

It was odd to think that her sister belonged here now. Didi was still working her notice in London. She was moving back in the next couple of months but Norah was glad she had her own time in Venice before Didi arrived. She wasn't sure she'd have applied for the internship if she'd known her sister would hook up with a glass-maker from a long line of Murano glassmakers and turn her life upside down.

First her mother, then her sister...

For years, Norah had been the only one in a functional, long-term relationship. But look at her now.

'Eccola, here she is,' Gianluca called from several metres ahead. The pride in his voice made her smile, especially when she saw the boat he was gesturing expansively at. Yeah, it was... small – no more than ten metres long.

Norah's equipment was tucked behind the bow, secured under a tarpaulin. By the end of the day she would probably have filled the entire boat with samples.

There was a single plank of wood across the middle, where she assumed she would be sitting as her bottom gradually went numb. And she'd have to squeeze her feet in behind her equipment. Where Gianluca was supposed to sit was a mystery to her. There was an oar strapped to the top and she had to admit the long, slim implement, made entirely of wood, was almost a work of art itself. It was probably twice her height, with a gently flared blade, painted with a red-and-white zigzag pattern.

'Well?' he prompted.

Norah arranged a smile onto her face. 'She's... lovely,' she said, unconvincingly, because Gianluca grinned. Norah blinked several times, trying to shake off the effect of that smile. Someone needed to do a PhD on his entire face and work out why the simple move-ment of his mouth could create such a reaction.

'Dai, come here,' he said, holding out his hands. She'd put her hands into his before she realised what she was doing. Then her brain stalled, leaving her staring up into his face. Stupid brain.

4

'Are you going to get in the boat?'

'Yes,' she said, releasing her breath on a huff and disengaging his hands. 'Just, a bit nervous,' she lied, regretting it immediately when his eyes dimmed with that familiar, goes-shopping-with-his-grandma concern. But she'd prefer to be nervous than to lose her mind over a guy at this stage – a guy who was probably in love with her boss. 'Here we go, then,' she said brightly and scrambled into the wooden boat.

It wobbled like crazy so she plonked herself down on the bench and dropped her cane onto the flat bottom. God, Gianluca was a good guy. He didn't even laugh and she'd forgive the quick, amused smile he gave her because it made her stomach dip in a much more pleasant way than the boat did.

He stepped gracefully onto the vessel, adjusting his balance. He untied the rope holding the boat to its piling and they immediately started to drift. Norah clutched the bench. She was so close to the water. A bunch of wooden planks was all that separated her from the lagoon.

Although '*Dafne*' was more than just a bunch of planks. Norah looked more closely at the dark, bowed wood of the hull and the paler planks of the deck, sanded and polished with precision.

Gianluca squeezed past her to open the straps holding the oar in place. Although the boat tipped with his weight, it felt surprisingly stable, which she was certain was something to do with Gianluca being born with sea legs. Had his father been an oarmaker, too? Or was everyone in Venice born to be on the water?

He had a tattoo on the back of his calf that attracted her eye. It was a schematic drawing, but she couldn't see it in detail. She appreciated the contrast of the ink on his skin and wondered what tattoo she would get, if she was game enough to get one.

He stepped over the bench again and grabbed the oar, taking up his position at the back of the boat. *Silly,* thought Norah. She shouldn't have wondered where he would sit. She was in the Venetian lagoon. The rower would stand.

Gianluca slipped the oar into the complex wooden bracket sticking up from the side of the boat – the oarlock, although he'd called it something else – then he straightened, the wind catching his hair.

'Just a warning,' he said, but his tone was... almost gleeful. 'This is not going to be fast.'

She shared his smile with an uncertain one of her own. She should probably be thinking of all the time wasted, of how she could have rushed back to the lab to analyse her samples much more quickly if she'd travelled in a motorboat.

But with the water close enough to dip her fingers in and the breeze gentle, she was looking forward to a quiet couple of hours on the marshes.

'Andemo!' he called out and he plunged his oar into the rippling water.

If Norah had felt like a Viking princess during the Festa della

Sensa, now she felt like a queen from antiquity, perched in a beautiful wooden boat with her own personal rower.

It was obviously hard work, sluicing the oar through the water as the boat bobbed at the edge of the channel, whipped by the wind. Norah would have felt guilty enough to want to help him, except he made it look so effortless. He used the weight of his body behind the oar, the muscles in his arms tensed and released, working in concert in this complex dance of man and boat.

There was a second oarlock, set near the bow, on the left – to port, she corrected herself. She'd been too long on land. The additional oarlock hinted at the possibility of a second rower, which, at the very least, would make the trip quicker.

Could she even row, with pins in her back and a dead foot? It didn't bear thinking about. She could barely contemplate standing in the boat, let alone standing *and* pulling an oar through the water.

They'd circumnavigated Murano, past its ancient brick basilica and innumerable glassworks, with a brief stop to grab panini, and *Dafne* was now bearing them to the wilds of the northern lagoon. Norah had her binoculars glued to her eyes and her heart in her throat. She'd read so much about the endangered salt marshes of the Venetian lagoon, a place with unique history and geography, that she was excited to see the first hints of grassy sandbanks.

Behind her, Gianluca kept up his easy rhythm. The boat was almost silent, except for the occasional muted splash and the creak of the oar. He stopped all of a sudden, when they were clear of Murano, and settled the oar next to Norah. He perched on the back of the boat, which was enclosed in wood, like the bow, and tugged off his shoes and socks.

He sighed – with relief, perhaps – and took up his position once more. He noticed her gaze. 'Sorry for my smelly socks.'

She smiled, taking a quick glance at his bare feet, planted on the polished wood. She hoped that meant he would eventually be comfortable with his passenger, rather than just tolerant.

'So,' she dared to begin, running her fingertips over the dark wooden bracket at the front of the boat, 'this is an oarlock? What was it you called it?' She studied it carefully. The shape was almost organic, thicker at the bottom to support the weight of the oar, and everywhere smoothly rounded.

'Yes, that's a fórcola. It is necessary for voga veneta, Venetian-style rowing. Some other types of rowing use oarlocks, too, but they are small clips, not like a Venetian fórcola.'

'You make these?'

'Yes.'

'How?' she asked, squinting up at him in the sunlight.

He took a deep breath and looked out over the lagoon. 'I don't want to bore you.'

'I think we've got time.'

He glanced at her and hesitated, but eventually nodded. 'It starts with a piece of walnut wood – a big piece. I have to cut it exactly into the parts that will form the fórcola, but they must come from the same piece of timber.'

'They absolutely *must*.' Norah nodded in mock seriousness. She couldn't help provoking him, since it teased out his smile.

'That is the way they've been made for centuries. But I use a machine to cut at first, then, once it's a manageable size, I use the traditional tools, mainly a two-handled saw. It takes a couple of days – more, if it's a decorative one for a gondola.'

Norah's fingers traced a dark line in the grain of the wood. Two days just for one fórcola. She could only imagine the patience that would take. 'That's what I call labour-intensive.'

He inclined his head, the breeze lifting his hair. 'When something is worth doing, it's worth doing slowly.'

'That sounds incredibly frustrating. Is that a job handed down from father to son?' she asked.

To her surprise, he shook his head. 'My father was a gondolier.'

'I'm sorry,' Norah muttered in response to his use of the past tense.

'That he was a gondolier? It wasn't that bad.'

Was that... a joke? She squinted up at him, responding to the twitch of his lips with a smile of her own. 'You didn't want to be one?'

'No, I... had to be different.'

She smiled ruefully. 'I know that feeling.'

'You're not from a family of scientists?'

'God, no. Science is... my way of dealing with a... rudderless upbringing, I suppose.'

'That's a very nautical expression.'

'I've got water on the brain.'

'I thought you had algae on the brain.'

'Gee, thanks, that sounds like a disease,' she quipped, ignoring the mocking niggle in the back of her mind that she must have *something else* on the brain, given the number of times she'd glanced up, just to take a look at *that face*. Perhaps he was one of those guys who didn't realise women went gaga over them. Trust him to be that perfect. 'Do you have to do a ten-year apprenticeship to become a fórcola-maker?'

'Not too far off,' he said drily. 'There are only four of us in all Venice. I had to train under one of the other three. Then I had to make my own tools. I can't just go across to Mestre to the hardware superstore and buy a traditional saw. And I needed a workshop – that's another story.' Norah looked up at him expectantly. He gave another reluctantly amused laugh and continued. 'My workshop is a pig's home, you know what I mean? It was an empty shell when I bought the building.'

'You own the building?'

'It's pretty hard to rent for a reasonable price in Venice. You buy a disaster and try not to throw your money into the canal. But at least I can live in an apartment above.'

'That's pretty impressive,' Norah said.

'What is?' he asked, in all his frustrating humility.

'You own a building. How old are you?' Eek, was that question too nosy? It also made her think of Manu. Would he be worried about her judging him? Norah couldn't care less about the age gap, if Manu and Gianluca wanted to be together. Besides, Manu could only be forty-five, tops.

'I'm nearly thirty.'

'That's so young to have bought a whole building. It's not even something I can imagine. I won't have a permanent job until I make Professor and God knows when that's going to be, now.' She hadn't pursued a research career for the job security – that much was certain – but to keep her mind busy.

Over the past year she hadn't even had that. Unless she got back into her research in earnest, all she'd have left would be a hatred of weddings and the ability to see monsters and gremlins in inanimate objects. She could do a PhD in that phenomenon where people saw faces in random things. That was the way she was headed.

'How old are you?' Gianluca asked warily, as though concerned about the answer. Did he think she was so young she couldn't take care of herself? Or had she aged ten years in the last one?

'I'm twenty-five,' she said.

'You look younger,' he replied, which answered her question, but also made her cheeks heat.

'I've completed half a PhD, so you shouldn't have assumed I was too young,' she pointed out. 'Just don't ask which half.'

'Let me guess, the half that was a lot of work, but counts for nothing?'

'You've got it, my friend.' She pointed her finger at him, as though she would have poked him in the chest if he'd been in range.

'Look!' he said, jerking his chin to gesture into the distance, since he obviously couldn't take his hands off the oar in the wind. 'Flamingos,' he said.

'What?' Norah swung around, even forgetting the wobbling of the boat as she caught sight of the flock of pale pink birds posing in the wetlands only a hundred feet away. 'Oh, my God. Are they real flamingos?'

'You're the biologist.'

She shared his grin. 'I'm a microbiologist. If there are microscopic flamingos in the water, I'd know about it.'

'I didn't know there was such a thing as microscopic flamingos. You learn something new every day when there's a scientist around.'

'Cheeky,' she muttered and lifted the binoculars to her eyes. The birds stood, goofy but dignified, in the shallow water. A chain of islands stretched along beside them, connected by patches of marsh grass and wooden poles. The only buildings she could see were some tumbledown ruins on a tiny island and the distant shore of Burano. They'd barely left behind the ancient houses and factories of Murano, but the wetlands were lush – turquoise and silver and green and utterly wild.

'Manu is a scientist, though,' she pointed out. 'Don't you learn from her?'

Gianluca's laugh was different this time, darker, and she wished she'd glanced at his expression. 'She's never around, though, is she?' he said.

* * *

Gianluca studied the clouds with concern. Rain had been forecast and they'd already been caught in a shower just before lunch, but the darkening skies in the west suggested the evening's thunderstorms might hit early. There was a reason for the local sayings about threatening winds rolling off Lake Garda.

Norah was engrossed in her vials and pipettes, her filters and nets. You wouldn't believe she'd been nervous on the boat that morning, given the way she leaned out to plunge a long plastic tube into the shallow water with what could only be described as jubilation. She'd been focussed all day, noting GPS coordinates and meticulously recording the environment of each sample. He supposed she'd been too busy to be worried about having another accident.

It had been a surprisingly enjoyable day. Norah was one of those stressful people who couldn't sit still or keep quiet – at least, not as quiet as he wanted to be out on the water. But he'd kind of enjoyed the curious questions she asked and even her busyness couldn't drown out the hush of the northern lagoon, the part the citizens of Venice had never tamed.

She swiped a strand of hair out of her face with the back of her hand, leaving a smudge. She looked up, a little startled to find him watching her. She should have been used to it by now. He felt as though his eyes had been returning to her face alarmingly often all day.

'I think we should head back,' he said.

'What? Already?'

'We've been rowing around all day.'

'All day? You insisted we stop at the taverna for lunch for a whole hour!'

'You don't come to Torcello and miss out on the taverna.'

'Is an hour's lunch break written into your contract?'

'It goes without saying. In fact I close my workshop for two hours every day for lunch.'

She looked him up and down. It would have made him self-conscious if it weren't for her wry expression. 'You don't look like you eat mixed fried stuff in a taverna for lunch every day. Or do you row it off?'

'You look like you could do with eating a bit more fritto misto – and taking a break occasionally.'

She sighed dramatically. 'Do you know how sick I am of people telling me to look after myself?' She was still joking, but he could sense an exposed nerve that'd he'd nearly hit.

He inclined his head in acknowledgement. 'Okay. We take lunch breaks for my benefit and my benefit only.'

She was fighting a smile. 'But... if you know of any other places where the mixed fried stuff is good...'

'I'm sure you'll be an expert on fritto misto before you go home.'

'I could do a PhD on it,' she muttered, almost to herself. 'But I can't really afford it, so maybe we should bring a picnic sometimes.'

He frowned. 'Manu can pay for your lunch.'

She studied him. 'What's up with you and Manu?'

His cheeks heated. Was it that obvious? He tried to feel as little as possible when it came to Manu. It was getting more difficult now she lived in Venice full-time – not that she had any more time for him. And why should she have time for him? He most definitely didn't want it.

'We... have a difference of opinion on a lot of things.' Like the existence of their relationship.

'Sorry, I get it. None of my business,' she apologised. The sky lit up with a sudden flash that made her face shine white. 'Shit,' she murmured. 'That was why you wanted to head back?'

He nodded. 'The storm wasn't supposed to arrive until tonight.'

A fat drop of rain landed on the deck near her bare feet. She grabbed for the lid of her equipment box and dragged the tarpaulin over the top. 'I'm waterproof now. I need to finish filtering this sample before we go.' She gestured to the pump that was whirring away, attached to vials and tubes and the large filtration chamber.

'We can come back another day.'

'It'll take five minutes tops.'

'We might not have five minutes,' he said grimly, looking up at the sky.

She shrugged, settling onto the bench and grabbing her rain jacket. 'We're going to get wet anyway, right?'

'Can't argue with that,' he said and reached for his own jacket.

He was regretting it five minutes later when she was definitely not finished and the drops of rain were getting fatter and more frequent. They'd come a long way east, through the chain of islands between Torcello and the distant mainland to the north. He didn't come up this far very often and he was struggling to plot the quickest route back.

'Norah!' he called out, alarmed at the way the wind whipped the words out of his mouth. She was on her belly over the bow of the boat, leaning out holding the tube that was connected to the purring pump. He was trying not to worry about her hurting herself – or falling off over the bow. She couldn't realise how precarious her position was. And he appeared to be talking to her backside.

She jerked her head up and had to grab for the side of the boat as it tipped. 'I'm not that wet, yet!'

'It's not the rain that's the problem. It's the wind.' A sudden gust punctuated his sentence and she tumbled sideways again. The tube in her hand slipped and she grabbed for it with a yelp. Gianluca swore and lifted his oar out of the water to go after her.

'I'm okay!' she called out, hauling herself upright before he could get to her, sliding again as the polished wood of the bow grew slippery in the rain. The boat tilted and she grabbed for the hovering oar to steady herself, making Gianluca wobble. 'Sorry,' she said. She let go in such a hurry that he stumbled and slipped.

In a farcical tug-of-war, set to a chorus of swearing in two languages, they tried to steady each other with the oar wobbling between them. Norah fell and landed heavily with a cry – mercifully onto the bow of the boat and not into the water – but she knocked the oar as she went down. It clattered against the side of the boat. Gianluca lurched after it, his feet slipping.

With a final curse, he gritted his teeth and prepared to hit the water as he heard Norah calling his name in alarm.

It was freezing. It had been a mild May day until the weather had rolled in, but May was a far cry from the sultry heat in August and the shallow lagoon responded quickly to changes in sunlight and air temperature. He yelped curses, hoping Norah's knowledge of dialect didn't extend to pig dogs and blasphemy, as the shock of the water temperature hit him.

It was shallow, but his feet sank into mud and he slipped as he tried to right himself until a pair of scrawny arms wrapped around him and tugged, pinching him in the ribs.

'I've got you!' Norah called, right into his ear. He froze in disbelief. The elven scientist who walked with a cane was trying to save him. He wasn't sure whether to laugh or scoff, but... he was touched, until the boat struck him in the back. He stumbled forward, nearly tugging her clean out of the boat.

The rain intensified all of a sudden. With another curse, he peeled her hands off his chest and set her firmly back into the boat. He straightened, grimacing at the feel of the mud squelching between his toes, but proving that the water was only just up to his ribs. He grabbed the oar, where it was attempting to float away, and turned back to the boat.

'Sorry,' she said. 'I thought you... might drown.'

He glanced up at her. Long strands of her hair were plastered to her pale face. She had fat water droplets in her eyelashes, and she looked as though the rain was slowly washing her away, except for her obstinate expression. She made him smile. Despite the rain and the inconvenience, and all his intentions to keep her at arm's length, he grinned at her. She stared back at him, disconcerted.

'Thank you, mariner,' he said with a mock salute. 'It's nice to know you're watching my shoulders.'

She recovered from her distraction and poked him. 'I was saving your life, not watching your shoulders.'

'It's the same thing. Did I say it wrong? You know... to look after someone?'

'Oh-h-h, you mean I've got your back. I sure do. But... are you patronising me?'

'Maybe a little,' he said. His smile stretched. He couldn't seem to help it. As if on cue, the sky flashed with sudden lightning, reminding him of where they were. She'd wanted to save him, but he was the one responsible for their safety.

She tried to help him up into the boat, but he slapped her hand away. 'Sit down!' Of course, she stayed where she was, taking the oar for him so he could haul himself over the side. The boat tipped and wobbled.

He grimaced at the muddy footprints he left when he made it back on deck. 'I'll clean her down for you when we make it back,' Norah said. 'I owe you that much.'

His gaze rose to hers. 'We're not back yet. You'd better sit down and hold on – and put on a life jacket,' he said, taking the oar from her. Lightning flashed, illuminating the marsh grasses and revealing just how dark the sky had grown. The wind slapped the water against the hull. Gianluca was not looking forward to the next hour. 'When we get back, you owe me a strong drink!' he added when she'd settled herself onto the bench and he was safely talking to her back.

'It's a date,' she said, then froze in alarm. 'I mean... not a date! It's just an expression.'

He couldn't believe he was smiling again. 'Okay, whatever it is, I'm going to need it after this!' he called back. He settled the oar into the fórcola and twisted, using the blade to turn the boat.

Burano and Torcello were distant smudges of beige. He squinted the other way. An uninhabited island, clustered with trees, blocked his view, but a few lights from Sant'Erasmo twinkled on the horizon. It was probably closer than Burano. Behind them lay only sandbanks and marshland – but no shelter.

'Do you have another oar somewhere?' Norah asked and he turned back to her in surprise. Her hand dropped to the fórcola on the front.

'No!' he called back. 'You wouldn't be any help, anyway.' She muttered something that reached him only partially. He recognised the bitter sarcasm in her tone, though. He didn't have time to explain the intricacies of voga veneta and, without time to learn, she'd only be working against him if he handed her an oar. 'Just hang on and put your hood up.'

'What about you?'

'I won't wash away.' He sighed. 'And I've got a big lunch to work off.' He gritted his teeth and headed for Sant'Erasmo.

5

It was raining so hard that the drops were bouncing off the water, dissipating into a fine mist among the sandbanks. Norah's jacket was useless, now, sticking to her under the chunky life vest. Drops of cool spring rain ran down her back in rivulets. She could almost hear Didi telling her to spray it again, but, of course, Norah was too contrary to take good advice, it seemed.

Good advice like: *I think we should head back.*

Then she'd all but tossed him into the lagoon. If she didn't laugh, she was going to panic. Luckily Gianluca was ridiculously capable. She had no doubt he'd get them to safety, despite the wind and the menacing sky that was dumping what felt like a year's worth of rain onto them. Gianluca just rowed on, despite the drips streaming down his face and the wind knocking the boat to and fro. Norah would forgive him for his slightly patronising comments. And buying him a drink? That wouldn't exactly be a chore.

She should have been used to feeling helpless after a year of it, but she struggled to sit still and do nothing as the wind whipped up the water and Gianluca stood alone against the elements. Her stomach dropped as the valiant *Dafne* crested a wave. It probably wasn't a very big wave, but it took Norah right back to that day off the Isle of Wight. Her back twinged, reminding her of the shock of falling on her backside a few minutes ago.

Was it the first time she'd fallen since the accident? A dull radiating pain had accompanied the fall, but she'd been distracted by Gianluca's dip in the lagoon and had managed to convince herself she was okay. Now, as the boat swerved and bobbed, her mind wasn't so sure any more. Her equipment hopped on the deck, banging against the wooden planks. She tucked her feet out of the way and hoped the pump survived.

Would *Dafne* buckle under the strain? Would Norah be tossed over the side and break her back again? She tried to tell herself that they weren't travelling at speed, that she couldn't get so badly thrown by a rocking rowboat. But her knuckles were white and she had to force her fingers open. An hour of this and she'd be finished. Melodramatic, but finished.

'Change of plans!' she heard Gianluca shout from behind her.

'What?' She looked up in alarm. His hair was plastered to his forehead, getting in his eyes.

'I made the wrong decision,' he said tightly. 'I thought we could get to Sant'Erasmo and take the vaporetto back. But we're not going to make it and I doubt the vaporetto is running anyway.'

Her throat closed. Her old friend nerve pain shot down her leg. God, she was so sick of it all. She stared at Gianluca, at his tight jaw. She hated that she'd caused such an inconvenience.

'Right, then,' she said with a firm nod, slapping her palms onto her thighs. 'What are we doing? Waiting it out on a sandbank?'

'There's an island over there. Just hang on while I try to get us there.'

He was right. Amongst the greys of storm and sky, there was a row of dark green cypress trees and a faint light. She slumped, dropping her forehead into her hand. 'What else had I expected?

There are islands everywhere in this lagoon. Why all the drama, then? And trust me, I'm hanging on!' He grumbled something that was whisked away in the wind.

She could make out a small port with a motorboat bobbing wildly on its piling. But as Gianluca tried to steer them in that direction, the bow veered off towards the stone spit, making Norah flinch away.

She considered writing down all of the words escaping from Gianluca's mouth. She'd had a beginner's tutorial on swearing in Venetian from Didi's boyfriend, Piero, so she understood when Gianluca was gritting his teeth and groaning about cock and balls, but she would like to have known what the more flowery ones meant.

In the midst of the chaos of wind and water, she started to laugh. God, she should have expected this. She wasn't a phoenix, rising from the ashes of her accident. She was a bad luck charm, bringing misfortune to every body of water she studied.

'I'm glad you find this funny!' he called out. She only laughed harder.

'Why don't we just pull the boat up on the bank?' she called back. She dropped down to the deck and rummaged for her binoculars. They were quickly obscured by drops of rain, but she wiped the lenses and looked again. 'There's a sandy bit over there!'

Gianluca squinted through the driving rain, clutching the oar. 'I can't see it. I don't know this island at all.'

'Oh. My. God. There is an island in the Venice Lagoon that Gianluca... Gianluca Oarmaker *doesn't* know at all?'

'I know which island it is, but I've never been here!' he shouted back drily.

'Well, there is a sandy spot over there! Let's get off the water before my samples are shipwrecked!'

He gave her half a nod and maybe a quarter of a smile, but he did as she suggested, leaning into the oar and steering them towards the misty island.

It wasn't much of a beach. It was more of a catchment of sediment that had been washed up against the rock wall.

'I'm going to have to get out and pull us in,' he said, tugging the oar out of the water.

She scrambled to her feet. 'I'll go. It's not deep, right? You stay and steer.' Refusing to think about the cold, swirling water, she stuck one bare foot over the side before he could protest.

She'd just yelped her own colourful profanity at the frigid water when she was promptly knocked over by the boat. She swallowed water. The life vest tugged her back to the surface and Gianluca's strong hand hauled her upright.

'I'm okay!' she spluttered, hacking a few times. She struggled to her feet, biting back a yelp as a stab of pain shot down her spine. Whether it was actual damage or nerve pain, she didn't have time to work out. She waded up to the bow and grabbed the rope.

She could feel the rocks beneath the sediment under the sole of her good foot. There was an ominous scraping sound as the bow made landfall, accompanied by a cry of alarm from Gianluca. He dropped the oar into the boat with a clatter and sprang into the water.

'Can you lift it?' he asked, his expression stricken. His poor boat.

She tried, but the twinge in her back brought panic into her throat and she had to shake her head. He took her place at the bow and started dragging the boat up onto dry land. Norah watched helplessly for a moment, before striding back into the water and grabbing hold of the stern. She lifted it as best she could, hoping she could at least save the worst of the damage.

When the bow reached the sandy grass, it slid easily and Norah lost her grip on the stern and toppled onto her hands and knees. She crawled slowly out of the water, groaning as a stone gouged her knee. But, as she looked up at the awesome stormy sky and the rain ran down her face, she felt... good.

She'd saved her samples. She'd hopefully saved poor *Dafne* a few scratches. She'd helped Gianluca get safely out of the storm. They were going to be all right. She was going to be all right.

Some of the water streaming down her cheeks was too hot to be rain, but luckily she was the only one who could tell the difference.

She stumbled to the boat and knelt to grab the other side of a flapping tarpaulin Gianluca was attempting to secure over her equipment. They worked wordlessly to tie down the boat and, with a final tug on the oar strap, Gianluca straightened and looked across at her.

Far from the wary reticence of that morning – was it only that morning? – his expression then held respect and... warmth.

'You okay?' he asked. He spoke too softly for his voice to carry over the wind, but she saw his lips move and understood enough.

She nodded, pretending all of her blinking was because of the rain running into her eyes. He came quickly around the boat and grasped her hands to haul her to her feet. She felt alarmingly limp and far too close to him. She was near enough to sneak a breath of him – fresh rain, with remnants of sunshine, sweat and a hint of lavender in his cologne. She shook off his grip and straightened.

'I don't need a hug,' she insisted. 'I'm okay.'

'Where's your cane?' he asked in alarm.

'Still in the boat,' she murmured. She leaned down to get it, but Gianluca was there first. He fetched her backpack, too, although she assumed her wallet and phone were so sodden they wouldn't be much use and the pump was secured under the tarpaulin.

'Can you walk? Should I carry you? We should get out of the rain.'

The unexpected pride welled inside her again. Mr Chivalrous had looked at her with respect once. She wasn't going to let him think she was helpless. She gripped his arm and squeezed. 'I can walk,' she said. 'But thank you for offering. Which way do we have to go?'

'I'm not sure, but I think I see a break in the trees over there. I imagine that's the way to the monastery.'

Norah drew back. 'Monastery? Like monks and matins and robes and funny hairdos?'

'That's it. That's where we are: the Isola di San Francesco del Deserto. The deserted island of St Francis.'

She laughed again, this time hard enough to wonder if she really was all right. 'Typical. My first sampling trip and we wind up on a deserted island. Is this the kind of luck that follows me?'

'It's not actually deserted. A brotherhood of Franciscan friars lives here.'

'Will they feed us?'

'I doubt you'll get fritto misto, but they'll definitely feed us.'

'Then I love monks. Let's go!'

* * *

Is this the kind of luck that follows me?

Gianluca couldn't get her bitter, rhetorical question out of his mind as they trudged through the soggy grass to the break in the trees. She marched on, keeping up with his longer strides despite leaning on her cane. Her hair was a sodden mess down her back and her face was almost the pallor of the rain clouds.

But she had the oddest smile on her face – stubborn and amused and crooked.

When the convento came into view, the warm beige of the bricks a beacon in the grey storm, she sighed loudly. 'I really love monks! Do you reckon we'll have to wear habits – or robes or whatever monks call them? Cassocks? I could really go a cassock right now, if it was dry and warm. But what do you think they wear under them? Calvin Klein?'

'I don't think I want to know.'

'We might be about to find out. I just really need to get these clothes off. My trousers are chafing so badly.' She pulled at the fabric plastered to her thighs, peeling it off her skin with a grimace.

They came to a paved path that felt tortuously long as their destination came in sight. Weak light shone through a door in the brick wall. They were going to shock the poor friars with their sudden drenched arrival at the back entrance, but Gianluca was more concerned that Norah's lips were turning blue.

'You do the talking, right?' she asked nervously.

It was his turn to chuckle. 'I'm sure they speak English. They do welcome guests here for meditation and prayer, I believe.'

'As long as they don't expect their guests to fast, I'll try to fit in. But solitude is not really my thing at the moment.' Her voice trailed off.

He prompted her with a casual, 'Hmm?' that was designed to cover how much he wanted her to explain.

'Have you ever been injured so badly that every movement hurts?' He shook his head wordlessly. 'It's not a walk in the park.' She gave a little laugh at her own joke. 'And it's isolating – fucking lonely,' she muttered stiltedly, through chattering teeth.

She quickened her steps up to the beacon of light and he hurried after her. They stepped through into a peaceful cloister of pale stone, lined with innumerable plants in clay pots, and blessedly dry.

'Oh, thank fuck,' Norah murmured, slumping against the wall. 'Or God or... whatever.'

He couldn't resist wrapping an arm around her. It was a waterlogged embrace, but she permitted it this time, wrapping her arms around his back with a squeeze.

'We made it.'

'You were amazing,' he blurted into her hair.

Her shoulders quaked with laughter, the sound muffled by his chest. He tightened his arms around her. 'I *was* pretty amazing,' she said, looking up at him with a glowing grin. 'But you were the hero. I was just your sidekick.'

'You can come along any time, Obelix.'

She snorted. 'I don't think we're Asterix and Obelix. What about Batman and Robin? I'd much rather be Chris O'Donnell than Gérard Depardieu.' She sighed, turning her head so her cheek rested on his chest. She felt entirely insubstantial, as if he were holding a mythical creature who could disappear at any moment. At the latest, she'd disappear in ten weeks – nine weeks, now. 'If I had more energy, I'd poke you in the ribs.'

Footsteps made them raise their heads. A young friar in a coarse brown cassock tied with a rope burst into the courtyard, his eyes wide.

He greeted them with a rush of stammered words. 'Mi dispiace,' he said, catching himself. 'Benvenuti sull'isola. Parlate italiano?'

'Sì,' Gianluca replied. He gave Norah's hand a squeeze and explained to the friar in Italian what had happened.

The friar exclaimed in surprise and in a matter of short minutes a whirlwind of monks had whisked them into a spartan guest room on the upper floor, delivered old, but immaculate, sheets and towels and had even produced some casual clothes and a dressing for the cut on Norah's knee. With instructions to join them in the refectory for dinner in an hour, the last monk solicitously closed the door behind himself, leaving them in privacy.

The silence fell heavily, all of a sudden. The rain dripping on the windowsill echoed in the plain white walls of the room, adorned only with an iron crucifix between the arched windows. The two single beds filled Gianluca's vision. He'd briefly considered asking for a second room, but he'd decided against it. He didn't want to leave Norah alone and he worried that, if he made a big deal out of it, she might feel awkward.

Norah collapsed onto the nearest bed with a groan, but jumped up again when she remembered her wet clothes. With a frustrated growl, she grabbed the hem of her shirt and Gianluca barely had time to turn around before she tugged it over her head.

'I'm way too cold to care what you see,' she said, punctuated by the swooshing sound of her peeling off her trousers. 'Or to look,' she added, 'if you want to get changed, too.'

He headed for his side of the room and pulled off his own shirt. As he hopped on one foot, wrestling with his saturated shorts, she was suspiciously silent. He handed her a towel – awkwardly, without turning around. He wasn't sure whether he let go too soon or she dropped it because her fingers had lost dexterity in the cold. But he snatched it up and handed it to her again.

'I'm decent,' she said a moment later and he turned to find her wrapped in the towel. She wasn't quite telling the truth. It was a small towel.

'Something wrong with the clothes?'

She shook her head. 'I just want to dry off for a minute.' She perched on the bed with a sigh. Her gaze dropped to his chest and stuck there, her expression blank. His fingers tightened on the towel slung around his waist.

'Eh... Norah?'

Her gaze snapped back up to his. 'Oh, God. Sorry.' She turned sharply away.

He studied her for a moment, her straight back, the tension slowly draining from her fine shoulders. 'You're getting in the spirit of the monastery,' he said. His own tension loosened its hold when he heard her tired laugh. Holding the towel loosely around his hips, he quickly stripped off his underwear and wrenched on the dry shorts.

'Somehow I don't think ogling you is in the spirit of the place.'

He nearly swallowed his tongue. 'You weren't... were you?' She laughed again. He pulled on the T-shirt the friars had given him – a Philadelphia Eagles American football shirt that was several sizes too big. 'I'm decent.'

'Thank God. I was about to give in to temptation and then what would the monks think?' She turned to him and something in his expression made her laugh wryly at him. 'Calm down, Gianluca. You must know you are ridiculously good-looking. Don't worry. It would take a lot more than a pretty face to make me lose my mind over a man right now.'

'Are you suggesting I'm only a pretty face?' he teased. Teasing her seemed a better idea than thinking too much about her admission. She spluttered and gaped and he struggled to keep a straight face. 'Lucky for you, I can also do first rescue.' He produced the dressing the friars had given them and hunched down in front of her to inspect her knee.

'First rescue?' she asked drily. 'Do you mean first aid?'

'It's the same thing, no?'

'One sounds more dramatic, but I suppose so,' she said with a smile. She stretched out her leg and he dabbed at it as gently as he could. The wound was already clean from the rain, so he dressed it quickly, ignoring her giggles when he held her knee. He didn't need to be charmed afresh because she was ticklish.

'Put your clothes on. It's nearly time to eat and we don't want to keep the friars waiting,' he said, getting to his feet and giving her shoulder a squeeze before he'd remembered it was bare. He snatched his hand back.

He pulled out his phone, relieved to see the device was as waterproof as advertised. He had a few bars of reception and enough battery for a phone call. He called Manu and explained what had happened.

'Oh, grazie Dio, Gianluca,' she exclaimed.

'You could say that,' he joked, speaking in Italian. 'We'll be back tomorrow,' he said, switching into the Veneto dialect for his usual passive-aggressive game with Manu.

'Tomorrow?'

'I wouldn't ask the friars to take us to Sant'Erasmo in these conditions and I'm not sure the vaporetto is running anyway. I'll check the boat and bring Norah back tomorrow morning.'

'You'll... spend the night?'

His brow furrowed. 'Is that a problem?'

'Well...' she began defensively, 'two young people, both single...'

He choked on a cough. 'Are you worried about her or me? Not that this has anything to do with... that.' Even though there was no way Norah could understand what he was talking about, he could still feel the colour sneaking up the back of his neck. Thank heavens Manu didn't know Norah was probably half naked right now and had just stripped off in front of him without a care. He rubbed a hand over his face and swallowed a groan. 'We're... just friends,' he said, something about the word striking him.

His gaze lifted to Norah without thought, but she was thankfully clothed again. She'd crossed her arms self-consciously over her threadbare tourist T-shirt that had 'Ciao Bella' emblazoned across her chest. But yes, they were friends, somehow.

'I'm sorry,' Manu said, her voice cooling with her customary detachment.

'Apology accepted,' he muttered. 'Don't worry. She's fine and we'll be back tomorrow.'

6

'Please don't tell me these monks are the silent sort,' Norah murmured as they headed through the cloister to the refectory. 'Or the creepy sort. I've seen *The Name of the Rose*.' She drifted closer to Gianluca. The delicious smell of garlic and onion and seafood kept her feet moving. She was so hungry it smelled better even than the fritto misto from lunch.

'The book is better,' he commented, making Norah squint up at him. Usually, she'd agree wholeheartedly, but *The Name of the Rose* was quite a tome and she'd never actually got through it. 'Which would you prefer?' he continued. 'Silent or creepy?'

'Silent over creepy any day,' she admitted begrudgingly.

'I don't think you have anything to worry about,' he said, leaning down to speak quietly into her ear as the door opened and a monk appeared.

She crossed her arms tightly. It had been too much to hope that the monks would have a bra lying around. She was hanging a little too loose for comfort in a monastery.

'Welcome,' the monk said warmly – in English for Norah's benefit. He was an older man with a white beard that reached his collar-bone. 'I am Brother Giuseppe Maria. We are pleased to have you as guests here in the convent. I hope you are not so cold now?'

The monk had such kind blue eyes that Norah couldn't help but smile. 'Thank you so much, Brother Giuseppe. I'm Norah York.' He clasped her hand, making her realise how cold hers were. The rain was still pouring down on the stone buildings that felt like an oasis in a tempest, protected from the weather by a religious forcefield.

'Gianluca Marangon,' Gianluca introduced himself, and shook hands with Brother Giuseppe.

'Marangon?' They exchanged a few words Norah couldn't understand and then Brother Giuseppe ushered them into the refectory.

'What did he say?'

'Brother Giuseppe grew up locally. He enjoyed the chance to speak some dialect. My surname gives it away.'

'Do they only speak Latin in the monastery or something?'

'I don't know. Italian, maybe, rather than Latin. I imagine the friars are from all over the country.'

The refectory was a small whitewashed room with dark wooden beams, lined with what looked like choir benches, with tables placed in front. The monks sat behind their tables in their brown habits, heads bowed, exactly as Norah would have expected. But she hadn't expected there would be only eight of them.

Brother Giuseppe showed them to their places and they slipped behind their table. The refectory was so still, with the rain beating on the windowsills, echoing from the bare walls and the large flag-stones on the floor. Norah had to stop her foot from tapping as a woman wheeled a trolley with a steaming pot into the room.

As guests, they were served first and Norah could have cried, she was so grateful to see the plate of risotto put in front of her. Her stomach rumbled as more plates were distributed. She clapped a hand to it ineffectually and she saw Gianluca was trying not to smile. Brother Giuseppe set glasses onto the table and poured wine.

'Am I allowed to drink that? I'm not Catholic,' she murmured to Gianluca.

'It's not a sacrament. It's a drink.'

'But... I didn't think monks drank!'

He dipped his chin, looked her in the eye and said, 'This is Italy,' as though that was all the explanation required.

The monks bowed their heads in prayer and Norah and Gianluca followed suit. She didn't understand a word, but the relief of being dry and clothed and about to be fed swept warmly through her body, along with the unintelligible words.

The 'Amen' was universal and she raised her head again. One monk took his place in the wooden pulpit at one end of the room, opened an ancient Bible and began to read. Norah picked up her fork and dug in.

The flavour was delicate and comforting. She couldn't see any fish amongst the rice, but the taste was there – salty and fresh and a little tangy. It was as though the monks had known two ship-wrecked visitors were coming, it was such a perfect meal to revive her. She took a sip of the wine, a light red that made her insides glow.

'This is amazing,' she moaned under her breath, unable to keep it in.

Gianluca stifled a chuckle. 'I can tell,' he murmured back.

She froze, realising her sighs of relief and appreciation must have been audible. She swallowed and glanced around the room, noticing the monks hastily dropping their gazes. Great. She was braless and groaning in delight in the presence of a bunch of celibate monks.

She finished her meal before any of the others and gulped

down her wine. She forced her hands into her lap and waited. Beside her, Gianluca was eating slow forkfuls, punctuated by measured sips of wine. He must have been at least as hungry as she was, but he obviously had more self-control. He scooped risotto onto his fork with the same capable movements as he swung an oar.

Norah released a breath on a huff. Now she was staring appreciatively at his hands. She was not built for monastic life, that was certain.

In her efforts to keep her eyes off her companion she stared at the ancient flagstones, on a spectrum from white to pale orange, and didn't realise she'd fallen asleep until Gianluca was gently rousing her with a hand on her cheek. Her other cheek was smooshed against his biceps.

She sat up groggily. 'Oh, God... I mean, gosh.' She winced. Gianluca was laughing at her again, damn him. He tugged her to her feet and they followed Brother Giuseppe back out into the cloister. Gianluca slid his arm around her waist and she didn't fight it.

At the door of the room, Brother Giuseppe smiled warmly again. Norah suddenly remembered the twin beds. At least it wasn't a double, but what did Brother Giuseppe think of them sharing a room? They'd changed their clothes together earlier. Did the monks think they were getting it on in the hallowed halls? Shouldn't they have been separated?

She kept her mouth firmly shut. She wasn't about to ask what Brother Giuseppe thought of unmarried guests sharing rooms and she didn't relish the thought of going to sleep in her own spartan chamber. She might have trouble keeping her eyes off him, but she'd rather Gianluca stayed with her.

'I wish you good rest. If you are interested, I can show you the convent tomorrow, and our gardens. The island is laid out for peaceful reflection. Perhaps you will find it of some benefit.'

'Peaceful reflection' sounded too much like 'stuck in bed with a broken spine staring at the ceiling', but, after a night sleeping in the same room as her gorgeous rower, perhaps she *would* benefit from a little peace in the morning.

Gianluca exchanged a few words with Brother Giuseppe, ending with, 'Bona note,' and then they were alone again. He shut the door and released a slow breath, rubbing his face with one hand. Guilt pricked Norah as she watched him. How much of this was her fault?

He strode to one of the beds and flopped onto it, stretching out and covering his eyes with his arm. Even in the enormous green T-shirt that looked like a muumuu, he drew her gaze far more than she liked.

She perched on her own bed. 'Is the mattress ridiculously hard? For the benefit of our spiritual life, perhaps?' she asked, hiding her nervousness. She stared around the room. As darkness fell, it was illuminated only by a single lamp on a side table. Aside from the constant sound of the rain, it was silent and that kind of silence would be heavy if she couldn't get Gianluca to keep talking.

'It's not too bad,' he said tiredly.

'I'm sorry.'

'Don't be,' he replied immediately. Norah stared at him, wondering how he could be so unquestioningly kind and whether she could accept it. He couldn't see her, so she let her fears out for a little play as she watched his chest rise and fall with his breaths.

Saffron had never been there for her when Norah needed her mother. Even Andrej, who'd known her longer and better than anyone, hadn't thought she was worth sticking around for, when she hit trouble. He'd sided firmly with their boss because his work was more important to him than she was. The worst part was, she understood where he was coming from.

How could Gianluca *not* blame her for all the trouble she'd caused?

She hadn't realised he'd moved his arm and was peering at her. She looked away with a quick breath. 'So, what do we do to fall asleep? No toothbrush, no book, no phone charger.'

'Try closing your eyes,' he muttered and rolled onto his side, facing her. A hint of ink peeked out from the sleeve of the T-shirt.

'I didn't expect you to have tattoos,' she blurted out, cursing herself for her inability to keep her mouth shut and go to sleep.

'Why not? What did you expect?'

She gave a little shrug. 'Not that. Did you have a rebellious phase or something?'

'You could say that. Are you going to lie down?'

She glanced between Gianluca's tired, tolerant gaze and the pillow that looked as if it was made from old jumpers. If she lay on the pillow, she'd be staring right into his eyes. 'Even if I lie down, I might not sleep for a bit. I feel too wired.' She pulled back the covers and stared at the bed. 'If you talk to me, it might help.'

'Are you going to ask more personal questions?' he asked wryly.

'If you want to be cagey about yourself, tell me about your nòna.'

'Nòna? Why do you want to know about Nòna?'

She swung her feet up onto the bed and tugged the covers up to her waist. She ran her hand over her plait, grimacing when she discovered it was still soaking wet. She decided to deal with it in the morning. 'Why not? You mentioned her yesterday. How old is she?'

'Eighty-four,' he answered, his voice softening again with impending sleep.

'And is she your mother's mother?'

'No. She's my father's mother. I didn't... know my mother.'

Norah ran out of words for a moment. She'd gathered that his father was dead. Now this. She could understand why he clung to his aging grandmother. Was he lonely? Maybe they could be lonely together.

She kicked herself inwardly. Unlike Norah, Gianluca at least had friends who wouldn't leave him in the lurch. And he still had his job. 'Do you have any brothers or sisters?' she asked.

'A bit difficult when I didn't know my mother. I have a couple of uncles, but otherwise it's just Nòna.' Norah pressed her lips shut and waited for him to fall for the old 'fill the silence' trick. It worked. 'And she's getting old – not that she'd let me say that to her face. She still lives in the same apartment she always has, which is good for when she's a little forgetful, but not so good because it's on the second floor. But she doesn't want to move Sissi. She's getting old, too, but even less willing to hear that.'

'Sissi?'

'Nòna's cat.'

Norah grinned, sliding down under the blankets. She wasn't quite ready to switch the light off, but the conversation was slowly settling her down. 'You're a cat person.'

'I didn't say that. Sissi can be a... minàcia. Catìva.'

'Catty?' Norah suggested with a giggle.

'Nòna, she tolerates, of course, and usually me. She sits on the windowsill bothering the fish seller. The way she makes noise, it sounds like she's swearing at him, the foulest curses.'

'Nòna, or the cat?'

Gianluca chuckled and tucked his arm under his head. 'Nòna does not swear.'

'But she does yell at the fish seller from the windowsill?'

'Only sometimes,' he said with a grin. 'And by "does not swear", I mean she doesn't blaspheme or let me get away with swearing in her presence, but she does have about a million sayings about taking a shit – a weird metaphor for life or something.' He paused. 'I suppose it's appropriate that there are so many sayings about that... function, given it's such a big part of life in old Venice. In some places, you can see the gatoli, the ends of the pipes where wastewater runs into the canals. I put in a water treatment tank, but when I bought my place, they couldn't tell me where the pipes led.'

'Wow, you're a really shit conversationalist,' she said, immediately regretting her joke, because it stopped him talking.

But he laughed again, louder this time. He eyeballed her. 'And you are a sarcastic... ladìn de boca.'

The warm, intense gaze he was shooting her scrambled her insides. 'Your English appears to be clocking off for the night,' she teased him back lightly.

'Could be,' he said. 'It means... agile.' He mispronounced the 'i', but she understood what he meant. 'Agile mouth.'

'An agile... mouth.' He couldn't mean what she thought he meant, but it didn't take much for her to start wondering what it would be like if they kissed. Stupid brain. Imagining a serial-killer monk being hunted by Christian Slater and Sean Connery, like in *The Name of the Rose*, would be better than wondering about kissing Gianluca right now.

'Yes, you know. A dirty mouth.'

'Oh-h-h-h-h,' she said with an unflattering snort. 'Dirty mouth' wasn't helping to banish her wayward thoughts of kissing someone she'd just decided should be her friend, but she at least understood his thoughts weren't on the same page. It was for the best.

'I'll have to be on my best behaviour if I ever meet your nòna.' It was a little weird how much she wanted to meet her.

'Once I tell her about you, meeting her is inevitable,' he said in a grumble, 'for food and... interrogation.'

'She might torture me, but I'll never tell her we spent the night together,' Norah joked. A choked cough came from the other side of the room. 'But seriously, I'd love to meet her.'

'I'll let you know when she issues the order – I mean invitation.'

'And here I was thinking you were a dutiful grandson, when she's just formidable.'

He didn't defend himself, which only convinced Norah that what she'd said wasn't true. He was dutiful. 'What about your family? Your mother is getting married again?'

'Not "again".' She laughed bleakly. 'My mother's never been married. My sister and I had some awful role models, so it's no wonder...' She trailed off.

'That's why you need more than a pretty face to... lose your mind over a man?'

'You have an inexcusably good memory,' she grumbled. 'But since you obviously know you have a pretty face, I think it's better to admit it and get on with life, rather than pretending. Besides, I think we should be friends.' She pressed her lips together. She hadn't intended that last part to come out.

He didn't reply for a long moment. She heard him swallow. 'I think so, too,' he said finally.

Norah grinned. She was stupidly satisfied with his agreement. She met his eye across the room, giddy with the success of earning his friendship. The storm had provided the opportunity, but she'd taken it. It felt like a step forward, which she'd been searching for – for a long time.

He returned her smile a little indulgently, but she didn't care. She trusted his friendship unexpectedly wholeheartedly. She must have been more of a mess than she'd thought, to want to trust someone – anyone – so badly.

His hair had dried in a wild swoop over his forehead. His eyes gleamed in the lamplight. And it was just as intense as she'd thought, staring at each other from their pillows, separated only by four feet and a side-table.

Norah rolled onto her back, wincing when it twinged. The pain was probably from the knock earlier. 'Yeah, my mum loses her mind over men all the time, so there's no way I'm going to do the same.'

'What about the guy she's marrying? Is it... better this time?'

'God, I hope so.'

'Light a candle in the chapel? Might reach God's ears,' he suggested playfully. She raised an eyebrow.

'Maybe she'd like to get married here. I wonder if they do that? Job done and all that.'

'I could ask in the morning,' he offered, 'but be prepared for them to say no.'

'I can't believe she's asked me to scout wedding venues,' she muttered with a sigh. 'Mothers,' she grumbled. But her gaze flew back to Gianluca. 'I'm sorry! I didn't think—'

'Don't worry about it,' he cut her off. 'I can imagine that rebellious mothers could be difficult to handle.' He stretched and rolled onto his back. Norah tried not to appreciate the way the muscles in his arms flexed.

'I think I was supposed to be the rebellious one, but my mum out-rebelled me.' She felt rebellious, coming to Venice, picking up the pieces of her career. It was satisfying.

Gianluca yawned and glanced at the lamp. Norah sighed. Just because he was willing to be her friend, didn't mean he had to stay awake listening to her chatter. She reached over and snapped the light off.

'Oh, shit, that's dark!' She snapped the light back on. Gianluca blinked back at her. 'Sorry. Could we leave it on?'

'Sure,' he said mildly.

'It must only be about eight-thirty. I mean, I'm exhausted, but I still can't sleep so early.'

'You can keep talking,' Gianluca said and Norah gaped at him. 'What? It's nice.'

'It's putting you to sleep!' she accused.

He smiled and there was a wicked glint that she liked a little too much. 'That, too.'

'What do you want me to talk about, then?'

'Anything. If you want to keep the light on, the least you can do is talk me to sleep.'

7

Gianluca was exhausted. He wanted to sleep because he planned to get up at first light to check the boat, but listening to her was like bingeing on a TV series: something new always grabbed his attention.

He didn't know why he'd asked her to keep talking. Perhaps it was because they'd otherwise be lying next to each other in silence – a decent distance apart, but somehow still together. If she didn't say anything, the intimacy would clog up his throat and he'd end up staring at her.

She shifted and winced again. 'Did you hurt yourself today?' he asked, on alert.

She sighed. 'I'm okay. Doctors say I'm fine, right?' She had that tone again, the one that made him feel powerless. 'But I bet you've been wondering why I was able to jump out of the boat and leave my cane.'

'It's none of my business,' he said carefully. 'Not that I don't care,' he added.

'Yeah, I know. But screw it,' she said and looked him right in the eye. 'Maybe I want to tell you the truth. It must be the influence of all these monks or something.'

'I didn't think you were lying,' he said gently.

'Huh,' she said. 'I suppose it's not a lie, that I need my cane,' she muttered. She took a deep breath. 'I broke my spine,' she said baldly.

'Ài, I'm sorry,' he blurted out. It sounded bad, but he'd seen what she could do today. She was either the luckiest spinal-injury sufferer in history or she'd pushed herself too far today. He couldn't say either to her face.

Her only acknowledgement of his inadequate comment was another wry facial expression. 'The paramedics and early therapy saved my spinal cord so I can walk. I can walk,' she repeated in a strange kind of tic. Gianluca froze. It was that or go over there and gather her up. He was accustomed to easy affection with his friends and family. If they were truly to be friends, he could hold her. But... something held him back. 'It hurt like hell. I wore a brace for months and I couldn't get far. The pain was too much. I had weird spasms in my leg and eventually the doctors worked out I had nerve damage.' He waited silently for her to continue. 'That's why I use the cane,' she said, her tone suddenly breezy, as though she wanted to shake off everything else.

'For the nerve damage?'

'No. That's the thing. I don't need the cane – at least, that's what the doctors tell me. So why, you ask, is she using the stupid thing when she doesn't need it? It's ugly and reminds me of the hospital and the pain and everything I lost in that stupid accident—' She cut herself off. 'Don't say a word right now. I don't want to cry.'

'Okay,' he murmured.

'And don't be too kind either.'

'Eh... sure?'

Her mouth wobbled and he wasn't sure which way she was

going to go. But a moment later, she smiled. She swiped her hand over her face. 'I can walk. I just feel... unsafe. I can't feel my right foot – so please don't step on it.' She laughed bleakly at her own joke. 'But I can walk on it. It doesn't even hurt.'

'You've said "I can walk" many times now.'

'Well, everyone tells me I'm supposed to be so bloody grateful for that.' She swore fiercely. 'God, I wish I'd just turned out the light.'

He forced his gaze from her face so she didn't feel so self-conscious. 'Thanks for telling me,' he said. 'Can I give you a hug? For my sake?'

'Ew, you are such a hugger.'

He couldn't help rolling his eyes. 'Friends hug, don't they?' he said lightly. Their earlier conversation came back to him with a tingle of warmth – the one where she admitted in the same breath that she found him attractive but was only interested in friendship.

He should be happy about it – he was happy about it. He'd done it once, falling in love over a single summer, and he wasn't prepared to put himself through it again.

'I don't know if I could control myself if we hug, big boy,' she said with a grin.

He hoped she was joking. 'No "big boy", please.'

'Okay, Lulu.' He shot her a dry look. She lay back on her bed, a little gingerly, he could tell. She stretched and rolled over, turning away from him. He should have felt relieved and done the same, but he stared at her back instead. 'Goodnight, Lulu!' she called over her shoulder. 'Bona note.'

'Bona note Norah,' he said. He stared up at the cracked ceiling. How was he supposed to sleep after that confession? His thoughts and feelings tumbled over each other, all coming back to the fact that he liked her a lot – unexpectedly – and it hurt to think of everything she'd been through. And she hadn't even taken pity on him and given him a hug.

* * *

Norah awoke with a shiver, confused about where she was and why her eyes refused to open. No, wait, her eyes *were* open, it was just ridiculously dark. Gianluca must have turned the lamp off.

Gianluca...

She lay still and stiff in the silence. The rain had stopped. She waited for a rustle of a bird, a hoot, a barking fox, but there was nothing. It was a far cry from Didi's Vauxhall flat, where Norah had been holed up for so long. Barely a night passed without a siren or two and the chicken shop across the road did a roaring late-night trade.

There wasn't even a daytime trade on this island. It was a place of peaceful reflection, but it was so bloody silent that Norah would start panicking soon. Except, a slight, muffled sigh came from across the room.

She could hear Gianluca breathing, deep and even, like when he'd fallen into a quick and easy sleep. Whereas she'd rolled around berating herself for spilling her guts.

Something cold and sharp landed on her face and she sat up with a yelp. She swiped at it, but it was only water. Running her palm over her face, she guessed it wasn't the first drop to have landed on her. No wonder she was so cold.

Why was the ceiling dripping on her after the rain had stopped? The convent had probably stood for centuries and *now* the roof had decided to fall in right above where Norah was sleeping?

She snatched the pillow out from under the drip and settled it at the other end of the bed, but, when she pulled the blankets back, they were sodden. The wall was wet. It was raining right over her.

Biting back a curse, she grabbed the pillow and hopped out of bed. She tiptoed over to Gianluca on the creaky wooden floorboards and stood over him, gnawing on her lip in hesitation. This was a crazy idea, right? She couldn't snuggle in bed with Gianluca just because her blanket was wet, could she? Would he get the wrong idea?

She patted the wall experimentally, and then the sheets at the end of the bed. They were blessedly dry. He wouldn't mind, would he, if she hopped in? It was either that or lie down on the bare floor with no blanket.

She settled her pillow at the end of the bed and gingerly tugged the blanket out of its neat hospital corners. She patted around for Gianluca, finding his ankles right in the middle of the narrow bed. He twitched, but didn't seem to wake. With a sigh, she shoved his legs over to the wall and climbed in.

She'd just settled her head on the pillow, marvelling at the warmth of the dry sheets and feeling rather pleased with herself, when his foot jerked, catching her on the chin.

'Ow,' she yelped, shoving his foot away.

He came awake with a shudder and rolled onto his side. His hand landed on her thigh, running down to her knee in hesitant confusion. His fingers brushed the back of her knee and she choked on a giggle and wrenched her legs away.

'Norah?' came his voice, gravelly with sleep.

'My bed is wet. The ceiling is dripping,' she said sharply. 'And your feet stink,' she added, needing to lighten the tone even though it was childish. Although now she'd mentioned it, there was a faint musty smell.

'How can the ceiling be dripping? It's stopped raining.'

'I have no idea. Maybe this place is like *The Shining*, but with water instead of blood. But do you really think I'd be snuggling up to your enormous stinky feet if I had another choice?'

'Why do I get the impression you've seen too many horror movies?' he asked. She could hear the smile in his voice.

'I haven't. But the ones I have seen... stayed. I'm impressionable.' An involuntary shiver ran down her spine. She always imagined those tingles reached the pins in her lower back and swore and beeped their horns at the roadblock before slowly driving on. Impressionable didn't begin to explain the wild landscape of her brain.

'You do have another choice,' he said with a sigh. She felt him stretch next to her.

'I'm not going to let you sleep on the floor. And my blanket is wet, too.'

'I didn't mean that,' he said, his tone hesitant.

'Uh, I don't see any other beds in here.'

'I can't promise fresh breath, after the garlic in the risotto and no toothbrush, but it's got to be better than stinky feet.'

Her breath whooshed out of her and she sat up. 'You mean... snuggle?'

He gave half a laugh that sounded distinctly embarrassed. 'Don't sound so horrified. You can be little spoon.'

She snorted. 'It's not such a big deal for you. You're a hugger, right?'

'I'll be gentle.'

'I'm not so sure about that,' she muttered, picking up one of his arms for emphasis. 'These weigh a tonne. Do you bench-press or something?'

'I row,' he said, his voice high. Poor Gianluca. She was embarrassing him – and kind of enjoying it.

She sighed. 'I was joking about your feet, by the way. They don't stink.'

'But I have a vague memory of kicking you in the face, so just come here so we can go back to sleep.'

'Well, if you're going to be so romantic about it...'

He chuckled and reached out. She felt his hand about to grasp her arm, but then he stopped. Aw, he was restraining his touchy-feelies for her. She was glad he couldn't see her grimace as she slid down beside him. He was so warm. She swallowed a ball of emotion as she stretched out, hovering over the pillow.

Was she going to have flashbacks of Andrej? Was she going to wake up with an embarrassing case of mistaken identity? She'd been blocking out the good memories and using her bitterness to get through the past year.

Her head fell to the pillow with a soft poof. She'd been part of a pair of scientists. They'd spent more time at work together than on dates. She'd gone back into the lab in Marghera without flashbacks to Andrej. This would be all right.

When Gianluca rested his arm over hers, she could only think he felt nothing like her ex – and she felt nothing like the Norah York who had dated Andrej for four years, carefully keeping herself in check with passions only for single-celled organisms and hypotheses and DNA.

Feeling her body go soft in the warm embrace, in an atmospheric monastery on a lonely island in the Venice Lagoon, she felt like Norah Phoenix York, Saffron's daughter, with a heart too big to fit in her chest.

She felt as blind as she was literally, at that moment, shuffling into the future without knowing where she was going. There was no way back. She'd been flung out of her old life by a motorboat. Remaining rolled up like a hedgehog wouldn't get her anywhere.

So, she swallowed her fear and allowed her bones to melt into the solicitous embrace of a friend. He said nothing, bless him. And she felt it when he relaxed heavily into sleep, breathing deep gusts into her still-damp hair.

A friend... She could do that. She probably needed it. She

certainly appreciated his presence, as exhaustion from the day – the year – leached from her and she could breathe deeply. She matched her breaths to his, feeling a tear drip down her cheek.

Things would look different in the morning. How different, she wouldn't realise until morning came.

8

Gianluca's eyes were gritty and wakefulness dragged at him like a fishing net caught on the seafloor. He was warm and comfortable and cocooned in deep, contented sleep, but the pounding sounded again and he struggled to force his eyes open.

The latch on the door lifted and Brother Marco, the younger friar with a Neapolitan accent, poked his head in.

'Oddio! Scusatemi! Mi dispiace tantissimo!' he spluttered and backed right out again.

A chuckle revealed that Norah was awake. She wriggled and he tightened his arm around her before he realised what he was doing and wrenched it back.

'Did we just scandalise a monk?' she said with a snort. She shuffled onto her back and turned her head to look at him. Her appearance punched him in the gut.

Her skin was blotchy with dried tears and probably a little sunburn. Her delicate mouth was twisted in a wry smile that was too wobbly for him to trust.

Her smile faded as they gazed at each other in the light of a new morning. Whatever had happened yesterday, it would stay with him for a long time, as though the sand had shifted under his feet. He brushed his thumb over her chin.

Then she stretched hesitantly towards him. Her lips opened slightly. And with halting slowness, she pressed her mouth lightly to his.

She made a choked sound and pulled away again immediately. It had been more of a breath than a kiss. But he felt a groan build up in his chest and forced himself to swallow it.

'Oh, God, what is *wrong* with me?' she said with a grimace. She hopped out of the bed like lightning. 'I'm sorry,' she said, crossing her arms over her chest and pacing. She detoured to the wall by her bed to grab her cane.

He sat up slowly. He couldn't un-know the things she'd told him last night and he couldn't un-feel the resulting protectiveness, no matter how much she wouldn't like that he felt it.

But would she misconstrue his protectiveness for romantic interest? What had that impulsive kiss been about? He couldn't take this attraction anywhere – certainly not for his own good – so he would rather not have experienced that half-moment of awareness.

He cleared his throat. 'Eh,' he began lamely, searching for the words to let her down kindly. 'I'm sorry, too. I'm not... I can't... We can't... interested.' Maria vergine, he'd mangled that sentence.

'Obviously we can't,' she agreed with an emphatic nod. Gian-luca waited for the relief to flood him, but her tone only tied him up more tightly in knots. 'I didn't mean... anything. I think my brain was asleep. Please believe me when I say I am not interested in a relationship with you.'

'I believe you,' he assured her. When she put it so baldly, it was impossible not to, and she'd pulled away from the kiss before it had even started. He must have misread that millisecond of tenderness. 'I'm not interested, either, but I understand we had a crazy day yesterday and a... strange night. I don't blame you – us.'

She nodded once, fiercely. 'I don't know what came over me,' she murmured, then turned away in a hurry to check on their clothes, which were drying on a rack in the corner. The air between them felt thick.

'We're still friends, right?' he blurted out before he could stop himself.

She turned back, emotions flittering across her face. Gianluca was unexpectedly breathless, waiting for her answer. A smile grew on her lips. It was lopsided and self-deprecating as usual and he realised he couldn't un-see the vulnerability, now he knew what it was.

'Friends sounds perfect,' she said. 'I need a lover about as much as a Venetian needs a bicycle, but I could do with a friend.' She stuck out her hand and he took it. She squeezed hard, which made him smile, now he knew how stubborn she was. 'It's kind of unavoidable after everything we went through yesterday.'

He studied the ceiling in thought. 'I hope we don't have any more days like yesterday, but I'm glad...' *It was you.* The words that came to his lips were too strange to say out loud. 'I'm glad we're friends now,' he finished, dropping his gaze again. He froze when he saw her slipping her arms out of the sleeves of the T-shirt and jimmying her bra on. He forced his mouth shut and turned away.

'Does that mean I can call you Lulu?'

'You didn't ask for permission before,' he pointed out.

'And maybe you'll actually keep talking to me instead of rowing in silence?'

'I talked more yesterday than I ever have out on the water,' he insisted. 'That was your fault.' He dared a glance and sighed with relief when he found her dressed again.

'Thank you,' she said, preening. She stepped up close and patted his chest with her palm. 'This is perfect. Since we're stuck with each other every weekend for the next few weeks, we can be friends and chat and it'll be great – I promise. It'll be like a summer fling, only with friendship instead of...'

'Sex?'

'Shhh, don't say that word in a monastery!'

'I'm pretty sure we already have a lot to repent. But okay. A summer friendship, eh? Just don't expect me to paint my nails with you.'

She burst out laughing. 'You have a sense of humour! You were holding out on me!'

'Of course I have a sense of humour. It's given to every Venetian child at baptism.'

Her laughter petered out and she patted him casually again. 'Please forget about that kiss, by the way. Truly, I think I'd just forgotten what it's like or something. I haven't kissed anyone in over a year.'

He tried not to wonder who she'd kissed over a year ago. 'It's been longer for me,' he said drily.

Her jaw dropped. 'Are you some kind of *monk*?'

He didn't give her the satisfaction of laughing, just a tolerant look, but he couldn't completely stifle his smile. 'Do you realise these aren't actually monks?'

'What do you mean? Are they just people in costumes? Re-enactors who take their hobby very, very seriously?'

He poked her in the ribs. She was so ticklish it was just delicious. 'They're brothers. Frati. Friars in English, isn't it?'

'What's the difference between friars and monks?'

'They're Franciscan. Monks are... not Franciscan.' He held up his hands. 'I'm not an expert. You'll have to ask them.'

'I don't know how I'm supposed to talk to them now they think we slept with each other in their monastery.'

'Shall I explain we didn't?'

'No!' she exclaimed, then turned to him, her hand on her hip.

'Just because we agreed to be friends, doesn't mean you can tease me now, *Lulu*.'

'It means exactly that,' he said with a grin. The banter came so easily between them that he didn't mind at all if she wanted to call him Lulu. They could have all of the benefits of a summer romance and none of the drawbacks – namely, being abandoned in the autumn.

She whirled away with a sniff, swinging her dishevelled plait. She grabbed the end and tugged off the elastic. 'Do you really think I'm the kind of girl who paints her nails?' she asked.

'No comment?' he ventured. She chuckled, running her fingers though her bedraggled hair with a wince. 'Can I help? With your hair?' He slammed his mouth shut. Even for friends, that was probably too much.

She eyed him. 'Not unless you have a brush, or could ask if the monks – or whatever – have a brush I could use.'

'Do you really think they would have a hairbrush?'

'I know!' she said, throwing a hand up. 'Brother Giuseppe must have a comb for his beard!'

'You'd really use Brother Giuseppe's beard comb?'

'You have a point,' she mumbled, turning her back. 'Go on, then. See if you can fix it.'

He stared at her long pale hair, which tumbled down her back in haphazard curls. He should have kept his mouth shut. He reached hesitantly for one rebellious curl behind her ear. He swallowed and reached up with his other hand. Lifting her matted hair, he ran his fingers slowly through it.

The flutters in his stomach needed to get a life. He and Norah were *friends*.

He just had to keep telling himself that.

* * *

Norah couldn't help thinking the weather was playing jokes on her later that morning, when she stood between the cypress trees and gazed at the sparkling lagoon, rippling innocuously. Sandbanks dotted the surface near the shore, teeming with algae, no doubt. The shallow water was a blinding turquoise, a colour of high spirits, contentment and delight.

In the distance lay a white, green and terracotta island, clustered with houses and a single wonky spire. Her sense of direction was terrible, but she guessed it was Burano. A sailboat meandered past, its pace sedate as there was very little breeze. Everywhere she looked was colour and light and benevolence. How such a day could dawn after last night was a mystery.

She understood the mechanics. She had done a meteorology course unit during her undergraduate degree, but the lagoon seemed to have a life of its own – replete with moods and whims.

Brother Giuseppe stood beside her quietly. The gardens of San Francesco del Deserto spoke for themselves – or rather, encouraged quiet reflection, a kind of solitude that was full of potential, because it wasn't a confinement.

Norah took a deep breath of the salty air, smelling the sharp chlorophyll of life. There was potential for her here, too.

She'd made a new friend. She couldn't think about that conversation without grinning like an idiot. This corny summer friendship idea had unlocked something between them. She shouldn't have kissed him – she'd almost managed to stop herself in time. But at least that short, startling brush of lips would serve as a warning. Definitely no more kissing. He was kind and wonderful and the very last person she wanted to mess around.

Safe in the knowledge that she wasn't pining for him, he'd crept out of his shell a little. Every new glimpse made her more certain that friendship with Gianluca would be good for them both. It was too sweet to ruin with a kiss that had exposed too many weaknesses.

They strode slowly back to the convent, Brother Giuseppe in his coarse brown cassock and Norah in her borrowed T-shirt. The buildings were prettily laid out at the end of the avenue of dark green cypress trees, all arches and warm bricks and rustic roof tiles. It would be the perfect setting for a wedding, she thought with a wry smile.

Brother Marco and Gianluca emerged as Norah and Brother Giuseppe approached.

'How's *Dafne*?' she asked in concern.

His smile went a long way to easing her worry. 'There's nothing to stop us heading back. A sand and a polish and she'll be as good as new.'

'Did you build *Dafne*?'

He shook his head. 'No, but I restored her.'

'Well, I'm sorry—'

'Psht,' he said softly. 'It's not your fault. Your equipment and samples are looking fine, too.'

'Oh... great,' she said. It was a very good thing that her hard work yesterday hadn't been for nothing, but the samples were somehow less important than the beautiful wooden boat that her friend had restored with his own hands.

They turned back to the convent together. 'You'll stay and eat some lunch before you go,' Brother Giuseppe said firmly.

'Grasie, frate, but we need to get back to Venice. My grandmother is expecting me.'

Norah looked slowly around at the palette of greens and browns, the restful panorama of her new favourite island. Perhaps she'd find a way to come back here.

'Do you do weddings here?' she asked, before she lost her nerve.

Brother Giuseppe and Brother Marco both blinked at her in

silence. 'You wish to get married?' Brother Giuseppe glanced at Gianluca, who was turning the colour of that famous pink hotel on the Grand Canal.

'Oh, no!' Norah denied emphatically. Brother Marco choked. Gianluca stifled a snort. 'I mean—' Her mind shifted into overdrive, trying to talk her way out of this one. 'I mean, yes,' she said, her voice high-pitched. Gianluca looked at her incredulously. Brother Marco seemed somewhat less scandalised, at least. 'Do you do weddings?' she asked again.

Brother Giuseppe hesitated. 'Not usually, but for our guests... I am a priest, as well, so I can perform weddings. If you would be willing to travel for pre-marital counselling beforehand. Are you both Catholic?' Norah's silence was enough of an answer. 'I'm sorry, but it's not something we would do at short notice, even when young love is involved,' he said with a kind smile.

It was Norah's turn to blush. To her shock Gianluca took her hand and threaded his fingers through hers. God, she'd forgotten how good *that* felt. 'Don't worry, nanarèla. I'll get you in front of a priest soon enough.' His dark eyes twinkled with amusement. He was a good sport, but she suspected he really meant he'd be dragging her to confession for lying to a bunch of friars.

She only hoped she'd never have to confess how good it felt to hold his hand.

9

Norah marvelled at their unique perspective of the old city of Venice, as they rowed back in the midday sun. First, she could make out little more than a set of spires on the horizon. After a while, Norah could differentiate the white houses from the beige ones, the red roofs from the green crowns of the tenacious trees. Gianluca pointed out the campanile, the orange bell tower with a copper spire that rose high over the other towers and cupolas.

The closer they came to old Venice, the more motorboats zoomed past, both pleasure craft and commercial vessels with cargo. All Norah could think about was the noise and the smell of petrol. She couldn't picture going into the protected salt marshes in a boat with such a disruptive motor.

Dafne was perfect: flat-bottomed, eco-friendly and very, very slow.

'What do you think when you see Venice?' she called back to Gianluca.

'Home,' he answered immediately with a quick smile.

It was a simple answer, but a wistful one for Norah. She'd grown up in the West Midlands, but she'd left her childhood behind with too many embarrassing memories of her unconventional family. Norah had spent more than three years in Portsmouth, completing her masters and starting her PhD, but it wasn't home, either. She hadn't been back since she'd been taken to London on a medical transport for surgery.

What would it be like to be so deeply rooted somewhere that you would always return, even if the memories there were mixed? Norah would never find out. If she got her career back on track, she'd be doing a PhD somewhere new and, after that, post-doctoral research. She'd be following algae around the world all her life.

It was one of the reasons a relationship with Andrej had made so much sense. He'd understood her commitment to science, to the career track that would make a normal life difficult, if not impossible. Working in the same field would have allowed them to take projects together.

They'd agreed to a long-distance relationship if they couldn't manage to get positions together. At the time, she'd taken it as a sign of his commitment to her. Now she realised they'd put work ahead of their relationship. Thinking she could have both was her mistake.

Now he was happily finishing his PhD in Portsmouth, while she was persona non grata in their department, for nothing more than making an insurance claim to cover medical expenses for extra rehab. She hadn't realised the subsequent investigation would ruin her relationship with her former colleagues, even though what had happened to her had been ruled an accident in the end.

With a sigh, she looked up, seeing the city suddenly up close, a raft of survivors who'd built a floating city from the crumbling remains of the old world. Why did this place make her mind swim with ridiculous ideas? Ideas like staying here until she was an old woman, when Gianluca could help her down the stairs of her apartment and take her shopping.

Dafne slipped deftly into a canal and Venice swallowed them up. Warehouses and fading apartment buildings with rickety shutters loomed over them. An ancient-looking brick church appeared on the right, with arched gothic windows and two tiny turrets that almost looked like minarets. The city looked different from the water, especially as it was low tide. She noticed the little holes just above the water level – and the occasional waft of something much less pleasant than the usual hints of fish and cooking oil. They must be part of the old sewerage system Gianluca had mentioned last night, the gatoli.

After dodging about a dozen gondole and several water taxis and negotiating sharp corners with aplomb, they arrived at Manu's palazzo. The canal-front façade was grandly decorated – or had once been – with ogee arches and columns that had been white, but were now flecked brown as the paint peeled. High above them, stone heads of solemn-looking bearded men emerged in bas-relief along with fishtails and a particularly buff merman that definitely *didn't* remind her of anyone she knew.

Gianluca nudged the boat against the piling outside the lower floor and efficiently tied off. He hopped onto the stone steps and held out his hands for her. He took her cane first, and then she placed her hands in his so he could haul her up onto dry land – if Venice counted as dry land.

'I'll take your samples down to the lab tomorrow morning. The university Biosciences lab in Marghera, right? Where Manu sometimes works? I'll get some tape and put your name all over it.'

'Thanks,' she said inadequately, feeling stricken at the idea of the goodbye that was coming.

'What is your surname?'

'Oh, it's York.' She spelled it for him, just to make sure. 'Um, how do I get in touch with you?'

'Manu has my number,' he said.

'Okay, I'll ask her when I've charged my phone.'

'Eh... maybe you could write down your number for me?' That request shouldn't have made her so happy.

She rummaged in her backpack for a pen, but the only paper she had was a sodden block of Post-it notes. 'Give me your hand,' she said.

His tanned skin, long fingers and thick knuckles looked alien in her small, pale hand, but she poked the tip of her tongue out and concentrated on remembering her phone number and not the warmth of his hand or the roughness of his fingertips. She wrote her name as well, for good measure.

'Norah with an "h",' she said, brushing her thumb over the word written in ink on his palm. She lifted her gaze to find his fixed on her.

'There you are!' came the sound of Manu's voice behind her. Gianluca wrenched his hand away and slipped it behind his back. 'Caspita, you two have had an adventure!' Manu squeezed Norah's arm and stretched up to place a kiss on Gianluca's cheek. 'Come inside and sit down. You must be exhausted!' The way she gestured made it clear that Gianluca was included in the invitation, but he stiffened and shook his head.

'Nòna is expecting me.'

'She's probably been keeping the sauce warm for you,' Manu said, her smile dim.

He nodded and turned back to Norah. 'I haven't forgotten I promised to take you to see Nòna. If I tell her you're coming next time, she'll start preparations tomorrow and there will be no going back.'

'She is an amazing cook,' Manu said. 'You should definitely go and visit her.'

Norah caught the quick grimace on Gianluca's face that was gone again in an instant. Norah was so damnably curious. Gianluca seemed to be naturally restrained, but Manu awoke some kind of passion in him that unfortunately made her jealous as hell.

Don't go there, she warned herself.

'I'd love to meet her, if you're sure she won't mind.'

'She'd mind if you *didn't* come. I'll send you a message about your samples and see you next Saturday.' He met her gaze for a wary moment, then lifted a halting hand to wave. She waved back.

'Thanks for... everything,' she said, her voice trailing off inadequately.

Gianluca looked as if he tried to smile, but it didn't get off the ground. 'It was nothing. See you next week,' he said without looking at her. He jumped back into the boat, slipped the rope through its knot with deft fingers and reached for the oar. In a few powerful strokes, he was gone.

Norah sagged against the damp stone wall, stifling a deep sigh.

'Come. Let's have aperitivo. You look like you need it,' Manu said.

* * *

'Te senta, amóre. Senta, senta! You don't help me cook today. You sit and drink graspa and then eat two plates of bigoli and a piece of amaretto cake and then you tell me why you look like you have been cleaning the gatoli.'

Nòna placed two colourful, long-stemmed schnapps glasses of clear liquid in front of Gianluca. He picked one up with a small smile, knowing she wouldn't be happy until he'd drunk it. He tipped the glass towards his nose to appreciate the fruity aromas that escaped the copious alcohol fumes of Nóna's grappa. 'Aren't you going to salute with me?'

She jerked her head at the glasses. 'They're both for you. I'll pour the wine.'

He chuckled and knocked back the first shot, enjoying the refreshing burn and the herbaceous aftertaste. He sighed deeply and Nòna turned back from the stove with a knowing glint in her eye.

He stared through the herbs rioting on her windowsill out into the sunny afternoon on the square, absently snapping a few basil flowers off the plant. It wasn't like Nòna to let them form at all.

It was too late for lunch and too early for dinner, but Manu had been right. It wasn't long before Nòna placed a steaming plate of pasta in front of him, in a sauce of aromatic sausage simmered with tomatoes.

'You always know when I need bigoli con luganeghe, Nòna. Grasie.'

She took his face in both of her lined hands and pressed a smacking kiss to his forehead. 'You were hard at work yesterday. Chiara came to help me with my shopping, the dear girl. Thank you for asking her.'

'She offered. I didn't have to ask.'

'It has been too long since she came for Sunday lunch.'

He swallowed a bite of pasta and reached for his wine. 'She teaches a few yoga classes on Sundays.' And he'd stopped bringing Chiara so often when Nòna's romantic hints had lost their subtlety.

Nòna crossed herself with a frown and quoted the old proverb: '"The woman of the world is never satisfied".'

Gianluca snorted. The saying reminded him more of Norah than Chiara. Everything reminded him of Norah today. 'You know there is mass at other times of the week,' he pointed out. 'And what makes you think Chiara isn't satisfied?' He knew he'd walked into that one when Nòna's eyebrows lifted. 'I know, I know: the same way I'm not satisfied because I'm single. Can I just finish my lunch before you pull out the list of people I could marry?'

She swatted him on the arm. 'I wouldn't need a list if you talked to me.'

'There's nothing to talk about,' he said. 'You know Chiara is only a friend and I don't meet new people every week.' He took a hurried sip of wine. It felt as if he was already tiptoeing around the issue of his newest 'friend' and he hadn't planned on introducing the topic of Norah right after a conversation about his love life – or lack thereof. He decided it was best to deflect. 'I saw Manu,' he said.

It had the predictable effect on poor Nòna. Her expression hardened to a grimace. 'Why? Are you two going to reconcile?'

'No,' he said, choking. 'She's hired me for the next few Saturdays – me and *Dafne*.'

'That sounds suspicious. She wants something from you.'

'She's got an intern from England for the summer, to work on her algae project. I'm taking Norah – the intern – out in the lagoon to collect samples. I won't even see much of Manu.'

Her expression softened. 'Was it okay for you? Seeing her?'

He shrugged. 'We can't avoid each other forever.'

'You can if you want to. You don't owe her anything, even if she reaches out. That woman has had enough of an impact on your life already.'

'I don't think she's "reaching out". I'm useful for her work. That's all. You don't have to worry.'

'I worry when you arrive late to Sunday lunch looking like *that*,' Nòna said, gesturing up and down his body with the spaghetti server. She took her own plate and sat heavily opposite him.

'That's nothing to do with Manu. We got caught in the storm and... we had to take refuge on San Francesco del Deserto.' He studied his plate, taking a careful mouthful so Nòna couldn't read anything in his expression. Not that he had anything to hide.

'With Norah, the intern?' Nòna asked. 'That is a pretty name. She is a young woman?' He nodded, trying not to show how carefully he was curating his facial expression. 'Pretty?'

He nodded again with a faint smile. 'And a lot like Manu,' he pointed out evenly. 'She's a PhD student and will be leaving after the summer.'

'Ah!' Nòna said with a frustrated swipe of her hand. 'What if she falls in love with Venice? What if she falls in love with you?'

'Nòna,' he said with a groan, 'she's not going to fall in love with me and, even if she did, it wouldn't mean she'd stay, so please don't wish that on me.'

She frowned and hauled herself out of her chair. She shuffled to the kitchen bench and poured a second glass of wine – a large glass. She sat heavily and took a long sip. 'I worry about you, toxàto mio.'

'I know you do,' he tried to deflect, but she took his hand and squeezed. She still had the powerful grip of a Venetian weaver.

'I don't want to see you hurt, but I worry your upbringing, your experience with Manu, with university and... that other girl has closed you off.' She patted his cheek. 'You needed brothers and sisters.'

'"Better a friend than a hundred relatives",' he quoted with his tongue in his cheek.

As he'd hoped, Nòna wagged a finger at him. 'Don't quote proverbs back at me! Invite Norah here – next Sunday!' she ordered sharply.

He resisted a smug smile. 'I already have.' The smug feeling vanished as Nòna's expression grew suspicious.

'You said she's pretty?'

Sissi landed on the windowsill and wailed an indignant demand. He'd never been so happy to see the damn cat. He stood in a hurry and lifted the sash window higher so she could strut inside.

'The cat smells suspiciously like fish,' he commented. 'Has she been stealing again?'

Nòna shrugged. 'If she has, she hasn't had the decency to steal two fillets. Take the plates, amóre. And refill my wine!'

10

Norah fell into the familiar rhythm of lab work during the week. She'd collected more than enough samples to keep her busy and spent every spare moment preparing them for DNA sequencing and propagation and mapping the species she'd identified.

Her work was engrossing, which was what she loved about it. On several evenings, she returned from the lab after dark, even though the days were long. She subsisted on crisps and chocolate bars and the occasional panino from the canteen.

The university lab was on the mainland in Marghera, connected to the old city by a long causeway over the western lagoon. Each time Norah took the bus back to the Piazzale Roma, the uninspiring Venice bus station, she experienced an odd itch, a feeling that she was missing out on something – like a social life. But what was the point?

No, it was better to be like Manu, she decided. Norah would grow old gracefully with no husband, no children and a glittering, international scientific career. Except, by God, if she had a hot affair with a man like Gianluca when she was in her forties, she'd try her best not to break his heart.

Manu let her in every evening when she returned. The heavy wooden door with its chipped black polish and the scary door-knocker had an ancient lock and a key that no locksmith had been able to duplicate. Norah could lock her own small apartment on the top floor, but she couldn't get into the palazzo by herself.

It was such an odd building, with its priceless chandeliers suspended from warped ceilings, fine, crumbling stonework and worn marble. Norah hadn't worked out if Manu spent her significant fortune entirely on her research foundation and had nothing left for the palazzo, or whether she simply had too little time to hire contractors, between her many meetings with politicians and developers.

As the week wore on, Norah noticed Manu attempting to feed her more often, but it was a case of the blind leading the blind, as Manu seemed to be unable to cook. By Friday, Norah felt as though she'd eaten her weight in olives and cod paste and she was thinking of stopping to pick up some fritto misto on her way home.

The lab cleared out on Friday afternoon and Norah forced herself to leave. She got off the bus and headed into the labyrinth of Santa Croce along the route she'd finally memorised. But, instead of following her nose to a hole-in-the-wall food stand for fritto misto, her feet slowed outside a hair salon.

There weren't many in old Venice – the property was too valuable, she imagined -so the fact that she'd walked past one at all was improbable. She tugged her long plait over her shoulder and ran her fingers over it.

'Take your hair down.' She could still hear the words in Andrej's voice and this time they produced a shudder of distaste.

Her long hair was a pain to wash and brush. She thought about cutting it every summer and it was mainly those words from Andrej that had stopped her.

She sucked a deep breath through her nose and pushed open

the door. An hour later, she wandered back to Manu's palazzo with a feeling close to elation. She could feel the breeze on the back of her neck, and the sharp hairline from the clippers.

Her girly plait was gone. She had the pixie cut of a scientist who meant business. It felt a bit like growing wings.

Manu gasped when she saw Norah, but clasped her shoulders and exclaimed approvingly, 'It suits you. Now come and drink with me!'

She ushered Norah up onto the rooftop balcony and sloshed wine into two coloured wine glasses that reminded Norah of Didi and her glassmaker boyfriend. Manu always poured far too much wine into each glass, but Norah didn't mind that night. She was exhausted from working long hours all week and restless from her crowded thoughts.

Luckily, she would see Gianluca tomorrow. His measured words and warm smile would settle her down – not to mention the peace of the lagoon. She couldn't wait. She wondered what he'd think of her haircut. If he thought she looked more like a boy now she'd shed that last vanity, that didn't matter, as they were friends and friends supported each other.

Thinking of tomorrow, she sat back and gazed over the red rooftops of Venice, the dark silhouettes of the trees and the glittering lights of the wooden terraces. The faint smell of barbecues and the sound of congenial voices rose over the city.

'I'm not paying you enough,' Manu blurted out, after Norah had taken her first sip of wine.

She spluttered and swallowed. The glass was so full it splashed over her hand. She studied the spilled wine, then shrugged and licked it off. Didi wasn't there to admonish her. 'It's a reasonable stipend, Manu,' Norah assured her.

'Well, then, you're working too much.'

Norah fiddled with the thick stem of the glass. 'That's just me.

I'm like a dog with a bone when you give me something to investigate. I'm glad to have something to do.'

'I'm lucky to have you for the summer, I think. Perhaps we're quite alike.'

'Perhaps we are,' Norah said. 'Where did you study? At some point, I need to finish my PhD, or start again, probably. But it's a bit overwhelming. I could go anywhere in the world, if I can get myself into gear and apply.' It was a big 'if'.

'I did my undergraduate here at Ca' Foscari. We did a masters as a basic degree back then. My PhD was in the States, at Woods Hole, and I did a few years of post-doc in Australia before returning to the States. Then I came back to Europe to set up the Biotechnology Centre in Stuttgart before I decided to start the foundation to move forward with the technological applications.'

'Your algae battery,' Norah said with a smile. 'I love the idea. I hope I'm the one to find you the perfect species.'

'If anyone can, it's you,' Manu said. 'The progress you've made already is impressive. I'll be writing the most glowing letter of recommendation.'

Norah gazed into her wine as warmth spread in her chest. Despite burying herself in experiments and documentation all week, her mind was still firing with ideas – like the idea that she'd come to Venice for a reason, that she was meant to be here.

Perhaps it wasn't her mind that was firing, after all, but her heart – that didn't want to be buried any more.

She grinned at Manu, shaking off the vulnerability she wasn't used to. 'Thank you. That means a lot. And thank you for pouring me wine and giving me food. I'm a terrible cook.'

'Me, too.' Manu chuckled. 'I'm not used to looking after anyone else and I'm not sure I'm doing a good job with you. Please tell me if you need anything. Or ask Gianluca, if I'm unavailable. He's... attentive, like that.'

Norah bit her lip, trying to force the question back down, but it wouldn't stay put. 'What's... what's up between you and Gianluca?'

Manu coloured immediately, her face turning pink under the fairy lights of the terrace. 'I think he needs to be the one to tell you. That would be fairer.'

Norah studied Manu's guilty expression. She must have broken up with him. It would have felt like kicking a puppy, breaking his heart like that.

'But he has reasons to... resent me. Reasons I fully acknowledge. But he's a very decent... man.' Did her voice break a little when she said that? Norah was more confused than ever. 'You won't get caught between us, or, if you are, then tell me and I'll fix it.'

Norah shook her head. 'No, it's nothing like that. You've both been very kind to me. It's just... a shame you're both... sad.'

Manu looked up sharply. 'Is he...?' She swallowed her emotion as quickly as it had risen to her face. 'I've no right to ask. But I'm... glad you two are getting on well.'

Norah froze, her throat thick with embarrassment. Was Manu suggesting there could be a romance between her and Gianluca? What should she say? Was she making an inappropriate assumption? Manu's attitude to all of this was... wrong, somehow. She was so full of bottled-up emotion, but voluntarily brought up the topic of Norah's relationship with her Gianluca. It didn't make sense.

'I will say, Norah,' Manu began hesitantly, 'it wouldn't be a good idea to... get involved with him.'

'That's the last thing on my mind, I promise you,' Norah assured her. Manu nodded with an apologetic smile. Norah racked her brain for a way to return the conversation to less personal territory. 'You know how it is. How am I supposed to have a relationship if I want to stay on track for a professorship?'

'I do know,' Manu said with a bleak smile. 'And, when you're a woman, it's doubly difficult.' To Norah's surprise, Manu's expression became even more haunted. If her work had come between her and Gianluca, surely it wasn't too late to change things? Norah, on the other hand, had no space in her life until she'd made a name for herself in her field.

'I haven't even finished my PhD, yet. If I want to keep doing this, then I have to focus. I'm well aware that a relationship isn't on the cards any time soon.'

Manu studied her with an expression that was difficult to interpret, but held a wealth of her own experiences and uncertainties. 'I'll order dinner, from now on,' she said, changing the subject. 'It's the least I can do. We shall eat like queens while you are here. I don't know a restaurant that can cook as well as Gianluca's nonna, but there are some that come close.'

'That sounds amazing.'

Manu lifted her wine and they clinked their glasses, sharing a smile. 'I have a list for you, by the way. And I made an appointment for tomorrow morning. Gianluca can take you before you head out.'

'An appointment?'

'At the Palazzo Contarini. They have a function room that your mother would *love*. It's in private hands, but I know the owner.'

Norah froze. She'd blissfully forgotten about her mother's harebrained idea to send her to scout wedding venues. Did Gianluca know what his first task would be in the morning? Her cheeks heated, remembering that conversation with the friars last Sunday.

'Um,' she said, her mind racing. 'I'm so sorry about that. I'm sure... Mum can just look herself. She was planning to visit in a few weeks, I think.'

Manu clapped her hands together unexpectedly gleefully. 'Wonderful! Invite her to stay with you. Is her fiancé coming as well?'

'I have no idea,' Norah said weakly.

'I would love to meet them.'

'I'm not so sure you would,' Norah said, her voice high.

Manu laughed. 'Nonsense. I gather your mother must be quite special.'

Norah resisted a grimace. 'That's one way of putting it.'

* * *

'I promise I won't pretend you're my fiancé, this time,' Norah said on a rush as she burst out of the doorway. A lick of hair fell over her forehead and he cocked his head, studying her.

'Did you—?'

'Yes,' she interrupted him abruptly. 'Well done for noticing. It's just a haircut.'

She turned to grab her backpack and he gazed at her hair, cropped short at the back. It *was* just a haircut, but... it made him itch to run his fingertips over the stubs of hair at her neck.

She set her cane in the boat and launched herself at him before he was ready. He fumbled for her elbow with one hand and grabbed the posto barca, the wooden piling by Manu's door, with the other.

'Bondí, Norah. Come xeła? How are you this morning?' he said, recovering himself.

She stilled, giving him a smile. 'Stago ben, grasie,' she responded carefully.

He chuckled. 'Where did you learn your dialect? I didn't think Manu would teach you a language she rarely uses herself,' he said, trying to ignore the feeling of anticipation as she settled onto the bench – her place. He couldn't wait to get back out onto the lagoon – that must be it.

The smile she gave him took him straight back to San Francesco del Deserto: the camaraderie of stumbling through the driving rain; the conversation in their twin beds. He skipped over the kiss-that-wasn't and landed right back at the friendship conversation that had been awkward but oddly pleasant with possibilities – although the only contact he'd had from his new friend through the week was a single text message.

And now she had a haircut that was probably supposed to be boyish, but it made him stare at her lovely neck.

'I learned a few phrases before I came – enough so I could impress the locals,' she explained.

'It works,' he said with a grin.

She pulled a hat out of her backpack, settling it over her short hair. 'Ready,' she said, glancing back at him. 'No storm forecast for today, I hope?'

'Clear skies and lots of sun, today. It'll get hot later. Have you got sun cream?'

'Yes, Mum,' she called back with a cheeky smile. 'Now let's get this wedding nonsense out of the way so we can get back to the lagoon.'

'Gianluca! Ciao, amore!' Manu appeared at the top of the steps. She leaned down and he placed the expected kiss on her cheek mechanically. Why the 'amore' all of a sudden? 'Raul will meet you at his palazzo. I'll call him now to tell him you're on your way.'

He nodded. 'We'll be ten minutes.' He steered *Dafne* back out from between the posts and along the narrow canal. 'Don't worry,' he said to Norah's back. 'I'm sure Manu has explained the situation.'

She laughed, but the sound was bleak. 'I hope so. I wasn't sure how I was supposed to explain that I'm looking for wedding venues for my embarrassing mother – and avoid the assumption that we're the couple.'

'I didn't mind you... lying to the friars.'

She snorted and her cheeks went pink. 'Yes, you did. You blushed like a little girl.'

'It was for a good cause,' he mumbled. 'Now, watch!' he

instructed as the sky up ahead opened out and he manoeuvred *Dafne* into the Canałasso, the Grand Canal. Norah whirled and gave a satisfying gasp as they entered the broad waterway, shining blue-green in the morning sunlight.

The ancient palazzi in bright white, orange, and shades of beige hovered loftily over the lapping water. With neoclassical columns or gothic windows, these buildings had been crafted to impress from the water and Norah was charmingly wide-eyed.

She fumbled for her phone and snapped pictures, cooing and gasping every few seconds as he pushed them out into the boat traffic. Purple petunias tumbled from the balcony of a pink palazzo. The red-and-gold Venetian flag flapped from the Palazzo Giustinian, with its countless gothic windows and striking quatrefoils.

Norah scrambled from port to starboard, snapping pictures and staring, slack-jawed, at the grand buildings in their myriad colours. Gianluca looked on in amusement as he rowed sedately behind her.

'I can't believe all you could say about this place was "home",' she muttered as she gazed at the stone façade of the Ca' Rezzonico.

A motorboat zoomed past, heading under the wooden Ponte dell'Accademia ahead of them. Norah startled and dropped her phone, clutching the bench with a curse.

'You okay?' he asked gently. She was already releasing the tension on a sigh. She hopped down to retrieve her phone from the deck.

'Yeah,' she said softly. '*Dafne*'s looking out for me.'

'She always is,' he said. 'Look.' He pointed. 'That's the Palazzo Contarini.'

Her jaw dropped as she gazed up at the pale façade, with its decorative stonework and rounded arches. 'You can seriously get married there?'

'Apparently, if you know Manu,' he commented drily. 'Just

quickly, you need to see the Palazzo Barbarigo and then we'll go in and talk to Raul.'

He rowed a little further and slowed in front of the famous palazzo, its façade covered in golden mosaics, the windows made of colourful glass discs. Norah leaned back to take it all in.

'Holy shit, who built that?'

'It's a giant advertisement, I think. It was built by some glass-making businessmen.'

'Those mosaics are made out of glass? Wow.' She continued to stare. 'Are those mer-chickens?' She pointed to a strip of mosaic under the eaves.

'Mer-what?' He followed her gaze to a coat-of-arms featuring two bird-like dragons. 'Phoenixes, maybe?' he suggested.

She shook her head. 'No flames, though. That's usually how you recognise phoenixes – they're on fire.'

He tilted his head in thought. 'I just thought so because the phoenix is a common symbol in Venice. Like the theatre – Teatro La Fenice means the phoenix theatre.'

She slapped her thigh all of a sudden. 'No wonder I feel so at home here,' she said.

'Hmm?' he prompted.

'Would you believe my middle name is Phoenix?'

'What?'

'I'm serious. My name is Norah Phoenix York. Did I already mention my mother is a weirdo?'

He gazed at her with a smile. 'Norah Phoenix. It's... ferocious.'

She burst out laughing, her shoulders shaking and her smile lighting up her eyes. It bubbled up inside until he was laughing, too.

'Do you think it suits me?' she asked.

'Without doubt,' he replied sincerely. 'Especially with that haircut.'

'I'll take that as a compliment.'

'As it was intended,' he said emphatically. She gave him a cheeky look and he got a bit tangled in her gaze so he cleared his throat and looked up, turning the boat around and heading back to the Palazzo Contarini.

'Your palace, siora,' he said, stepping past her to grab the post and tie off.

The swirling wrought-iron gate before them swung open. 'Ciao, hello, welcome! You must be the happy couple thinking of hiring our beautiful palazzo for your wedding!'

Norah froze. She shot Gianluca a look, as though it was his fault Manu had given Raul the wrong impression. He stifled a laugh and stepped off the boat onto the stone steps. He shook Raul's hand warmly.

'Yes, thank you for showing us the palazzo.' He turned to Norah and held out his hand. 'Honey? Are you coming?'

11

Norah was wondering if she'd accidentally sloshed a generous shot of amaretto into her coffee earlier. Between all the laughing and the surreal splendour of the Grand Canal, she certainly felt tipsy. Perhaps it was these wings that she'd grown after she'd chopped her hair off.

The feeling only grew stronger after Gianluca hauled her ashore and tugged her against him, clutching her hand.

'Dai, come on, *honey*,' he said with a straight face as Raul preceded them into the sparse ground-floor entrance and up the stairs to the main floors above.

They spent half an hour inspecting the ancient frescoes on the walls, the intricate baroque cornicing and the grand marble doorways, while pretending to be an engaged couple. There was no way Saffron could actually book the place after that.

Norah could barely think with Gianluca leaning close, pointing out the little gilded leaf motifs over the door, or tugging her out onto the balcony and slinging an arm around her. Every time she sneaked a scowl at him, Raul would appear and Gianluca would redouble his efforts to make her feel silly. Not that silly was what she felt, with his fingers brushing the back of her neck.

Her haircut was supposed to protect her from romantic feelings, but either Gianluca was a great actor, or that plan had backfired and he really liked her new look.

It would have been immensely frustrating if she'd thought Saffron would love the palazzo, but, although it was a fairy-tale wedding venue made real, Norah couldn't imagine her mother and Neal here. Saffron would be wearing something hand-sewn by Sherpas in Nepal, or dyed in Bali and smelling vaguely of incense. Neal would have a loud tie and an awkward grin and the whole picture would make Norah's head explode.

She had no idea how she was supposed to help Saffron choose a wedding venue, when she was deeply uncomfortable with Saffron's engagement and not feeling too keen on relationships in general. And if Gianluca insisted on making a charming nuisance of himself at every venue, she had no hope.

Her mind was tied up in knots by the time they took the stairs back down to the canal.

'Grasie,' Gianluca said as he firmly shook Raul's hand.

'It's beautiful,' Norah said, in all honesty. 'Thank you so much for showing us around.'

'You're welcome, you're welcome,' Raul said. 'You just tell Manu if you need anything.'

Her mind whirling, Norah stumbled back into the boat without waiting for Gianluca to help her. It was odd that Manu had put herself out for a couple of strangers, odd how quickly she'd grown so comfortable with Gianluca. Strangest of all was the sense of well-being she had here, in this strange city.

'Do you want to stop and get a water sample while we're here?' Gianluca said, pulling her out of her deep reverie.

She grinned up at him. 'Is this your way of apologising for that stunt at the palazzo? Or did I really train you so well last weekend?'

He tilted his head in thought and the wind caught the swirl of dark hair on his forehead. 'A bit of both, I think.'

'I won't get any samples from the old city today. We might not make it back out to the northern lagoon, so I'll save space for that.'

He nodded once, turning his face up to the sun. If he was bothered by the idea that she might never go to that part of the lagoon again, he didn't show it. Venice for him was *home*. It was only for Norah that it was a magical place where both her passion for science and her disorderly imagination lived in contented parallel.

Maybe it only felt so extraordinary because she knew she was leaving again.

'I'm going to cut through the city to head north. Do you want to go under the Bridge of Sighs?' he asked.

'As long as that's not some excuse to kiss me, *honey*.' She gave herself tingles with the stupid joke, thinking of his hand on the back of her neck once more.

He chuckled and she turned to see him leaning out to turn the boat with his own weight and the gentlest movement of the oar. She studied the long oar with its flared blade. It looked as though it had been grown, rather than manufactured, and a smile tugged on her lips to think of Gianluca as some kind of oar farmer, planting bits of wood and digging up oars.

He ducked to fit underneath the stone bridge next to the Doge's Palace and caught her watching him. 'What?' he asked.

'Did you make that oar?'

'Of course,' he responded evenly. 'Why?'

She shrugged and turned towards the bow again as he gestured to the bridge they were rapidly approaching. 'I suppose I've just been thinking of you as my personal gondolier and I forget you have a whole other life.'

Stone heads peered down at her from the arch of the famous white bridge, like a Greek chorus for her life. She smiled as she studied the various expressions, from grimaces of pain to puzzled smirks. At least, now she'd escaped from Didi's apartment and the endless physical rehab, she felt as though her life could be a comedy, rather than a tragedy.

'Maybe if you visit my workshop, you might see I'm real and not just your fairy gondolier,' he said.

She laughed. 'You realise I'm going to call you my fairy gondolier from now on.' He winced with chagrin, making Norah smile. 'I will,' she said with a firm nod. 'I'd love to come visit your workshop.'

'If you can tear yourself away from the lab, you're welcome any time.'

* * *

Gianluca thought Norah was unexpectedly quiet during the sedate circumnavigation of San Michele and Murano. After they'd cleared the old city and set off past the brick walls of San Michele, she'd stretched out in front of him to soak up the sun. Her ankles were crossed and her bare feet swung from side to side in typical Norah's restlessness. Well, one foot swung from side to side, nudging the other into sluggish movement. In a pair of blue shorts, with the tie of a bikini visible at her neck, she was distracting.

'You're quiet,' he said, when he couldn't hold it in any more. He usually craved the silence of the lagoon, amongst the tiny inlets where no motorboats ventured. But Norah's silence was eloquent and he wanted to know what was going through her head.

'I'm just waiting until we're far enough out that no one can hear you scream,' she called back.

'That answers one question,' he muttered.

'You didn't ask a question,' she pointed out. 'But yes, your stunt turned that visit into a waste of time.'

'I am sorry. I couldn't resist. I'll make it up to you somehow.'

'I'm sure you will,' she said in a suspiciously suggestive tone. 'Do you think Manu did it on purpose?'

She turned to look at him, her expression pinched. 'To embarrass me?'

'No,' he insisted immediately. 'More like a poor attempt at... matchmaking.'

'Matchmaking? Us?' Her voice was so high with disbelief that at least he could be certain the thought was far from her mind. 'No way.'

He wished her tone didn't prick him. 'It must have been a misunderstanding. I didn't think it through. I'm sorry.'

'Stop apologising so beautifully. I want my revenge.' He stifled a smile. She mustn't be too angry. 'I don't think the palazzo was right anyway.'

'And?' he prompted.

She hauled herself back up onto the bench. 'I don't know how I'm supposed to find my mum a venue. I can't even picture her truly going through with it.' Norah sighed, staring out at the marshes, as though she found them as soothing as he did. 'To be honest, I always thought I'd get married before she did.' She tugged off her hat and ran her fingers through her cropped hair.

'It was probably a reasonable assumption. It's surely unusual to get married at her age.'

'It's not that.' She paused, glancing up at him. 'I'm not sure you really want to know.'

He hesitated, feeling the pressure to word his next sentence correctly. 'If you want to tell me,' he said. 'I care, Norah. Friends, right? I meant it.'

This time, when she peered up at him, her eyes had lost a little of their shadow. 'I meant it, too,' she said softly. She took a deep breath. 'I was with a guy for... years.' She stared up into the sky as though trying to work out how many years they'd been together. It made his jaw tense up in chagrin. If he and Norah were together and she couldn't remember how long it had been, he'd be quite put out. But that was the difference between them. 'I really thought that was it. I thought we'd get married one day. We never argued. We both understood the pile of work we have to do – publish or perish and all that. But...'

A new feeling twisted deeper inside him – anger in his blood, at what he suspected was coming.

'When I got hurt, I thought he'd stayed behind at the university because there was no point following my worthless body to London when there was nothing he could do that the doctors and nurses couldn't. It made sense.'

Gianluca cursed, rubbing a hand over his mouth before clutching the oar again tightly.

'Yeah,' she said flatly. 'Actually, he'd already broken up with me in his mind. He just hadn't had a chance to tell me because I was on heavy drugs. Then I applied to get the insurance paid out and... all hell broke loose. The university department basically turned on me because they got investigated. All I did was fill in the forms, but they thought I must have said something to arouse suspicions. It was awful,' she said with a vehemence that was too obviously covering hurt. 'He... my boyfriend sided with them. He told me over the phone that he didn't want to see me, that I'd made everything awkward in the team. And that was it. He kissed me goodbye that morning when I went out sampling and I never saw him again.'

Gianluca took several deep breaths through his nose before he managed to speak. 'Norah,' was all he managed to say at first. 'He was... is a coward. And that's the last word I would use to describe you.' She squinted up at him, her eyes grave.

The words weren't enough. He hauled the oar out of the water and set it in the boat, stepping down to her level. She shuffled over on the bench and he sat next to her. They were only touching at the shoulder and hip, but he slowly breathed out. He didn't know what else to say. He wasn't going to push her for a hug, but the silence, the soft touch of her shoulder and the simple act of gazing out at the lagoon together dulled the sharpness of her confession.

After a long moment, she leaned her head gently against his shoulder. He had to fight to keep his eyes open, he was so gratified to have her come to him. 'I'm sorry he put you through that,' he said, the words coming a little more easily now. 'And thanks for explaining it to me.'

She squeezed his arm and lifted her head again. He had to let her draw away. 'Thanks for being angry on my behalf.' She smiled up at him unexpectedly and it caught him like a punch. 'But don't crack a tooth.' She brushed her thumb teasingly along his jaw and he swatted her hand away.

He pulled himself together. 'I would be saying some pretty foul things in Venetian right now if you understood,' he managed to joke.

'Something about penises, right?' she guessed.

He snorted, giving her hand a quick squeeze in one final, inadequate gesture of his feelings. 'What have you been learning?'

'My sister's boyfriend is from Murano.'

He winced. 'Glassmaker? They're almost as bad as the gondoliers.'

'What? Are the oarmakers paragons of good language?'

He cocked his head in acknowledgement. 'But seriously, Norah. Your ex-boyfriend is a... bad guy.' He wanted to say something stronger but resisted.

She sighed. 'I know. But... if it didn't work with him, what hope do I have?' She shook herself. 'So I need to be alone, right now, and that's another reason why we should avoid a holiday romance.' Her smile became a little wicked. 'It's nothing personal. If I was going to have a wild fling, I'm pretty sure it would be you, Lulu!' she said with a grin.

He forced himself to laugh but she wouldn't joke about that if she knew how much he'd been staring at her neck that morning, more Nosferatu in Venice than fairy gondolier. Mind you, if she knew how tightly he'd held onto his last girlfriend... Norah Phoenix would fly in a second.

He stood, stepping around her to retrieve the oar and set them back on course.

'Does someone actually live there?' she asked, pointing to a small island with an orange brick wall all around. He couldn't remember the name of it.

'I don't think so. There are a lot of uninhabited islands in the lagoon, even ones like this with buildings on them.'

'No monks, then,' she joked.

'Or nuns, or psychiatric patients, or plague sufferers, or former Doges. There are islands for each of those – or there were in the past.'

'Which one shall we get stranded on next?'

'We're *not* going to get stranded anywhere today!' he insisted emphatically. 'I'll have you home safely for dinner.'

'You're no fun,' she said and gave him a wink. 'I'm sure I can work out a way to strand us *somewhere*. Somewhere with really good fritto misto.'

He shook his head with a smile. The sun was beating down on them with unseasonal strength. There would be no dramas today – if he could at all help it.

12

The sun was remorseless that afternoon, reflecting off every surface and baking poor *Dafne* in a zillion-degree heat. It was almost too warm to concentrate on sampling. It was only the end of May and somehow Norah had to survive all of June and most of July.

Gianluca slowed the boat to a drift at the next sandbank. One hand keeping the oar steady, he grasped the hem of his T-shirt with the other and wiped his forehead. Norah whipped her gaze back to her sample kits.

They were somewhere north of Burano, further than last time, deep in the salt marshes. The further they rowed from Venice, the wilder the landscape became. The islands were flat and scrubby, with no houses or structures of any kind. The only evidence of the impact of humans on the area was the silver posts sunk into the water delineating the channels and the narrower sticks marking fishing nets under the water.

The sky was enormous overhead, swept with clouds, a blue so bright it was almost painful to look at. The water was a turquoise green, silty and earthy, but so clean on her fingers, after the hint of oil that tainted the canals of the old city.

The gentle drift of the boat, the bright colours and the languid heat seemed to slow Norah's entire metabolism. A shaggy heron picked its way through the mud a few feet away, half-heartedly poking its head into the water as though it, too, had lost its appetite in the heat.

'It's so beautiful,' she commented as she leaned over the bow with the vacuum borer to grab some sediment.

'What's left of the natural lagoon,' Gianluca said slowly.

She glanced back at him curiously. 'I read about the retreat of the salt marsh. Do you remember it differently?'

'Not really,' he said. 'But that's the problem, isn't it? Preserving something people don't appreciate anyway. It's hard enough to preserve old Venice and it's one of the most well-known cities in the world.'

He waved his T-shirt, trying to get some relief from the heat. Norah finished up with her sample, recorded the GPS data and filled out the label. After she'd placed it in the box, she decided to take pity on him. She slipped off her T-shirt with an appreciative sigh. She was glad she'd put her swimsuit on underneath. Hopefully he'd get the message that he could feel free to take his shirt off, too. She wouldn't even check him out, she promised herself.

'Is it always this hot in May?'

He made an odd choking sound before speaking and she looked up in confusion. He was staring with unexpected focus in the direction of Burano. 'Not always, but it's not unusual,' he said finally. He wiped his brow again with his forearm. He wasn't taking the hint.

She clapped her hands together. 'Let's go swimming!'

'I thought you needed samples.'

She gestured to her neat box of samples, which was nearly full. 'I've got so much I could probably work in the lab for the next eight weeks just with this stuff. Is there somewhere we can swim?'

'Is it okay for you to swim?'

'What a stupid—' Her gaze flew to his as she realised what he meant. Her hand flew to her back, her fingers finding the indentations and raised rough patches she still wasn't used to. God, how had she forgotten she had some pretty nasty scars on display? Her stomach dropped. 'It's fine,' she said tightly. 'Can we go somewhere?' She turned back to the bow.

'Ciò,' Gianluca said, clearing his throat. 'Norah, ehi... I'm sorry.'

'It's not your fault,' she forced out. 'My back is right in your face. I don't know what I expected.' She grabbed for the T-shirt, but his hand landed on her shoulder, squeezing for a short second before he took it away again.

'To be honest, I didn't notice at first.' She responded with a sceptical look. 'I'm serious. Without your hair... I don't know. You... have nice shoulders.'

Tingles flared all over her skin as some unwise part of her believed him. When she'd swallowed her feelings, she gave him a wink. 'So do you.'

He chuckled and shook his head wryly. His gaze was warm and amused. She grinned back. She should look away, but she didn't want to. Eventually, he laughed again and reached forward to ruffle her hair with one hand.

'Hey!' she protested half-heartedly as his heavy hand thoroughly mussed the short locks.

'I've wanted to do that all day,' he said as he smoothed his hand once down the back of her head.

'I look like Albert Einstein now, don't I?' she said drily.

'Your hair is too short for that.' He clamped his hand back around the oar and looked up. 'Do you really want to go swimming?'

'Yes!' she cried. She glanced back at him. She hadn't forgotten the stunt he'd pulled at the palazzo that morning. She'd get her revenge when she'd lured him into the water.

'Bón,' he said with a nod. He dipped the oar in, carefully manoeuvring the boat back out of the marsh and into the twisting, natural channel. 'Andemo! Let's go.'

Dafne was never fast, but she moved jauntily through the water. Norah sighed and, on a whim, raised her arms to soak up the sunshine and sweet, tangy air of the wetlands.

'Why did you cut your hair?' Gianluca asked.

'Why do I need to have a reason? Why do women have to have long, annoying hair?'

'You have a point,' Gianluca said after a moment of consideration. 'Nòna always tells me to cut mine.'

It was a small thing, but she was gratified that he'd shared something about himself without her levering it out of him.

'It would be a shame for you to cut that adorable floppy bit on top.'

'It takes some effort to keep this... floppy bit just the right length.'

'And what does Nòna think of your tattoos?'

'Nòna doesn't know about all of the tattoos.'

'But she must know about the one on your leg.'

He nodded. 'I got that one when I opened my workshop. It's a... schematic drawing of the movements of an oar.'

When she peered rudely at him, he twisted his leg and showed her. She saw the oar in the diagram, surrounded by arrows denoting movement, angles represented by Greek letters and several equations.

'Wow. This makes the nerd in me weep for joy,' she muttered.

'Here, this is the force applied by the rower,' he said with a smile in his voice, pointing to the first equation.

'And the resistance of the water.' Norah pointed to the second equation. She cocked her head, fascinated in equal measure by the maths, the ink on his skin and the fine dark hair on his leg. 'And this one is something to do with the fórcola.' She looked up at him. 'Most people would just tattoo "I heart Nòna" or something.'

He shrugged. 'Well, I heart fórcole.'

They reached a long sandbank among a labyrinth of narrow channels and Gianluca tossed the anchor out and put down his oar. It was a little sandy beach, hidden behind the marsh grasses of other islands. The smile on Gianluca's face suggested he knew the place well.

He tugged off his shirt – finally. Norah stifled her smile and counted the seconds, taking the opportunity to study the tattoo on his upper arm. It was the head of a bird, drawn to look fierce. But now was not the time to ask him what it meant. She was hell-bent on revenge for him pretending they were a couple that morning. 'What?' he asked warily.

She tried to look innocent, but the amusement in Gianluca's expression suggested that wasn't an improvement. She stood carefully, choosing her moment.

'If you think—'

Now. 'This is for calling me "honey",' she cried, and she gave him a shove.

As she'd intended, he headed straight for the water like a human sinker, a satisfying expression of shock on his face. What she hadn't intended was for *Dafne* to wobble manically and throw Norah off in revenge. She hit the water backside-first and sank.

She had a moment of panic as she unravelled herself, but she had been a good swimmer before the accident and the lagoon was cool and refreshing, rather than the frigid shock of the waters around the UK year-round. It also wasn't deep. She brushed the sand on the seabed with her fingertips. She hung suspended for a moment, enough salt in the water for a little buoyancy, but not so much that she could taste it.

It was glorious under the water – cool, still and clean – until

Gianluca hauled her up. Then it was glorious for a few more reasons.

He wrapped his arms around her as he lifted her. They were both warm and slippery and he struggled to get a secure hold on her, but that feeling that the embrace would end any second now, that she could slip out of his arms without effort, made her want to stay.

'Are you okay?' he asked. He was so cute with that concerned expression on his face.

She put her feet down – the water was only up to her thighs. She answered his question with a cheeky smile and raised her arms slowly around his neck. But instead of continuing the embrace – which was strictly *friendly*, she reminded herself sternly – her fingers travelled up the back of his head to ruffle his hair.

She took her time, tangling her fingers in his thick hair until it stuck out in all directions. Her revenge was complete, but it didn't feel as satisfying as she'd expected when she dropped her hands and stepped away.

'Finished?' he asked tolerantly.

She tapped her finger against her chin. 'Almost.' She tugged one strand of hair straight up, grinning at his goofy expression as he tried to look up at his hair. 'There,' she said and stumbled back to the boat to retrieve her phone. She snapped a picture as he tilted his head and gave her a long-suffering smile.

'My fairy gondolier.' She giggled.

'Do you realise the problem with revenge, Norah?' he asked in a thoughtful tone.

'What?'

'It starts a cycle.' All he had to do was eyeball her and she shrieked, dumped her phone back into the boat and took off. He caught up with her without any trouble, nabbing her ankle – her good ankle. She splashed him with all her might and wriggled free.

When he eventually dunked her, *Dafne* was a hundred feet away and they were in a deeper basin, but the warm water and the pale reddish buildings of Burano in the distance gave Norah the feeling that nothing could go wrong in this protected lagoon – a sanctuary for birds and plants and scientists who'd lost their way. In the water, she didn't feel so panicked about her balance – or about her future. She didn't have to be anyone. She could just be.

The hazy sunlight shimmering on the water took the fight out of her quickly and she kicked her legs up until she was floating, dead-man style, under an endless sky. 'This is perfect,' she murmured. 'Thank you.'

'I love this part of the lagoon,' he said softly, stretching out to float beside her. 'I used to come out here to fish with my father. We'd take Nòna to her vegetable garden on Sant'Erasmo and continue up here. Dinnertime in summer was always the best.'

The water lapped at her ears, but if this was what it took to get him talking, she'd put up with it. 'My mum is a terrible cook,' Norah commented.

'So is—' He cut himself off.

Norah swallowed, fighting a frown. She was certain he'd been about to say 'Manu'. The sudden sting was sharper than she'd expected. She struggled for a light response to shrug off her change of mood before he noticed something.

But before she could think of anything else to say, an angry shout cut through the silence. Gianluca jumped and righted himself with a grimace. A torrent of harsh words and the rattle of a motor made Norah flinch as she stood as well. Gianluca's hand closed around her upper arm.

The motorboat pulled up in front of them with a splash. Two men were on board, one of whom was still castigating them loudly.

'Merda,' Gianluca groaned.

'What's he saying?' Norah asked.

'You don't want to know,' Gianluca muttered.

'Actually, I do. Translate for me – especially the bad words.'

But Gianluca's attention was on the newcomers. 'Scuxa,' he began with a deeply apologetic expression. He exchanged a few sentences with the men on the boat, gesticulating with one hand while he held Norah's forearm with the other.

'What've I done now?' she whispered when one of the men raised a frustrated hand to his head.

'*We*,' Gianluca said, 'have strayed into their fishing area.'

'Oh,' Norah said, suddenly noticing the sticks poking up out of the water all around. 'I'm sorry!' she called out.

'Eh? Forèsta?' the man called back.

'A forest?' Norah asked in confusion.

'No, it means a foreigner – anyone who's not from around here.'

'Oh,' she said with a grimace.

The men hopped out of the boat in shallower water a few feet away, their long waders keeping them dry. With a deft movement, one of the men grabbed the end of a net below the water and tugged, hauling it in efficiently.

'Uh, can we help?' Norah called out on an impulse. All three faces looked at her as though she'd lost her marbles. She shrugged. 'I'm truly sorry for disturbing your... fish.'

The older man, who wore a crushed blue baseball cap and a perpetual grimace, looked to Gianluca, as though expecting an explanation.

She poked Gianluca in the ribs. 'Translate for him.'

'I understand you,' the man said. 'We don't need your help.'

'Oh,' she said. 'Can we buy some of your fish, then?'

He laughed then, tipping his head back with a howl. He waded closer to study them. 'It's not fish. And you would be lucky to buy.'

Gianluca squinted at the net. 'Moeche,' he said, a grin breaking out. He dropped her hand and strode over to the fishermen. He beckoned to Norah with quick fingers. 'It's crabs. Look!'

At the word 'crabs', she shrank back. Crustaceans were her least favourite form of marine life, coming in after gelatinous zooplankton and ectoparasitic flukes. She shook her head fiercely at Gianluca.

'I do not believe my ears,' the older man continued. 'The lady does not want to buy moeche?'

'*I* do,' said Gianluca with enthusiasm. 'Come on, Norah. These aren't just any crabs.'

'These,' explained the fisherman grandly, 'are *nude* crabs. Or they will be in some days, I hope.'

'Did he say "nude crabs"?' Reluctantly curious, she approached and inspected the specimen in the palm of the older man's hand. '"Nude crabs",' she repeated drily. 'That's *carcinus aestuarii*, the common green crab. And it's about to moult. Natural behaviour for this species in spring, I believe.'

'But have you ever eaten it, fried lightly in oil?' Gianluca said, his face lit up. 'Nòna would love some of these.' He turned to the older man and spoke in rapid dialect. A moment later, they were shaking hands and clapping each other on the shoulder like long-lost friends.

Norah watched with a smile tugging on one side of her mouth. Her brain filled in the blanks of the conversation:

'*For your nòna, I will give you a good price – and because you can speak my dialect!*'

'*I have always wanted to meet a nude crab fisherman!*'

'*Lucky for you the crabs are nude and not the fisherman – bahahaha.*'

Okay, that last bit was unlikely, but it seemed their trespassing had been forgiven. Gianluca introduced himself and it all started up again: the back-slapping, exclamations and the flood of warm words.

'This is Emiliano,' Gianluca said, gesturing to the older man, 'and his son Daniele.'

She stretched out her hand. 'I'm Norah.'

'You cannot help, not dressed like that, but you can watch from your boat,' Emiliano said grandly. 'And you must come back with us to Burano. I cannot let Gianluca Marangon come to my island in moeche season and *not* eat! You can leave the boat at my posta and take the vaporetto back after eating.'

Norah trailed Gianluca back to *Dafne*, alternately swimming and wading. 'Are you famous or something?' she asked as he hauled himself up, the boat tipping wildly.

'No,' he said dismissively. 'I made his brother a fórcola last year and...' When he didn't continue, she prompted him with a look. 'I've been doing some things for a local campaign against large cruise ships entering the lagoon. Emiliano's niece is involved, too, so he's heard my name.'

'You're a local hero,' Norah muttered, not sure whether she was teasing him or simply impressed. His response was a predictable and quite inarticulate denial. He shook off the topic and held out his hands to haul her up into the boat.

They followed Emiliano and Daniele back to the island of Mazzorbo, where they sorted the crabs into submerged baskets according to the imminence of their moulting and retrieved the jelly-like specimens that had already shed their shells and were crawling around nude.

Norah's stomach rumbled as Gianluca rowed up to Burano. Earlier that day, they'd stopped for lunch at an osteria on the eastern side of the island, but she hadn't seen the main canal. The fondamenta was bustling with tourists visiting the lace ateliers or stopping at market stalls, and locals wandering to their favourite spots for their evening aperitivo. The brightly coloured houses – sky blue, hot pink and lime green – were a shock after the graduating greens, blues and browns of the lagoon. Flapping laundry hung from ropes under the upper windows. The buildings were only two or three storeys high, making the island feel like a village in comparison to its grand old sister to the south.

They met Emiliano outside a restaurant with a weathered sign that read 'Pasta, Pizza's', the unnecessary apostrophe making Norah cringe, but instead of eating at the restaurant, they strode straight through it, to a walled garden out the back. Emiliano presented a large bag of his prized crabs to an ancient woman whose hands looked as though they could tell everyone's future, and then Gianluca and Norah were shown to a large table like honoured guests. Daniele poured Prosecco liberally. They nibbled on bread with fish paste or prosciutto as the sounds and smells from the kitchen wafted into the garden: the sizzle of oil in the pan, sharp words from the old woman and a sweet seafood smell.

Norah's glass was never empty and her mind was chock full of boisterous conversations she couldn't understand and good humour she definitely could. Emiliano answered all of her questions about the changing lagoon and Daniele asked her about London with a wistfulness that was not appreciated by his family.

While the last rays of the sun dabbed the island in gold, it was finally time to eat. They greeted the arrival of the cooked crabs with a cheer and the pop of another wine bottle, this time a dry Soave, which went down even better than the Prosecco Norah had been slurping. Seeing the crabs, fried in a light dusting of flour, she suddenly understood why they needed to be nude – they were fried whole.

She was tipsy by the time she picked one up on her fork. Emiliano and his family howled with laughter at her grimace as she nibbled at the legs. But the smooth, lightly crunchy texture and the unique flavour – brackish water and seaweed, with the sweetness of crab meat – made her groan with delight. As she enthusiastically crunched the rest of her crab, she felt as though she'd passed some kind of initiation ritual and had become one of them. She wasn't, of course, but she was getting too drunk to remind herself she was a stranger.

It didn't hurt that Gianluca had draped an arm along the back of her chair. Whenever the conversation went over her head, she just leaned back to recharge against his warm forearm. Occasionally, his fingers would brush her shoulder.

'Do you know what a good man you have there, Norah?' Emiliano's wife leaned in to ask her.

'Oh, I... No, we're not...' Her mind was disturbingly sluggish. She had no way of knowing how much wine she'd drunk. 'Solo amigos,' she said, her tone a little too perky. 'Wait, is that Spanish?'

'We all understand you,' Gianluca said, resting a hand on her shoulder. Was he drunk, too? He gripped both of her shoulders with a gentle squeeze. 'I think it's time to go home.' Probably not drunk, then. That was just her.

Gianluca took her hand and hauled her to her feet, steadying her with both hands on her upper arms.

'Phew!' she said. 'I am such an embarrassing lightweight.' She heard Emiliano laughing, but it sounded distant. Only Gianluca felt real. 'Why aren't you drunk?' she asked accusingly. She dropped her voice low to answer her own question in a poor imitation of Gianluca. 'Because I am twice as big as you, squirt, and these enormous muscles soak up the alcohol.' She flexed her biceps.

He wrapped an arm around her. 'Time to go... squirt.' He retrieved her cane and it took her two attempts to grasp it properly.

She wriggled out from under his arm and turned back. '*Grasie*, Emiliano,' she gushed, kissing his cheek. 'Daniele, Lidia, thank you! You are all so beautiful and I love you!'

* * *

Gianluca suspected the feeling was mutual. Norah was an adorable drunk. It took him another ten minutes to drag her out of there; she was too keen to kiss everyone's cheeks and soak up the endless smiles and endearments.

He tried to reconcile drunk Norah with bitter Norah, from last weekend, but it was difficult. He'd thought she wasn't comfortable with casual touches, but here she was hugging with abandon.

Emiliano saw them back through the restaurant and shook his hand. 'It was a pleasure to meet you, Gianluca,' he said warmly.

'And you.'

Emiliano glanced at Norah with a chuckle. 'She's not so much of a forèsta any more, eh?'

Gianluca responded with a forced laugh and steered Norah back along the canal towards the vaporetto stop, waving to Emiliano.

'He called me a "forèsta" again, didn't he?' she said with an exaggerated frown.

'Actually, he said you weren't so much of a foreigner any more,' he commented lightly.

She turned to him, her eyes wide. 'Really?' she asked, her tone high-pitched. 'I *did* pass some kind of test!'

He didn't trust himself to respond. The one test she would never pass was the test of time. She was one of those people destined to leave Venice.

Whereas he'd been born *venexian*, to a gondolier and a woman of an old Venetian family, and every time he'd left, it had not ended well.

'You know,' she said, 'I keep oversharing with you.' He wasn't sure if she planned to continue. She seemed to grow fascinated by the stars all at once, staring up with her mouth open. He tightened his arm around her as she took no care for her balance.

'Maybe you needed it,' he said mildly.

'Of course, I needed it. I need a *friend*,' she said pointedly. 'But you don't. And that sucks.'

'What makes you think that?' he asked carefully.

She snorted and poked him. 'I vomit verbally all over you and you just stand there and say nothing back.'

'As long as you don't vomit literally.'

She pushed away from him with a grumble, wobbling along the fondamenta. 'Fine, be that way! I still want to be your friend because I'm sad and lonely and inadequate!'

'Ehi!' he gasped and grabbed for her as she tottered on the edge of the canal. He took her hand firmly, wondering why her words had got to him just as much as the concern that she'd fall into the water. 'You think you're the only one who's sad and lonely some-times?' he snapped without thinking.

She stopped suddenly, tugging him to a stop as well. 'Oh, God,

I'm sorry Gianluca. I'm sorry,' she repeated, her voice breathy and tight. 'Here I am whinging about my shitty ex-boyfriend and lack of friends when you've lost both of your parents.' She lifted her hand to his cheek and the curl of emotion tightened its hold on him. Part of that emotion was guilt. He'd wondered whether he should have simply told her the truth right from the beginning. It was more awkward now than he'd pictured it being then.

But he hadn't been thinking of his parents when he'd suggested he was also sad and lonely. He'd been thinking of Nòna and her shrinking chances of ever seeing him settle down and have a family.

'Don't be sorry,' he said with a shake of his head. 'I meant you're not the only one who's... been disappointed in love.' He winced as he said it, waiting for her nosy questions.

If anyone would understand, Norah would. He opened his mouth to tell her – about university, about Milan and about his ex, who he should have been able to leave in the past by now.

To his shock, she pressed her palm to his mouth. 'It's really none of my business.'

'That hasn't stopped you before,' he said gruffly after she carefully retracted her hand. After steeling himself for the confession, he deflated slowly. 'You said you wanted me to talk.'

'I do...' she said. 'But not if I'm forcing you.'

'Okay,' he said on a confused huff. 'You probably won't remember this in the morning anyway.' He tugged her hand to get them moving again. She drifted against him and he lifted his arm around her shoulders.

'I hope I remember this,' she said, looking up at the sky again. 'I didn't feel sad or lonely today,' she said softly.

'Neither did I,' he responded before he could overthink it.

'That's the good thing about a summer friendship. And the bad thing about it is probably you having to drag me home after I've thoroughly embarrassed myself.'

'Don't worry,' he said. 'You're a cute drunk.'

'What kind of drunk are you?'

'A heavy drunk.'

She giggled. 'Yep, you'd be spending the night on Emiliano's table if it was up to me to drag you home.'

'Lucky it's the other way around.'

She nodded, leaning her head on his shoulder. After a few minutes of walking in cosy silence, they reached the vaporetto stop.

She fell asleep before they'd cleared Mazzorbo. By the time they rounded Murano, he'd given up catching her every time the boat lurched and had settled her head in his lap. Her hair was smooth under his fingers, except for the short crop at the back. He found a kind of fascination running his fingertips over the back of her head.

He nearly forgot to grab her cane when the vaporetto pulled in at Fondamente Nove. He hauled her up, supporting her against him as he stumbled off the boat. She was dead asleep and he propped her up on a bench with an exasperated huff while he considered his options.

He realised with a start that he hadn't contacted Manu and he hadn't looked at his phone in hours. A glance at the screen showed low battery and several missed calls. He quickly shot her a text, hoping she was still awake.

He nudged Norah's chin. 'Oi, nanarèla,' he said softly. 'What did you say in English again? Squirt? Come on, squirt.' He shook her shoulder. 'I can't carry you all the way back to Santa Croce.'

'Yes, you can,' she mumbled. 'I feel like death.'

He rummaged in her backpack until he found her water bottle. There wasn't much left, but he handed it to her and she guzzled it. She blinked at him with sleepy eyes and a double chin.

'All right, let's give this a go,' he said and hauled her to her feet. He clutched her cane in one hand and wrapped his other arm around her. He managed to flag down a water taxi for the last part of the trip, bundling Norah into the polished wood motorboat next to a pair of startled Americans.

His muttered explanation of, 'She's just drunk,' didn't appear to put them any more at ease, but it wasn't long before he was hauling her back out again at the steps beneath Manu's palazzo. He rang the bell urgently, too tired to care if he was disturbing her.

'You're starting to feel like a really heavy bag of groceries,' he murmured, more to himself than to her.

'Gee, thanks,' she replied.

'If you're awake enough to joke, you could have helped me out a bit.' He heard footsteps and set Norah away from him. He didn't want to know what Manu would think if she knew he'd basically cuddled her all the way home.

But as the door swung open, Norah swayed and he grabbed for her with a gasp before she could fall down the stairs into the canal. Manu appeared at the door, her eyebrows shooting up at the sight of Gianluca clutching Norah desperately to him, her face squashed into his chest.

'Non è come sembra, Manu. It was an accident. I didn't think to tell you we'd be late. We ended up eating moeche in Burano and... she got drunk.'

'I'm okay!' Norah said with a hiccough, lifting her head. He eased her out of his hold, but she stumbled and he had to grab her again. Her arms closed around his waist.

'You might have to take her upstairs,' Manu commented tightly. With a sigh, Gianluca hoisted her up into his arms and headed inside.

Three very long flights of stairs later, he stood waiting for Manu to find Norah's key and open the small apartment. Norah's fist closed in his shirt.

'Thanks for being my hero,' she murmured, her breath on his

neck. Manu looked up sharply. When the door finally swung open, he stepped inside and settled her on the bed.

She grasped his upper arm. 'I know we're just friends,' she said with a sigh, 'but I still like your muscles.'

Luckily Manu couldn't see how that sentence made him feel, but he was painfully aware that she'd heard every word.

14

Norah's eyes were scratchy and her head pounded. She squeezed her eyes shut and then forced them open, until her room came into focus. The first things she saw were a glass of water and two little pills on the bedside table. She hauled herself up and grabbed for them greedily.

In her desperation to unfuzzy her mouth, she spilled water down her shirt. She patted her chest in surprise to see she was still wearing yesterday's grimy T-shirt, with her bikini top underneath.

Then the memories flew into her mind, of Gianluca staring down at her in the moonlight, telling her she wasn't the only one who was sad and lonely sometimes, and she doubled over, light-headed.

When she remembered plastering herself to him all the way back, like a needy, drunk barnacle, the guilt twisted and pinched. Shit. She'd clung to him in front of Manu. He must have been mortified.

A sudden shot of panic had her sitting upright again, clutching her head in one hand. Had she pushed his patience too far? She could barely believe he'd agreed to be her friend in the first place.

Sad and lonely...

Oh, God, she'd cut him off when he'd tried to talk to her about Manu. Norah groaned. She was a shitty friend. Of course, he should have been able to tell her about his love life, even if it made her feel awkward. That was what friends were for, right? To stick by you, even when times were tough? She'd fallen at the first hurdle because she'd selfishly thought that not knowing would make her feel somehow closer to him, as though it didn't matter that she was Manu's intern.

If she wanted a friend, she had to *be* a good friend, which meant finding him this morning and grovelling.

That thought, combined with the paracetamol, got her out of bed and into the bathroom. She stank of seaweed and silt and fish. She vaguely remembered Gianluca grumbling about having to carry her. God, couldn't she have just said no to more wine?

She showered and slipped on a light T-shirt and shorts, fluffing her hair. As she ran her fingers through it, she had a niggling memory of him doing the same – gently, affectionately? Had she imagined that?

Gianluca was easy to find. He had a nice website with an earthy colour palette and a few awkwardly posed photos of him working. Most importantly, he had a contact section with a big red pin on a map and Norah knew he lived over his workshop.

It was still early, so Norah slipped out quietly, resolving to text Manu later. Her stomach grumbled and she could really do with a coffee, but this was important.

She found his workshop down a tiny alley, in a narrow building, set a few steps above ground level. A forest of fórcole filled the sales window, sticking up haphazardly like fists. Didi, who was a visual merchandiser and created displays like this for a living, would have a field day – or a breakdown – if she saw it. A few oars were stacked to the side, and strung from the ceiling was an old piling, sawn off, bearing his name in burnt lettering. She cupped her hands around her eyes and peered through the window.

The workshop was very definitely closed. The little sign with the opening hours – also scratched onto a piece of old wood – showed he didn't even open on Saturdays, let alone Sundays. If he did, he couldn't take her out in *Dafne*. But, as he made his living from orders and not gawking tourists, she supposed it made sense.

She stepped up to the polished green door next to the workshop and rang the bell. She didn't hear it ring and, after several minutes, she was wondering whether it worked at all, but perhaps he was still sleeping. She should have thought of that. They hadn't got back too late the night before, but it was fair enough if Gianluca needed to sleep late after dragging her home. It was only nine.

But he didn't strike her as someone who regularly slept late and she wasn't ready to give up and go home. She rang the bell again, longer this time. Still nothing. She took out her phone. She probably should have texted him first anyway. What had she expected, that he'd hear she was on her way and hide? She glanced up at the windows with their rickety green shutters. Perhaps he'd seen her.

'Norah?' a voice called from the end of the alley.

She recognised Gianluca's voice immediately. He hurried towards her. He had a gym bag slung over his shoulder and he was wearing a loose vest top and a tiny pair of shorts. His hair was mussed and the tattoo on his arm glistened as though he'd been working out.

She tried to say something – she wasn't sure what – but nothing would emerge from her tight throat.

'Is everything okay?'

'Yes!' she forced out. 'But I'm so sorry.' After that, the words tumbled out in a rush. 'I didn't realise how much I'd drunk – not that it's an excuse. Really, you've been nothing but kind to me and I can't believe I... took advantage of you like that last night and... in front of Manu... and... can I make it up to you somehow? I meant it when I said I want to be friends, I just keep... screwing up and that's just where I'm at right now and you don't deserve it, but I'm going to try harder. I can explain to Manu, if you like, that there's nothing between us except friendship. I really hope I haven't... screwed things up for you.'

'What are you talking about?'

'Last night,' she said in a pleading tone.

'I remember what happened last night – probably better than you do,' he said carefully. He tugged a set of keys out of the gym bag and gestured to the door. 'You'd better come up.'

She nodded, trying to temper her eagerness. The stairwell was cramped and the steps rickety and uneven.

'I live on the top floor,' he explained as they ascended and ascended. 'How are you feeling?'

'I was a bit rough when I woke up, but Manu left out some water and paracetamol, so I'm okay. I'm never drinking that much ever again,' she said vehemently.

He smiled faintly as he stopped on the landing outside a wooden door. 'It's almost impossible to say no when a host is refilling your wine glass.'

'God, you're so ridiculously kind!'

'You say that like it's a bad thing.'

'I just don't deserve it.'

He eyed her as he swung open the door of his apartment. 'Prego, come on in,' he invited.

She stepped through into a little wood-and-brick wonderland. The beams were exposed, revealing the slant of the roofline. A brick feature wall separated the living room from what was presumably the bedroom. An L-shaped sofa faced two dormer windows that were set high enough to catch the natural light. Their dark wooden frames had been sanded and polished to showcase the natural beauty of the material.

The rendered walls were white, with only a few photos – of boats, rowing crews and the lagoon – decorating them.

'Do you want a coffee?' he asked.

'Is the Pope Catholic?' she responded before she remembered she was supposed to be penitent and not making jokes.

He smiled at her. 'Come on through to the kitchen. I need to head back to Burano to collect *Dafne*, but stay for breakfast first.'

She nodded in reply, too relieved by his apparent lack of resentment to say anything. She trailed him into the kitchen, which was small, but well designed, with polished wooden benchtops and space-saving corner units. He gestured to the small table with two benches and she sat down.

He moved through the kitchen in a slow, relaxed manner, grinding coffee beans and filling a moka pot. It was all very domestic – normal, for a pair of friends, Norah decided. And the cappuccino he put in front of her smelled heavenly.

'Thank you,' she groaned.

'Can't Manu even make coffee?' he asked.

Wouldn't Gianluca know better than Norah if Manu made coffee? 'My apartment in her palazzo is self-contained. I'm supposed to make my own coffee.'

He gave her a small smile. 'Ah, but I guess you haven't been taking the time.'

She shrugged. 'There's a machine in the lab.'

He grimaced. 'Press-button coffee? What's the point? I need a shower, then we'll eat and you can tell me what you think you screwed up last night.'

'Is there really a gym in Venice that's open on Sunday mornings? And do you really need to work out? You've got to row *Dafne* back later.'

'I thought you liked my muscles.'

Her eyes widened as that memory returned sharply. 'I'd like you even if you didn't have so many muscles,' she insisted.

He grinned. 'That's nice to know. But I wasn't at the gym. My crew trains on Sunday mornings. I already missed last week's training and I can't let them down again.'

'Ah,' she said stupidly.

'Enjoy your coffee,' he said and disappeared into the bedroom. He emerged ten minutes later, his hair wet, wearing a clean vest top and smelling of lavender again. It suited him somehow, especially combined with a note of citrus and spice.

He repeated the coffee process, unhurried and apparently unbothered by Norah's presence in his kitchen. While he waited for the moka pot to sputter to life, he cut up a bread stick and toasted it under the grill. In a few leisurely minutes, he'd set the table with a breakfast spread that was making her stomach groan in anticipation. There were two types of jams, as well as fresh tomato and mozzarella and a little jar of fish paste. Along with the bread and toppings, he'd cut up some plums and nectarines and set a large jar of plain yoghurt on the table.

'You look like you want me to mix it all together and pour it down your throat,' he said with a chuckle. 'But it's Sunday morning. You're not allowed to rush breakfast on Sunday morning.'

'I don't normally rush breakfast,' she said defensively.

His brow twitched. 'You don't normally eat breakfast, I'm guessing.'

She scowled at him in response, but grabbed a piece of bread and slathered it with jam. The jam jar had no label, only a date written in permanent marker. Nòna's jam, then.

'What's got your nerves up under your skin? I was there last night. I know you were drunk and I really don't mind. You're not even that heavy. I'm sorry I called you a bag of groceries.'

She stared at him. He truly didn't seem upset. She couldn't understand him. Every time she mentioned Manu, he got all prickly, but when she'd basically rubbed herself against him in front of his ex, he didn't seem to care.

'But... Manu...' she mumbled helplessly.

He tilted his head in acknowledgement. 'I felt a bit bad for letting you get so drunk in front of your boss, but, ultimately, I don't think she's going to cancel your contract – or mine,' he said drily.

'But I... I mean what I want to apologise for is... I... you know, I was all over you and... she doesn't know there's nothing... I don't want to ruin your chances.'

He frowned. 'My chances of what?'

'Of getting back together with her!' Norah blurted out.

Gianluca froze, his hand paralysed on his coffee cup. He stared at Norah, horror gradually transforming his expression. She cringed, wondering how she'd managed to make everything worse.

And then he burst out laughing. He dropped his hands heavily to the table. He stared at her, disbelief clear in his expression and the huffs of laughter making his shoulders jerk. He tried to speak several times before he managed it and Norah's worry gradually transformed to chagrin.

'You thought *what*?' he said, his voice at least an octave higher than normal.

Norah swallowed. 'You... obviously have some kind of history with Manu. I didn't want to pry, but... you get upset when I mention her and there's this awkwardness when she touches you.' Her voice trailed off when he snorted again and rubbed both hands over his face.

'Just to be clear: you thought Manu and I used to be lovers?'

'Obviously I was wrong,' Norah mumbled, her jaw tight.

He made a choking sound and shook his head. 'Norah, she's not my ex. She's... my *mother*.'

15

Now they both felt sucker-punched – at least Norah looked as sucker-punched as he felt. He'd thought it would be easier not to say anything about his dysfunctional relationship with the woman who'd given birth to him, but he certainly wished he had now.

The more he thought about it, the more he understood that her wild assumption hadn't been as strange as he would have thought. Manu had had him when she was only twenty-two and she looked younger than her fifty-one years.

'But—' Norah began, but cut herself off again. 'I thought Manu didn't have any family.'

'She doesn't,' he said – too harshly, if the stricken expression on Norah's face was anything to go by. 'I mean, she handed me over to my father and Nòna when I was six weeks old. Then she left for the States.'

Now Norah looked as though she'd been sucker-punched and then swallowed a bee. 'You were an accident?'

His throat clogged up and he searched around for the resentment to clear it again. 'More than that. I was a career-ending *mistake* – or I would have been, if she'd kept me.'

'Oh, God,' Norah said under her breath. 'And here I am, complaining about my mother. At least we have a relationship.'

'I'm glad I can give you some perspective,' he said grimly. He finished his coffee and stood. He wasn't hungry any more.

'But—' She grabbed his wrist to stop him. 'You said you didn't know your mother.'

'I didn't,' he insisted. 'I *don't*, not really.'

She stared up at him, her expression unexpectedly fierce. 'I'm sorry for jumping to conclusions,' she said, letting go of his wrist, 'and I'm sorry for always making everything about me. But if you want to talk about it, I want to listen.'

She dropped her gaze as the silence stretched, but he studied her: the mop of hair that he liked so much, the restless fingers fiddling with the jam spoon. She looked so normal in his kitchen. Maybe that was what friendship was about. Maybe he needed a friend more than he'd realised.

He was close to Chiara and Pino – as close as siblings – but he'd got in the habit of not talking about the mess of feelings he had about his mother and now he wouldn't know where to begin.

I wasn't sad and lonely today...

He lowered himself slowly back to the table. 'I'm sorry to brush you off,' he murmured. 'It's not... I'm not used to talking about this.'

'I know what you mean,' she said softly. 'When I got to university, I was so relieved no one knew my mum or that I was the kid in the second-hand clothes whose "dad" looked different every month. I could just study. That's why I love science. I can kind of... lose myself in it.'

'But losing yourself doesn't sound good.'

She perched her chin on her fist. 'You've just got a hero complex now because you had to protect me in the storm.'

'I thought you were protecting me,' he said lightly.

'Ha ha,' she said drily. She watched him critically for a long moment and he could almost hear her repeating her offer to listen if he wanted to talk. Her hand meandered haltingly to his. She curled her fingers around his hand and held on. 'Manu must be older than I thought,' she prompted gently.

'She's fifty-one.'

'Wow, okay. She missed your whole childhood while she was away studying, then?'

He nodded. 'I wasn't lying when I said I didn't know my mother. I didn't meet her at all until I was ten.'

'Oh my God,' Norah muttered.

'You understand, though, don't you?' he pushed. 'Something to do with being a woman in a scientific field.'

'Yes, but... I can't imagine it was an easy decision.'

'Probably not, but it was the decision she made,' he said flatly. 'This is why I didn't tell you,' he continued. 'You're trying to make this okay for everyone, but it's not and that's the way it has to be. Manu and I usually avoid each other so it's not uncomfortable.'

'For you? Or for her?'

'Both of us, I imagine.' She stared at him, so many thoughts crowding her expression. 'Go on, say it all, Norah. I don't mind.'

She struggled for one moment longer, then, blurted out, 'I just can't imagine if I got into a great PhD programme now and then discovered I was pregnant. I mean, I would make it work, I'm pretty sure. But back then? Science is still a field where women who take time out for kids are penalised professionally – less time working means fewer publications, less networking and there are still a few dinosaurs among the professors. I don't think she would have got where she is if she'd...'

'Kept me?' he prompted her, knowing the words would make her flinch.

'Shit, that's awful. I can't believe she did that.'

'You just said you *can* believe it. I don't want to put you into a difficult position with Manu.'

She shook her head. 'You're not. She's just my temporary boss.'

'But you... admire her, right? She's achieved a lot. I understand that.'

Norah's expression hardened into one of her fierce frowns that she probably didn't realise were utterly captivating. 'But you're my friend,' she insisted, as though it was self-explanatory. It knocked the wind out of him. 'Understanding or not, I admire her less now.'

He struggled for words for a moment. 'I'm sorry it's difficult for you—'

'It's not,' she said, cutting him off. 'Stop thinking about me. What about your future? Do *you* want anything to change with her?'

'No,' he insisted immediately. He didn't need a relationship with Manu. If he did, he'd be disappointed.

'Wait a second,' she said. 'What were you talking about last night, then?'

'Which part exactly?'

'The part where I thought you were about to tell me about a romantic relationship with Manu, so I shut you up because I was too selfish to hear it,' she said with an apologetic grimace.

There was some emotion behind that statement, but he didn't dare try to work out what it was. 'I can't believe you thought she was my ex-girlfriend,' he groaned, rubbing his hand over his head vigorously.

'Don't worry, I'm feeling pretty stupid right now.'

'No, it was... someone else.'

'Chiara?' she asked, wide-eyed.

'No!' he said with a choke. 'Do you think every woman you see me with is a lover? Chiara is and always was just a friend.'

'Who was she, then? Who caused your disappointment in love?' Norah asked.

'Maybe I was being dramatic,' he mumbled.

'Dramatic? Lulu? I don't believe it.' She flung her arms up to punctuate her sentence.

'I... had a... an actual summer fling once.'

'Only once?'

'Yes, only once,' he said sharply. 'Just because I live in a tourist magnet doesn't mean I look for opportunities to sleep with visitors!'

'Ouch, I'm sorry,' she muttered.

'Her name was Anna and she was from Torino. She was here for an exhibition, but she extended her stay for a bit. And then, because I'm me, it became more than a short-term thing and I asked her to stay, to move in with me. It lasted another two months – shorter than the summer itself. That was five years ago and I haven't had a girlfriend since. *That's* what I was going to tell you last night. Do you want another coffee?'

Norah didn't take the hint about the change of subject. She was staring at him with an odd expression on her face – perplexed and worried and, yes, pitying. 'Did she break up with you?' she asked, her voice high with disbelief.

'I would hardly have been disappointed if I'd been the one to end it.'

'But... why?'

He coughed. 'You want a post-mortem on my relationship from five years ago?'

She smiled, catching him completely unawares. It made his heart thud loudly – probably because he felt as though she'd opened him up like a surgeon. 'I like you when you're grumpy.'

'I'm not grumpy!' he insisted, but wondered if he was okay to be grumpy if she liked it.

'Of course not,' she said with a poor attempt at a straight face. 'I just meant, what woman in her right mind would break up with *you*?' He coughed again, this time choking at the same time. 'Do you have reflux or something?'

'No,' he rasped, not sure whether to laugh or cough and choke some more. 'You make it sound like I'm some great catch, but I'm just a Venetian remèr, tied to my city by blood and identity and the past.'

Her smile dimmed. 'That's a really depressing way of thinking about yourself. I know this city is something special, but you are, too, regardless of all that stuff. She shouldn't have made you feel like you weren't enough.'

He took a heavy breath to clear his lungs. 'She didn't – not the way you're thinking. She wasn't happy here. For most people, Venice is nice for a visit, but who wants to live in a city where you have to take all your rubbish to a boat? She gave me an ultimatum: Venice or her.'

Norah made a sound as though someone had stamped on her toe. 'But you... you couldn't leave! In my mind, you *are* Venice.'

'I suppose I'll take that as a compliment? But you're right, of course. I left Venice for university and it didn't go well. I suffer from mal di terra – land sickness.'

'Is that a thing?'

'Cioè, I was unhappy,' he admitted.

'I didn't realise you went to university,' she said. 'Not that... not that I didn't think you were intelligent. You're obviously... And I'm sure being an oarmaker is...' He just smiled and waited for her to talk herself more tightly into a corner. 'It's my problem, obviously.'

His smile widened. He patted the back of her hand. 'You're a sweetheart, Norah.'

She snorted in reply, then asked, 'What did you study?'

'I have a masters in physics.' It was her turn to choke. 'I am the son of a scientist, after all,' he said drily.

'Wow, I'm even more of a shit friend than I thought,' she muttered.

'Don't blame yourself. You said it last night: you verbally vomit on me and I say nothing back. Maybe I wanted you to judge me. Maybe I wanted to keep pretending I had nothing to say in return.' He paused, his gaze catching in her eyes. 'To keep pretending I didn't need a friend.'

She bit her lip and nodded slowly. 'I know I'm nosy and selfish and my sense of humour is off sometimes, but I really want that – both ways. I want to be your friend as much as I want to have you as a friend.'

'I know,' he said gently. 'And I like it when you're nosy, I understand when you're selfish, because aren't we all? And because you shared what you've been through over the past year. I love your sense of humour and I really should have let you be my friend sooner, because you're... inevitable.'

Her smile twisted. 'I'm not sure that's a compliment. Although you are stuck with me for the summer.'

'That's not what I meant,' he insisted. 'More like... well, you know how Italians like the idea of il destino. This summer we're... helping each other move on... or something like that.'

'The summer of moving on,' she repeated with a wistful smile. 'I'd drink to that, if I didn't have a raging hangover.'

He stood to clear the table. 'Speaking of hangovers, are you coming out to Burano? I could use the company.'

'I suppose it's only fair, after my behaviour last night.'

He leaned on the table to look her in the eye. 'Will you stop apologising for that? Getting each other home safe on a night out is what friends do, right? And I liked drunk Norah, too.' He ruffled her hair, adding a little more force so it felt like rowdy camaraderie, rather than the desire to run his fingers through it.

She wrinkled her nose at him and made a vain attempt to tidy her hair. 'Well, on behalf of drunk Norah, I'll come out to Burano with you.'

'And after that, prepare for an interrogation. Nòna is expecting you.'

16

'I love this lagoon,' Norah said with a sigh as they slowly splashed back towards the old city in the afternoon. It wasn't as remorselessly hot as the day before. The sun was just warm enough to make her languid and relaxed as she gazed at the familiar jumble of red rooftiles, beige buildings and brick belltowers of old Venice.

'You wouldn't have said that last Sunday,' Gianluca joked behind her.

She smiled up at him. 'Since every week here feels like a lifetime, that doesn't seem strange,' she said thoughtfully.

'If you've already spent two lifetimes in the lab, shouldn't you know everything there is to know about algae by now?'

'I've spent half a lifetime with you and I'm only just scratching the surface,' she quipped. It was getting easier to swallow that twinge of something, when she made jokes like that with him.

He laughed, deeply and openly. She'd heard that laugh many times throughout the day of lazy conversation.

She now knew about his work with a group of young business owners – Chiara included – to lobby for sustainable tourism and the retention of essential local services for residents. She'd heard about his plans to develop his business with *Dafne*, taking visitors on eco-friendly tours of the lagoon and accepting charters.

She asked him about Pino and Chiara, about Nòna and her years of working as a weaver. She especially enjoyed it when she made him talk about his oars and fórcole like a physicist – force and momentum and resistance. He was such a nerd.

It was mid-afternoon when he tied *Dafne* up near his building – his own posta barca, he explained. Then he grabbed the bag of moeche he'd bought from Emiliano and hopped out of the boat, hauling her up after him.

Whether he slowed his steps for her benefit or was simply a leisurely walker, she wasn't sure – both options sounded like Gianluca. She leaned heavily on her cane because her eyes were up, soaking in the ancient buildings, which had fewer storeys and more washing strung up outside the further they travelled from San Marco. It felt like a village, where neighbours spoke loudly and rapidly to each other with Sunday afternoon gossip.

Two people stopped to speak to Gianluca, one a friend of Nòna's and another an acquaintance associated with the rowing club. Both were dismissive of Norah and continued speaking in dialect – at least, she was fairly sure that nasal, slightly lazy speech was dialect, rather than standard Italian. Norah was a 'forèsta' after all. She was only borrowing Gianluca's legitimacy for a few weeks.

Nòna was just as tiny as Norah had pictured, but her voice boomed unexpectedly and she had a grip of steel, covered in wrinkled skin that was as tough as crocodile leather. She spoke no English, but made up for it by speaking more loudly than was necessary.

Norah stammered the Venetian phrases she'd learned as Nòna crooned in delight and held up her powerful hands. She cupped Norah's face and patted her cheeks, before smacking kisses on both.

'Che bella ragazza!' she said with emphasis. Then she cocked her head and spoke rapidly to Gianluca, expecting him to translate. But instead of complying, he responded, lifting his hands to punctuate the words Norah couldn't understand.

'Let me guess, she's asking why I ruined my hair with this haircut?' Norah asked.

They both turned to her, the enormous grandson and the tiny grandmother who'd raised him. Norah grinned at them, wondering if she was allowed to tell them they looked ridiculously cute together.

Nòna said something more that made colour rush to Gianluca's cheeks. As she ushered them into her tiny flat, Norah eyed him until he spilled.

'Yes, she was asking why you have a man's haircut.'

'And?'

'I said I liked it and... she said I'm blinded by infatuation.'

Norah snorted. 'I thought I was the only one who thought you fell in love with every woman you see.'

Nòna demanded a translation with little more than a gesture and a nasal, 'Eh?'

Because he was a good boy, Gianluca obviously translated faithfully, blushing adorably in the process. Nòna cackled and clapped Norah on the shoulder so hard she stumbled.

She sat Norah down at the kitchen table with an enormous glass of wine and bustled around the kitchen, shouting orders at Gianluca like a pint-sized army commander. As soon as she opened the bag of crabs, Sissi the cat appeared on cue. Nòna alternately scolded the cat and shot nosy questions over her shoulder, giving Gianluca a challenge with the translations.

'Stupid cat,' he muttered as he placed the enormous ball of grey fur onto the floor for the fifth time. But he stroked down her back, making the cat preen and purr and undermining his words completely. 'She's asking why you walk with a cane.' Norah assumed he didn't mean the cat.

'You can tell her,' Norah said with a smile, taking an appreciative slurp of her wine, thankful it wasn't Prosecco, because she doubted she'd be able to stomach that for at least a week.

'She wants to know how old you are,' was the next question.

She scrambled around in her brain for a moment, before calling back, 'Venticinque,' with too much satisfaction. The cat was looking at her as though she'd butchered the pronunciation.

'She's asking what you think of Venice,' came next.

'Bellissima!' Norah said, kissing her fingertips. 'Is she going to ask what I think of you?'

He coughed quietly. 'She already did.'

'Bellissimo!' she repeated, blowing him a kiss and winking at Nòna.

'Don't encourage her,' he grumbled. 'You have no idea how many times she's already told me you'd make a great wife.'

'Wow, she's really taking advantage of the fact that I can't understand her.'

'Actually, she's just tactless.'

'I love your nòna.' The statement was worth saying just for Gianluca's grin. As though Sissi understood, she approached the table and rubbed against Norah's leg.

'And you haven't even tried the food yet.'

'Manu told me her cooking is legendary. Wait, does she know that I don't cook?'

He shrugged. 'It doesn't matter. She taught me.'

She couldn't help whistling, impressed, and giving him a cheeky look up and down, which Nòna unfortunately caught. Poor Gianluca had to stammer the translation. Nòna exclaimed something in response and picked up Norah's hand in her steely grip.

'She's offering to teach you to cook,' Gianluca translated.

'Does she have insurance?'

He gave her a withering look. 'She doesn't need insurance to teach you to cook.'

'I can't believe you haven't worked out I'm a disaster area yet.'

'That normally becomes obvious in two weeks?' She hoped the next eight felt as long as the last two. 'Besides, if you can work in a lab, you can cook. You just don't want to.'

'I don't want to disappoint Nòna.'

Gianluca translated the conversation. Norah understood the eye-roll he used to punctuate the explanation. He and Nòna talked over each other for a short conversation. Norah watched their mirrored body language with interest. Gianluca hunched, both bringing himself closer to Nòna's eye level and relaxing his habitually straight back.

He said one last sentence, before stealing the first crab that Nòna had placed in a dish and escaping from her ire with a kiss to her cheek.

He sat down next to Norah and stretched his arm along the back of her chair. The hairs on the back of her neck stood on end. Norah was worried what Nòna would think of the ease in that action, of course. Surely, after all the conversations they'd shared, she'd be used to his platonic presence close to her.

But he snatched his hand back before Nòna turned from the stove, startling the poor cat, who gave him a filthy look and left with her tail in the air. Perhaps he thought Nòna would never believe they were just friends.

'I know this is eating the same thing two days in a row, but I had to bring some moeche back for Nòna and they're coming to the end of the season now. Yesterday you ate your first moeca, today will be your last.'

She couldn't help chuckling. 'You make it sound like it's some kind of lagoon secret: if I try it you'll have to kill me.'

He translated the joke for Nòna. 'She says you're not wrong. Once you've eaten enough moeche, you belong here and you can never leave.' He said it in a mock-threatening tone that Nòna definitely hadn't intended, as though he assumed being stuck in Venice would be a terrible fate for Norah. She could think of worse fates.

'But these are so delicious, I could probably eat them every day.'

'Even Manu isn't rich enough to eat these every day!'

Norah gave him a sidelong glance, but didn't pursue the subject. She didn't have to ask what his ideas about Manu's inherited wealth were. He didn't consider himself her heir.

Nòna's moeche with fried vegetables, fresh salad and polenta was worthy of the highest ratings on Tripadvisor and probably a Michelin star, if Norah had known anything about those. Gianluca saved her from another day of overindulging in wine only by having sharp words with Nòna. After Norah and Gianluca washed up, they played a few rounds of cards out on the tiny balcony, interrupted occasionally by nosy neighbours on their rooftop terraces – called altane – or across the courtyard. Sissi had the place of honour on the armchair in the corner and woke occasionally to hiss at them. Nòna exclaimed that the grumpy old cat liked Norah and that it was a very good sign.

Gianluca sank lower into his chair, mimicking the sun's trajectory. Norah couldn't imagine how tired he must be after rowing training early that morning, followed by a long trip back from Burano. He stretched between rounds of cards, his feet reaching across the small balcony and nudging Norah's.

Nòna made a comment that Norah imagined was something like: 'You work too hard.' Norah nodded in agreement without thinking.

A smile curled up the corners of his mouth. 'Do you know what you just agreed with?' She shook her head warily. 'She said I look good in blue.'

Norah snorted. 'You look good in anything,' she admitted with a grin. 'I thought she was telling you to go have a rest or something.'

'Do you want to go?'

The tiredness hit her all of a sudden. She didn't want to go, but daytime drinking, the drunken sleep last night and the enormous couple of days in the sun had drained her. 'I probably should. But you stay here. I can find my own way back.'

He shook his head. 'I should get an early night, too.'

Nòna kissed them both profusely on the cheek before they left. It was still bright and sunny, despite the approach of evening. Diners sat under parasols along the canals and the sunlight hit the windows of the boutiques and delis of Cannaregio – their doors firmly closed for the day of rest.

They walked quietly, side by side. Even the locals kept to a relaxed pace. Norah thought about threading her arm through Gianluca's – companionably. But her walking rhythm with the cane probably wouldn't suit that action. She scowled at the ugly thing, so sterile and out of place among the ancient buildings.

Gianluca caught her scowl, but he said nothing. For once, both of them were content to be silent. They arrived at Manu's palazzo much more quickly than Norah had expected and she was suddenly reluctant to go inside.

'If you need anything through the week, just call me – or text me,' he said. He gave a little shrug with one shoulder. 'Or just text me anyway, even if you don't need anything. Take a break sometimes.'

'I do take breaks,' she insisted. 'If I texted you every time I took a break, you'd get sick of me.'

'I won't get sick of you,' he said with a scowl.

'I like a challenge,' she quipped.

'I know you do,' he said drily, but her stomach twisted and flipped at the statement that should have been casual, but felt... big.

'Allora... thanks for coming out to Burano with me,' he said to fill the silence.

'If I'd stayed here, I would probably have ended up working, so...'

His eyes clouded – only a touch, but she was sensitive to his emotions, now, after coaxing him out of his shell. She remembered with a start that his *mother* was a scientist – one who had chosen science over him a long time ago.

'I'll, uh, I'll plan next week's trip and let you know. Sant'Erasmo and the nearer islands, right?'

She nodded, cold creeping into her chest at the return of practical subjects. 'Thanks for taking me to see Nòna,' she said, knowing it would make him smile. 'She's amazing.'

He inclined his head in acknowledgement. 'If I hadn't brought you, she probably would have scaled this building and knocked on your window to meet you.'

She laughed – more loudly than the joke deserved, but she was nervous. She hated being nervous. 'Well, um, I'll see you...'

He ducked towards her and she froze. He froze in response and his eyes flew to hers, only inches away. 'Sorry,' he muttered. 'No kiss on the cheek?' he asked weakly.

Norah stared, her eyes refusing to blink. How was his face even more beautiful up close? She wanted to run her thumbs over his lips. She blew out a measured breath, trying to stop her head spinning.

He drew away, leaving her wondering if she'd breathed on him too much. 'Sorry, I'm not a big cheek-kisser. My family are hug people – not that I'm asking for a hug!' she added.

'Okay,' he said with what looked like relief. He lifted his hand in an awkward wave as Norah knocked on the door. It swung open immediately, startling both of them.

Gianluca tripped in his hurry to go, mumbling something to

Manu, who'd appeared in the doorway with a tight smile. A few seconds later, he'd disappeared around the corner.

'Sorry to bother you,' Norah said.

'No, no, don't apologise. I should get the lock changed,' Manu replied. Norah felt the older woman's eyes on her as she came inside and Manu shut and bolted the door. Her ears were hot. She wasn't sure what to say to Manu – if anything.

I know Gianluca is your son, seemed a poor conversation starter. Should she pretend she didn't know?

'Forgive me asking,' Manu began, sending shivers of foreboding down Norah's spine. 'Are you and Gianluca...?'

'No!' she insisted before Manu could find the awkward end of that sentence. 'We're just friends. We left the boat at Burano last night and I felt kind of responsible, so I went back with him and then his nòna cooked for us. We found moeche.'

Manu nodded faintly. 'You'll be spending... a lot of time with Gianluca as it is.'

Norah nodded. 'That's why we decided we should be friends.'

'Rather than... more than friends, you mean?'

She shook her head emphatically. 'That's not what I mean. Although... yes, I kind of mean that.'

'He's been hurt before. I wouldn't like to see it happen again.'

Norah nodded vigorously. 'You don't need to worry about him. We're cool. Nothing is going to happen like that.'

Manu watched her as the heat pooled in her chest and rose steadily up her throat to her cheeks. 'He told you,' she said softly.

'Yes,' she replied. 'I mean, what? He told me a few things.'

'But he told you... that I'm...'

'His biological mother, yes,' she finished for her, as kindly as she could. Manu still flinched. 'But it doesn't change anything.'

'Of course, it doesn't,' Manu said, recovering. 'You'd understand better than most – not that I'm excusing myself. But you can understand what it was like to be pregnant during my undergraduate study.'

'That must have been terrifying,' Norah replied carefully.

'You know the pressures of a scientific career,' Manu continued. Norah nodded slowly, just once, as the hairs on the back of her neck lifted. 'And at least I... made something of it, even though it came at a high cost.' Manu's voice lost its strength. She took a deep breath 'And now, we need to find that perfect species of algae to power the homes of the future, hmm?'

Manu turned away, putting an end to the conversation, but Norah's mind flooded with questions. Why did she book Gianluca for these trips? What did she truly want from him? How much had it hurt her to give him up? And the most futile: would she do the same thing again, if she had her time over?

17

June arrived and, with it, a heatwave that made the old city muggy and bloated. Norah took Gianluca's offer seriously and texted him pictures of everything strange that amused her, from an ancient TV sitting, abandoned, on a bridge, to a door knocker with a naked man on it – a rather ripped, naked man, who, she suggested, must have been doing a lot of rowing two hundred years ago when he was cast in bronze.

She sent him a series of photos of a pair of pigeons near the bus stop, with the conversation she imagined they were having:

C'mere, gorgeous.

Nah, I found some bread.

But c'mere, look, I'm puffing up my chest for you. You're supposed to be impressed.

Pigeon eye-rolling I've got bread, I'm good. If you want bread, there are some cheapskate tourists over there having a picnic. Get your own bread.

Gianluca replied asking if that was her opinion on the males of all species in general and she sent him back a picture of her raised middle finger in the foreground of a blurry selfie. He replied with a gif of the Italian chin flick, which she'd gathered from context meant 'I don't give a damn'.

She teased him about the nerdy photos he sent of oars from all angles, asking for more photos of people – by which she meant himself. Of course he didn't oblige, but instead sent her a few pictures of his smiling clients with their wares. Every evening, he'd send her a picture from his altana, with the sun low over the red roofs, asking if she'd left the lab yet. Her answer was usually a picture of a petri dish, or a forgotten half of a panino from lunch.

One evening, his photo featured Chiara holding a bright orange spritz, staring out at the sky from his altana. Norah was frustratingly jealous, no matter how many times she reminded herself that friendship wasn't exclusive. She was jealous of Chiara's spritz, that was all.

She reluctantly visited wedding venues for Saffron in the morning before heading to the lab. After she complained to Gianluca via text about the awkwardness of going alone to the first, he offered to come to the second for moral support. It was a larger venue, with no personal connection to Manu, so this time she pretended they were an engaged couple, mainly to ruffle him.

To the first employee, she gushed that they'd met by chance in a cramped water taxi, got talking and switched to a romantic gondola. A few hours and five hundred euros later, they were a couple. To the next one, she claimed he'd fallen into a canal and she'd fished him out, only for him to insist that she'd neglected to mention that she'd *pushed* him into the canal first.

'Fished out of a canal? He was never going to believe that one,' Gianluca murmured as they wandered away from the palazzo in the direction of the bus stop.

'Why? Because it wasn't the man who saved the day, but the woman?'

'It's not that,' he insisted. 'It's... no one would believe *you* would be able to get me out of a canal.'

'Whatever do you mean?' she asked sweetly.

He scowled, but she did a pretty mean innocent face. 'It's just... you're...'

'Hmm?'

'Nanarèła,' he muttered.

'I've been meaning to ask what that means.'

He made a disgruntled noise with a hint of apology. 'It means you're short.'

Her face fell. 'Oh,' she said.

'Literally: a duckling. It's an affectionate term,' he insisted. 'And you're short, but you're also...' She let him squirm for a minute, keeping her mock serious expression. 'You're not really offended, are you?' he accused drily.

She grinned. She secretly liked being called a duckling. 'Nope. But I get to call you bigfoot.'

Their journey to the islands between Venice and Sant'Erasmo on Saturday was oddly uneventful – a fact they joked about unceasingly until Norah decided she needed to at least push him into the lagoon to mix things up.

'I can see what you're planning,' he said with a smile, 'and I can't believe you'd disturb this endangered salt marsh – not to mention the grumpy flamingos.' He was unfortunately right, even though his smug smile tempted her afresh.

'You're a grumpy flamingo,' she muttered.

When they headed back out of the marshland, they stopped for a picnic lunch and a voluntary swim instead.

'I understand your "physics of rowing" tattoo now,' she said as they lounged in the warm water of the lagoon. 'But what about that one?' She pointed to a stylised bird on his upper arm.

'It's a duck.'

'A very angry one.'

'My rowing crew has the nickname "the Ducks". Don't laugh. We won the regatta at the Festa della Sensa, remember,' he said with mock defensiveness.

'What about the other one?' She gestured to the tattoo on his shoulder blade. She thought it looked like a snail or a nautilus shell.

'That's just a pattern – a tattoo artist's attempt at Mandelbrot fractals.'

'God, you are such a nerd! I can't believe I didn't realise it before.' He didn't reply and she worried he'd started brooding about Manu again, although he hadn't brooded as much since he'd told her. 'I'd love to get a tattoo, but I don't think algae would look very good.'

'Surely there's something else you'd get a tattoo of? Rather than algae?'

She shrugged, staring up at the sky. Saying she'd like a tattoo of something to remind her of Venice sounded naïve and kitschy. 'Nope,' she said instead. 'Nothing much else in my life except marine microbiology.'

She joined Gianluca and Chiara in a bar one night the following week and, when Pino joined them after dropping off his last fare, they bought a pizza and a bottle of wine and took Pino's gondola for a spin, taking turns to row.

Norah made sure her glass wasn't filled every time someone

offered and only got just drunk enough to join in with the shouts of, 'Oi!' when another gondola approached.

Norah couldn't stop herself analysing Chiara and Gianluca's behaviour for romantic potential, even though her data set was far from complete. Norah noticed touchy-feely Gianluca didn't fluff Chiara's hair or squeeze her shoulder as much as Norah had expected. But Chiara would definitely be able to fish him out of a canal, if he ever fell in. She was slim, but tall and toned. She seemed to be one of those strong women who went out and got what she wanted. She would have realised sooner that her relationship was a dud, if she'd been the one with Andrej.

Chiara enthusiastically took up Gianluca's new nickname 'bigfoot', which Norah also secretly resented. She wanted to like Chiara. She wanted to feel a part of this little crew for a few weeks, but her stupid feelings kept getting in the way. She wished Gianluca weren't so gorgeous so she could just get over it and settle into their summer friendship the way he obviously had.

'Baioco can't come on Saturday,' Pino said after they'd parked the gondola at his post and were wobbling their way back through Cannaregio. 'Do you want to come, nanarèła?' he continued, turning to Norah. 'Now we've got a spare ticket.'

'Ticket? To what?' she asked.

'Remember I said I can only take you out for half the day on Saturday,' Gianluca spoke up. 'We're going to a music festival on San Servolo.'

'I'd love to come!'

'What kind of music do you like?' Pino asked. 'This is a punk rock festival, with some electronic music later at night. It might get a little... crazy.' She was unexpectedly, probably inappropriately excited at the prospect of a wild night out. She suspected she looked as giddy as she felt, if the twinge of concern in Gianluca's eye was any indication. 'I can do crazy. Count me in.'

* * *

Heavy showers broke the heatwave early Saturday morning, giving them a wet trip out past the Isola delle Vignole, an island not far from the Castello district of old Venice. But the showers were already clearing to mist by the time Norah and Gianluca returned.

They split up to go home to change, having arranged to meet Pino and Chiara at the San Zaccharia vaporetto stop. Gianluca wasn't sure how he was supposed to find Norah amongst the sea of revellers in band T-shirts from the Ramones or the Misfits. He found Pino and Chiara easily and squinted at the crowd, searching for a familiar dainty head with a boyish haircut.

Pino was pumped, chatting about his favourite bands while Chiara gave indulgent responses. They fell silent behind him, but Gianluca barely noticed.

'Oi, vècio!' Pino called, finally getting Gianluca's attention.

'Cosa?'

Pino and Chiara shared a look. 'I was just checking you knew that training is cancelled tomorrow, since we're all going to the festival,' Pino explained.

'E?'

'I'm not sure he's interested unless it's something about Norah,' Pino pretended to whisper to Chiara.

'Shh! You're embarrassing him,' Chiara said with her own amused smile.

Pino shrugged. 'I don't know why. They could just give in and do it. She's a bronzsa cuerta, that girl. Maybe he needs a bit of fire.'

He opened his mouth to defend himself, but got distracted by Pino's description of Norah as 'covered embers', a banked fire with hidden heat. She'd probably like that. He did.

'Well, I don't want to mop him up off the floor again when he hands over his heart,' Chiara said. 'So, you have my blessing to pretend you're not interested in her that way,' she said, patting his arm. He gave a shrug, searching for a rejoinder that would get his friends off his back. His phone vibrated and he glanced down to see Norah had sent him a picture of a couple of goths kissing in front of the Bridge of Sighs. He grinned and looked up to watch for her. Chiara leaned over his phone to look at the picture.

'Is she sending you all her holiday snaps?'

He quickly put his phone to sleep, not wanting to tempt Chiara to scroll through and see the true extent of their texting. It wasn't something he was eager to explain.

He saw little more than a ripple through the crowd coming from the direction of the Piazza, before Norah appeared beside them in a loose vest top and a pair of tight shorts, a bag around her waist.

'I left my Iggy and the Stooges shirt at home,' she said.

'You have a—?'

'I'm joking,' she said wryly. 'Think we can push onto the next vaporetto?'

Pino chuckled and draped an arm around her shoulders. 'You fit in even better every time I see you. You just need a glass of wine in your hand and to say ghé sboro in answer to everything and you'll be a real Venetian.'

'Ghé sboro,' she said with a grin and Pino hooted with laughter. 'Is that the rude one about getting off on things? You guys are like five-year-olds obsessed with bodily functions.'

'That's Venetian men for you,' Chiara said with a shrug.

'I feel sorry for you,' Norah said, squeezing her arm in mock sympathy.

'Yeah, once you're a member of a rowing club, you aren't allowed to leave, so I'm stuck here with this *very* limited choice in men.'

They both glanced at Gianluca, which made heat rise to his cheeks. 'I thought we solved your problem, Chichi. We're going to lie in wait on the Lido for when that Turkish actor you love arrives for the film festival.' He hopped away to avoid Chiara's attempt to slap him on the arm, grinning unrepentantly.

'Insemenìo,' she grumbled, calling him a fool in dialect.

'You guys think *you* have a hard time. What about me? The only other gay guy in the rowing club thinks I'm an idiot,' Pino piped up.

'He's not wrong,' Gianluca quipped. Pino's punch unfortunately made contact, but Gianluca flung an arm fondly around his friend's shoulder regardless. The sun was shining again; they were all together and headed out to a festival. He was more content than he remembered being in a long time – if he could just shut down the urge to hold Norah's hand.

It had become a bit of a habit. He'd been helping her in and out of *Dafne* so much that the thought came unprompted. That must be the reason he had to force himself to let go after she settled beside him at the railing on the ferry.

She lifted her face as the vaporetto pulled out of the stop and headed east, away from the old city. She was smiling and the wind whipped her hair around her head, making it stand up.

'A nice change from Lulu's snail speed, right?' Pino asked her with a smile.

It didn't take long to arrive at San Servolo, which was set between old Venice and the Lido. The island was built up with old brick hospital buildings and a church. It was a far cry from the wild islands Norah and Gianluca had been exploring.

'This used to be an asylum for people, you know,' Pino explained with a tap to his forehead.

'The museum's horrible,' Chiara added with a shiver. 'But the island's a popular place now.'

'Meaning, too many tourists make it out here,' Pino completed.

'I don't know if I believe you about the tourists,' Norah said with a smile. 'We had a picnic last Saturday where there were more flamingos nearby than other people.'

'You'll be surrounded by people soon enough,' Gianluca said. 'Both in Venice, as the summer season starts, and right here, at the festival.'

Norah had an odd look on her face as the vaporetto pulled up to the pier. 'Bring it on,' she said with a small smile.

18

Gianluca looked on with a grin as Norah and Chiara counted to three and lifted their plastic cups of beer to their lips. Pino was filming. The video would be full of his tipsy laughter.

Chiara finished first and whooped, even as the last trickle of beer ran down Norah's chin and dripped onto her top. Norah laughed and swiped the back of her hand over her mouth.

The sun was low, glowing on the stone arcades in the courtyard of the museum. In another hour, it would be dark and strobe lights would replace the rays of the sun, illuminating the festival-goers as they danced.

Two acts down and Gianluca wasn't quite as tipsy as Pino. He kept forgetting to drink. He was too busy enjoying himself. A large part of that had to do with Norah. She didn't know any of the bands and she occasionally clutched at her back when she danced a little too enthusiastically, but she was in high spirits – from the alcohol, but also from more than that.

He knew the feeling. There was something exhilarating about that afternoon of music and laughter and friendship. Pino was at his engaging best. He knew the words to a lot of the songs – in

English and Italian – and he taught Norah the chorus to a few of his favourites until she was singing along, out-of-tune, with terrible Italian pronunciation and no idea what she was singing about.

The next band was a popular local group and Pino pushed them all forward as the crowd swelled. Norah was jostled from behind and clutched Gianluca's arm. He pinned her hand in place before she could snatch it back.

'You okay?' he asked her quietly – as quietly as the crowd allowed.

She grinned, right up into his face, and his heart stuttered. Time seemed to slow and the crowd lost focus as he gripped her fingers and stared.

The deafening ring of an electric guitar sounded and Norah jumped. 'Shit!' she said, rubbing a finger over her ear. He slipped an arm around her and she didn't pull away – the opposite. She leaned into him, soaking it all in from the safety of his arm.

The band stepped onto the stage and the crowd went wild. Norah was a good sport, but she was stepped on and jostled and, even though they weren't far from the stage, she craned her neck and probably couldn't see much, peering between the sea of heads in front of them.

Two songs into the set, it became too much for Gianluca. 'Give me your cane,' he said into her ear.

'What?' she called back.

In explanation, he dropped onto his haunches and beckoned to her. 'Come here! You'll see better.' He looked up at her when she hesitated. Her eyes were dark in the fading light. Her gaze flickered over him with uncertainty and a wobbly smile that was probably a result of the alcohol.

But she nodded, turning so he could grasp her legs and hoist her onto his shoulders. She squealed and spilled some of her beer as she settled. He swiped her cane from her hand so she could grab hold of his head to steady herself.

'Okay?' he asked.

She wriggled for another second, before falling still, her hand in his hair. 'I have the best view in the house!' she called out, glancing down at him. He watched her take in the crowd, the courtyard between the two stone buildings and the band on stage. 'This is amazing!'

'I think the concert sounds better from between your legs!' he called up, but choked on his words when she snorted with laughter, clinging to his face to stay upright. 'I didn't mean it like that!' he insisted.

'I don't care what you meant. I heard what I heard!' she called back, still laughing. She threw one arm out and shouted, 'Today is awesome!'

* * *

She didn't quite believe the concert sounded better for him with his head squashed between her thighs, but it was certainly better enjoyed from her vantage point on his shoulders. It was glorious.

The darkening sky stretched above the old buildings. The air was thick with revelry and the heavy vibrations of the music. She'd enjoyed dancing, throwing her head around even though she couldn't quite do the same with her back any more. But this was better. She cuddled his head to her stomach, ostensibly for balance, and listened to him tunelessly shouting along with the band.

She'd learned he was an adorably bad dancer. She guessed his limbs were simply too long to move to the beat with grace. He was built to have an oar in his hands, not to swing his body to the music. But he'd joined Pino singing along and cheered like a maniac.

Norah had felt part of... everything. Something about the way he drew her to him made her feel like less of an outsider. Pino and Chiara were welcoming, too, but with Gianluca... She felt wanted.

She knew, on some level, it was just a feeling. She didn't really belong, but she'd decided to enjoy it today. She'd be the actor in a play that kind of looked like her life, but wasn't. As she sat on Gianluca's shoulders, running her fingers through his floppy hair and peering down at him as he smiled, her character was melting inside.

'Pino, hold this!' she called between songs near the end of the set, handing him her beer. She grabbed a hair tie out of her bum bag – one of many she kept finding, scattered during her former life. 'You need this more than I do!' she said to Gianluca.

She smoothed his hair up between both of her hands and gave him a little topknot. He tipped his head back to look at her and she grinned down at him, pleased with herself.

She tapped his cheek. 'Aren't you cute, bigfoot?'

His brow quirked and even that was adorable. He looked back at the band with a chuckle, his hand squeezing her calf. It was odd, how her blood seemed to be singing, but she was deeply peaceful. It was the magic of their summer – all the best parts of a holiday romance, without the agony of uncertainty. She ran her hand over his topknot again, just because she could, and because she couldn't quite believe that this gorgeous human liked her and wanted to be her friend. It made her want to press a kiss right next to the topknot – and maybe another one on his cheek.

When Norah's voice was hoarse, her legs were numb and the band had ripped through two encores, Gianluca finally swung her back down to the ground. She clung to him for a second, getting her balance, and his arms came around her automatically – at least, she thought it was automatic.

She realised how tired she was with her face half an inch from his chest. The temptation to slump into him was strong. But she wasn't as drunk as she'd been that night on Burano. She'd remember it, this time, which was perhaps an argument in favour.

There was so much about that night on San Servolo that she wanted to remember.

'I need to pee,' announced Chiara. 'Want to come, Norah?'

Norah realised she probably should. She hauled herself back from the warmth and familiar tangy lavender smell of Gianluca and took her cane.

When she caught sight of herself in the mirror while washing her hands, it was a timely reminder. She no longer had the long, sleek hair of the old Norah. Her short hair better reflected the woman she was becoming: strong, committed to her career and answering to no one but herself. A woman who would find her place in life and fight for it.

Chiara stopped her on their way back to the stage. 'I don't really want to say this,' she began.

'Then don't,' Norah sighed. 'Trust me, you don't need to.'

Chiara studied her with a frown. 'What do you mean?'

Norah shrugged, surprised the action felt oddly defeatist. 'I'm not interested in Gianluca romantically. You have no idea how many times I've had to say that already.'

'But... that won't stop him falling for you and getting hurt.'

That statement made her blink in surprise. 'He's not going to fall for me.' The sceptical look on Chiara's face had the opposite effect to the one intended. A thrill of possibility ran up Norah's spine. Could he? Did he touch her casually and talk gently to her because...? No, it couldn't be the case. He was just being... Gianluca. He was kind and attentive to everyone. God knew, Norah wasn't anything special.

'I'm just... protective of him,' Chiara explained, 'because he's been hurt before.'

'I know,' Norah said with a sigh.

'You know?'

'He told me.'

'Gianluca never talks about Anna. I only know because I was there.'

Norah searched for words, but none came. She cleared her throat, which had clogged up with something unbearable. 'We're... stuck with each other because of my work. We decided it was better to be friends than polite and distant acquaintances.' That sounded plausible.

Chiara's brow furrowed, but she said, 'Allora... okay,' and headed back to the others.

Norah tried to recapture the carefree feeling from earlier, when they returned to Pino and Gianluca, but she was tired and tipsy and mixed up. She tried not to think about Gianluca and romantic relationships, but the thoughts came anyway.

'Do you want to go?' he asked over the pumping music an hour or so past midnight. Norah stifled a wince. She hadn't realised she'd been so obvious. 'I'm tired of the crowd,' he added sheepishly. She suspected he was waiting for her to tease him for getting old, but she wasn't in the mood.

'Okay, let's go,' she agreed.

Pino threw his arms up in disbelief when Gianluca explained they were going, when the music would continue until dawn. Norah caught Chiara's eye, hoping she understood the invitation to come back with them, if she wanted. She hated to think Chiara suspected she was trying to catch Gianluca alone – which was ridiculous given the many long hours they'd spent alone out on the lagoon.

Chiara shook her head and patted Pino on the shoulder. 'Someone will have to drag this one home.'

'Thanks for letting me come today!' Norah yelled over the music.

Pino shook his head and exclaimed something she didn't understand. 'You're one of us now, Norah!' he said.

She wasn't, of course, but the sentiment was nice.

The vaporetto wasn't too crowded, as most of the festival-goers were still bouncing to the electronic beats in the courtyard of the museum, but they still couldn't get a seat. She chose a spot at the side, leaned her cane against the barrier and held onto the railing, staring at the blinking lights of old Venice in the distance, under the black sky.

Gianluca stood behind her, his arms reaching around to the railing, holding off the small crowd of other passengers. Norah froze, staring at his hands, feeling the warmth in the air between them. He wasn't touching her, but he was close. Her thoughts and feelings were a jumble.

'Are you okay?' he asked conversationally.

'Yeah, of course,' she murmured. 'I just... you guys are great.'

He made some kind of odd huff. 'And that's making you sad because...'

'I'm not sad!' she insisted, turning to eye him, but realising he was far too close and turning back. 'I just know I'm a forèsta and it's really nice of you and Chiara and Pino to adopt me for a few weeks.'

'I didn't "adopt" you because I'm nice,' he said thoughtfully.

'Yes, you are – you did!' she said indignantly.

'I mean I'm not friends with you out of... pity.'

'Of course not, but... you've already got friends,' she pointed out. 'Not that I don't... well, I kind of don't. I lost touch with everyone, even the few people who were nice to me after the accident.'

'Why don't you get back in touch with them?'

The words formed in her mouth before she was brave enough to release them. It was frustrating to realise she was still working through the changes in her life. 'I feel like a different person,' she said as quietly as she could, not sure if she wanted him to hear.

His hands clenched on the railing in front of her. If he offered her a hug, she would take it. 'They'll still want to know you, Norah,' he responded evenly.

'I don't know,' she said, shaking her head. 'I have no PhD in progress and an awkward break-up with a mutual friend. I've spent the past year buried in pain and rehab. What am I supposed to talk about?'

'Pigeons,' he said suddenly. 'Door knockers. Abandoned TVs. Monks.'

She laughed. 'Now I *know* you're being nice.'

'I liked those messages,' he said softly.

'Well, maybe you're just as wacky as I am,' she murmured.

'Maybe I am,' he agreed.

'You're not,' she said with a snort, before continuing softly, 'but it's nice to feel... some new kind of normal with you and Pino and Chiara.' Talking through her feelings brought her enough peace for now and she smiled wistfully out at the twinkling lagoon. 'Because it's kind of okay not to feel like the old me with you guys. I've never skulled a beer in my life.'

'Really?'

'Did I look like that much of a pro?'

She felt him shift behind her. 'Yeah, you did.' She heard the smile in his voice.

The silence stretched as Norah stared at the approaching lights and tried to ignore the irregular thump of her heart. Stars twinkled overhead. The lagoon was dark in all directions except the old city, where it was a labyrinth of reflections and silhouettes.

The little stone lighthouse of San Giorgio Maggiore was ghostly white. Norah looked ahead to the campanile on the Piazza San Marco, the tallest tower among the ancient buildings glowing yellow with artificial light.

And she straightened with a start. 'What time is it?' She

fumbled for her phone. The clock read 1.45 a.m. 'Shit!' she exclaimed. 'I didn't even think. How am I supposed to get in without disturbing Manu? Should I send her a message?' She winced, imagining ringing the bell at this hour, or waking Manu with a text. 'I'm a lousy guest,' she mumbled.

Gianluca cleared his throat quietly. 'You're more than welcome to my sofa. Or I can take the sofa.'

'You're not taking the sofa,' she responded automatically. 'I don't want to be a lousy guest twice over.'

'Does that mean you'll be my guest?'

'*Friend*, rather than guest, right?' she said. 'Like a friend crashing. That's totally normal.' She risked a glance at him to see him bite his lip and then lick it. Eek, that switched on the lights in places inside her that she didn't want illuminated right now.

'It is the main reason I have a sofa.'

She smiled, determined to clear the tension. 'Well, I wouldn't want your sofa to have an existential crisis. Thanks.'

'No problem,' he said lightly. 'And this way I can make sure you have at least one decent meal tomorrow.'

'Because that is the main reason you have a stove,' she responded with a grin. He made an inarticulate grumble and fluffed her hair. She ducked away, but it was mainly because, if he kept his fingers in her hair, she would start purring. She had too many new, fragile emotions to share them with anyone. And on top of it all, her friendship with Gianluca had become far too precious to risk. She had to make sure nothing happened between them that night.

19

Gianluca peered out of the bathroom to check if the coast was clear.

A sleepy mumble of, 'I'm not looking,' came from his bed, where a Norah-shaped lump lay under the sheet on the far side.

'You're in the bed!' he said, stupidly stating the obvious. He cleared his throat. 'Are you trying to give my sofa an existential crisis?'

The sound she made was an attempt at a laugh, but she seemed to give up halfway. 'The bed was... there,' she said, her voice trailing off.

'Do you want me to sleep on the sofa?'

That woke her up. 'No!' She tried to rise, but flopped down again. 'No,' she repeated on a sigh. 'If you try to sleep on the sofa I swear I will get out of this bed and stop you.'

'I'm terrified.'

'It's a big bed and I don't mind sharing it – if you don't,' she murmured.

He bit his lip, glad she couldn't see his expression. When she didn't say anything further, he tiptoed into the room with the small towel around his waist and rummaged for a T-shirt and a pair of boxer shorts. Norah didn't move. When he was dressed, he slipped into bed with a sigh, stretching out on his side and trying to get comfortable.

Norah rolled over and flopped an arm in his direction, but she was clearly asleep. Her finger brushed his shoulder. He glanced at her and quickly away again. With another sigh, his gaze returned to her face and stayed there. If circumstances were different...

The next thing he knew, daylight was streaming in around the edges of his blinds and he was slowly waking from a dream where he'd caught an enormous cod and had to wrestle it into the boat with his bare hands.

The fish punched him in the stomach and he realised it wasn't a fish. It was too warm and too soft.

'Get off me, you brute!'

He sprang back and tumbled right off the bed, landing on his backside with a shout.

'God, you're heavy! Are you okay?' She peered over the edge of the bed.

'Just shock and a few bruises,' he muttered. 'If you're going to fall asleep in my bed, you could at least stay on your side.'

'I was asleep. I didn't realise I was drifting into bigfoot territory,' she said. He resisted a smile. That was probably all the apology he could expect. He hauled himself to his feet, trying not to look at the tangled sheets and limbs on his bed.

He headed for the kitchen and she followed a few minutes later, looking adorably dishevelled with her hair sticking up and his T-shirt and shorts hanging loose on her small frame. He set the moka pot onto the stove and turned on the oven to warm a stick of bread.

She offered to help and he directed her to the plates and cutlery. She set her cane against the table, moving fairly confidently around the small kitchen, and he tried not to watch her too closely. She found Nutella in the cupboard and set it on the table.

'I'll make you eggs and there's prosciutto in the fridge.'

'I want Nutella,' she replied happily.

He gave her a withering smile. 'Child,' he teased gently.

She shrugged. 'It takes one to know one,' she said, stealing an olive out of the fridge. 'You wouldn't have a jar if you didn't eat it yourself.'

They took everything up to the altana, although she had to grip the railing tightly as she navigated the rickety stairs up from his kitchen door. Once up, she turned her face into the morning sunshine. 'Your photos always made me want to be up here with you,' she said with a smile, her eyes closed.

'You need to experience breakfast on an altana at least once when you visit Venice,' he replied mildly.

'Manu has one, but she doesn't seem to use it much and I haven't been brave enough to head up there on my own. She's quite... private, although that's a good thing because ten weeks is a long time to have a guest and my apartment is pretty self-contained.' She eyed him speculatively. 'Have you been inside the palazzo much? It's kind of your family seat.'

He scowled. 'I'm not a Delfini and I never will be. Manu understands that. She wanted it that way.'

'Sometimes what we want changes over time,' Norah said thoughtfully. 'And sometimes we've made decisions that sabotage what we want in the future.'

'I hope she doesn't suddenly want a son.' He heard the bitterness in his own voice.

'When did your father die?' she asked.

'Six years ago,' he answered, trying to match her matter-of-fact tone. Her hand landed on his and gripped it tight, suggesting he hadn't managed to keep his voice even.

'You were at university?' she guessed. He nodded in answer. 'Is that why you came back?'

'One of the reasons. Leaving home was an experiment.'

'What was your hypothesis?'

'Well, Manu always left. I wondered whether... I'd find the same... satisfaction away from home.' He glanced at her. 'I didn't,' he added when she continued to stare thoughtfully at him.

'Were you trying to impress her? Studying physics?'

'No!' he insisted, but Norah was watching him too closely and was far too cynical herself to dismiss the possibility so easily. 'Maybe,' he corrected. 'But I also failed to prove that hypothesis, so I'm done with it – done with her.' Norah squeezed his hand again, her expression sombre. 'That came out very harsh, but it's... fine.'

'You were worried she hired you as an excuse to funnel money to you, weren't you? That first day, the Festa della Sensa, you didn't look happy she'd hired you.'

He nodded. 'Since my popà died, she's been reaching out with offers of money occasionally, but I don't need it. I mean, I do need money to get this business off the ground and to finish sorting out this house, but I don't need it from her.'

'I wondered whether you were annoyed about having to take *me* out.' She mimed walking with a cane, although she'd left her cane behind in the kitchen. 'And I nearly fell into the lagoon that first day.'

'You nearly pulled me in with you,' he said with a smile. 'No, it had absolutely nothing to do with you, Norah,' he said softly. She returned his smile. She almost looked as though she believed him.

She helped him clean up after the leisurely breakfast and then he had to accept that she would leave soon.

She stepped back from the kitchen bench and wiped her hands on her – his – shorts. 'I suppose I should...' she said, retrieving her cane.

He resisted offering her another coffee. It was only delaying the inevitable. 'I'll walk you back.'

They chatted their way through the alleys and over the bridges back to Santa Croce, discussing the wedding venues they'd visited and Gianluca's open studio day scheduled for two weeks' time, when he might finally lure Norah in to see his work. She joked it couldn't be hotter than watching him row a sanpierota single-handedly through a storm and he had to poke her in the ribs because he'd lost the ability to speak for a moment. He hadn't forgotten how ticklish she was.

They arrived at Manu's door and Norah hesitated before ringing the bell. 'Thanks for letting me come along last night. It was... great. You guys are amazing.'

He took a deep breath. 'We were all happy you came. And I'm happy... you had a good time.'

'Um,' she began, licking her lips. 'Do you reckon we're up to hugging now? I mean, now we're real, proper friends.'

He nodded wordlessly and tugged her against him so abruptly that she fell into his chest with an 'oof'. Her arms came around him, one hand still holding her cane. One of his hands drifted to the back of her head and the other tucked around her waist as he held her against him. What was it about holding Norah that felt so good?

She sighed into his chest and the moment came back into sharp focus. She tucked her cheek against him and looked up, her eyes lazy and a small smile on her lips. She looked so content, it touched him deeply.

He must have dipped his head. He hadn't consciously intended to kiss her, but somehow that was what he was an inch away from doing. Her eyes were wide and close and sincere. He felt her startled breath, and then he felt her mouth on his, hot and soft and full of uncertainty.

* * *

Norah's synapses were overloading. At least, she thought that must be what was happening. Why else would a kiss have such a burning effect on her? It was a good kiss – if she had more oxygen available to her brain, she might have been able to describe it better, but her brain was currently reacting with base instincts like 'more' and 'omigod'.

His mouth was warm and firm, but with a halting restraint that shot longing down her spine. Before any of her reservations could surface, she pressed into the kiss, her hand lifting to his face. His mouth opened and hers did the same in automatic response.

The kiss unfolded and deepened, drawing something beautiful out into the sunlight. She chased after it, giddy with the feeling of his familiar features under her fingertips. His hand tightened in her hair. His tongue brushed her mouth.

And then he pulled sharply away. He squeezed his eyes shut, rubbing an agitated hand through his hair and down his neck. He turned his face briefly into his arm as he swallowed and took several uneven breaths.

Norah leaned heavily on her cane. She could be certain she wouldn't have stayed on her feet without it at that moment. His eyes shot open and he gripped her shoulder with one hand and dropped his forehead to hers, blinking fiercely. She turned her face up to him, not to repeat the kiss, because she wasn't ready for that, but to look at him – his thick, dark lashes and bottomless eyes up close.

'Maybe,' he began, but he had to pause to clear his throat. 'Maybe that's why we don't hug?' Something like a grimace crossed his face.

'Maybe,' she agreed as the helium inside her that had sent her flying high began to seep out.

The door behind them opened suddenly and Gianluca straightened.

'Sweetheart!' came a familiar voice, which had Norah freezing to the spot. Really? Right now?

20

'I thought I heard you—'

Norah turned slowly to see what had cut Saffron's gushing short. Her mother was staring, her mouth comically ajar, at Gianluca. She had one of her long colourful scarfs wound around her head and wore a flowing tie-dyed dress with spaghetti straps that made it obvious that she didn't wear bras. What she should find strange about Gianluca, Norah had no idea.

Saffron clutched Norah's arm with steely fingers. She leaned close, to speak into Norah's ear while not taking her eyes off Gianluca. 'He's... *gorgeous*,' she said, failing spectacularly in her attempt to whisper. Norah froze and Gianluca turned decidedly pink.

'Is this your gondolier?' Saffron asked. He caught Norah's eye and raised his eyebrows.

'Uh, no, this is Gianluca. He's my... friend and... driver, I suppose.' She risked a look at him and was relieved to find a hint of an amused smile on his face. 'He's been taking me out into the lagoon to collect samples. This is my mum, Saffron,' she muttered to Gianluca.

'Your... friend,' Saffron repeated, instantly unravelling all of Norah's attempts to make this moment less painful.

The door swung wider and Manu appeared, completing the axis of awkwardness. 'Gianluca, Norah. I'm... surprised.'

Perhaps she should just go and leap in a canal right now. Where was Neal? For once, she hoped he would appear so his overdone politeness and strange ties could take the heat off Norah.

'We got back from the festival late and Norah didn't want to disturb you,' Gianluca said woodenly to Manu.

'Um, his sofa is very comfortable,' Norah lied. The perplexed look Manu gave her suggested she might have been better off saying nothing.

Gianluca took a step back, making Norah wonder just how close they had been standing when Saffron had appeared. 'Allora, I'm... going.' He raised a hand in an abortive wave.

Manu's head jerked up. 'You're welcome to stay for breakfast,' she blurted out.

He shook his head. 'Grasie, we already ate.' Manu nodded stiffly in reply. If Norah had had to guess, she'd have said Manu was disappointed. It was none of her business and had no easy solution, but the gulf between them made her ache.

Gianluca squeezed Norah's forearm briefly before he turned to go. She'd never been so glad he was touchy-feely. That second of warm pressure was the reassurance she'd needed. Whatever that staggering kiss had been about, they were still friends. Norah took a deep breath and turned to follow Saffron back inside.

'Darling, your hair looks *amazing*! I might have to find that hairdresser and get the same cut. It looked great in the pictures, but in real life, it's *gorgeous*,' Saffron said, taking her daughter's hand as though Norah were still five years old.

But a conversation about her haircut was preferable to any further words about Gianluca, so Norah smiled and mumbled some kind of thanks, trying to ignore the fact that Saffron had just called both of them 'gorgeous'.

'Oh, Norah, I am so glad to see you getting out and living your life! I mean, how can you regret breaking up with Andrej, when *that* was in your future? You don't have to tell me any details, darling, but I am *so* pleased for you. He looks just wonderful.'

Norah regretted not jumping into the canal when she'd had the chance. 'Mum, you've got the wrong end of the stick. Gianluca and I aren't together, in any sense.' She risked a glance at Manu, to find her boss with a sour expression on her face. Ouch. 'I'm serious,' Norah mumbled.

'I'm glad you got home from the festival safely,' Manu said tightly. 'Saffron arrived last night, but she didn't want to disturb your fun.'

'I remember the festivals in my day,' Saffron said with a grin that made Norah wince. She'd been dragged to a handful as a small child. Her memories were of Didi feeling stressed and miserable while Saffron shirked her responsibilities.

'I'm sorry,' Norah murmured to Manu. 'I didn't realise she was coming.'

Manu eyed Saffron. 'Yes, I gathered the trip was last-minute.'

Norah's stomach rolled with a cocktail of emotions, but this was a mix she was familiar with. She was Saffron's daughter; embarrassment and defensiveness were her old friends.

'I set up a guest room for Saffron because I couldn't let her into your apartment,' Manu continued, pricking Norah further. She knew Manu had better things to do than set up guest rooms for strangers.

'Thank you,' she said softly. 'She can stay with me now.'

'Oh, I wouldn't want to be in the way,' Saffron said, eyebrows raised. Norah stifled a groan. 'The room was lovely, even if the bed was...' Norah eyeballed Saffron urgently, trying to get her to shut up before she made things worse.

'Saffron is more than welcome to stay wherever is most comfortable,' Manu said.

'She'll stay with me on the sofabed,' Norah said firmly. Whatever reason Manu had for being hospitable to Saffron and even offering to help with the wedding venues, it was nonetheless clear that the two women hadn't clicked. 'And it won't affect my work schedule. She can come out with us on the next sampling trip, perhaps.'

'Oh, no, darling. I would only get in the way,' Saffron said with a wink, making Norah want to beat her head against the frescoed wall.

'Either way, thank you for taking her in last night,' Norah said earnestly to Manu.

Her boss finally smiled. 'It's all right, Norah. Is... is your fiancé going to arrive soon?' she asked, turning to Saffron.

Saffron's pinched expression did not look promising. Norah groaned inwardly for the fiftieth time. 'Perhaps. I just... wanted to come out first to check on Norah... and the wedding venues. She's sent me some incredible pictures. I wanted to choose one and surprise Neal.'

'*I* was certainly surprised,' Manu muttered. 'Please do feel welcome here. Neal, too.' Norah wondered why she didn't quite believe Manu.

'Come on, Mum. Let's move your things into my apartment. Thank you again, Manu.'

'You're welcome, cara.'

Norah ushered Saffron away as quickly as politeness allowed. As soon as they were safely shut inside Norah's little studio, she turned to her mother in exasperation. 'Mum! You can't just show up unannounced! Manu is my boss!'

Saffron sighed and took Norah's arm. She shook it off. 'I'm sorry, sweetheart. I just... I feel all at sea at the moment and I... I thought seeing you, seeing Venice again on my own this time, might provide some clarity.'

Norah released an enormous huff and sat heavily on the bed, setting her cane next to her and rubbing her palms over her face. 'Don't look to me for clarity,' she warned darkly. 'Our family is like the blind leading the blind.'

'You're still using the cane,' Saffron commented, giving the aluminium tube a critical look. 'Didi said...'

Norah groaned. 'Didi knows what the doctors said, but she doesn't know what it feels like.'

'I'd just hoped... you'd be well.'

Norah wished Saffron weren't so good at triggering an emotional response, but it was probably built into children's DNA. She wanted to insist that she was well. She'd seen and done so many amazing things over the past four weeks, pushing through when she was afraid, or when her balance wasn't perfect. But there was a little voice in her head telling her she should hate her cane. It was such an obvious sign of disability, but she wasn't ready to walk without it, no matter what the doctors said. She was still too afraid. The memory of trying to walk at rehab while her back felt like a teetering pile of dominoes was too fresh. Part of her was attached to that cane and she wasn't ready to deal with the psychological challenge of giving it up.

'I am well, Mum,' she insisted. 'The cane is... nothing.'

Saffron studied her with a growing smile. 'Your hot young man obviously agrees with you.' She stuck out an elbow to catch Norah in the ribs, but she shifted away.

'Mum,' she said through gritted teeth, 'firstly, whether I walk with a cane or not has nothing to do with potential romantic relationships. And, secondly, there is no romantic relationship with

Gianluca. *Please* don't suggest there is. It's... awkward here at Manu's house.' She suspected telling Saffron about Gianluca and Manu's true relationship was a bad idea, but if she didn't, Saffron might develop some ideas even wilder than Norah's original misunderstanding. 'It's not widely known, but Manu is Gianluca's biological mother. But they're estranged, so don't put your foot in it!'

'Oh,' Saffron said slowly. 'That is awkward. And what makes you think I would put my foot in it?'

'Just... best behaviour, Mum.'

'Oh, I will. Anything, if you'll let me get to know your beautiful young man.'

'Shut up about the beautiful young man! What happened to your lovesickness over Neal, anyway?' Norah expected one of Saffron's signature facetious sniffs of offence, but her expression was disconcertingly stony. 'Mum?' she prompted warily. 'Has something happened with Neal? After making me go to all of these sappy wedding venues for you?' Her voice rose at the end.

'Nothing's... happened,' Saffron said tightly.

'But?' Norah asked.

Saffron threw herself onto the sofa and stared out of the window, although she obviously wasn't seeing the sun-bathed gothic windows with riotous begonias across the canal. 'I'm just not... sure.'

Norah grunted to stifle some less appropriate words. 'This is why normal people don't rush into engagements,' she said peevishly.

Saffron scowled at Norah. 'You waited four years and you were still wrong.'

'Mum!' Norah cried, but the stab of hurt didn't land where she thought it was going to. The wound from her broken relationship with Andrej was closing over. It was her relationship with her mother that pained her.

'I'm sorry, Norah,' she muttered. 'God knows I'm usually wrong about everything.' Her statement was enough to silence further censure from Norah, but not enough to garner much sympathy. 'I... Neal is wonderful. It's... me, that's the problem. That won't be a surprise to you.'

'You're afraid to commit?'

'Everyone's afraid to commit, sweetheart,' Saffron said matter-of-factly. 'I'm afraid... I'm just waiting for the day when Neal wakes up and realises I'm... well, I'm *me*.'

Norah recognised the feeling far too intimately. But this wasn't about her. Andrej was in the past. Neal could be Saffron's future, although why Norah was now so hopeful for her mother, she didn't know.

'You don't think he's realised already?' she asked gently.

'He can't have realised. He's still there,' Saffron replied. 'Every crazy idea I have, he listens. This Venice wedding? He keeps saying I can have anything I want. And that's the other thing...' Saffron's chest heaved as though she was panicking and Norah scooted onto the sofa and took her mother's hand. 'He's rich. I don't mean rich, rich. I mean *stinking* rich. He founded a business when he was in his twenties and now... I didn't realise. I just met him on a normal sort of cruise and I had no idea he would give me diamonds – *real* ones – and look at houses with me and agree to getting married in a historic palazzo in *Venice*!' Saffron turned to Norah, her eyes wide with panic. She clutched her daughter's other hand. 'What am I supposed to *do*?'

'Mum, have you been *trying* to push him away?'

Her mother took a deep breath. 'I don't know,' she said softly. 'Maybe I have. What if I push too far? What if he gives up on me, but it's too late!'

'Too late for what?' Norah asked. 'To be honest, if he agreed to the Venice palazzo thing, then he must *really* love you.'

'Oh, God, he can't seriously love me.'

Norah's skin crawled. She'd never had such an honest conversation with Saffron and the emotions she was expressing were uncomfortably familiar. Norah understood enough about inheritance of traits to start to worry she was doomed to her mother's fate. But wasn't that a moot point now? Like Manu, she'd decided to disavow love and relationships in pursuit of excellence in her field.

Manu had chosen that life – even given up a relationship with her son – whereas Saffron had stumbled unhappily through it. Which one was Norah, really? As much as she understood Manu's reasons for her actions thirty years ago, she was more and more convinced that she would never be able to do the same. Did that mean she wasn't as committed to her career as she'd thought?

No, she would have tried to make it work – and perhaps lived in doubt, as she suspected Saffron had her entire life.

'Do you love him?' Norah asked tentatively.

'There's no simple answer to that question, darling, and that's what scares me.' Norah started to say something, but Saffron shook her head to silence her. 'It's not something you can understand, until you've loved someone with everything you have – and then lost it all again.'

'Um, I was with Andrej for a long time, Mum. And then I lost it in an instant,' Norah pointed out.

Saffron waved a hand dismissively. 'You didn't love him,' was all she said, ignoring Norah's indignant huff. 'I've always loved... irresponsibly. That's part of the package for me. And it's why I've been hurt – and hurt others. Except with Neal. It's all so... normal. We don't even argue.'

'You want to argue?'

Saffron's shoulders drooped. 'No, but I'd like to see his... passions somewhere outside the bedroom, too, you know.'

Norah clapped a hand over her mouth. 'Too much information,' she mumbled.

'I'm honestly not sure,' Saffron said with a weak smile. 'And I wanted to see you. Didi has been... amazing these past few months. Since she went a bit crazy in love herself, she's more tolerant of me and... Yes, yes, I know I was entirely to blame for the distant relationship I had with her and not the other way around, but I've learned to trust that she will stick with me and I... I want a good relationship with both of you. I don't want to feel like the difficult child in this family any more.'

Norah slipped an arm around Saffron's shoulders and squeezed. 'I'm pretty sure you saved me from being the difficult child,' she joked.

'Maybe you'd like to have the mantle for a few weeks? Your cute haircut is a great start!'

Norah patted her hair self-consciously, wishing she could switch off the memory of the feeling of Gianluca's fingers in it. 'This haircut isn't supposed to be cute. It's supposed to be real. I'm a scientist. Why should I have long hair when no one needs to look at me?'

Saffron gave her an odd look that suggested dissent, but she merely nodded in response. 'It didn't seem to stop that beautiful young man from touching it,' she said wryly.

'Mum!' Norah admonished. 'I will not let you within a hundred yards of Gianluca if you keep this up!'

'As long as you get within an inch of him, I don't mind.'

'Not going to happen!'

Saffron made a poor attempt at a serious look. 'Oh, it'll happen, sweetheart.'

21

It took until Thursday, when Gianluca sent her a text reading
simply,

You OK?

for Norah to realise she'd buried herself in work because everything else was just too hard.

She had filled an entire wall in the aquarium lab with samples
she was propagating under different conditions and her observa-
tion spreadsheet was getting out of hand. She sometimes thought to
herself that she could spend her entire life just documenting the
different species of algae in this one lagoon and working out the
best way to propagate them. Manu and the other researchers could
then work out how to use them and they'd be some kind of science
dream team for eco-tech.

But she knew the project would continue without her when she
left in a few weeks. At least she would give them a ream of compre-
hensive data to work with and was nurturing a few ideas for PhD
proposals herself.

Every evening she came home to Saffron, draped on the sofa in exhaustion from a day of exploring and visiting wedding venues even though Norah wouldn't want to bet on whether the wedding was going ahead or not. She was perplexed by her mother's vacillations: visiting every palazzo in Venice and planning a grand event on the one hand and secretly doubting and crying when only Norah was watching. Norah had given up trying to diagnose Saffron's feelings. She'd spent the week grumbling to Didi via text and they'd come to the conclusion that Neal needed to get his backside to Venice because they didn't know what to do.

Norah had had no desire to text Gianluca whining messages about her mother's love life or any algae nerdiness and, since those had made up her entire week, she'd been left only with a few feverish and confusing memories about that kiss.

She replied to his text as she sat on the bus back from Marghera, assuring him that she was okay, just busy, and he replied with a picture of an art deco dresser that had been abandoned near a bridge, with the caption:

Thought of you.

She was too alarmed by her racing heartbeat at first to reply. Another message popped in a minute later.

Do you have any pigeon updates? I was wondering what happened next.

Norah sighed with relief as the text banter returned her heart rate to normal. When she hopped off the bus, she snapped a picture of some pigeon poop and sent it with the caption:

It all went to shit for him.

He replied almost immediately, starting with a row of laughing emojis.

Oh, well, sometimes a woman just wants to eat.

It was a stupid text exchange that had her grinning like an idiot, but it was much better than dwelling on the kiss. She should probably put them both out of their misery and confirm it had been a big mistake. They'd agreed to a summer friendship, not a summer of kissing. But she didn't have the heart to snuff whatever it was out, not quite yet.

Want to do the old city sampling sites on Saturday? You could bring your mum.

His sensible text made her inexplicably grumpy. Didn't he want to get her alone after nearly a week apart? She'd certainly been looking forward to catching up... properly, with no one watching.

But his suggestion unfortunately made sense. Norah should pay a little more attention to Saffron while she was there. She might leave again at any moment – if Norah was lucky. She typed a reply.

Okay, sounds good. I apologise in advance for her calling you 'beautiful'.

Norah wished she could have seen his face when he read that message.

As long as you don't assume I'm in love with her, I can handle that.

Norah choked, as she'd imagined Gianluca had done a minute ago. On a whim, she called him. He picked up on the first ring.

'Hey, beautiful,' he said, a smile in his voice.

'That's my line!' she scoffed.

'Are you on your way home from the lab?'

'How'd you know?'

There was a short pause and she imagined him shrugging his big shoulders. 'Where else would you be at this time of night where you'd be free to talk?'

She was surprised it had been so easy for him to tell she wouldn't talk to him in front of either of their mothers. 'Sorry I didn't make you sick of me with texts this week.'

'You're busy. I get it.'

'I'm not just busy. I'm... boring.'

He gave an odd laugh. 'That's about the last word I would use to describe you, Norah.'

'You wanted texts about algae and Venice weddings? My mum kills something off in me, I think – or sucks it out. Are you sure we can't go to some distant island on Saturday and accidentally leave her behind?'

His only response was an inarticulate huff of amusement.

'We know the monks would look after her if she washed up on San Francesco del Deserto. But then she'd probably fall in love with Brother Giuseppe and we'd be dealing with the wrath of God on top of everything.'

'Norah,' he interrupted her with a cough.

'Too much?'

'Yeah, too much. It'll be all right.'

Norah gave a disgruntled sigh, even though she knew she was venting selfishly again. 'Everything okay with you? Have you seen Chiara or Pino?' she asked after a moment of silence.

'I caught up with Chiara for a quick drink last night, but Pino works different hours.'

Well, that had turned into a conversation killer, since Norah was now wondering whether Chiara had asked about his relationship with Norah.

'Ehm,' he began and his tone set off some kind of panic response in her. 'Do we need to—?'

'No!' she insisted. 'We're good. I just want to... leave things be. I promise you more pigeon pics. Everything's fine.'

'Okay,' he said, but his tone was deflated. 'I look forward to the pigeon pics.'

'I'm nearly... home,' she said, her voice sounding odd to her own ears.

'Take care of yourself, nanarèɫa,' he said.

'You too, bigfoot. See you Saturday.'

* * *

'I thought you'd visited every palazzo in town by now!'

Gianluca heard Norah's voice before he manoeuvred *Dafne* around the corner to the steps of Manu's palazzo.

'I saved this one for today, because I wanted to approach it from the water,' her mother replied evenly.

'What do you think *Neal* would think of it?' Norah's sardonic tone made him eager to arrive, even if he certainly couldn't give her a hug.

'He'll say it's fine,' Saffron replied with a little sniff.

'Mum...?'

Gianluca pulled back on the oar, wondering whether mother and daughter needed another minute to talk this through, but it was too late. *Dafne* glided into their view. Norah and Saffron watched expectantly as he drew up to the post.

Saffron exclaimed over the quaint woodwork as she settled on the bench and Gianluca took advantage of her distraction to squeeze Norah's hands as he helped her into the boat. They shared a look that felt like a conversation. It would have gone something like this:

She's a mess. I'm a bit of a mess.

I know. It's okay. Can I help?

Only if you can manage to strategically dump her into the Grand Canal so her life can flash before her eyes and help her work out what's really important to her.

Don't know if I can do that. Would a kiss help?

You want to kiss my mum?

No, silly.

He bit his lip to fight back the strange thoughts. He was so accustomed to their easy banter that he could do it inside his own head – except he wouldn't actually say the thing about kissing.

'Do we have a wedding venue to visit before we start sampling?' he asked carefully.

'Yes,' said Saffron.

'No!' Norah contradicted her at the same time. They eyed each other. 'I'm not wasting any more of Gianluca's time – or Manu's money – on this. I'll get Pino to take you another time, if you want to arrive from the water. You've been looking at stupid wedding venues all week!'

Saffron swallowed. 'Stupid? Is that what you think of all this?'

Gianluca watched the dismayed expression settle onto Norah's face. 'What do you want me to say?' she asked bitterly. 'Do you even realise I thought *I* would be the one getting married soon? All this wedding shit...'

Saffron glanced at Gianluca in surprise. 'I didn't know that, you two!'

'Not *him*! God, Mum. I'm talking about Andrej – the one who actually was my boyfriend for years.'

'Oh,' Saffron said with a start. 'You thought you'd marry *Andrej*?

But... all you ever talked about was... DNA and... test tubes and stuff.'

'That's what I wanted,' Norah insisted. Gianluca's skin prickled as he realised it probably wasn't good for him to overhear this conversation. 'I get scared that I'm like you, that I'll give up everything for some guy over and over again. What I need is a career.'

'Is that what you think I'm doing with Neal?' Saffron asked in a small voice. 'Only ten times worse, because this time I'm actually marrying him?'

Gianluca wordlessly cast off and set the oar into the water. This was the kind of conversation that required motion. If he stayed still, he'd start thinking about Manu and her choices, wondering whether Norah was made from the same cloth.

'I don't know!' Norah answered Saffron's question, oblivious to Gianluca's uncomfortable ruminations. 'You haven't been together long and... I don't know who you're going to be with him.'

Saffron clasped Norah's hands. 'Oh, sweetheart, I'm always *me*!'

'No, you're not,' Norah insisted. 'Do you know what it was like getting to know you again every time you had a new boyfriend? At least, when you were alone and depressed, it was real. Is it any wonder I settled with a guy who felt safe?' She sucked in a sudden breath, as though only just realising what she'd said.

She glanced at Gianluca. He couldn't interpret her stormy expression, but it started up an ache inside him.

'Look, I'm sure we don't need to inflict this conversation on poor bigfoot here,' Norah said, extricating her hands from her mother's and giving Gianluca an apologetic smile.

'Bigfoot,' Saffron said. 'Is that indicative—?'

'Don't you dare, Mother,' Norah cut her off sharply.

Saffron was obviously stifling a smile. 'Of course, sweetheart. Because you wouldn't know anything about his—'

'Mum!'

'—you-know-what if you're just friends.'

Norah gave a dramatic sigh, but her expression was wry. Gianluca smiled, touched and amused by the honesty of their relationship as the torrent of emotion subsided and only the gentle splash of the oar remained.

'I can see where Norah gets her sense of humour,' he said lightly. He glanced at Norah, who was wrinkling her nose at him. 'You can punish me later.'

Gianluca was fascinated by the push-pull of Norah's relationship with her mother as the day progressed. One minute they were snapping at each other, and the next, Norah was taking her mother's hand and pointing out the most beautiful buildings. Seeing them together completed a picture for him – a picture he found more and more beautiful.

At lunchtime, he took them to his favourite bacaro in Cannaregio, which had no tables. He ordered a selection of his favourite cicchetti and Norah and Saffron contributed by pointing at plates of things they couldn't identify and he sometimes had trouble translating.

The woman behind the bar set the plates of bruschetta, fried meatballs, pickled vegetables, fish and prawns on the counter, along with three glasses of wine.

'What happened to Venetians eating a leisurely lunch?' Norah asked with a teasing look that also hinted that she wished he'd taken her there sooner.

He leaned on the bar and gave her a smile. 'We can have a leisurely lunch standing up. It just requires more wine.'

'I'm all in favour!' Saffron added, taking a generous sip from her glass.

'As we say in Venice, "eat and drink, because life is short"!' he said, clinking his glass with Saffron's.

'Do you need a stool, Norah?' she asked, eying the cane.

Norah shook her head wordlessly, but Gianluca sensed there was a lot she could have said on the subject. It felt as though they had so much to catch up on.

They continued their trek through innumerable canals after lunch, past little patches of grime that made Norah vibrate with excitement at the possibility of finding a different species of algae in the water nearby. He only had to haul her backside back into the boat once, when the wake of a passing motorboat surprised them as she was leaning out.

'Gosh, this is dangerous work,' Saffron commented.

'Not really,' he defended on Norah's behalf, as she was settling back on the seat and tugging her trousers back into place. He might have tugged too hard on her waistband. 'It's not a big deal if she falls in.'

'It's nice to know that's how important you think I am,' she said drily.

'I didn't mean... I caught you, didn't I?' he said, belatedly recognising her teasing look.

The afternoon grew heavy with heat and by the time he steered them back up the canal to Manu's palazzo, Saffron was sprawled along the bow, fanning herself. Norah was hunched behind the bench, looking over her data.

'Just imagine my mum thirty years younger, wearing a bikini,' she muttered, briefly looking up from her tablet.

He laughed. 'I thought I told you not to suspect I was in love with her.'

She made a sound somewhere between a snort and a choke. 'I deserved that.'

'You could sit in the bow wearing a bikini next time.'

'You're the beautiful one,' she quipped, stowing the tablet in its waterproof case. He couldn't think of a way to contradict her that still sounded like light banter.

He tied up to the post at Manu's and helped Saffron out of the boat. Manu opened the door and ushered Saffron inside with a tight smile. Gianluca watched for a moment. He didn't know Manu well, but there was something... off about all of this. Why would Manu be so supportive of the search for a wedding venue if she obviously found Saffron tiresome?

'Oh, this heat is stifling,' Saffron groaned as she headed inside. 'I need some water and a rest.'

'You go ahead, Mum,' Norah called as she opened up her samples one last time to make sure everything was secure. 'I'll be in soon.' She glanced up at Gianluca and then slid her gaze to Manu. 'We got some... really good samples.'

'I'll come out to the lab this week, now you've made so much progress,' Manu replied. 'We need to start discussing PhD proposals for you. I've been speaking to the Director of the Biotechnology Centre and I have an idea of what they're looking for, so let's see if that's of interest to you. I'd love to send you in my footsteps.'

Norah's mouth hung open for a moment. 'Wow, thanks. I'd... love to throw around some ideas. I've been thinking about it, of course.' Had she? He'd been trying not to think about what she'd do after she left Venice.

Manu smiled at Norah, then glanced warily at Gianluca. 'Do you want to come in? For a drink?' He stiffened, more out of habit than anything else. She'd asked so many times he was beginning to think she actually wanted him to accept. 'Or do you have to go and see Fernanda?'

'Fernanda! That's her name!' Norah muttered. 'I thought it was funny you just introduced her as Nòna!' Her smile died when she looked up to see the tension between Gianluca and his mother.

'Does she...? Is she all right, these days? On her own?' Manu asked, her voice stilted.

'She's been on her own for six years.' *Since Popà died.* He didn't need to say it. Understanding was written onto Manu's face. He wasn't used to sharing thoughts with her, as though they had a real relationship.

Manu drew in a sudden breath. 'I'll just go... check on Saffron. I'll leave the door open for you, Norah,' she said, disappearing quickly into the palazzo. So much for that relationship. He should have known better than to suspect Manu had feelings.

Norah was watching him when he came back to his senses. She grabbed her backpack and her cane and hauled herself to her feet. He reached for her when the boat wobbled, his hands slipping around her waist before he could stop them.

She stilled and took a deep breath. He slowly dropped his hands. 'I'm sorry for... this morning, with my mum.'

'Bòn, it's okay,' he insisted. He gazed up at the shaft of sky between the buildings on either side of the canal. 'In a strange way, I was jealous.'

'What?' She stepped nearer and took his hand. Her small hand didn't get far around his, so he twisted his arm and closed his hand over hers. He tugged until she sat back down on the bench and he sat in the stern, holding her hand and looking into her face.

'You two obviously care about each other. I know it's probably not helpful to hear that.' Her hand tightened on his.

'It is,' she said softly, with surprise. 'It is helpful. Sometimes I wonder... whether Manu secretly does care about you too – a lot,' she said warily.

'What difference would it make?'

'I'm pretty sure that's exactly what she would say,' Norah commented with a small smile. 'I'm... I'm glad you were there today. That sounds weird and I really am sorry you had to witness that crap, but... I don't know.' She smoothed her hand along the side of the boat, the polished wood that he'd sanded and smoothed over and over again until it felt right. 'This boat... you... it's been good for me.' She met his gaze with a rueful one of her own. 'This is the best summer friendship I've ever had.'

'I know what you mean,' he added softly.

She looked away. 'Thanks for sharing your life with me for a little while.'

Her choice of words set something to burning inside him.

She'd been in Venice five weeks. That was half of her time. *Half* of her time had already ticked by. The thought was hard to take.

'If it helps you get back on your feet – figuratamente – then I'm glad.'

She sighed and her hand went limp in his. 'I definitely needed to get out on my own and... the work has been really good.'

'I hope Manu's help with the PhD stuff will get you wherever you want to go,' he said, his tone sounding grim to his own ears.

'She knows everyone in the field. It's... an incredible opportunity.'

'Good,' he said firmly and dropped her hand.

She retrieved her cane from the bottom of the boat and scowled at it. 'Sometimes I wish I could walk without this, just to shut Mum up,' she said with a sigh. 'But I know it's because she's my mum and it's hard for her to see changes in me.'

'I didn't know you before...' he began, feeling his way through the sentence, 'but I think you've taken a difficult experience and... made yourself stronger.'

She smiled – a little self-deprecatingly, but it was bright and sweet. 'A phoenix, rising from the ashes,' she said, raising a hand in a mock dramatic gesture.

He chuckled and ruffled her hair. 'Dai, come on. Are you getting off my boat or are you coming home to Cannaregio with me?'

'I have to hang out with my mother,' she grumbled. 'Next time you go out with Pino or Chiara, can I come?'

'Certo, nanarèla,' he said, tugging her to her feet. He had a sudden idea. 'And, do you know what?' he said. 'Since you keep inconveniencing me,' he began with a teasing smile, 'could you help me with something?'

'Anything,' she answered firmly.

'Next weekend is my open studio. I'm usually quite busy with demonstrations and... Maybe you could do the money for me?'

'I'd love to,' she said with a smile. 'I'll get to see the carpenter at work!'

'Carpenter?!'

She laughed and gave him a playful shove on his shoulder. He grinned back, and then held out a hand to steady her as she stepped off the boat.

'I'll... text you,' she said. He nodded and she turned to go before he could say anything else. They shared a wave as she pulled the door closed behind her. He should have been relieved that their friendship appeared to have returned to normal after the kiss, but he had a niggling suspicion that it hadn't – at least not on his side.

But he looked forward to showing her his workshop and spending the day together in a different setting. They'd get back on track and everything would be easy between them, as it had been before.

22

Norah spent her week as usual in the lab, occasionally with Manu, who seemed to carefully avoid the topic of Gianluca. Saffron was not as diplomatic, but she was increasingly distracted and managed to restrict her questions about Gianluca to a couple a day.

Norah confided to Didi on the phone that she thought Saffron might be missing Neal and somehow the suggestion made its way back to the man in question, and before she knew it there were romantic plans afoot for the following weekend. At least Didi had been dragged in to help, too, and was on her way to Venice. Norah was dying to see her.

On Saturday afternoon, Norah hurried to the meeting place she'd arranged to kick off Neal's plan, which she had greeted with much eye-rolling, as well as relief. She rushed at Didi as soon as she saw her sister approaching over the bridge and threw her arms around her.

'I'm so glad you're here,' Norah murmured.

Didi pulled back to study Norah, her hands clutching her younger sister's shoulders. 'Wow, your hair really is short. I missed you, noodle.'

Norah hugged her tight once more. 'I missed you too. But don't dare call me noodle in front of anyone else!'

'Ciao, noodle.' Didi's boyfriend, Piero, took his turn giving her a hug and a kiss on the cheek. Norah gave a muffled grumble, but he just grinned at her with a glint of mischief in his eye and wrapped an arm around Didi.

'It's so quiet without you at home,' Didi said earnestly.

Norah bit back a grin. 'I'm kind of glad to be out of your hair.' Piero had moved into her sister's flat a month before Norah had left, unwilling to wait in Venice while Didi worked her notice. He was great for Didi, but Norah knew they'd held back because she was always around.

'How do you like the city?' Piero asked.

'Pretty good,' she said with mock nonchalance, casting a quick glance along the shimmering turquoise canal lined with ancient houses.

Didi shared a look with Piero. 'Just don't ask her if the city knows her like a lover.'

Norah snorted. 'What?'

Piero shrugged apologetically and pressed a kiss to Didi's forehead. 'Norah doesn't need to be riled up like you did.'

'You must be Norah,' the man behind Didi and Piero said, coming forward with his hand outstretched. 'I'm Salvatore.'

Norah smiled and presented her cheek – she was getting better at this. 'I've heard so much about you.'

'And yet you haven't come out to Murano to visit yet.' He tsked.

'Leave her alone, Popà,' Piero said to his father. 'She's finding her own Venice, right, noodle?'

She scowled at him, but Piero had one of those cheeky smiles that were utterly irresistible, especially on someone she suspected would one day be her brother-in-law.

'Noodle?'

Norah whirled. Just her luck that Gianluca and Pino would arrive within earshot right at that moment. Piero draped an arm over Norah's shoulders and held out his hand to Gianluca and Pino as they climbed out of Pino's gondola. 'You must be Norah's friends.'

'And you're Piero Zanetti,' Gianluca said with a nod as he shook Piero's hand. Norah found it easy to forget that Piero was a world-renowned artist and even more famous in his home city.

'This is Gianluca and Pino,' Norah introduced them as Didi came forward. 'My sister, Didi, and Piero's father, Salvatore.'

'Pino?' Didi said, studying the gondolier. She met Piero's eye. 'Our Pino?'

Pino's face broke into a grin. 'I remember you two now! A certain kiss under a certain bridge at sunset.' He chuckled and mimed gagging as Didi's cheeks went pink and she looked decidedly sheepish. Pino turned to Piero and shook his hand. 'You told me to eat tuna!'

'Only because your singing ruined a perfect moment. And we're not naming our first child after you, no matter what you demanded.' Piero was grinning, but his hand drifted, seemingly of its own accord, to clasp Didi's.

Norah was struck with the sudden, unexpected image of her sister as a mother. Didi had always been so level-headed about love, but she was head-over-heels now. How odd that she could change so much in such a short time – and all it had taken was a sojourn in this crazy city. Norah grimaced at her own sappy thoughts.

'Hey, you okay?' Gianluca said, drawing up beside her. 'Noodle,' he added with a grin.

'I'm great, Lulu,' she replied lifting her chin. She took a deep breath. 'Sorry for dragging you into this.'

He shook his head. 'You're still going to help me with my open day tomorrow, right? It's only fair.'

'I would have done that anyway,' she insisted.

'I would have done this anyway. Where's Neal?'

'He'll be here any minute. He's just getting into his costume,' Didi said, her straight face slipping when she caught Norah's eye.

When Neal arrived a few minutes later, there were no straight faces left. He'd swapped his usual loud shirts and bow ties for a Venetian carnival costume, complete with a curly wig and an effusion of lace flounces at the neck.

He hurried towards them over the bridge, as quickly as the heeled court shoes allowed, and went straight to Norah. 'How is she?' he asked earnestly.

Norah stifled her laugh with some difficulty, trying desperately to ignore his silk tricorne and the dark beauty mark some committed person at the costume hire shop had added to his chin. 'She's fine,' Norah managed. 'You guys need to talk, but, if you're serious about her, I think you've got a shot.'

He theatrically mopped his brow with a lace handkerchief and his whole body drooped with relief. Norah caught Didi's eye and they shared a cringe. She drifted over to her sister as Pino showed Neal the gondola.

'I can't believe it takes so many of us for them to sort out a simple problem,' Norah grumbled.

'You do know our mother, right?'

Norah shared a smile with Didi, but there was a shadow of something new in her sister's eyes. 'What?'

Didi's smile faded. 'Just... baggage,' she said with a huff, glancing at Piero. 'Stuff I didn't know we carried around with us – *I* carried around with *me*, I should say.'

The statement gave Norah a prickly sense of awareness. 'I think I'm beginning to have some idea,' she murmured. She had inherited a lot more than simply DNA from Saffron, and sifting through to keep the good legacy and release the bad would take a lifetime.

Didi squeezed her arm. 'Gianluca looks strangely familiar, too,' she said thoughtfully.

'Oh, thank God. I thought you were going to make some comment about our relationship.' She caught Didi's surprised look. 'We're just friends,' she added quickly.

Didi's slow nod was a little too sceptical and Norah inwardly groaned. 'Does he live in Cannaregio? Near the Campo San Felice?'

'Yes!' Norah exclaimed. 'Don't tell me you met him, too.'

Didi shook her head. 'No, I never met him, but I think he was my neighbour in Ava's apartment. I saw him get in a boat dressed like an old woman with lace on his head.'

'What?'

'It's a long story,' Didi said drily. 'And this is a crazy place.'

'A crazy place that will soon be home for you,' Norah pointed out.

'The unexpected twists in life, huh?' Her eyes drifted back to Piero.

'Made in China, as I suspected!' Salvatore huffed as he studied the lace at Neal's neck.

'Well, it's too late to get a replacement from Burano and we can't just rip it off, so we'll have to hope that Saffron doesn't notice,' Piero said. He clapped his hands and rubbed them together. 'If we're all in place, who's ready for a romantic spectacle?' He raised an eyebrow at Didi as he said it.

Didi ignored him. 'Is Mum wearing the dress?' she asked Norah.

'She was putting it on when I left. I'll go get her and... we'll get this show on the canal.'

* * *

'If this is such a fancy café, where's your dress, darling?' Saffron huffed ten minutes later as Norah ushered her through the alleys of Santa Croce towards the Ponte del Gaffaro.

'Erm, these are my best trousers,' she said lightly. 'Come on.'

Saffron came to a sudden halt. 'Is Neal here?'

Shit. Norah's jaw clenched. Had she ruined this? Who had put *her* in charge of a stupid romantic gesture? But the sheen of panic in her mother's eyes doused the self-reflection.

'What is it? Have you decided you're breaking up with him?'

'I should,' Saffron said, her voice weak.

'Why? Has he done something? Why "should"?'

Saffron swallowed heavily. 'I can't stop thinking we're going to be disastrous together.' She clutched Norah's arm. 'He's a member of... a *golf club*!'

'Does he have a skull and crossbones tattoo that says "Birmingham Golf Club until death"?'

'I'm serious, Norah! Do you think I belong in a country club?'

'You don't have to go there with him!'

Saffron's panic only crept up a notch. 'But... what if he meets another woman there?'

'I imagine he's thought this through and, if he asked you to marry him, he's not intending to look for any other women. You need to work out if you trust him.'

'Do you think I can?'

Norah snorted. 'I'm not the best person to ask. I don't know Neal from a bar of soap and I just got my backside kicked by a guy I thought I loved,' she grumbled.

'You'd trust Gianluca, though, wouldn't you?'

Norah's throat clogged up. 'With anything,' she muttered before she could stop herself. 'But that's beside the point. I can admit that being friends with him has dragged me out of the "all men are bastards" phase, but that doesn't mean I'm going to fall in love again any time soon.' Her voice trailed off and, after a long silence, she glanced up to find Saffron studying her. Norah didn't give her the satisfaction of asking what she was thinking. 'Are we going to put Neal out of his misery or not?'

'He really came all this way for me?'

'No, he's a real bridge fanatic,' Norah joked.

'His business *is* something to do with architecture,' Saffron commented.

'I was joking! Of course, he's here for you. I bet he even blew off a game of golf to be here!'

'And he's planned something romantic and... undignified?'

'Very undignified.'

A smile tugged at Saffron's lips. 'I don't know how... I – I don't know why...'

Norah felt an annoyingly violent stab of emotion at her mother's flustered stammering. She knew exactly how Saffron felt. And she didn't know if she'd be brave enough, if she was faced with the same decision.

'What should I do?' Saffron said pleadingly.

Norah swallowed. 'There's no science to it, Mum.'

Saffron gripped her hand and looked ahead, to the glimpse of the Rio del Gaffaro at the end of the alley, glinting green in the afternoon sunlight. 'I suppose not,' she said with a sudden laugh. 'Well, except chemistry!' Saffron smoothed the frilly red dress and took a deep breath. 'I have always been good at leaping right in!'

'Just please not into a canal,' Norah muttered to herself.

Saffron rushed off and Norah had to pivot quickly to follow. Her back complained with a grumpy twinge and she sighed. Had she just talked her mother into behaving recklessly? She didn't know what was going on with life any more. Along with the niggle of pain was the suspicion that uncertainty was something she would have to learn to live with.

23

'I hope she realises that stunt is going to end up on YouTube,' Piero grumbled into his glass. After witnessing Neal ardently serenade Saffron with Chris de Burgh's 'Lady in Red' from Pino's gondola, while Norah's mother stood on the Ponte del Gaffaro, they'd waved them off with Salvatore and collapsed into seats at a café on a nearby square for a spritz – or ten. 'I counted at least five phones trained on them,' Piero continued.

'Not everyone is as averse to the Internet as you are,' Didi said, nudging his shoulder with her own.

'I guess when it's true love, you don't care who's watching,' Pino responded drily, swirling the ice cubes in his glass. Gianluca gathered his friend had rowed Didi and Piero on a romantic gondola ride back in the winter. Looking at Norah's sister and her boyfriend, it was hard to believe they'd only been together a few months.

Didi was darker than Norah, taller too, and she was obviously protective of her younger sister. He enjoyed seeing how close they were. If it made him feel excluded, that was his own problem.

Gianluca was quiet as the others bantered and bickered, trying not to watch Norah too intently. He realised he'd only met Venice

Norah, who was a little lonely and a little fragile. Was that what drew him to her? He liked the feeling that she needed him, although he knew she wouldn't like that idea if he made the mistake of voicing it.

But today it felt as though *he* needed *her*. *Tomorrow*, he needed her, he corrected himself. Having her in the workshop tomorrow would allow him to focus on demonstrating his work, while she could handle the annoying customer service.

Salvatore returned from bringing Saffron and Neal to their holiday apartment on the Lido and immediately began bickering with his son about where they were going to eat. Pino stood and tucked his phone into his pocket.

'I should go and find some fares,' he said, shaking Piero's hand and giving Didi a kiss on the cheek. He hugged Norah and kissed her cheek. 'Don't take any strange gondolas,' he said, wagging his finger at her. 'And protect Gianluca from the flirting tourists tomorrow.'

Gianluca gave him a withering look. 'I hope you'll come some time tomorrow,' he said.

'Of course.'

They clapped each other on the back and, once Pino had left, suddenly everyone was staring at Gianluca. He drained his glass and pointed awkwardly in the rough direction of Cannaregio. 'I should... prepare for tomorrow. It's my laboratorio... workshop open day.'

'You're not coming to eat?' Piero asked, a belligerent expression on his face. Gianluca opened his mouth to say something, but Piero continued, 'You should join us. Give you a bit more time to stare at my... Norah before I confront you about your intentions.'

'Piero!' Didi said sharply, but she was obviously stifling a smile.

Norah stood quickly and grabbed her cane. 'I'll walk you back to Cannaregio,' she said, giving his back a shove to get him moving.

'I'll meet you at the restaurant,' she called to the others over her shoulder. She gave him another poke when he turned to say goodbye rather than leaving with all speed.

'I'm sorry they're so embarrassing,' she groaned when they'd turned enough corners that they were out of earshot. He had to lengthen his strides to keep up with her. Perhaps that was an advantage of the cane: it allowed her to walk at her accustomed speed.

'It's fine,' he said mildly. 'Nòna was the same.'

'I don't know why everyone keeps thinking it's impossible to be just friends, especially when they know what I went through last year. Only Manu seems to think we have the right idea, not leaping into bed together.'

'Ciò, we already did that.'

'You know what I mean,' she said with a frown.

'What did Manu say? About us?' he asked, trying to keep his voice light.

'Nothing specific. She probably thinks you have an abandonment complex because of her.'

'And you are going to abandon me at the end of your internship,' he added, hoping she didn't detect the thrum of emotion beneath his joking words.

'That's the good thing about this. You don't abandon friends.' She glanced up at him, her eyes clear. He wasn't sure he shared her certainty, as much as he wanted to. It was getting harder to ignore all the other things he wanted when he looked at her.

She squeezed his hand, aiming for reassurance, he thought, but once their fingers tangled, it was difficult to force them apart again. Their steps slowed as they walked the length of an alley, hand in hand.

Norah's pace picked up again and she extricated herself. Sadly, Gianluca suspected it would always be easier for her to extricate herself than for him.

He trailed her to the Campo San Felice, smiling faintly at her turbo-charged figure. She stopped and leaned on her cane at the spot where his street met the square. 'I'll see you tomorrow, then. What time?'

'I just realised you might want to spend time with your sister,' he heard himself say, although he wasn't sure he was happy with himself for saying it. 'You don't have to help out if you don't have time.'

She frowned deeply. 'I love my sister, but I lived with her for a year and I'm still happy to be out here on my own. What's the matter with you?'

His skin prickled at the knowledge that she could read him so well. 'I just... I don't want to hold you back,' he murmured.

'You're not holding me back. What gave you that idea? You've... done exactly the opposite since I've been here.' She took a step closer and looked up into his face.

He shrugged. 'I'm glad you think so, but you're... pretty amazing on your own.'

She studied him, making him wary of what she saw in his face, but she straightened quickly. 'Let me be amazing for your open day, then! You can whittle to your heart's content and I'll sell stuff for you. Besides, I promised Pino I'd protect you from the flirting tourists.'

'Whittle?' he asked. He'd learned English for years, but had never heard that word before.

'Look it up after I've gone so you can't get annoyed with me,' she said with a smile. 'Don't kiss me. I'm going in for a hug,' she announced, before throwing her arms around his chest. He closed his arms instinctively around her, one hand cradling the back of her head.

He smiled. He couldn't help it. Without thinking, he brushed a kiss to the top of her head.

'Oi! I said no kissing,' she said, her voice muffled by his chest. She pulled back with a deep breath, keeping him at arm's length with two fistfuls of his shirt. 'You're pretty amazing on your own, too,' she said evenly. 'But I like... us.'

He couldn't have got any words out, even if he'd known what to say in response.

'Friends, us,' she clarified. It was concerning that she needed to clarify that. 'When there's no one else around making stupid assumptions.'

He studied her. 'Me, too,' he admitted. 'See you tomorrow? At nine?'

She nodded and gave him a jaunty salute.

* * *

She rushed into the workshop the following morning and thrust a box of biscuits at him as a kind of peace offering. It wasn't much, but she couldn't handle him doubting how much their friendship meant to her.

'I tried to get coffee, but the bar pasticceria doesn't do takeaway,' she complained.

He grinned and everything inside her calmed down all of a sudden. 'You don't take your coffee with you to litter the streets of old Venice. You swallow it down at the bar.'

'I was in too much of a rush to get over here,' she said. 'And I thought Venetians did everything slowly on Sundays.'

'Not always,' he said, brushing his hands on his thick work trousers. He was wearing heavy boots, which made her realise she was used to seeing him barefoot. She tried not to notice the full view of his muscular arms, revealed by his sleeveless shirt.

He took the box and set it on the counter next to the cash register, before leaning down to kiss her cheek. It was a quick, soft kiss, but it somehow communicated everything she'd wanted to hear: he was sorry for being weird last night; he wanted their friendship back on an even keel; surely they could touch like normal people without being terrified they'd accidentally make out.

'Anyway,' he said, 'I already made you a coffee.' He placed two cups onto the bench, both frothy with steamed milk.

'I forgot you are an all-round perfect human being,' she joked, taking an appreciative sip of her cappuccino.

'I haven't even cooked for you yet,' he commented, as though surprised to realise it himself.

'There's still time to remedy that,' she said with a wink.

He chuckled, promising a dinner party on the altana one day that week.

'So, this is your workshop,' she said, nursing her coffee cup.

'You have your laboratory. I have my laboratorio – that's the Italian word.'

'From "labour"! I get it. All these Latin roots.'

'You can already swear in Venetian. If you learn Italian, too, you'll practically be a local.'

'Don't I have to join a rowing club?'

He grinned. 'That too, but then you're not allowed to leave.' He cleared his throat and continued, taking her around the various stations within the workshop. 'I'm going to make a fórcola today, as a demonstration, but I... *whittled* several small articles that might sell – I don't know. I don't know how many people are going to come, but I'll be happy if you can take their money so I can just...'

She failed to stifle her smile. 'Whittle?' she joked.

'Exactly,' he said with a straight face. 'Because I am a carpenter.'

She snorted. 'Okay, I'll take their money while you stroke your wood.'

His brow furrowed and she couldn't hold back her laughter. 'Is that... rude?' he asked.

'Yes, I'm sorry!' She giggled.

They alternated between working in parallel to ready the workshop and the light banter she'd missed. He fetched an enormous hunk of wood and set it on the workbench as though it weighed little more than the biscuits she'd brought. She tried to keep her focus on her own tasks, rather than appreciating the strength in his hands as he set up his equipment.

She ran her fingers over one of the fórcole in the window, tracing the bracket where the oar sat.

'That's called the mouth and the two tips are the noses,' Gianluca explained. She picked it up and made silly faces with it until he was doubled over with laughter. 'You'll scare away the customers!' he accused.

She set it back in the display and took in the variety of wooden implements, all of which he must have made himself. There were polished platters that displayed the intricacy of the wood grain. A board carved with a twisting, erratic pattern was shoved behind a few fórcole. She drew it out to run her fingers over the complex geometric carving, before settling the piece more prominently in the window.

'I should have got Didi to come by,' she commented, almost to herself. 'She's a visual merchandiser. She'd know how to set this stuff up so it would sell.'

'Are you suggesting I've done a bad job?' he joked.

Norah eyed him with a smile. 'You do seem to be hiding some of your best work.'

'My best work is a functional fórcola.'

A few visitors trickled in from ten o'clock and it wasn't long before Norah was busy behind the till. Her lack of Italian was only a problem on a handful of occasions, when Gianluca would wipe his forehead with his arm and come over himself.

Usually, Norah would gesture to him, call him the 'maestro at work' and encourage as many 'oohs' and 'aahs' as she could get away with. She called it a success when he looked up from his work to give her a withering look.

Gianluca's patience appeared inexhaustible. After making the initial cuts, he hacked away at the wood incrementally with his hand tools, painstakingly forming the mouth and checking his work with hypersensitive fingertips.

The stream of curious customers was so constant that they grabbed pasta in takeaway boxes, Gianluca for once foregoing a leisurely lunch break – although he vetoed the plastic forks and fetched some of his own cutlery. And then it was back to work, if smiling at customers and watching Gianluca could be called work.

He rarely broke concentration as the day wore into afternoon. Even when she said outrageous things about him to visiting tourists, his eyes remained trained on the wood, his expression endearingly earnest. His floppy hair fell over his forehead and he swiped at it unconsciously, making Norah want to find another hair tie – or just run her fingers through it.

The stream of visitors slowed as the June afternoon grew stifling. Norah had fewer transactions to ring up and more time to watch Gianluca and think.

Even though they'd reset their friendship, watching him work made her feel things a friend probably shouldn't. The physical aspect was familiar enough: his deft fingers gave her far too many ideas. But it was the yearning that disturbed her more. He was steady and sure and gentle, patient and content with his quiet work.

She wanted that. Or maybe she just wanted him, to balance out her slightly manic approach to life, which only came from her own fear anyway.

Fear of what?

He glanced up right when her thoughts were bogged down with dangerous questions. She had pushed her career zealously because she'd had little else to pursue, with her restless hands and busy mind. She was afraid that, without her studies, she wasn't worth anything – the same fear that had got Saffron into trouble over and over. But Norah's commitment to her research to the exclusion of all else had made that true. When she'd lost her colleagues and her work, she truly had been nothing.

Until she'd come to Venice and let Gianluca chip away at her with his kindness, to reveal the grain of the wood that had always been inside her. When he looked at her, she could believe she was worth knowing. Yes, she wanted a successful scientific career, but she wanted to be just herself, too.

Gianluca put down his little saw and approached, his brow furrowed. 'What's up?' he asked, hunching to look her in the eye. His rough fingertips fluttered on her cheek. She wanted to kiss him. She wanted to stay friends too. It wouldn't work.

'Watching you work makes me all philosophical,' she murmured, glancing up to catch his amused smile.

He ran his fingers through her hair. 'I think that's the biggest compliment you've ever given me.'

'Really?' she asked. 'Have you forgotten I told you I think you're hot,' she said before she'd thought it through.

'I haven't forgotten,' he said softly. He paused, a rueful expression on his face and his eyes trained on her. Something in his expression made Norah's breath hitch. He seemed to make a decision and finally spoke, his voice soft. 'And I haven't forgotten how hard I had to try not to tell you the same.'

24

'I didn't think that would be a news bomb to you,' Gianluca muttered, drawing back so he could take a breath and rub a hand over his face.

'A news bomb?' she said with a quick, flummoxed smile. 'It is, kind of,' she murmured. She was staring at him as though she'd never seen him before. 'Maybe if we just kiss a little...' she said, trailing off and biting her lip.

His emotions were coiled tight and she appeared to be an expert at turning the screw. He shook his head slowly. 'I don't think... kissing "a little" is an option.' He swallowed, watching her do the same.

'But I don't... but you...'

He wasn't prepared when she closed her hands in his shirt and tugged, bringing his lips to hers. But he reacted quickly, steadying them against the bench and deepening the kiss before she could change her mind.

If the kiss outside Manu's palazzo had knocked him flat, this one made him fly. He opened his mouth against hers, letting go, giving in, and she stayed right with him, sharing the rush. It felt like the final pieces of her slotting into place; she was funny and tough and vulnerable and kissed with her whole body – her whole self.

He lifted her onto the counter and tangled his fingers in her hair. Her thumbs stroked his cheeks and she angled her head, drawing him closer. The kiss grew deeper, wilder, until they were gasping for breath and friendship was the last thing on his mind.

The bell over the door tinkled and Norah pulled back with a jerk. Her hand flew to her mouth. The newcomer reacted with a startled and slightly amused, 'Oh-h-h.'

Gianluca stepped away quickly, reaching back to catch Norah when she leaped off the counter. Without looking at each other, they shifted apart.

'Oh, hi, Pino,' Norah said, her voice breathy and high, which was more than Gianluca could get out at that moment. Norah froze. 'Hi, Chiara. And... Nòna.' The tone of her voice changed entirely.

Gianluca whipped around to see his grandmother on Chiara's arm, her expression frustratingly inscrutable. He rushed over to kiss her cheeks.

'You forgot to turn the sign to "closed",' Chiara said evenly. Gianluca couldn't tell how much she'd seen. Pino, on the other hand, had clearly seen more than he'd expected and he was blinking at Gianluca with a smug smile.

'What?' Norah asked, staring at the door of the workshop.

'It's four o'clock,' Chiara explained. 'You should be closed by now.'

'Oh, right.' Norah sprang into action, locking the till and gathering her bag and her water bottle. Gianluca realised he was still watching her too closely and tried to shake it off, but it was difficult.

'Are you... leaving already?' he asked lamely. She stared blankly at him and it made everything a little better to know she was just as unsettled as he was. Except that the long look between them attracted the attention of their inconvenient audience.

Pino rubbed his hands together. 'I thought we'd go for a drink.'

'Uh huh, a drink,' Norah said, dumping her bag down again.

'I'll just... tidy up,' Gianluca said and returned to the tools he'd put down in order to kiss Norah senseless. He'd just gathered up his saws when the door tinkled again.

'Oh, hi, Manu!' Norah sounded like he felt.

Gianluca jerked his head up in shock and lost his grip and before he realised what he'd done, he'd nicked himself on the saw. But despite the sting, he couldn't drag his gaze away from the scene unfolding by the door.

Manu was here, in his studio, for the first time. Nòna was white, gaping at Manu as though she'd seen a ghost. And all he wanted to do was lock himself in a closet with Norah until he'd sifted through everything he was feeling.

'Shit, you're bleeding!' Norah cried, snapping him out of it.

He waved his hand dismissively and fetched the first-aid kit from the back wall, so numb he couldn't even say how badly he'd cut himself. Norah snatched it out of his hands and rummaged for a dressing. She dragged him to the sink and washed his hand, patting it dry on an old towel.

'Stai bene?' Manu asked from her place by the door, as though she were afraid to enter his domain. Given Nòna's body language, he could understand her reluctance.

'Mi stago bèn,' he muttered in reply. He glanced at Norah, her brow pinched in concentration as she wrapped the dressing around the cut. 'I'm fine,' he translated. He wanted to tell her he'd just realised that speaking in dialect to Manu was a barrier he put up between them. He wanted to ask her if she thought it was immature, if it mattered at all. In the middle of this farce, he just wanted to talk it through with her.

Norah looked up at him, her eyes wide with wry sympathy. He took a deep breath, gathering himself for the unexpected confrontation. When he was brave enough to look up, it was Manu who looked upset, while Nòna appeared to have recovered.

'I—' Manu began with the look of an animal about to bolt.

'We're going for a drink,' Gianluca said before she could continue. 'Would you like to join us?'

Her mouth dropped open, but nothing came out, as though his words had choked her. He didn't know what he was doing, inflicting his broken family on his friends, but she'd been kind to Norah. She'd turned up here, at his workshop. And he couldn't ignore the look on her face as she tried desperately to hide her uncertainty.

'I'm not sure... I don't think it's a good idea,' she finally managed. Gianluca stiffened. They'd taken a step towards each other, but it was only a small step. 'I wouldn't want to... intrude.'

'He invited you. It's not intruding!' Nòna piped up.

'Even so,' Manu said, unable to meet Nòna's gaze for longer than a moment, 'I'm sure no one wants me to come. I hope your open day went well.'

'Grasie, it did.' He felt compelled to say something, to make something happen, but he wasn't sure what. Either the two women needed a confrontation with shouting and fireworks, or wailing and tears. He'd reached a point where he could almost handle either, as long as the tension broke.

But both women were too tough to break down.

He glanced at Nòna. It wasn't like her to hold her tongue. But the older woman wasn't looking at Manu, she was studying Norah, as though she had the same feeling that Norah's presence in this situation changed everything.

'Are you all standing around waiting for me to keel over?' Nòna snapped, recovering herself. 'If Manu's going to wallow in self-pity, she can go home and do so alone. I need wine.'

'I need something stronger,' muttered Pino, trying to stifle a smile. He clapped Gianluca on the back. 'Since you're so keen for our company, let's go. Is Manu coming or not?'

Chiara glared at Pino and took Nòna's arm again. Manu's cheeks burned pink and her gaze flickered around the studio before settling on Norah. 'I'll see you back at the palazzo.' She pasted a smile onto her face and turned to Nòna. Before his eyes she lost some of her starchy pride and he could imagine what she would have looked like thirty years ago – young and uncertain. 'Fernanda. It's a pleasure to see you looking so well. Le auguro ogni bene,' she finished, her voice and attitude stiff with formality as she wished the older woman well. 'Arrivederci.'

She turned and left without saying anything further. Gianluca shared a brief glance with Norah and they both started after Manu. 'Un momento,' he called back to Nòna and his friends as he chased after his mother.

Manu heard them emerge from the workshop and stopped, her shoulders sagging on a long sigh. 'You can go back in. Unless you're coming home with me, Norah?'

'Are you okay?' she asked.

'Of course, I am!'

Gianluca wasn't sure whether to believe her. Norah certainly didn't, if her expression was any indication.

'Maybe I should stay with her,' Norah murmured. He wanted to protest, but his throat was too tight to get anything out. Then her eyes darted to his. 'Maybe we could meet up... this week? Do we have... stuff to prepare... before we head to Pellestrina on Saturday?' He tried not to smile at her terrible poker face.

'Tomorrow,' he said firmly, making her smile. 'I want to show you something I think you'll like. It's a tradition on the evening before Saint Peter's Day.'

Manu turned back. 'The barca di San Pietro?'

'Oh, if you're going to do it, that's fine. I can... I'll go to Nòna's.'

Manu sighed. 'No, I've never done it before. You'd better show Norah. I'm not a very good host, am I?' The bitterness in her tone was stirring. He studied her, wondering what she'd thought to achieve by coming to his studio. He was unexpectedly disappointed he hadn't had the chance to show her his work.

'Shall I...?' It took another attempt before he could get the words out. 'I could cook dinner... for both of you.' It wasn't quite what he'd pictured when he'd imagined showing Norah the local tradition, but it was better than not seeing her at all.

Manu froze and he knew she appreciated the significance of the suggestion. 'That would be lovely,' she replied, her voice betraying little. Gianluca wasn't the only one with barriers up. 'I'll... we'll see you tomorrow, then.'

He gave her the required kiss on the cheek in farewell and glanced apologetically at Norah. She was studying him, her eyes wide.

He mouthed, 'I'm sorry,' and squeezed her hand when Manu wasn't looking. She shook her head almost imperceptibly and squeezed his back.

He leaned down to kiss her cheek, knowing the action would be vastly inadequate, and he swallowed as he waved them off. 'See you tomorrow.' He returned to the workshop with a pensive sigh to find three pairs of eyes trained on him. 'Whatever you're thinking, I don't want to talk about it,' he mumbled.

'Why did you let her take Norah?' Nòna asked, flicking him with the backs of her fingers. 'Just when you were finally getting somewhere.'

He choked, wondering when he was going to get a chance to calm down.

'You've been hiding that dear girl,' Nòna accused.

'I haven't been hiding her,' he defended, his ears heating. 'She's here to work.'

She tut-tutted. 'You made her work on a Sunday – a step towards hell. And you didn't even cook her dinner in thanks. What kind of child did I raise? Manu's son?'

'Yes, Nòna. You raised Manu's son.' It was surprisingly easy to say it. 'Are we getting a drink?' he asked, rubbing a hand over his face.

As they turned for the door, he couldn't help glancing back at the counter and remembering Norah standing there, charming his customers – and that kiss that was unfinished in so many different ways.

Pino came up behind him and clapped him on the shoulder. He leaned close and dropped his voice. 'Caught in the act in your own studio by your nòna!' he guffawed. 'Fio, next time it's andare in camporea o gnente.'

Heat rushed up Gianluca's face. He didn't like the suggestion that he should sneak around with Norah in the fields, like a teenager from the countryside, but what was the other option? He'd kissed her, properly kissed her. Plausible deniability was gone. Although he probably should have, he didn't wish it back.

* * *

Norah was distracted in the lab the next day. She nearly set the wrong species of algae under the lights in the aquarium lab. It wasn't like her, but it was hardly unexpected, given the latent processing power her brain was expending on that kiss. She wasn't sure where she could file it – or if she wanted to file it. She wasn't done dwelling on it yet.

She probably shouldn't have left so abruptly, but her emotions had careened from pure adrenaline from the kiss to an indistinct fear of what would follow. Just the thought of trying to process everything while going out for a drink and pretending nothing was happening had been exhausting.

Added to that had been the concern that Manu was genuinely upset by the scene she'd walked into. Norah had tried to ask her if she was all right, but, of course, Manu had returned to business, which was unfortunately her right. Norah didn't belong in the family picture, but her heart broke a little every time a glimmer of emotion escaped Manu's composure. She was growing more certain that Manu wanted to make something of her relationship with Gianluca.

Norah had no more answers that night, only more adrenaline, when he arrived at the palazzo with a trolley of groceries. Manu granted access to her kitchen, which was a little rustic, but enormous, like the rest of the palazzo, and Gianluca set about cooking a three-course dinner.

Given Manu's presence, there was no opportunity to discuss – or repeat – the kiss so Gianluca roped her into being assistant chef and they fell back into the easy chatter that had made those trips out onto the lagoon so special. Manu contributed occasionally, but she was pensive, as she sipped her wine and watched them cook.

The banter protected Norah only marginally from the sensual experience of watching him cook. He prepared the meal with the same careful, capable hands that made his fórcole, but with a little more naked enjoyment.

She'd expected to feel awkward, not knowing where they stood, but it didn't seem to matter. Friendship or summer romance were both labels that didn't feel right. Norah and Gianluca just were. He touched her casually on the shoulder or the arm and she enjoyed it. Yes, she was wondering what would happen when they were alone, whether he wanted to take things further or not, but what they had was... good.

After they'd eaten the tagliatelle with sausage and a secondo of chicken in white wine sauce and polenta, Gianluca went through all of the cupboards, searching for something and making sharp comments to Manu that Norah couldn't understand.

'He sounds like his grandmother,' she muttered at one point. 'It's wonderful.' Her tone reminded Norah of Gianluca's comment that Manu hadn't wanted him to be a Delfini, but with a different interpretation than she'd first assumed. Perhaps Manu had thought it would be better for him to be raised a Marangon, not that he didn't deserve to be a Delfini.

Gianluca eventually found a large glass jug, which he declared would do. He filled it with water and cracked an egg, separating the yolk and the white.

'Make a wish,' he instructed as he poured the egg white into the water with a drop of vinegar. He glanced at her with a smile, as though he knew she'd wished she could kiss him again. Then they carried it up onto the altana. 'It stays outside overnight. Take a picture of it in the morning and I'll tell you what it means,' he explained.

'Is this like reading tea leaves? Don't you need a degree in hogwash for that? Oh, I suppose physics is close enough,' Norah teased.

'I'll stop my tongue, since I'm outnumbered by biologists,' he quipped.

In the morning, Norah and Manu tramped up to the altana to find that a little ship had formed in the water overnight – or a deformed, upside-down jellyfish, depending on your imagination.

'What do you think it means?' Norah asked as she took a photo to send to Gianluca.

'It means that Venetians are very superstitious,' Manu said drily.

'Did you make a wish?' she asked.

'Did you?'

Norah's cheeks heated and she acknowledged that Manu had won that round. 'Fine, I won't ask,' she mumbled.

'And I don't have to ask,' Manu muttered in reply.

A few minutes later, Gianluca's answer pinged into her phone: the 'sails' of the boat were open, meaning good health and happiness for their families for the year to come.

'I should bloody well hope so, after the year I've had,' Norah commented. 'I suppose that means Mum is going to marry Neal after all,' she joked.

'I was hoping to meet Neal sometime soon,' Manu said, 'after everything I've heard.'

Norah frowned at Manu. She hadn't realised she'd had so much to say about Neal. 'I'm sure they'll come by soon. I'll... introduce you if you like.'

'That would be great,' Manu said evenly. 'And you are headed to Pellestrina this weekend?'

'Finally into the southern lagoon.' Norah grinned, as though that were what she was looking forward to most.

'Are you staying in the house on Pellestrina?'

'I think so,' Norah answered carefully.

Manu nodded tightly. 'I wondered if it was still in the family.'

Norah suddenly realised Manu's awkwardness wasn't about Norah's relationship with Gianluca, but her own. 'Do you... have you been there?'

Manu's slow nod revealed more than her words. 'Once or twice, a long time ago,' was all she said. 'When you get back, we need to sit down together and discuss the Biotechnology Centre proposal. I have an idea for you.' The switch back to business should have surprised Norah, it was so swift, but she was getting used to Manu's methods of avoiding difficult subjects.

'That's amazing. Thanks, Manu. For everything.'

The look on Manu's face was perplexed. 'I'm not sure you'll thank me in the end.'

'What?'

She shook her head. 'I need to get to my office. Keep up the good work in the lab.'

25

Norah met Gianluca at the rowing club early on Saturday morning with her backpack stuffed with extra clothes. It was a golden summer morning, as July had arrived during the week, already stinging with heat that would be languid and muggy by afternoon. Norah was already warm in her vest top and shorts, looking forward to cooling off in the lagoon later.

Dafne was moored to a post near the boathouse, but she wasn't the *Dafne* that Norah had grown to know and love. She stopped and stared as Gianluca threaded ropes and looked up at the mast.

Because *Dafne* now had a mast – and not just a mast. A yellow sail billowed in the gentle breeze, the tips an eye-catching orange. At the stern, another man was checking a thick wooden attachment that was also new.

Gianluca glanced up to see Norah staring and grinned. He hopped up onto the fondamenta and squeezed her arm in greeting. After a few hesitant seconds, he pressed a kiss to her cheek. She smiled back.

'*Dafne* has turned into a sailboat!' she blurted out. 'She's beautiful!'

Gianluca's proud grin stretched. 'She's ready to go. Conditions are good for a trip to Pellestrina.'

'I can't wait,' Norah said, dumping her backpack into its usual niche next to her equipment. 'Why haven't we sailed before?'

'It's difficult in shallow water. Because the sanpierota is a flat-bottomed boat, it needs a drop keel for stability, but the rudder...' he motioned to the wooden attachment on the stern '... needs to be lifted in shallow water – especially in the endangered marshes.' He shrugged. 'Plus I like to row.' He glanced up at the sail. 'The southern lagoon is much deeper and further away, so it makes sense to sail.'

He exchanged a few words with the other man and then they shook hands in farewell. He beckoned for Norah to get in. She passed him her cane and then held out her hands, but, instead of helping her in as he usually did, he grasped her around the waist and lifted her down. She steadied herself with her hands on his shoulders, smelling the early morning sunshine on him, as well as the familiar lavender and spice scent she recognised well.

His hands tightened on her waist. 'She's going to feel less stable. It might take a while for you to get used to it.'

She nodded, letting him help her to the bench, which was now right behind the polished wood mast. When he cast off, she understood what he meant. The boat tilted dramatically as he fought the wind in the sail to row *Dafne* out into the lagoon. Norah threw her hands out for balance and cursed.

'Is the sail a little... off?' she asked as she squinted up at the smooth wooden mast. There was something jaunty about the little sailboat. It felt more like a historic cutter than a yacht. It was so... Venetian somehow.

'It's a vela al terzo,' he explained, 'a traditional sail, hung at an angle from the mast. Here, hold this,' he said, handing her a thin rope that ran through a metal bracket and attached to the smaller front sail. 'Pull on it when I tell you to.'

Once they'd cleared the canal, he stowed the oar and settled at the stern, rudder in hand, tipping his face up to the sun. Norah took a moment to watch him – his contented, comfortable body language, the quietness in him.

'What?' he asked, making her realise she'd been staring.

She chuckled. 'You and *Dafne*. You're both gorgeous. Can I get a photo?'

'Sure,' he said with a self-conscious shrug. After she'd rummaged for her phone and snapped the picture, he gestured for her to give him the phone and took a picture of her, perched on the bench, the breeze lifting her short hair. She grinned self-consciously, before fluffing her hair and reclining in an exaggerated pose with her leg up on the side of the boat. Gianluca took a few more pictures and handed her back the phone.

'Send it to me,' he said.

'Which one?'

'All of them,' he said with a glint in his eye that made it impossible for her to tear her eyes off him. It took a sudden lurch of the boat to snap her out of it. She stowed her phone again and clutched the side as they sailed past the orange-and-white crenenellated buildings of the old Arsenale, the military shipyard.

She rattled off the names of the islands as they sailed past: Isola delle Vignole, Certosa, the Lido and then San Servolo. She could have rattled off the species of algae she'd found at each – with the exception of San Servolo, where the only thing she'd sampled was beer. But more deeply embedded in her memories were the experiences she'd shared with Gianluca in these waters – the conversations, the stunning views of trees and marsh, sky and lagoon, and a feeling of freedom, of finding something she hadn't known she'd needed.

She didn't feel like the same person who'd arrived seven weeks ago, dwelling on the challenges of the past, instead of the future. She still used a cane and had hardware in her back, but that was just a part of who she was now and it didn't have to be everything.

They spent a lot of the day under sail, visiting sampling sites along the marshy coast of the mainland south of Marghera and pulling into Malamocco on the Lido for lunch. Crossing the main channel was a bit hairy, as an enormous cruise ship lumbered by. Gianluca had to trim the sails in earnest to keep *Dafne* in check and they bobbed like flotsam in the wake.

The afternoon saw them making their way along the island of Pellestrina, to a few deeper sampling sites in the natural channels. Gianluca fetched a fishing rod and cast bait into the water, setting the rod in a little niche Norah guessed he'd made for the purpose. He shouted in excitement when he pulled in a mackerel, holding it up proudly and making Norah take several photos.

'You'd think you'd never caught a fish before,' she teased.

'Mackerel isn't easy to catch in the lagoon,' he replied. 'Dinner is one frying pan away.'

'I didn't realise your fishing skills were so advanced that you could make a rare fish take your bait.'

He smiled drily and poked her between her shoulder blades until she squealed. 'Don't make fun of my skills or I might not share the bounty.'

'Oh, I greatly appreciate your skills,' she assured him with a smile.

When the heat of the afternoon became unbearable and the wind had died down, *Dafne* meandered lazily down the long coastline of Pellestrina, before Gianluca steered them towards a post and tied off.

Norah dropped some of her sample containers over the side of the boat, attached to a rope, to keep them out of the heat and covered her equipment with a tarpaulin. Gianluca had already stepped out onto the wooden planks that served as a makeshift pier.

'The house is just through here,' he said, gesturing to a paved street that was too narrow for cars and lined with two-storey houses with shutters and crumbling render.

Norah retrieved her cane, taking his hand to step onto the pier. He glanced at their joined hands, as though he, too, was wondering whether they could keep doing it. But he dropped her hand again once they set off across the street. More sun-baked houses in various colours stretched along the promenade. Norah saw a church with a stately baroque façade by a little square dotted with riotous purple petunias.

The house, which, Gianluca explained, had belonged to his grandfather, was wedged in a row of narrow, squat houses painted in warm colours, with contrasting green shutters. It had probably once been pink, but the render was now faded and coming away in places. Kids' bikes were parked along the narrow alley and there were potted plants growing exuberantly by each door.

Gianluca retrieved a key from over the doorframe and unlocked the house, giving the door a shove to get it moving. He winced as he entered.

'Just let me open the window. I haven't been out here in a while and Nòno only ever used this place for fishing trips.'

She followed him inside to find a quaint, ancient-looking room on the ground floor with a bench, two chairs and an open fireplace at the front, between the windows. 'Wow, I've travelled back in time,' she said.

'You did that seven weeks ago, when you arrived,' he quipped. He opened a cupboard under the stairs to reveal a complex electrical device with flashing LEDs.

'Except you've got solar panels,' Norah commented with a smile.

'Keeping the connection to the grid was complicated, although the power is a bit hit and miss in the winter. But today, I can promise you electricity and, I hope, hot water.'

'Five-star luxury! You are spoiling me,' she teased.

Upstairs was a bedroom with a single bed, a bathroom and a roof terrace. Gianluca fetched a camp bed and glanced at Norah questioningly. 'Up here? Or should I sleep downstairs?'

He'd asked the question casually, but she still felt the heat of a blush in her cheeks. 'Up here,' she said, before she could think it through and come to a more sensible conclusion. 'A sleepover, like San Francesco del Deserto,' she said with a chuckle.

'Not exactly like San Francesco del Deserto,' he said with a dry smile. 'Unless the roof leaks and we both end up in the camping bed.'

'You'd better hope the roof doesn't leak,' she replied. 'I wonder what Brother Giuseppe and the other monks are up to.'

'Friars.'

'Whatever. They were a good bunch. I'd like to go back someday.'

'They'd welcome you anytime.' He met her gaze. He didn't voice it, but the question was there: would she come back to Venice? He looked away again, as though he'd had a sudden thought that didn't please him. Norah knew what that felt like: she'd bet her expression looked similar every time she thought about the 25th of July and her flight home.

'Perhaps I left my heart with some Franciscans,' she joked, shaking off the moment. '*I left my heart...*' she started to sing a poor imitation of Tony Bennett, but her voice, never particularly strong, wobbled even more than usual when she listened back to the words she'd sung. 'You probably don't know the song anyway,' she muttered.

'I think I've heard it,' he said, his voice soft and an amused smile on his face. 'But that was the first time I've heard your real singing voice – not just shouting along with a punk band.'

'It's not much to write home about,' she said ruefully.

'It's cute. Like you.'

'Yeah, yeah,' she said, rolling her eyes to compensate for her stuttering heart, 'I'm your little duckling. I know. Come on, bigfoot. Take me to the beach. I want to swim in the Adriatic.'

* * *

Gianluca was tired but happy and relaxed, and deeply content, as the afternoon wore into evening. He loved letting Norah splash him in the cool sea, and giving her a lick of his pistachio ice cream as they walked along the promenade. He grilled the mackerel and some sliced vegetables over the fire in the house while she watched, her mouth agape, and they ate it on the beach, staring at the horizon. She buried her toes in the sand and leaned against his shoulder.

It felt natural to wrap his arm around her and pull her tight against him. They talked quietly – about everything and nothing – as the air slowly cooled after the heat of the day. She draped her legs over his lap and leaned her head on his shoulder. He rubbed a hand up and down her arm and breathed in.

She reached out for him as they clambered up the dunes and over the sea wall. After they joined hands, neither one let go and they let their hands dangle together between them all the way back.

Gianluca bought two cold beers and a stick of salami from a restaurant while Norah washed off in the old bath and then they sat on the dusty sunloungers on the terrace. Norah was yawning, although she showed no signs of wanting to go in to bed.

Gianluca leaned his head back and studied her. She was wearing short pyjamas with pineapples on them and her hair had dried a sticking-up mess. She looked the way he felt: tired and content – and maybe a bit sunburned.

Venus was winking brightly in the sky when they finally decided to go in to bed.

'I'll take the camp bed,' she said.

He shook his head vehemently. 'I'm not letting you sleep on the camping bed.' He eyed her pointedly.

'I'll be fine.'

He took a deep breath. 'I know your back is okay, but I also know it bothers you a little sometimes, so I'm not letting you sleep on that bed. Accepting that isn't a sign of weakness.'

'All right,' she responded softly after a long moment.

After brushing his teeth, Gianluca sighed and sat heavily on the fold-up bed, but before he could stretch out on it, something went *ping!* and he fell through the material, landing heavily on the floor. The frame groaned and crumpled and before he realised what had happened, he was fighting the stupid thing off as one side tried to close on him.

He scrambled to his feet as Norah held it down, giggling helplessly. The bed made one more ominous groan, before settling on an angle. One side had completely buckled. Norah was still laughing, pressing her hand to her mouth and clutching her stomach.

Gianluca chuckled with her, unable not to, when he looked at the sorry bed and heard Norah's snorting laughter.

'It tried to attack you,' she panted. 'How's your bum?'

He rubbed his backside as his laughing eased. 'What a piece of shit.'

'It's probably just old. It needed someone to put it out of its misery.' She turned to him with a wide smile and a glint in her eye. 'Looks like we're cuddling again. Can I be little spoon?'

'I can—'

'We've slept in the same bed twice. It's not a big deal. Come on, bigfoot.' She grabbed his hand and tugged him to the single bed. 'Get in before I whack you with a pillow.'

He pulled the covers back and stretched out, tucking his feet under the light sheet. She scrambled in after him, lying on her side and pulling the sheet over her.

'All normal, see?' she said with a little laugh.

'Completely,' he agreed evenly, draping an arm over her because he didn't know what else to do with it. She sighed and relaxed against him and he allowed his muscles to do the same, closing his eyes. Perhaps she was right and they would just get a good night's sleep cuddled up together. He could feel the comfort seeping from her to him. She made a little happy sigh and she smelled good – some kind of tangy soap, like citrus, with a light vanilla overtone.

His face drifted to her neck, following the scent that was stronger now he'd closed his eyes. When the heady warmth of her skin reached his nose, he breathed in sharply. She smelled like a lot more than comfort and sleep. He froze, wondering if he should pull back to a distance where he wasn't tempted to press a kiss to the back of her neck.

She wriggled. He opened his eyes to see her peering over her shoulder at him. 'You okay?' she asked. 'Have you got enough space?'

He nodded, ruffling her hair and turning her back over. 'I've got space. Don't worry.'

But she didn't stay turned away from him. She shifted until she could lie on her back, her head turned towards him. And suddenly she was taking up all the air in the room. Her face was close, her grey eyes dark in the twilight of the long day. They stared at each other across the pillow.

He brushed his thumb along her cheek. Her eyes didn't leave his, open, focussed, as though she were soaking him up. Her lips parted, just enough to release a choppy breath, and he lifted his head to respond in the only way that felt possible.

The first kiss was soft and slow. Her hand curled around the back of his neck and played with his hair. He lifted himself up onto an elbow and kissed her again.

One kiss became several, until there was no way to tell who was kissing who. She wrapped her arms around his neck and his hand rested on her hip. Norah opened her mouth and stole his breath all over again. His hand tightened on her as the kiss heated.

It was the most natural progression in the world when he kissed her neck and moved his hand under her shirt. She did the same, clutching him to her and searing his skin with her palms.

They undressed each other in between kisses that gradually grew in confidence. She smiled at him, eager and tousled, but so full of wonder and vulnerability that he had to stop and press his forehead to hers, tangling their fingers.

But Norah didn't stop. She tipped her head back to capture his bottom lip between her teeth, drawing a startled groan from him. When she pulled their joined hands to her ribcage and higher, his throat closed with emotion and he struggled to remember to breathe.

It appeared he didn't need to breathe. Norah was breathing adequately for both of them, her chest rising and falling under his hand. And she reached for him, bringing his mouth to hers.

26

Making love with him was so beautiful it might break her, when she left, but in that moment, she didn't care.

The way he kissed her was reverent, as natural as their friendship. As though they both sensed that the moment was right, they kept silent, communicating with touch instead of words.

She understood, from the brush of his fingers over her lower back and a single look, that he knew this was the first time she'd done this since the accident and he trusted her to tell him if her back was hurting. She responded by pulling him closer, until more of his weight was on her.

She paused briefly, her fingers pressing to his lips, as she searched for a condom in her backpack and he thanked her with another kiss, quick and affectionate, this time, as he took the packet.

With aching touches, smiles and hitched breaths, they found their way together. As the intimacy grew, it became almost unbearable. Norah couldn't look away from his face as his expression tightened with emotion.

He murmured something inarticulate, his voice choked, and she clutched his face, wanting to feel everything he did and give him everything she was feeling. They stared at each other until the last moment, when he dropped his forehead to hers as their breath came in gasps and they held desperately on to each other.

She noticed how heavy he was several long moments later. He tried to pull away, but he didn't get far. His head fell to her shoulder and his arms wobbled like jelly as he attempted to lift himself. He peeked up at her from where his head lolled on her chest.

She grinned and poked him in the arm. 'What happened to your impressive rowing muscles?'

He smiled, a little sloppily, and blinked. 'I should ask you what powers you have,' he mumbled, 'to take away all my strength.'

'Pfft, you need more stamina.'

He laughed, jostling her, and lifted his head. He fluffed her hair and hauled himself off her to go to the bin. 'You might be right.' He returned a moment later and pulled her against him. 'Is this going to be okay?' he asked, pressing a kiss to her shoulder.

'Yep,' she said, her confidence mostly genuine.

'Does this make us friends with benefits?' he asked sleepily.

Something about the term didn't feel right, but Norah was too tired and happy to think it through. 'I don't know what we are,' she said with a sigh that was part-contentment, part-confusion. 'But I like it.'

'Me too,' he murmured into her hair.

* * *

Norah would later remember the following day as the time they pretended to be a couple for real. Although she did grab some samples, mostly they lounged in *Dafne* as they made their way south to Chioggia. They wandered the calli of the mini-Venice in the south lagoon and along the canals, enjoying the sunshine that penetrated further in the wider streets of Chioggia than the narrow alleys of Venice.

Brick byzantine churches dominated little squares and the earthy houses with their coloured shutters were at once so reminiscent of its more famous neighbour and strikingly different, because they weren't rammed so closely together.

Strangest of all were the cars and bicycles. Gianluca had to tug her out of the way of a bicycle as they meandered along one paved alley. He used it as an excuse to curl his arm around her and leave it there.

When they weren't walking arm in arm, they were holding hands, and whenever they stopped – to photograph a double-masted sailboat that looked like a miniature pirate ship, or to inspect the fórcole in the window display of a restaurant – Norah hung off his arm until he leaned down to give her a kiss.

She dragged him around the marine biology museum, cooing at the samples of rare sea creatures preserved in alcohol and formaldehyde, while he quietly gagged at their bleached, lifeless forms. After a fish lunch and a spritz in a little osteria, they wandered across the causeway to the wide sandy beach facing the Adriatic. It was teeming with holidaymakers sunbathing, swimming and parasailing.

Norah's cane was useless on the soft sand, so she took her shoes off and hung onto Gianluca for extra balance, while he carried her cane.

'You'd think I'd be used to my different feet by now. It's weird,' she commented quietly as they stared ahead at the beach stretching into the distance. 'I can feel that the sand is warm, but not the texture of it.' She stopped to wriggle her feet deeper.

'I can't imagine, but it's plausible that you're still adjusting.' He paused, looking out to sea. 'A bit like grief, maybe. You might never stop remembering what you used to feel.'

'Are you thinking about your dad?'

He nodded. 'I had a great childhood, thanks to him. And holding onto the memory... maybe that's part of the reason I don't want to get to know Manu, even though my childhood is clearly over and Popà is gone.'

'I did wonder whether that was something she wanted from you: a connection to your father,' Norah said as casually as she could.

'What?' His tone was sharper than usual.

She stopped, linking her fingers with his before she continued. 'I know it sounds a bit wild, but, I don't know, something she said made me realise they had a relationship once – she and your father.'

'It can't have been much of a relationship,' he muttered.

Norah's feelings wobbled. Why couldn't it have been much of a relationship? Because Manu had left? Norah was leaving, too, so what did that mean for her and Gianluca?

They walked along the spit that protected the waters of the beach from the traffic in the channel between Chioggia and Pellestrina. Norah took photos of the enormous concrete dumbbells that made her feel as though she'd been shrunk. She asked Gianluca to explain the trabucchi, complicated fishing contraptions along the spit, mostly because it was sexy to listen to him talking about force and tension and mechanical advantage.

By unspoken agreement, they didn't discuss returning to Venice until well into the afternoon. Norah wanted to keep pretending, in this place where no one knew them and they could forget the future. She wanted to blow off all of their other responsibilities and just stay there.

Gianluca caved first. 'We should... head back,' he said with a gratifyingly dismayed expression.

Norah stepped in front of him and wrapped her arms around his neck. 'What if we don't?' she asked.

His smile was indulgent. He kissed her, for the zillionth time that day, but it reached to her toes, as usual. 'You want to stay here?'

'Or Pellestrina,' she said softly. 'I don't want to go back yet.'

'I know what you mean. It's not the same when there are others around.'

'Exactly. Can we stay another night?'

'If you're willing to get up early tomorrow morning. I have to get your samples to the lab and open up shop.'

She nodded readily. 'We sail at dawn,' she said, dropping her voice dramatically.

He laughed and caught her around the waist. 'For a scientist, you have a weird sense of humour,' he said with an affectionate smile. 'You're almost Venetian.'

'I feel almost Venetian,' she said before choking on the admission. 'That sounded really naïve,' she said dismissively. 'Like the time I had to talk myself out of getting a Venice tattoo.' She laughed ruefully.

His smile was light and playful as he tightened his arms around her and lifted her high. 'Nothing wrong with a genuine tatuajo. How about a duck, nanarèła?' he suggested with a smile.

She swatted him on the arm. 'I'm not going to get a tattoo that reminds me I'm short.'

'You're not short. You're adorabilmente diminutiva,' he said with emphasis, rubbing the tip of her nose with his.

She snorted and wriggled until he put her back down. 'I'll show you adorable.' She dragged him into the water, giving him a playful splash. Ten minutes later they were soaked and stumbling out of the waves, exchanging clumsy kisses.

When they sailed back to Pellestrina, it was to a quiet evening of sitting curled up together on the terrace. Norah sat in Gianluca's lap, studying the line of his jaw and neck, as she asked about his business, his family and plans for the future.

I feel almost Venetian... It had been a throwaway comment, but it stuck in her mind. She *wasn't* Venetian and she never would be, but the city had its claws in her, making her think foreign thoughts about home and belonging. She'd never thought a home was something she wanted or needed. She was Saffron's daughter, after all. She didn't stay still.

The hesitation from the day before was absent when they retired to bed. Instead, they clung together, pushing each other higher because they didn't know when they'd have another opportunity to do so. He made her feel physically whole, unleashing the full force of his passion on her wounded and healed body. And she felt privileged to see this kind-hearted man letting himself go with her, letting her appreciate the turbulence in him, as well as the gentleness.

When they finally stilled to fall asleep, Norah was overwhelmed, so full of feelings that she threaded her fingers through his to sleep, needing the anchor to stop believing she might float away.

He woke her early with a lingering kiss that held a taste of the intensity of the night before. But he smiled wryly at her attempt to keep him in bed and peeled her hands off, tugging her after him. She grabbed her cane and followed him down the stairs and out into the dim light and cool air.

They cast off and steered towards Venice on a gentle breeze that would power them back to reality – if Venice could be called reality. Gianluca pointed out the ball of the sun, scorching the horizon over Pellestrina and turning the lagoon gold. Norah's breath caught; she was struck, not only by the beauty of the scene, but also by the quietness of her heart. She glanced back at Gianluca, his hair whipped by the wind, his face kissed by early-morning sunlight.

'This is the most beautiful lagoon in the world,' she murmured, because she had to let something out so she didn't burst.

'It's worth getting up early for.'

'It's beautiful at every time of day, in every spot,' she said with a sigh. She kept the added *when I'm with you* to herself. He wasn't hers to keep – she only had these next three weeks and she wanted to make the most of them.

The clay rooftops and ancient buildings of Venice glowed molten gold in the sunlight as they sailed past San Servolo and skirted the Lido and Castello, heading for the rowing club. It was as though the sun wanted to remind the world that it was just as beautiful as the ornate interior of St Mark's – if any tourists were watching the slow sunrise. Norah doubted they were, and was glad of it. The moment was hers and Gianluca's alone.

Gianluca steered *Dafne* towards the boatshed with a sigh, hoisting his oar when they got close. He rapped on the door and it was pulled open. Someone called a greeting and he answered. They weren't alone any more. Norah had to accept the slow tarnish of reality at the edges of her golden morning.

Gianluca's hand landed on her shoulder and squeezed as he spoke to the man on the wooden pier. She brushed her cheek against his fingers and heard his voice falter. His hand moved to the back of her neck, a proprietary touch that melted her again.

She was tired and distracted. When the man walked away to calibrate the crane to remove *Dafne*'s mast, Gianluca turned her towards him and pulled her into a hug.

His palm on her cheek turned her face up and he pressed a fierce kiss to her mouth. 'I wish we could have stayed out there longer,' he said between kisses.

She wrapped her arms around his neck and deepened the kiss. 'You were the one who dragged us home,' she complained.

'Someone had to be reasonable.'

'Reasonable is overrated,' she said before pulling him in for another deep kiss.

'I'll see you again in a few days – maximum,' he pointed out.

'That's too long,' she said, her kisses turning clumsy with smiles and swingeing emotion.

He chuckled. 'You can come to my place whenever you like.'

'But what do I tell your mother?' She gave him a wide-eyed look. 'I'm just off to sleep with your son! Be back later!' She wiggled her fingers in a pretend wave.

He caught her around the waist with a groan and they kissed a little more. Someone cleared their throat from along the pier and they lifted their heads, expecting to see the attendant. But it was Chiara.

Norah jumped back so quickly the boat wobbled and Gianluca had to grab her. Norah stared at Chiara in horror as his hands landed on her waist again. When she was stable, she stepped sedately back and fetched her backpack. Gianluca wordlessly handed her the cane and she struggled out of the boat alone, straightening in front of Chiara, who was eying her warily. All Norah could think about was the assurance she'd given Chiara that night at the festival.

'I heard you were expected early this morning,' Chiara said lightly, ignoring Norah. 'I haven't seen *Dafne* with the sail in a long time.'

'I'll... head off,' Norah said, her voice losing strength.

'I'll get your samples to Marghera as soon as we've got the mast off,' Gianluca replied, clearing his throat halfway through the sentence.

'Thanks,' she muttered. His eyes met hers, but only briefly. He lifted his hand in an abortive wave. 'I'll text you,' she said, the words sounding brutal to her own ears. But what could she say in front of

Chiara? *That was the best weekend of my life* wasn't exactly for her ears.

'I need to get sick of you, remember,' he replied and her stomach flipped. She understood what he meant: she was supposed to text him as often as she could. But the strain in his tone made her wonder if he *wanted* to get sick of her – conveniently in three weeks' time, when she left.

Her stomach sank as she walked away from him. As she slipped out of the boatshed she heard Chiara speaking, her voice high. She recognised Gianluca's flat tone in his reply, although she couldn't understand the words. It was a fall back to earth that neither of them had been prepared for.

As she made her way back to Santa Croce, she couldn't help wondering if, one day, Gianluca would realise he and Chiara could have a love to last a lifetime. If not Chiara, then another woman with deep roots in the city.

Norah didn't grow roots. She floated with the tide. And the tide was slowly taking her out and away from a person she hadn't realised had grown so dear to her.

27

The scent of coffee greeted her when Manu swung the door open for her. 'Come to the kitchen with me,' she said curtly, making Norah feel as though she were in trouble. Did Manu suspect what had happened on Pellestrina? Norah winced, remembering their brief conversation about the house the week before. Manu had been there – with Gianluca's father.

'I have a few meetings this morning, but I have something for you.' She thrust a ropey cappuccino with a mountain of froth into Norah's hands and then woke up her tablet. 'Here,' she said, gesturing to an email on the screen. 'The head of research at the Biotechnology Centre in Stuttgart wants to see your doctoral research proposal.'

Norah choked on a mouthful of froth. 'Are you serious?' An email from Manu could open doors just like that? But she hadn't developed a proposal or even looked at their requirements.

'I'll work on it with you, but, for now, they want to see your CV. I've sent them what I had, but you'll need to update it with your experience from LiveVenice.'

'But... For *this* year?'

Manu nodded impatiently. 'You'll need to move fast. I assume I don't need to tell you what an amazing opportunity this is. They want a research assistant as soon as possible, with the option to switch onto a PhD track once we've sorted the paperwork. The work you've done here will fit nicely with one of their projects and I'm sure we can whip up a PhD proposal that will... kick proverbial ass. And in the meantime, they'll pay you a lot more than I can.'

'Thank you,' Norah said, too floored to know what to think. She had a new way forward. With a PhD from the Biotechnology Centre, she had a guaranteed career – whatever she made of it. But it felt as if she'd lost an anchor, rather than gained one. Science, her career – they were her anchors. Why didn't it feel that way any more? 'When do they want me to start?' she asked through the fog.

'They want a research assistant by the beginning of August, with a view to starting the doctorate in October.'

The ground might as well have shuddered and cracked, she felt so abruptly unstable. 'Beginning of August,' she repeated dumbly. 'My return flight from here is booked for the 25th July. That's cutting it fine, if I'm going to collect my stuff.'

'If you want to leave earlier, you're welcome to. You've achieved so much in the time you've been here and everyone in the lab sings your praises.'

Norah coughed in response to her clogged throat. 'I'll... think about it,' she managed to say as she mumbled a farewell and escaped to her apartment.

To confuse matters further, Saffron called when she was dressing after a shower. 'We're having such a wonderful time here at the Lido, sweetheart, but I'm so sorry to have just disappeared on you.'

'It's okay, Mum.' Norah chuckled ruefully. 'I'm glad you're back together.' She was surprised to find she meant it. She stilled, wondering why she was so full of hope that her mother might find a fulfilling love after a lifetime of misjudged relationships.

'Yes, I... it was all my fault, darling. I want you to know that Neal is... wonderful. He really tries to understand me – the real me. If I can just keep believing that I deserve him, then I want to be with him for the rest of my life.'

Norah hadn't changed so much that that statement didn't make her slightly nauseous. 'That's great. So, the wedding's back on? Will you be back to venue scouting soon?'

'Oh, I don't know about venue scouting,' she said, an odd tone in her voice. 'How are you? And Gianluca?'

'Good,' she said firmly – too firmly, given the surprised huff that Saffron made. 'How much longer are you thinking you'll stay?' Norah asked, changing the subject before she blurted something out about Manu's bombshell. She wanted to tell someone – more specifically, she wanted to tell Gianluca – but she couldn't explain how she felt about it and she wasn't sure she was ready for the discussion that would follow. She couldn't handle it if he gave her his congratulations and a casual goodbye.

And then there was the part of her that was afraid she would hurt him when she left. She knew she couldn't stay for him, in this place that wasn't quite real, leeching off Gianluca and his peaceful life when she couldn't be certain that she was welcome. That she was even picturing staying shocked her. She'd only pictured a stable future with Andrej because they would be rootless together – and even that sliver of stability had proved insubstantial.

'We'll be here another couple of weeks at least. There's a holiday coming up, the Festa del Redentore. There'll be fireworks and it sounds like we *must* stay for that.'

'Oh,' Norah said, thinking, rather stupidly, that Gianluca should have told her about that.

'Neal is going to book a table for dinner. Didi and Piero will be back for the weekend. I was wondering if you could ask Gianluca if we could watch the fireworks from his boat.'

'I'll ask him,' Norah said automatically.

'Are you all right, sweetheart? Have you been working too much?'

She hadn't been working enough. There was too much time to agonise over what she meant to Gianluca – an utterly pointless line of inquiry. That would have to change this week, if she was going to get her CV sorted and prepare to head to Germany by the end of the month.

* * *

By Friday night, she was fed up with the few short moments she'd stolen with Gianluca through the week and was looking forward to spending all weekend with him – without having to explain too much to Manu, she hoped.

But, of course, Manu caught her on her way out with an overnight bag. 'I thought we'd agreed you had enough samples,' she said.

Norah tried very hard not to feel like a teenager caught sneaking out of the house, but the fact that Manu was Gianluca's mother added to the awkwardness. 'I'm not going sampling. I'm just... going away overnight.'

'To Cannaregio?' Manu said with a raised eyebrow.

'Is... is that a problem?' Norah asked, trying to be an adult about this.

'Is he the reason you haven't sent me your updated CV yet?'

Norah froze, worried that Manu might be right. She had been dragging her feet on the CV. 'No, I'm keen to apply.'

Manu nodded, as though interpreting more from the statement

than Norah had intended to communicate. 'Just don't do anything you'll regret.'

Norah stared at her, trying to swallow her unease. 'Are you suggesting you regret... having Gianluca?' she asked, her voice high.

Manu straightened on a breath that would have been a gasp on someone more used to emotional roller coasters – God, Saffron would have fallen in a dead faint.

'I'm sorry, that was uncalled for,' Norah muttered, wondering if the offer to arrange her job with the Biotechnology Centre was about to go up in smoke. The thought made her queasy, but not because she was particularly desperate to go. She hated to think Manu was pulling strings to set up something she didn't deserve. 'Truly, I'm sorry. I didn't intend to... get involved with your personal life. That was inappropriate.'

'I know you're close to Gianluca and I don't want him to think I... regret anything. But I wasn't in a position to be a mother to him. Fernanda and his father gave him the close family I never belonged in. Of course, I don't regret having him. I just wish...' She released a breath on a huff. 'I wish there had been a way for me to stay.'

There was no way Norah could refrain from asking. 'Wasn't there a way? Would you make different choices if you had your time again?' Had she been imagining Manu's willingness to reconcile these past few weeks?

'No,' Manu said with a note of finality. 'Well, perhaps I would have better enjoyed the time I had.' Her gaze settled on Norah's face with a perplexed sort of grimace. 'I'm not a... mother figure or an old-fashioned Venetian. I just made the mistake of loving a man who wanted different things.' She sighed. 'Go – and enjoy your weekend.'

But Norah didn't take the offered ticket out of there. 'Do you... still think about him?'

'Every time I see Gianluca,' she answered, her voice losing

strength at the end. Norah wanted to ask if it still hurt, after all this time, but there would be no point. She could see the answer in Manu's face and felt too much sympathy for her to make her say it. 'I wasn't sure if I'd be strong enough to get to know him,' she continued quietly. 'Or if I have a right.'

'You know he's the kindest person in the world, right? He's not going to be angry with you for asking,' Norah said. Manu's glance held a glimmer of such vulnerability that their relationship shifted from mentor-student to... something like family, even if it was just for a moment.

Manu recovered herself quickly, making Norah wonder what had made her so eager to hold herself apart from everyone around her. But then Manu turned around the question, which was probably what Norah deserved for her nosiness. 'Are you going to think about Gianluca after you leave?'

'Yes,' Norah admitted with unfortunate certainty. 'More than I even realise right now.' She looked away. 'We're friends first, and I suppose we'll stay friends, but I—' *love him so much...* The sentence finished itself. Her throat constricted. Of course, she loved Gianluca. He had become her favourite person in the world – a fact she'd acknowledged several weeks ago.

It didn't mean they belonged together. She'd find a way to keep this in her heart, while they pursued their separate paths. She just hated to think of another woman in his life. She'd have to get over that when the time came.

'I—' Norah tried again, but cut herself off with a shrug. 'Friends are the new family, right?'

'Especially when you're sleeping together,' Manu responded wryly.

'Yikes,' Norah squeaked. 'I'm going to go. But maybe you should talk to Gianluca some time? He's not going to stay angry at you, but you're the parent here, so don't expect him to build the bridge.'

* * *

'I just had the weirdest conversation with your mum,' Norah blurted out before she was even completely over the threshold. Gianluca turned from the stove to catch her and her careening conversation as she tumbled back into his life. 'Hello,' she added as an afterthought, throwing her arms around him.

Gianluca grinned, hugging her tight and lifting her a few inches off the ground. He'd seen her every day this week, although sometimes only for a quick coffee at the lab, but every time he'd felt as though he'd missed her. He was probably projecting ahead to the 25th of July, when she'd fly off for good.

He gave her a lingering kiss, then a glass of wine and settled her at the kitchen table. 'Do I want to know about this conversation with Manu?'

She grimaced, another wild, typically Norah expression that made him smile. 'Probably not. She implied that... I don't know, that we were repeating history or something.' She shuddered and took a large swallow of wine.

'What?'

She shrugged carelessly. 'I suppose she has a point. Female scientist, leaving behind a relationship with a deep-rooted Venetian.'

'No, I—' He shook his head fiercely as he tried to determine why it wasn't right on so many levels. 'If anything, Manu leaving is more like my ex leaving than *you*.'

Norah had an odd expression on her face, hinting that he hadn't expressed that quite right. 'Because... because you loved her?'

'No...'

'You didn't love her?' Norah asked in confusion.

'No,' he repeated, not sure if he meant 'no, he hadn't loved her' or 'no, he had'. He couldn't remember any more. 'I just mean... I know you're leaving,' he forced himself to say. 'I've always known that and I understand why. With her... she could have stayed, but she didn't.'

Norah's expression smoothed to pensive and he found he didn't like that either. He sighed and sat down opposite her. He picked up her hands and fiddled absently with them, running his fingertips over her delicate knuckles.

'I'm not going to blame you for leaving, like my dad blamed Manu.'

She eyed him. 'I thought *you* blamed Manu.'

'I did – I do.' All Norah had to do was study him and he caved with a little groan. 'She's regretful. I can see that. And it does mean something to me,' he admitted. She curled her hand around his, somehow enclosing him in warmth although her hand was so much smaller. He smiled faintly at their joined hands.

'I'm glad. I... I get the impression she loved your dad.'

'I wouldn't go that far,' he grumbled. 'She left.'

'A-a-a-and we're right back to the place where I get terrified you're going to hate me when I go.'

He gripped her hand tightly in both of his. 'No. We've gone over this. If you want to think like that, then remember that I'm the one who's chosen to stay – like maybe my dad chose to stay.'

She snorted. 'As if you'd ever leave. You're part of this city. But I get it. You're one of the kindest people I've met and for some reason you like me. We're both a bit lonely and it worked out like this. Sorted. We don't have to go over it again. Trust me, I'm relieved that this isn't some life-altering love affair.'

'You're misunderstanding me, Norah,' Gianluca said softly, the word 'life-altering' echoing in his mind. 'This isn't because of circumstances. If anything, those are keeping us apart. Despite all the things that shouldn't work between us, it *does*. No matter what happens when July ends, I care about you a lot and I will continue to care about you.' She looked like a rabbit in the headlights, but he needed to drive home his point, if only to stop her thinking she didn't deserve everything. 'I'm not going to keep you here and I'm not going to resent you for going, because I know how important your research is to you and I love that about you – I love *everything* about you.'

When she was silent for a long moment, her chest heaving, he wondered whether he'd made a mistake, telling her the truth. He still wasn't sure she believed him. Saffron had a lot to answer for.

'Did someone, like, create you out of all the best parts of all men?' she muttered. 'I love you, too, hey?' she said softly.

It was his turn to freeze, to feel the words, even though he wasn't sure if she meant them the way he wanted her to mean them. But he would cherish those words, even if she meant them in friendship, as he suspected from her tone.

He wanted to turn her face up to his and stare into her eyes and tell her he loved her – *loved* her, like a partner, another half, like his *life*. But that wouldn't be fair. She was pulling away, hiding in the easy banter that made every emotion bearable – even impending heartache. He would never make her give up her future for him and he understood only too well from watching Manu's career that Norah's future would take her all around the whole world.

Instead of a heartfelt declaration, he pressed a kiss to her forehead. 'Is that an emoji? I love you, too, hey?' He ruffled her hair.

She scowled and poked him and he slipped out of her reach, standing to check on the stove. 'I'll give you an emoji,' she said and raised her hand with her fingers pinched in the Italian hand gesture, shaking it at him.

He howled with laughter and wrapped his arm around her for another hug. 'And this is why I love you,' he murmured in her ear, wanting to say it again.

'Yeah, yeah, don't burn the dinner,' she responded, a little breathlessly. 'That's why I love you.'

He smiled and leaned down to her, very slowly. 'Even if I burn the dinner, this is worth it,' he murmured just before he brushed his mouth over hers.

28

It seemed silly to leave a toothbrush at Gianluca's apartment when she was leaving in less than two weeks, but it was a symbol of the slightly desperate days after... that Friday when everything and nothing had changed. She turned up at his apartment whenever she finished work, which was usually late. She was writing up some of the propagation experiments so the work would be tied up for the team to refer to at a later date. She was also drafting a PhD proposal under Manu's guidance, but she was struggling to find her usual enthusiasm – she suspected because Manu's influence showed in every paragraph and she found herself questioning whether Manu secretly wanted her to leave Gianluca.

But Norah had no other immediate options and no time to look at alternative PhD topics, so she worked with Manu diligently. And, since her boss knew already that she was sleeping with her son, she didn't bother sneaking out, she just declared that she was staying at Gianluca's.

Didi flew back to Venice on Thursday night and came to the lab to catch up with Norah the following day. They spent an hour sharing their irritation at Saffron's latest demands, which involved finding cocktail dresses and turning up to a romantic bridge for some kind of surprise on Saturday afternoon before the dinner Manu had booked for the Festa del Redentore.

'I worry she's celebrating this engagement so much to compensate for something,' Didi muttered into her coffee.

'She is,' Norah agreed. 'She's compensating for the past. I kind of hope she gets it right this time,' she added wistfully. Didi gave her an uncertain look that made Norah think of the person she'd been nine weeks ago. She wasn't physically any different, no matter how much Didi and Saffron might wish she could quit the cane, but she felt different.

'We bought a house,' Didi surprised her by blurting out. 'It all happened so quickly in the end. I sold my flat. I'll show you before you leave.'

'In Murano?' Norah asked.

Didi nodded. 'I'm sorry—'

Norah shook her head fiercely. 'Your flat wasn't my home, so don't apologise. It was the perfect place for me to curl up and play dead for a few months, but... I don't need to come back. I can... move forward.' Although a house in Murano gave her an odd feeling of longing.

She'd watched Didi fall in love with the last person she'd expected last winter. Her sister hadn't fundamentally changed, but she'd... opened. It was one of the reasons Norah liked Piero so much, even though he'd taken so long to come to his senses and drag Didi back to Venice.

Could Norah have the same, even though she couldn't stay? She inwardly winced. Threading two lives into each other was something that couldn't be forced, no matter how strongly those threads pulled together.

'Do you... need to talk?' Didi asked warily.

'You seem terrified that I'm going to bite your head off. I'm sorry I was such a bitter hag last year.'

'You weren't,' Didi insisted. 'You don't need to feel so bad. You're allowed to struggle sometimes. And family is there to stick with you. Even Mum, in her own way.'

Norah rolled her eyes. 'Even Mum. Now she's so interested in our lives, I'm wondering how we can get her to stick less.'

'But... you seem...' Didi frowned. Norah waited for her sister to dig the hole deeper. 'I don't know. But talk to me when you can – when you need to.'

Norah nodded and leaned her head on Didi's shoulder.

'At least tell me you've had a bonkfest with the hot oarmaker!' Didi finished, making Norah laugh. Norah had said something along the same lines in February, when Didi had returned to London after leaving her heart in Venice.

Norah shrugged. 'Just a... little bonkfest.' She gave up on her straight face and giggled, clutching Didi's hand when her sister joined her.

* * *

Saturday morning dawned with a heavy summer shower that Gianluca assured Norah would burn off by afternoon. They enjoyed a lazy breakfast that dragged into lunch – 'The Venetians are born tired and live to rest,' as Gianluca explained with a proverb, while tugging her back to the sofa with the promise of coffee and more cuddling.

The sun was struggling through the low clouds when Norah tugged on the dress she'd worn to the 'wedding' on Ascension Day all those weeks ago. It was a little tight around the middle, but Norah told herself she'd just gained some abs – fritto misto abs that couldn't be a bad thing because they'd come from happy times.

Gianluca glanced at her with a glint in his eye that had everything to do with memories of the day they'd met and nothing to do with her new abs.

She grimaced when she caught sight of her mussed hair in the mirror. 'I have no idea what to do with it at this length,' she muttered to herself.

'I like the "just rolled out of bed" look,' Gianluca commented from the second sink, where he was shaving. Norah glanced at him, not daring to look for any length of time. He was too gorgeous and the scene was too pleasantly domestic.

She borrowed some of his hair gel in the end, but it didn't stop him trying to mess it up. She retaliated by attacking him with a hair tie and the result was a series of selfies of them, looking ridiculous – and ridiculously happy. Then he gave her a clumsy kiss, as though he treasured the memory of that night at the festival on San Servolo as much as she did.

'Are we late?' she asked, glancing at her phone as she grabbed her cane.

Gianluca shook his head and tugged on her hand. He was holding his other hand behind his back. 'Wait a minute. I have something for you.' He caught her alarmed expression and pulled her closer. 'Don't worry. One day you'll give me an algae battery for my building.' She gave him a wry look.

He cleared his throat and instructed her to close her eyes. She always felt as though she was swaying when she shut her eyes, but she took a deep breath and did as he asked.

His hand closed over hers – the one clutching her cane. As he eased her cane out of her grip, she almost panicked, until, instead of leaving her to sway, he slipped something else into her hand – something cool and polished. Her fingertips discovered a series of indentations, while her palm settled onto the perfect curve at the top. She closed her hand around it and opened her eyes.

It was a wooden cane – the most exquisite cane she could ever have imagined. The handle felt as though it had been made for her hand, because it had been. Around the top was an ornately carved panorama of boats and sea grass, flamingos, cypress trees and distant bell towers.

Gianluca cocked his head, staring at the cane as though he couldn't bring himself to note her reaction. 'It felt... good recording our trips to the lagoon.' He hunched down to look, shifting her hand experimentally and nodding. 'I had to guess exactly how small your hands are.'

She belatedly registered the tears running down her cheeks. She loved the cane and everything it represented. She hated the thought that all she would have was this cane when she left.

'It's beautiful,' she managed, before a snort-hiccough betrayed the state of her emotions. He looked up in alarm. 'My hands are big enough to slap you on the arm for reducing me to a blubbering idiot,' she murmured, whacking him half-heartedly on the biceps.

'I needed to make you something...' he said apologetically. 'I thought you needed a... formidable cane, Norah Phoenix.'

She grabbed him around the neck and kissed him because with him she almost believed she was formidable Norah Phoenix. She just had to work out how to take that with her, when she couldn't take *him*.

They arrived five minutes late, to find their small party milling on the Ponte delle Tette. Piero and Salvatore wore grey suits and matching scowls, as though they hadn't intended to turn up in the same outfit. Didi wore a blue dress with an embroidered bodice and a flirty skirt. Saffron and Neal were nowhere to be seen.

'I have no idea why Mum told us to meet them here,' Didi said, tapping her foot. 'I don't like surprises.' The warm look that Piero gave Didi at that comment pricked Norah's eyes with happy tears again. She'd never imagined someone could love her sister so much and know her so well.

'Do you think she knows this is the bridge of tits, where the prostitutes used to advertise their...?' Piero's voice trailed off and he tugged on his collar.

'Assets?' Didi finished, her straight face slipping. Norah snorted and met Piero's eye. 'Don't encourage him,' Didi censured drily.

'Her? Encourage me?' Piero said, pressing his hand to his chest in mock outrage.

'When's *their* wedding?' Gianluca asked in Norah's ear, making her smile afresh.

Piero raised an eyebrow. 'I heard that.' He glanced pointedly at Norah's waist, where Gianluca's palm was pressed. Piero blinked and opened his mouth so Norah grabbed Gianluca's hand and tugged him up onto the bridge before Piero could comment.

'Yoohoo!' Saffron's voice carried along the narrow canal and the sun came out all of a sudden, turning the water a bright, cloudy turquoise. The buildings in yellows and reds, leaning over the canal and holding drunkenly onto one another, looked charming and quaint in the light, accented by red begonias in window boxes.

Five faces turned to see an elegant black gondola cutting through the water towards them with its tilted prow. Standing to the stern in his full gondolier regalia – striped shirt, boater hat and a red handkerchief tied around his neck – was Pino, who gave them a wry look and a mock salute. Saffron and Neal sat in the plush gilded seats, both decked out in their finery. Neal wore a fancy suit with a buttonhole of baby's breath and Saffron had flowers woven through her wavy grey hair and she wore a crocheted cream dress with thin straps and a flowing skirt.

Norah and Didi shared a look of alarm. As the gondola approached, a woman who'd been hunched in the bow stood and opened an official-looking book.

'Dearly beloved, we are gathered here today...' she began.

Norah saw stars. Her mother was getting married. Today. On a gondola in a canal in the middle of old Venice, while her family stood on the bridge of tits and watched in surprise. It was so... *Saffron*. And Neal... he looked like the proudest man in the world, as he stood and took Saffron's hand, the sun glinting off his bald patch

Norah was certain that even the prostitutes of old would be watching this display with their jaws slack and a drop of undeniable sentimentality. It made her want to laugh and cry at the same time, which seemed to be the theme of the day for Norah. They were actually doing it. Neal had nursed Saffron through her crisis, where most men would have interpreted her doubts as a personal slight.

After a life of low self-esteem and correspondingly disastrous relationships, Saffron was taking this step, if not with complete confidence, with at least a measure of healing and hope. Norah's eyes stung and her heart hurt. She wasn't sure why the ridiculous image of the two of them making vows to each other on a gondola was wreaking so much havoc with her own feelings.

Her legs wobbly, she leaned back, knowing she'd find Gianluca there. He slipped an arm around her waist and propped his chin lightly on her head as she settled into him for support. Was this for real? Did someone really love Saffron so much? The question sounded awful as it echoed in her mind. But the answer was in front of her, in the form of a man wearing an ugly gold bow tie and earnestly pronouncing a marriage vow that he'd obviously written himself.

'Before I had your free spirit by my side, I didn't know how to enjoy life. It's a precious gift you've given me, and I want to be with you as we both grow old. I want to hold onto you as you drag me out of my comfort zone. I want to watch your brush strokes – whether it's your brilliant landscapes or your terrible portraits.'

Everyone laughed – a disbelieving, touched sort of laugh. Tears were running down Saffron's face and Norah even noticed Didi groping for Piero's hand. As the gondola passed under the Ponte delle Tette, the celebrant declared them husband and wife. When they appeared again on the other side, they were locked in an embrace worthy of the cover of a romance novel.

Pino glanced meaningfully up at the stunned party on the bridge and used his hand to rouse a cheer. Then he eyed Piero, before breaking into a jaunty song. Saffron and Neal broke apart in surprise, but Saffron laughed, which encouraged Pino to continue.

He reached what sounded like the chorus and glanced at the bridge again, looking pointedly at Piero and Salvatore and waving one hand. He sang a line and then, in low, grumbling voices, Piero and Salvatore sang an answering line. The call-and-response was repeated and this time Gianluca sang as well, shaking with laughter.

Saffron clasped her hands together in glee as the four deep voices lifted in the last line of the chorus, before Gianluca's voice cut off with a laughing snort.

'When Piero and I were in Pino's gondola,' Didi began, 'he tried to sing "O sole mio", but Piero swore at him because that song isn't Venetian.'

'So, he's chosen the stupidest Venetian folk song this time,' Piero added with a shake of his head.

'Is it romantic?' Norah asked.

'Not at all,' Gianluca said with a laugh.

'It has a whole verse about the stench of Venice and the last line is about eating fish!'

Norah laughed. 'Don't tell Mum. I don't want to burst her bubble.' She turned back to see Saffron and Neal waving.

'Wait for us there!' Saffron called out. 'We're going up to the rooftop of the Fondaco dei Tedeschi together!'

'Sounds great!' Didi called back. 'Might help me accept that that actually just happened,' she muttered.

'I know what you mean,' Norah commented, giving Didi's hand a squeeze. 'But, wait, was that even legal? What about the paperwork? It was all in English and we didn't sign anything as witnesses.'

Didi rolled her eyes. 'It doesn't matter. They got married in secret at the town hall in Birmingham a few months ago. They submitted the forms on a whim apparently.'

'What?' Norah cried. 'She put me through all of that planning for a ceremony that didn't take place, for a marriage that's technically already happened!'

Didi winced and wrapped her arm around her sister. 'You know the saying: marry in haste, repent at leisure.'

'And then marry a second time in haste?' Norah harrumphed, that troubling feeling of guilt and disbelief returning. Things were changing and, as much as she didn't wish her old life back, she also couldn't trust the future. What was she supposed to do with this laughing, crying mess of emotion? Would losing herself in research work at all this time? Did she even want to lose herself again?

Manu had booked the finest dining experience for the Festa del Redentore later that evening, at a function room in a palazzo right on the Grand Canal. As a wedding 'breakfast', it was everything Saffron could have wished for. The room spanned the length of the palazzo, with floor-to-ceiling windows on either end, and was frescoed and stuccoed and gilded with renaissance opulence. The antique Murano glass chandeliers had impressed even Salvatore and Piero as they caught the fading sunlight, painting little rainbows throughout the room.

Manu was dressed in fine silk and playing the role of charming hostess, welcoming Norah's motley crew of family and friends as though they were her most valued business associates. She congratulated Saffron and Neal effusively and chided them for not telling her so she could have made more grandiose plans.

Saffron had said exactly what had been in Norah's mind: 'Even grander than this?'

Pino arrived, dressed in a suit, with his beard carefully groomed. He greeted Norah with a kiss on the cheek and a brash smile.

'Ready for the fireworks?' he asked.

'I thought they weren't until midnight,' she replied, confused.

'You're right, but I was making a joke about the fireworks right here in this room. You and Lulu... your families are a fantastic soap opera.'

'God, I know what you mean,' Norah said, sharing his wry smile. 'Thank you for today.'

'It was an honour. Lulu's on his way,' he added, noticing Norah's gaze straying to the door again. 'His nòna is slow on the steps.'

'Of course,' Norah mumbled.

'This is a strange sort of party,' Pino commented. 'Manu and Fernanda in the same room. You and your family as temporary in-laws. If you'd asked me two weeks ago, I would never have believed it would happen.'

Norah coughed as the term 'temporary in-laws' stuck in her throat. 'I think Manu wants a relationship with Gianluca,' she said when she'd found her voice.

'That's a live horse waiting for the grass to grow.' Pino snorted.

'You don't think he should let her into his life?'

Pino shrugged. 'There's a lot of water under that bridge and...' He glanced at Norah and quickly away again.

'Were you going to say he has a fear of abandonment?' she said with a rueful smile. 'And you think I'm going to make it worse.'

'No...' he insisted weakly. He squeezed her elbow. 'If you weren't leaving I'd say... you're good for him.'

'Thanks, Pino,' Norah murmured, biting her lip, hard, when she felt the tears pricking again. 'If only I was as Venetian as that song you sang my mother.' She gave Pino an artificially bright smile.

Gianluca and Chiara arrived a moment later, assisting Fernanda, who was wearing a navy dress that glittered with sequins. Norah rushed over to greet her. She'd eaten with Nòna on both days the previous weekend, enjoying charmingly incomprehensible conversation and lots of jokes about marrying Gianluca that she hadn't minded half as much as she should have.

Nòna patted her on the cheek and said something with the word 'bella' in it. Then she looked past Norah to the rest of the party and her smile slowly faded and her brow knitted.

Manu approached, her posture regal as always, but with a tension that was palpable. She stopped in front of Fernanda and stared at her for several long moments, her lips opening and closing several times before she could speak. 'Fernanda,' she began, and then she said something Norah couldn't understand.

Gianluca's eyebrows shot up. Norah wished she could understand the words. She wished she belonged in this moment, when Gianluca's only living family members were finding their way through the quagmire of past mistakes.

'Manu's speaking in dialect.' Pino whispered an explanation to Norah. 'To be honest, she's not very good at it. But it's a gesture. The fine Delfini woman is speaking to the mother of a gondolier in the vernacolare.'

'Are they being friendly?' Norah asked urgently.

Pino nodded. 'Lulu looks like he's about to faint from shock. Fernanda is made of tough stuff.'

Norah balled her hands into fists, wishing she could go and tuck herself against Gianluca. But she was nothing more than a bystander, even though detached was the last thing she felt. It was his family. She didn't have a place there – not like Chiara and Pino, his real friends, who shared roots and deserved to be there.

Then Fernanda smiled and allowed Manu to help her to the table. When Manu turned, Norah caught sight of her expression, which was marked with regret and relief, a lifetime of choices reflected on her face.

What would Norah's face look like in thirty years' time?

The tense moment was quickly forgotten as the odd mix of

guests drifted towards the long table, set with coolers holding bottles of Prosecco. Chiara gripped the back of the seat next to Gianluca's, before lifting her gaze to Norah and stepping away with a wary frown. Norah felt like even more of an interloper as she took the seat next to him.

The starters consisted of many small plates: clams and mussels with herbs and tomato, whole fish and fillets, shrimps and octopus, all served with bites of polenta, rice or grilled vegetables. Saffron was her usual, unfiltered self, gushing over everything and insisting she'd never eaten anywhere so posh.

Norah wished she could numb herself a little with the Prosecco, but it settled badly in her stomach. She had the most awful feeling that her weird family was ruining the lovely meal for Manu and Fernanda – or perhaps it was just her, for selfishly believing she deserved Gianluca's devotion, even if it was only for a few weeks. His friendship, she could just about accept. She only wished she'd left it at that.

When a waiter brought out the main course, roasted whole duck topped with sprigs of sage, the smile she shared with Gianluca was almost unbearable with memories and tenderness.

'Does your rowing crew have to flee the hunters every July?' she joked, resorting to banter. She pretended to punch him on the shoulder, on his duck tattoo in honour of his team.

'You'll have to be careful, too, once you're all grown up,' he said, giving her a wink. 'Nanarèla,' he added in a whisper, pressing a kiss to her hairline that nearly made her weep.

Norah caught Saffron watching her with interest and eased away from the familiar warmth of Gianluca with a sigh. No catching bouquets for Norah.

She made it through half of the meal before she needed air – or space, or something she couldn't name – to relieve the restless

tension in her. She excused herself as graciously as she could and
went to find the restrooms.

* * *

Gianluca felt numb as he watched Manu converse openly with
Nòna. They hadn't spoken properly, except for a few awkward
exchanges when Gianluca was a teenager, for thirty years. And yet,
to look at them as they politely discussed the food, the resentment
appeared to mean nothing.

That wasn't quite the case, of course. He knew Nòna too well
not to recognise her wavering body language. But Manu's gesture –
inviting Nòna and reaching out to Gianluca, in her reserved
manner – had begun the task of bridging the gap of the years.

He could picture Nòna inviting Manu to the apartment to cook
for her and they would frown and drink grappa and then look at
photos together until they cried. Gianluca realised that Norah had
been right about a lot of things. Manu wanted a closer relationship
with him, although neither of them expected emotional intimacy.
And, perhaps, she'd truly loved his father.

But his father had chosen to stay when Manu left. The truth of
that choice still sat uncomfortably with him. Manu was not blame-
less; she'd not only left her child, she'd made few attempts to
connect with him since. But it wasn't the simple betrayal it had felt
a few months ago – when he'd been his old self.

He felt adrift and he wanted to hold Norah.

He'd wanted to hold Norah all afternoon, through the whirlwind of the strangest wedding celebrations he'd ever attended – as
strange as the Festa della Sensa, the day he and Norah had met.
They'd snapped selfies on the famous roof terrace of the Fondaco
dei Tedeschi and Saffron had thrown her bouquet of daisies point-

edly at Norah's sister. He'd felt a detachment in Norah that he hadn't expected, which made him want to hold on tighter.

Of course, he knew that she was leaving the following Sunday and he should gradually let her go, not hang on so tight his fingers would get cramps. Gradually letting go seemed to be what she'd been doing ever since she'd witnessed her mother's wedding ceremony and he couldn't shake the feeling that something had upset her.

When she left the table and headed in the direction of the bathrooms, he saw his chance. He waited a few moments and then got up to follow her.

He snagged her around the waist when she emerged from the ladies' restroom and tugged her close. She slumped against him, squashing her face into his chest and clinging to his shirt.

'You okay?' he asked casually.

She sucked in a wobbly breath. 'I don't know,' she murmured.

'Talk to me,' he instructed gently.

'I shouldn't,' she whispered. 'I'm leaving.'

'You're not leaving right now.'

'What difference does it make? I don't belong here. I don't belong with *you*.'

'You *do*,' he contradicted her. He couldn't help it. He narrowly stopped himself from saying she always would.

Her eyes clouded. 'I know you think so, because you're the best human being in the world.' His stomach dipped at the combination of the touching words and her defeated tone. 'And I'll never deserve you,' she muttered, almost to herself.

'It's not a question of deserving each other,' he countered immediately, although he couldn't interpret her exact meaning. He certainly had the strong sense that whatever she felt for him, it wasn't enough. In his life, love had never been enough. There were stronger forces in the human heart after all: identity, the drive for success – and fear.

She looked up at him. 'What about you? Nòna and Manu... It went well, didn't it?'

He hugged her tighter and rested his cheek on the top of her head. Yes, she wasn't leaving *yet*. 'Yes, it went well. Manu... has definitely had a change of heart.'

'Does that hurt? To think she's had a change of heart *now*, years too late to be the mother you could have had?'

'Yes, it does,' he admitted softly, marvelling at her perceptive words. She knew him so well. 'To hear her speak in Venetian to Nòna, after I've refused to speak Italian to her for years out of a stubborn, weak sort of rebellion...'

'Tell her,' Norah mumbled into his shirt. 'Talk to her – about the past.'

'If you'll hug me afterwards,' he whispered. Her arms tightened around him, but she didn't respond. He knew what she would say if he pushed her: *I'll hug you afterwards if you talk to her this week. But after that, I'll be gone.*

It hurt, that flash of comprehension that he might never see her again – certainly not like this, as lovers. He'd known it in his head, all this time, but he hadn't known it in his heart. His heart had been hanging onto the dream that love might one day be enough.

She raised her head for a kiss and he readily gave her one – a lingering, silent conversation, but she pulled back, far sooner than he would have liked. She took his hand with her free one and they made their way back to their party.

He stared at their joined hands as they approached the table, marvelling that he'd even miss holding her hand, when she suddenly stiffened. He tuned back into the conversation, seeing Norah staring at Manu. His mother was deep in conversation with Neal, who was nodding tolerantly.

'And you see the potential return on investment is huge, for this sort of technology, because it's a new field, but the science is proven. We just have to perfect the manufacturing processes and then get it into households, but that's only a question of time and money. The concept is sound.' She looked up. 'Tell him, Norah. You understand better than anyone the potential of algal fuel cells to power the environmental revolution.'

Norah opened her mouth, but it was more in shock than to say anything. Gianluca gripped her hand more tightly, but she didn't seem to notice.

'I'll admit, it sounds very promising. It's exactly the sort of investment I look for, but, of course, I'll need to see all of your accounts and projections,' Neal said.

'Yes, of course. Perhaps we could make an appointment before you leave.'

Norah sucked in a sharp breath. 'Is this why you wanted to meet him?' she asked so quietly she wouldn't have been heard if anyone else had been speaking.

Manu swallowed. 'Yes, I thought that was clear.'

Norah shook her head. 'No, I never imagined... Is this why you offered to help me look at wedding venues?' Manu's answer was only a faint blush and a purse of her lips. 'And why you organised this dinner for all of us? Because you wanted a chance to *pitch* to Neal? How did you even know who he was? *I* didn't know, for God's sake!'

'I heard you mention his name in that phone conversation you had with your mother,' she admitted, having the good grace to look sheepish.

Norah gave a humourless laugh. 'So, you were never really interested in me as a person – or my family or my future. I thought it was odd, but I just assumed...' She laughed again, but it didn't begin to hide the hurt in her voice. Gianluca's emotions churned and turned sour. What had Manu done now? 'I just assumed you were a nice person,' Norah said, her weak voice tugging at his heart.

He thought of the gutsy, jaded woman who'd got stuck in a storm with him all those weeks ago. He'd loved watching her come out of her prickly shell and he hated the thought that Manu's inconsiderate actions might make her retreat back inside. He clung to her hand, wishing there were more he could do. Anger bubbled – anger he'd only recently thought about laying to rest. Manu had caused this. She'd used Norah. He might have been ready to consider moving on from the mistakes of the past. But this was a mistake of the *present* and he wouldn't overlook it.

'I do care about your future, Norah. I'm sure it will be a bright one.'

'Especially if I can land you an investor?' Norah said accusingly. Her eyes widened. 'Oh, God. The Biotechnology Centre. Did you call in a favour for me? Was this the only reason you want to send me there? Because my new stepfather is *rich*?'

Gianluca reached for Norah, but he knew she wouldn't come. Manu rose slowly to her feet, but he'd seen enough in her expression. There was too much truth in the hurtful things Norah was taking to heart. He glared at Manu and her expression sharpened to alarm.

'You are a very capable scientist, Norah. I had no reservations in recommending you to the Biotechnology Centre and I have no doubt you will start a brilliant career with them,' Manu insisted.

'But?' Norah prompted bullishly.

'But I felt responsible for your future initially because... I intended to secure financial support from Mr Brunswick.'

Gianluca hated that Manu was doing this to Norah. He hated that Norah thought she didn't deserve him. He'd thought she'd left all that behind. But, although he saw the strong woman she'd become, she was still stumbling through years of baggage – baggage he suspected had a lot to do with her own mother. It broke his heart. And it closed that part of him that had been thinking of letting Manu in.

His mother continued, her voice pleading now. 'But this opportunity... it's everything I have been working towards with Live-Venice. An angel investor is the quickest way to—'

'And you are always looking for the quickest way,' Gianluca interrupted Manu, his voice quiet. 'The right way be damned. If there's a way you can take a shortcut to, forse, for example, your son's adult years, you'll walk over people to take it!'

He realised everyone was staring at him, but he was too angry to care. Manu went white.

'Gianluca,' she began, her voice weak.

'Everyone in this room, you've used in some way or another,' he said, throwing his hand up for emphasis. The build-up of thirty years of resentment became palpable. 'It's always your noble objectives. You excuse your mistakes because what you are working on is more important. But people work on important things all over the world while still having empatia – still having feelings. Norah did an amazing job for you and you paid her shit and you treated her like shit.' He dimly registered Norah's hand, fisting in his shirt and tugging, but he didn't stop. 'If that's the sort of person you are, I don't want to—'

He couldn't ignore it this time when Norah shoved him bodily away from the table, muttering an apology over her shoulder to her mother for ruining the wedding. He glared at Manu as he allowed Norah to shepherd him away as though he'd been in a brawl. He wasn't finished – not by a long shot – but he could see this wasn't the time or the place. He ran an agitated hand through his hair and clutched Norah's shoulders.

'Are you okay? I'm so sorry.'

She shook her head fiercely. 'Don't.' She took a deep breath and he noticed the agonised expression on her face. His anger cooled immediately. Norah swallowed. 'Don't say anything rash. What she did hurt, but she was my boss. I never should have... been personally involved.'

He frowned. 'With me?'

'Among other things,' she mumbled. Cold seeped slowly under his skin as she considered her next words. 'She's your *mother*. I know she's not perfect – no one's mother is perfect, damn it.' Her voice broke and he slid his arms from her shoulders down her back, but she stepped away and wrapped her arms around herself. 'But *please* don't wreck your chance of reconciliation with her just for me.'

'What do you mean, *just* for you?'

'I mean... I'm... temporary. She's... a fact of life.'

'You're not *temporary*. You're *you*. And you shouldn't be treated like that. She has no idea what treasure she found when she hired you!' He'd stunned Norah into silence. After all these weeks, she still wouldn't accept what she meant to him. '*You* have no idea what you're worth to... everyone.'

She glanced back at Manu. 'I have some idea,' she muttered and he simply *knew* she was thinking about her ex, her colleagues who hadn't stood by her. When her gaze moved to Saffron with a wince, his breath left him. If Norah wouldn't fight, how could he? She swallowed and turned back to him. 'Don't let this be the end with Manu. I'm angry at her and still saying this. I hate to think of you alone.'

Then stay... It was the one thing he couldn't ask. He couldn't make her give up her future, only for her to find she hated his crazy city, his weird life, a few months later. They'd only known each other nine short weeks.

'I won't be alone,' he said, mainly to ease her mind. God knew he would feel alone, and it had nothing to do with his relationship with Manu.

'No,' she said thoughtfully. 'You belong here.' She stroked her palm down his chest, following the movement with haunted eyes. She sighed. 'I think I need to leave.'

He wanted to protest, but he understood her point. 'Can I get you your bag?'

'I meant Venice,' she said, her voice so soft he nearly missed it. She *was* leaving Venice. Next Sunday. 'I can't stay at Manu's house, can I?'

'Stay with me,' he offered immediately.

Her gaze rose slowly, forlornly to his. 'I can't do that either.' The breath rushed out of his lungs. He wasn't ready for this to end. The memories he had stored would barely last a week, if he thought of them as often as he suspected he would. 'I was leaving anyway.'

'But not until next weekend,' he said, alarmed at the panicked tone of his voice.

'Maybe this will be easier.'

'And maybe it won't!'

Her expression hardened, reminding him of Manu and her choices – her choices that had knowingly hurt people. Perhaps Manu had really loved his father, but it still hadn't been enough. Norah loved him in some way, but she knew she was hurting him and she was doing it anyway. When would he learn that love was never enough?

30

Norah wasn't sure if she ruined the fireworks for everyone or just for herself. She heard them, from her little apartment at the top of the palazzo, at 11.30, but she couldn't even muster the enthusiasm to go up to Manu's altana to peer at the distant bursts of colour.

She wanted to be out on the lagoon in Gianluca's boat, watching from the best seat in the house – which was next to him, wherever he was. She hoped this would stop hurting soon.

She suspected she was acting on impulse and emotion when she madly emailed several contacts in the microbiology field in the middle of the night, but she couldn't stay still. She'd been stuck for too long staring at the walls in misery last year and now she had to move. The Biotechnology Centre felt like a dead end, since she'd need Manu's blessing to go there and she didn't want that if she hadn't earned it.

So much for getting back on her own feet these past few months and rediscovering what she was worth. She'd let Manu manipulate her. And what did she have to show for it? She didn't even know what her next steps should be, except for the certainty that it needed to be her own path. She couldn't rely on anyone but herself and she couldn't stay any longer than necessary with the woman who'd betrayed her trust – or her good-hearted son who was too easy to love. She needed a plan B, somewhere she could go fast.

How she managed to drift off to sleep despite her restlessness, she wasn't sure, but morning came quickly and she was surprised when the team administrator from Portsmouth phoned her early.

'Norah, hi!' Risha squealed when Norah connected the call. 'How are you? I've been wondering how you were doing, but since you didn't call me back... Oh, that doesn't matter.'

'When did you call me?' Norah asked with a frown. She'd always got on well with Risha – as well as she could, given how busy Norah had always been with work.

'I called a couple of times... To be honest, it was probably last year. When you didn't call back and deleted all of your social media, I just assumed you wanted to move on and I thought that was fair enough after how horrible Stanten was to you.'

Risha's statement gave her pause. Perhaps she'd been wrong to think everyone had sided with her boss. 'I-I'm sorry,' she stammered. 'I wasn't in a good place last year. I missed your calls somehow.'

'But you're okay now?'

Aside from the wobbles of awareness of how poorly she'd handled the past year? Or the feeling that she didn't know what she was doing with her life now? Yeah, she was okay. Her eyes strayed to her wooden cane and she bit her lip to stop the tears.

'Yeah, I'm getting better. It's good to hear from you. I'm sorry I went off the radar.'

'It's okay. So, I got your email,' Risha began, 'and I wanted to call you back straight away, even though it's Sunday. Let me check I have this right: you want a temporary job of some sort anywhere in the world that will have you at short notice.'

'That's it,' Norah confirmed. It sounded like an escape because it was one. But escaping was better than curling into a ball and scrounging off her sister again.

'All right,' Risha said softly. 'Are you sure you don't want to look for any PhD positions that have opened up because of drop-outs? There are always a few of those, if you're not fussed where you go.'

'Send them through, but I'm not sure I'm ready for that,' Norah admitted. After everything she'd been through, did she want to restart her career with a programme she'd chosen out of desperation?

'Otherwise, you know they're always looking for people on the algae project in Svalbard in August.'

'Ha. I might be desperate enough for that.'

'I can phone them for you tomorrow. They put out a call for research assistants just last week, so I'm pretty sure they'll have you.'

Norah didn't have to think for very long. The pay was good, since most researchers had no desire to spend August in the Arctic on a rock in the Barents Sea. She could get away without having to work anything out with Manu – or see the kicked puppy expression on Gianluca's face again. What better way to forget her idyllic summer on the Venice Lagoon than by freezing her memories away?

'Sounds great,' Norah confirmed with as much enthusiasm as she could muster.

'Any chance of you coming back here for a visit before you head off? There are still a few things of yours hanging around the lab.'

Norah's brow pinched as she thought of the little knick-knacks she'd had in the lab: a mug that read 'Keep Clam and Study Marine Biology'; probably about a million hair ties. It felt like another life, a life that seemed naïve and somehow shallow to her now.

Risha continued tentatively, 'You know... most of us would love to see you. I'm so sorry—'

'It would be good to see... you,' Norah heard herself say, wondering if she meant it. 'I'll see how I go for time. I'll be at the mercy of the flights.' It was difficult to get on or off the island where the research station was based in the Norwegian archipelago of Svalbard – another plus in the circumstances. 'Thanks, Risha,' she said before disconnecting the call.

Trying to drown her restless thoughts, she went straight online and booked a flight back to the UK – the following evening was the earliest she could find. Then she sat and stared at the screen. She was really going. When she stepped off the plane at Stansted tomorrow, she'd be asking herself if she'd ever really been here, if her Venice really existed.

When she'd been staring for so long that her screen went black, she shook herself and woke up the laptop again. Knowing she'd agonise constantly if she didn't do it, she snapped a grainy picture of the flight details and texted it to Gianluca with the comment:

This could be my last picture from Venice.

Worried he would think she was trivialising their messaging, she quickly added:

I'm sorry. Don't miss me.

It was vastly inadequate, but she hated the thought that she might have hurt him. Remembering his expression at dinner the night before, she was doubly certain that she had to go – as soon as possible, perhaps without saying goodbye. It was cowardly, but the easiest way for both of them.

She waited a long time for his reply, packing a little and doing those nothing things that drove her crazy. When he finally texted, two messages came through in quick succession. The first said simply:

I miss you already.

Norah smiled, despite her discomfort. Her smile died when she read the second message.

Did you send that because you want me to come to the airport?

If they'd been speaking in person, she would have said she was tongue-tied. As it was, she was finger-tied, with no idea what to say so she took the easy way out.

You don't have to.

He responded quickly.

Let me know if you need any help packing or getting to the airport.
Dafne and I are at your service.

She had a sudden pang of memories and gave a miserable sort of laugh but she didn't reply, because she couldn't bear the thought of things between them not being comfortable. She kept busy instead, forcing herself to eat lunch with Saffron, Neal, Didi and Piero before their flight home that night. Saffron's concern was cloying, but Norah had no choice but to bear it.

'Isn't there any way you can stay?' Saffron asked during a lull in the conversation, as though the question had been stewing inside her.

'For what?' Norah asked bleakly.

'For... *love*,' Saffron said, gripping Norah's hand. Norah looked to

Didi for their usual eye-roll, but she looked concerned, too. Before Norah could mumble any kind of response, Saffron continued, 'You will make something amazing of your life. Alone or... not. I admire you so much, my dear sweetheart – for your commitment to your research, and for bravely being your own unique self, even though I know I haven't been the best role model or parent. You and I are alike in many ways, but you... you haven't got bogged down in my mistakes.'

Norah frowned. That had been her goal, but it didn't feel as though she'd achieved it. She knew she'd reacted against Saffron's example by committing to Andrej, when she probably shouldn't have. But did it go deeper than that? Was she secretly afraid she would repeat Saffron's history if she ever truly fell in love? She swallowed.

One thing was clear: she hadn't loved Andrej – not the way she loved Gianluca, with that togetherness that was so simple and so wonderful and went beyond interests and goals and careers. But what did that mean for the future? She still couldn't stay. She couldn't give up her career, her choices, when there was a good chance it would all go wrong. Saffron had been a perfect example of how spectacularly wrong relationships could go and how much she had to lose.

And if she couldn't stay with him... she had to escape these feelings that were already there and already hurting.

'I'm sure everything will work out,' Norah said, knowing it was an empty platitude. Didi squeezed her arm under the table and, although Norah appreciated the solidarity, she didn't want to tarnish Didi's happiness with Piero by revealing how bleak she truly felt.

She gave into temptation and sent Gianluca a text with a frowning emoji and bad photo of Didi and Saffron. She felt even worse when he didn't reply. Her farewell to Didi and Saffron at the vaporetto was wooden.

She wanted to avoid a lengthy conversation with Manu and, true to form, Manu shared the wish and kept their exchanges to a clipped minimum. Only on Monday afternoon, after Norah had bumped her suitcase clumsily downstairs while clutching her cane, did Manu approach with an ominous look that foreshadowed a conversation that Norah wasn't ready to have.

'You don't need to say anything,' Norah cut her off. 'I shouldn't have got so upset. You are my boss, after all.'

'I'm a terrible mentor,' Manu blurted out.

Norah gave her an unimpressed look. 'You were trying to be a mentor?'

'You can still take the job at the Biotechnology Centre. It would make me happy if you did.'

'I'm sorry, Manu, but I'm no longer in a position to make you happy – unless you're happy I'm leaving Gianluca in peace,' Norah snapped before she could stop the words tumbling out. Manu looked stung. 'I will find a PhD position somewhere, but I can't go there now. I'll never know if I truly deserved it and I'll feel like a fake.'

'You're a good scientist, not a fake,' Manu said. 'I'm so sorry for making you think otherwise.'

'Well, the damage is done,' Norah mumbled. 'I'll dig my way out of it, but it's something I have to do for myself.'

Manu nodded at that, a look of understanding passing over her face. Norah winced, thinking of these two female role models she currently had, neither of whom had made perfect choices. It only made her more confused.

'If there's any way I can ever help you... I owe you any assistance and I will gladly give it.'

Norah nodded, Manu's words giving her an idea that was very

different from what Manu had imagined when she'd made the offer. 'There is one thing you can do for me,' she began. 'Can you try to show Gianluca that he's important to you? Can you try to make up for what your actions did to him in the past?'

Manu drew back in surprise. 'I meant—'

'I know what you meant, but that's what I want most from you.' Manu continued to stare, making Norah want to cry all of a sudden. 'I have to go,' she muttered. Manu nodded silently, clutching her arms around herself as though Norah's words had shocked her.

But Norah was too fragile to handle Manu's shock, so she turned away, walking out of the palazzo for the last time. She strode furiously through the familiar alleys and squares, finally crossing the Ponte degli Scalzi and allowing herself one more look along the Grand Canal, at the moored gondole and mix of slender gothic buildings and neoclassical ones of floating solid stone that appeared to contravene the laws of physics.

The sky was painfully blue and the balustrade of the bridge bright white. Venice was an impossible place, once more, married to the water, with miraculous roots that extended deep into the silt. Norah wished for one last look at the lagoon and decided she'd soak in everything she could when she got onto the train. She'd squash her face to the window, even if all she could see from the causeway were the little uninhabited islands Gianluca had warned her were only used by criminals, drug users and fly tippers.

God, Venice was a weird place, but she loved it.

She stopped to check her phone when she arrived at the square in front of the station, but she had no new messages – nothing for over twenty-four hours. Gianluca hadn't even responded to the photo of the truly awful tourist magnet she'd bought, featuring a wonky Campanile di San Marco that looked like a child's interpretation and a gondolier who looked as though he was possessed by the ghost of George Clooney. She'd hoped at least that he'd respond with a joke about Pino getting royalties for them using his image, but – nothing.

It appeared he wasn't coming to say goodbye. She'd thought it was what she wanted, but it still made her sad – deeply. She knew it was only a moment, a farewell, and part of her wanted to avoid it, too. But this way meant their relationship was somehow incomplete, as though they needed to return to even ground.

An emotional farewell was perhaps not the way to do that, anyway.

With a sigh, she stowed her phone and headed for Santa Lucia station. She took one more look around, glancing up and down the platform, before she forced her feet onto the steps and boarded the train. When she took her window seat, staring out at nothing but the concrete blandness of the station, she wasn't sure she was going to be able to take that one last look at her lagoon.

Someone took the seat next to her, jostling her shoulder as he sat down heavily, taking up far too much space, as male passengers always did. She turned with a scowl, only to have the expression die on her face and her heart leap into her throat.

31

Gianluca dipped his head and looked warily into her eyes. He'd waited until the last minute to board the train, afraid she'd insist on a farewell here in Venice, rather than at the airport in Treviso. Amidst all of the confusion in his mind, he was certain of one thing: he was taking Norah to the airport. His feelings demanded at least that.

The instant he saw the expression on her face, any lingering resentment fled. He couldn't blame her for his painful feelings, not when she was hurting, too. She let out a choking sob and threw her arms around him and he released a breath and enfolded her in a tight hug.

The conductor's whistle sounded and the departure of the train was announced as they held each other. Her head was tucked against his neck. She still felt like family in his arms.

She drew back slowly, taking a drawn-out breath, then she settled back into her seat, facing forwards. 'You came,' she croaked, clearing her throat.

'You said I didn't have to, but, allora... I wanted to.'

'I'm glad you did,' she murmured before she could stop herself.

He shared her smile – tentative and a little bit stubborn. 'Good, because I was worried you'd try to elude me.'

'I wanted to show you how ugly my magnet is in real life,' she said, biting her lip as she fished it out of her backpack.

'It is very ugly,' he said, not looking at the magnet. He was too busy feeling his skin prickle in amazement that they were sitting here, shoulder to shoulder, as together as always, despite everything. 'I'm sorry I didn't text you. I was worried I'd spit the toad, as we say... tell you I was coming. That and... we won the regatta yesterday, Pino and I.'

She inhaled a sharp breath. 'The regatta? Why didn't you tell me...?' Her shoulders drooped and she looked away again. She patted his hand and he stared at the hesitant gesture with a sense of loss – until she closed her hand around his more firmly and held it there. 'Congratulations. Victory for the ducks,' she said with half a smile.

They fell silent, facing forward as the train made its way along the causeway and onto the mainland. Their shoulders touched – firmly. He kept his hand still in hers. Her thumb stroked his.

'Why do you smell like lavender?' she asked.

He smiled at her. 'All the big questions, hmm?' She just lifted her chin and waited for an answer. 'My aftershave, I suppose,' he answered with an awkward smile. 'Why? What's wrong with lavender?' He eased his fingers in between hers.

'Nothing,' she replied. 'It usually makes me think of English gardens and old people, but on you it's...'

'Virile? Masculine? Please?'

She snorted. 'Virile,' she muttered with a chuckle. 'It smells like you,' she said softly. 'It'll remind me of you. Maybe I need one of those little pouches of lavender potpourri to help me sleep,' she said, almost to herself.

He leaned down and sniffed her hair. 'I have no idea what that scent is – except eau de Norah.'

'Ew,' she said with a laugh. 'That would not sell this shampoo to anyone.'

'It would to me,' he insisted.

She bit her lip and poked him, and he loved making her fall silent like that, blushing and touched. He used the opportunity to ask the question that wouldn't stay silent in his mind.

'Do you know where you're going?'

'First, back to Portsmouth,' she said softly. He turned to her questioningly. 'Not to see Andrej,' she said with a snort. 'But the others... I might still have friends there.'

'I can believe that,' he said softly.

She squeezed his hand. 'Of course, you can.'

'Are you going to take a position there?'

She shook her head slowly. 'I don't think so. I'll go back to visit and then, for August, it looks like I'm going to the Arctic.'

'The... *Arctic*? Do they have algae there?'

'Yeah, the midnight sun makes the algae go crazy. The research station there is very remote, but it's an amazing phenomenon.'

He studied her with a smile. 'Sounds fascinating.' She eyed him. 'To you,' he added, his smile stretching.

'Yeah, we're both nerds, you know,' she said.

He untangled their hands and wrapped his arm around her, tugging her against him. 'I know,' he murmured. She settled her head on his shoulder as the train moved them inexorably towards the end.

At Treviso station, Gianluca headed for the taxi rank with her suitcase, while Norah went for the bus.

'You're that cheap?' he asked.

'It's right there.'

'What about all those other passengers?'

She smacked him playfully on the arm. 'You snob. It's that Delfini blood!' They shared another smile.

'Maybe we could—' Gianluca hesitated before finishing the idea that had tumbled out without thought.

'What?' she prompted him gently, nudging him with her shoulder.

'Do this again sometime,' he said, blinking back a range of emotions. 'As friends or... whatever. We could go on a road trip or... something.'

Norah was giving him the strangest look, as though a lighthouse beacon had flicked on in her eyes. She'd instructed him not to miss her, but she felt it too – the inability to snuff this out. The realisation made the adrenaline surge in his blood, but it also made him ache. She wasn't supposed to leave. 'Yeah,' she said, her voice soft. 'Let's do that.'

He took her hand, holding it fiercely as he stared straight ahead. 'Do you... think they have pigeons in the Arctic?'

'They probably have terns or something,' she said with a shrug. She peered up at him. 'I'll send you a picture.'

'A selfie,' he corrected.

'Of me with a tern?'

He nodded, failing utterly at keeping a straight face. 'I'm still not sick of you,' he explained. They stared at each other. He was full of things to say to her – mundane things and enormous ones, but he was struggling to tell one from the other and there was no time.

The bus pulled up to the airport far too soon. He waited as she checked her bag and then they stood, staring at the departures board together, neither seeing anything. The sign blinked 'Go to Gate'. He grabbed her hand, regretting not spending the past hour – the past nine weeks – telling her how amazing she was and how much she meant to him.

He risked a glance at her face and saw it was stained with tears.

'Ài, Norah,' he muttered. He clamped a hand on her shoulder and pulled her against him. How soon could they conceivably go on that road trip? Was the Arctic nice at this time of year?

* * *

Norah clung to him, tears flowing too freely to show her face in the crowded airport. Maybe this was worth risking her career for, risking everything on the chance that they could make it work. Maybe if she loved him this much, it was enough. How the hell was she supposed to know? There were no experiments she could run, or hypotheses to test. It was the mess of life she'd tried her hardest not to get mixed up in.

She pulled away, blinking wildly to stem the tears. She held him at arm's length, but undermined her own action by gripping his shirt in her fist. 'You're my best friend... bigfoot,' she murmured. 'Don't... hate me for leaving.'

He covered her hand with his own. 'Does it look like I hate you? I'm not built to hate you, Norah. I love you.'

The words made her eyes swim with fresh tears. There were far too many feelings inside her that had no outlet. Well, there was one outlet.

She twisted her fingers in Gianluca's hair and pulled him down for a kiss. It was like the kiss in his studio, when they'd finally been honest with themselves and each other about their attraction. It was like the kisses on Pellestrina, full of heat and the miracle of mutual feelings that both completed and surpassed friendship.

And no matter how Norah wanted to think of this as a farewell kiss, it didn't feel like the kiss of two people who were saying goodbye.

Hearing the word 'Stansted' among the jumble of Italian words coming through the loudspeaker made Norah panic and she wrenched away.

'I'll see you—' Gianluca didn't finish the hopeful farewell. 'I'll... be here,' he said, his expression suddenly miserable. He leaned in to press a lingering kiss on her forehead. 'Go take over the world,' he murmured.

'I was serious when I said you're my best friend,' she said firmly.

He smiled. 'And I was serious when I said I love you.'

She pressed one last soft kiss on his lips, imagining she was transmitting the same words back to him, and then she walked away.

With his cane in her hand, she managed it. She even managed to turn around and give him one last long look.

32

Stones crunched under Norah's boots as she stepped off the gangway and made her way up the spit. She adjusted the rifle on her shoulder, still slightly disbelieving she had to carry it everywhere with her – or that she'd passed the rifle training on her second day at the station. If she actually had to shoot a polar bear, she'd probably lose her lunch, but Svalbard was one of those inhospitable places that brought out different sides to people.

She had no idea what time it was. The sun just made a circle around the sky to denote the passing of the days. With the glacial ice glinting in the summer sun on the rolling brown hills of the island, Svalbard made Venice seem positively normal. This was a frigid lunar landscape, covered with hardy brown grass and a few desperate flowers on the lower plains.

She'd been there a week, working twelve-hour days out on the research vessel and then returning to the lab until she keeled over at night. In the evenings there was nothing to do but play cards with the motley crew of other scientists and technicians. Truthfully, Norah still had far too much time for her brain to wander off and the places it kept returning to felt just as treacherous as an ice sheet populated by polar bears.

A bird call overhead snagged her attention and she snatched up her phone and a pair of binoculars. She snapped a picture of the two birds of prey that were swooping and circling in the swirling breeze. It was easy to create a dialogue about these two:

Hey, you! Long time no see. What are you doing back here?

I missed these winds. Nothing like it. And... the other winds aren't as good without you.

These winds are always better with you, too.

The birds dived and banked in concert, in a little celebratory reunion that was entirely a projection of Norah's mind.

You going to stay this time?

I might have to go check out some other winds sometimes... But if you'll wait for me, I'll come back.

The scene in Norah's imagination got a little too real and she turned away to clear the sadness. She brightened her expression artificially and snapped a selfie with the birds in the background. She'd have to wait for the Wi-Fi at the research station later for the message to send, but she drafted it already, along with a caption:

Norah with gyrfalcon.

It was a sign of her state of mind that she'd ordered a bird identification book for Svalbard before arriving. She wasn't going to change her scientific field, instead she'd bought the book purely to prepare for the messages she planned to send to Gianluca. Although they hadn't talked, they exchanged texts every day – mundane things that were incalculably precious because she sometimes caught glimpses of his face amongst the terrible photos of oars and fórcole.

After she'd admitted that she missed Venice, he'd sent her a flurry of pictures of creepy doorknockers, gargoyles and carved faces in unexpected places, as though he'd known she was still a little freaked out by that stuff. Then he'd sent her a picture of the lagoon, calm and glinting gold in the early morning sun, and she knew all the gargoyles in the world wouldn't scare her off.

She was going to go back, she knew that now. It was just a question of when and how and what her relationship with Gianluca would be when she went. She couldn't keep moving in and out of his life, taking advantage of his warm heart, but she couldn't promise him she'd never leave either. She refused to be a dead weight in Gianluca's life, no matter how much he meant to her.

As she walked back to the station, trailing behind the other researchers who laughed and joked and carried containers of samples, her thoughts snagged on the idea that she needed to do her PhD. As much as she'd discovered another side of life in Venice, she was still a scientist to her core.

Instead of sequestering herself in the lab for hours the following week, she opened up her laptop and skimmed the list of PhD positions Risha had sent. She'd felt too mixed up to face them straight away, but Risha had kept sending them through, until she had a list of about ten positions across the globe that had opened up due to problems or cancellations.

She forced herself to think them through rationally: *Australia*: terrifying. *Singapore*: very hot. *Ohio*: she always got those four-letter states mixed up. *Montreal*: very cold. *Lima*:... Peru! She should just pick one and get on with her life.

But as she sat there staring at the screen, the problem with each of the positions was unfortunately crystal clear: they weren't in Venice. A PhD in Venice would make a lot of sense, if she ignored the practical challenges of finding a position at late notice. That way, if things with Gianluca didn't work out, she'd have her work to fall back on. The research programmes in her field were world-class. Her recent internship positioned her well for any places that might be available. If that was what she really wanted, she could always apply next year if nothing opened up.

As the days passed, she considered it obsessively. She couldn't work in Venice forever – a research career wasn't structured that way. She would have to take a placement elsewhere at some stage. She couldn't imagine how much it would hurt to leave Gianluca if they'd been together for years instead of weeks. But what if they had a chance to make something real, that might survive a separation? Having Gianluca's texts was nothing compared to seeing him in person, but she'd rather have them than nothing at all.

It would never work... He was too wonderful and she was... a mess.

Norah was diluting a sample into a test tube in preparation for DNA sequencing and ruminating as usual, late one night as the sun blazed into the windows, when she came to a realisation so obvious and yet so surprising that she nearly dropped the sample. She hastily placed it back in the holder and grabbed the bench in case she lost her balance.

It wasn't her career keeping her away from Gianluca. It was fear. She was afraid he didn't love her enough – did she even believe that he loved her at all? It seemed too good to be true. As a child, Norah had always felt like Saffron's afterthought – loved, yes, but not enough for Saffron to get her life in order. To Didi, she'd been the little sister who'd made Didi grow up too fast. Andrej had found it far too easy to let her go.

She hadn't been enough for Manu, either, despite her willingness to work long hours in the lab. She'd been little more than a means to an end.

Norah had never been enough for anyone. How was she supposed to believe Gianluca loved her enough to make this work, despite the obstacles and the uncertain future, despite the short time they'd known each other?

She thought of Saffron and Neal and their unconventional wedding vows, the culmination of a relationship of less than a year. It didn't make rational sense, and yet she couldn't doubt their relationship any more. Saffron had worked through her lifetime of disappointment to trust in happiness with Neal and he obviously appreciated her eccentricities in a way no one had before.

The same way Gianluca had stood at the back of his boat and allowed Norah to discover who she was. He'd never made her feel any less than welcomed and then wanted.

Didi, too, had worked through her heartache, her years of wanting to be close to her family, but needing the feeling of control more. Norah now understood what Didi had gone through, and how her sister had made room, not only for her relationship with Piero to grow, but also for a more open relationship with Saffron. If her uptight sister had fallen in love with an artist who was far from orderly, why couldn't Norah find a way to keep Gianluca in her life?

Norah eventually stumbled to her room and pulled the blinds on the eerie sunshine. Although her thoughts were in turmoil, there was a new measure of peace in her heart and she fell into a deep sleep. Tomorrow, she needed to make some phone calls. Time to stop anticipating and worrying about other people's mistakes and take a risk for what she truly wanted.

* * *

Gianluca's phone rang, but he ignored it. His mind was blessedly blank for once and he was hoping to keep it that way. He had a tiny chisel in his hands and was carving an artichoke-flower motif into a fórcola for a client in the US.

He'd started receiving requests from the US a couple of years ago and had investigated reliable shipping. Since then, the niche group of gondola enthusiasts based across the Atlantic had come to him for their requirements, which had provided a nice extra stream of income.

This fórcola was going to be a masterpiece – not because he was charging more or even because he knew the client well. It was simply proving a successful way to distract himself from how lonely he'd felt since Norah had left three weeks ago.

He'd tried to reason with himself, that he had good friends and Nòna. But it was glaringly obvious that a part of him had been lonely, even before he'd met Norah – a part he'd never realised was there until she'd fitted into it. And he knew he couldn't go and put himself on Tinder and simply date his way out of this.

He didn't believe in the existence of a single soul mate, but, certainly, he'd never felt so... *together* with anyone else.

But that didn't help him work out what to do about it. Gianluca had spent a few days agonising, looking up the place where Norah had gone, only to discover it didn't even have any roads, which felt symbolic after they'd talked about going on a road trip. He had to assume she'd left because she wanted to let him down as lightly as she could. It wasn't the same as what Manu had done, so he couldn't be angry with her, but it was similar enough to sting. Which only proved Norah right.

She'd tried to protect him from more heartbreak, especially knowing, as she had, about his previous relationship, but he'd ploughed ahead as though he would be saved by some miracle of circumstances, because they belonged together and the world would make it happen.

The bell on the workshop door tinkled and he cursed under his breath. He had no patience for tourists. Norah had dealt with them much better than he did. He wasn't a salesman – especially not of his own work. He just wanted to get this spiky leaf on the artichoke flower *just right*. But he couldn't keep a customer waiting forever.

He looked up – and slammed the chisel down onto the workbench in shock. At the door of his workshop stood Manu, watching him with a grimly determined expression, and leaning on her arm was Nòna. He looked between the two of them, blinking wildly.

'Is this some kind of intervention?' he blurted out.

Nòna clucked her tongue. 'You admit it, then? You have not been looking after yourself since Norah left?'

'I am looking after myself,' he defended himself weakly.

'You are working too much,' Nòna scolded him. 'I've never seen that from you, even when you want to start your second business! As the saying goes, "Who pisses against the wind gets a wet shirt"!'

His brow furrowed. 'I'm pissing against the wind?'

'You think this work will help? No, you are making everything worse. What will help is Nòna's risotto – and grappa,' Nòna declared.

Gianluca sighed. Nòna solved everything with grappa. 'Sometimes I think your proverbs are full of shit,' he muttered.

'"We have had our backsides a hundred years in the rain before making *you* a proverb!"' she quoted dismissively. 'Come, now. We need food for this conversation.'

'What conversation?' he asked warily. Nòna and Manu exchanged a look that was a little wild. 'Have you two been drinking together?' he asked.

'Only a little,' Manu muttered. 'Come on, Gianluca. You can't pretend we don't need to talk – about a lot of things.'

He remembered with sudden sharpness the time Norah had told him to speak openly to Manu, but that had been before Manu had shown how ruthlessly she could use people.

'You do know how strong Nòna's grappa is, don't you?' he asked softly as he followed the two of them out of the workshop. 'She still gets it from the co-operative on Sant'Erasmo.'

Manu made an unexpected snort and gave herself a shake. 'That would explain it. But a bit of liquid courage is probably what I need right now.' He studied her with reluctant curiosity as she sighed dramatically and then hiccoughed. 'I don't want to be... a personal failure any more.'

'Is she drunk already? What kind of woman did my son...' Nòna's voice trailed off, as though she'd just realised what she'd been about to say.

'Come on,' Gianluca said softly, pressing his hand lightly to Manu's back and taking Nòna's arm himself.

They walked silently along the grid of canals to Nòna's flat, three generations of an incomplete, accidental family. He stood between the woman who had given him up and the woman who had had no choice but to raise a boisterous boy when she'd been ageing herself. Both of them clung to him.

They settled at Nòna's kitchen table with bread and olive oil and steaming fish risotto in front of them, as well as an unlabelled bottle of grappa and three glasses. Nòna filled them. Her hands shook more and more as she aged, but she could still pour the perfect amount of grappa into a glass with the deftness of youth.

She lifted her glass and paused, giving both Gianluca and Manu her evil eye. They lifted their glasses obediently. 'You two – you sit and drink until you are ready to talk.'

33

She fixed her gaze on Gianluca. 'She doesn't deserve this, but it might help you to hear what she has to say.' Then she knocked back her grappa in one gulp and poured another.

Gianluca and Manu followed suit, not looking at each other. They all ate a few mouthfuls of risotto in silence, before Nòna pointedly cleared her throat and muttered, "'You can't force a donkey to take a crap.'" She huffed and glared at their glasses until they drank the next one.

Gianluca and Manu finally shared a wary look.

'I promised Norah I would talk to you,' Manu began all of a sudden. Gianluca's brows shot up and Manu smiled faintly. 'That got your attention. She made me promise before she left. I offered her anything – any help within my means for her career, for instance – but what she wanted was for me to try to talk to you.'

Gianluca's breath was stuck, emotions leaking in all directions. 'Why are you telling me this?'

Manu swallowed. 'Because I want you to know that, in some ways, she's a lot like me.'

'No, she's not,' he insisted.

Her eyes clouded. 'I mean, we both left you, but not for the reasons you might expect.'

He knocked back the grappa so he could blame his spinning head on the alcohol. 'How is this supposed to help?' Nòna's steely hand gripped his. Her habitual scowl for Manu was present, but there was something else in her expression that made Gianluca pause. Her eyes were dull with hurt and grief and he marvelled at how long she'd held those emotions with no resolution.

Manu gripped the stem of her glass and stared into her next shot, but she didn't drink it yet. 'I gave you up because I was afraid, Gianluca,' she said softly. 'Yes, I had the excuse of the research programme in the States, which complicated things, but there were any number of other solutions for that.'

'Popà wouldn't go with you,' he supplied.

She stared at him. 'You worked that out? But I won't blame him. I didn't give him that option. I could have stayed, done a PhD somewhere else. I could have at least visited you in the semester breaks,' she pointed out.

His feelings pricked again, each word a fresh sting, when he already felt like Nòna's ragged pincushion. 'What are you saying?'

'I grew up with every advantage and many luxuries, but... it came at the cost of a close family. My father was a hard man and my mother reacted by betraying him. They were both miserable. I grew up being pulled between the two of them until sometimes I thought I would break. Then I went to university and I found... life. I found a measure of independence from them. And I found your father.' Manu looked down into her food, pushing it around and forgetting even to pretend to eat.

'You loved him?' Gianluca asked, because he couldn't not, and because the question reminded him again of Norah.

She nodded slowly. 'I was young... It got too serious – not the relationship, but my own feelings. And then I discovered I was pregnant.' Her voice broke. 'I was terrified. I thought my father would pull me out of university if he found out. I saw myself under his thumb again, but with him turning his scorn on me, as he always had on my mother. He'd speak of me so proudly – of my good grades and my scientific study. I was... too weak to stand up to him and too afraid of what would happen to *you* if you grew up with that man in your life.'

Gianluca suddenly understood. Manu had deprived him of a mother, but it hadn't been out of selfishness – or not entirely. 'You didn't visit because you thought he'd find out?' he asked.

Manu's cheeks coloured and she took another sip of her grappa. 'Partly. I was also afraid, at the beginning, that my heart would break. I thought it would be easier for me not to know you. I knew Fernanda and your father would make an excellent family for you. They had shown me hints of what family is supposed to be.'

'What you've never had,' Gianluca commented quietly.

She shook her head dismissively. 'I learned not to want what I couldn't have.'

'But you've been trying to reach out to me.'

'When I heard your father had died, I... got a shock. I didn't hear the news for nearly a year.' She shot a look at Nòna, who didn't flinch. 'I suppose I always thought I'd see him again one day,' Manu continued, her voice losing strength. 'And when I knew I wouldn't, I realised my mistakes were... final. It wasn't a good feeling. I didn't know what to do at first. I know I don't deserve to be a part of your life. When I heard you were starting your charter business, it was too good an opportunity. I could... see you without having to face it all right away.'

Gianluca was surprised how much it hurt, knowing she'd grieved his father, too, but with the pain of the past unresolved. The sympathy coexisted with his anger, rather than replacing it. 'Instead of calling me or coming to my workshop, you arranged for me to work for you and then took advantage of my girlfriend,' he accused. Calling Norah his girlfriend made him want to sit up straighter and take on the whole world if necessary.

'I made a terrible mistake with Norah,' she admitted, her voice quiet. 'I... I can't defend myself. All I can say is that I realised that all I had, my only legacy, is this project. And that will fail, too, without funds. I've bet everything I have – finances, my professional reputation, all of my life's work. It's all I have.'

Nòna clucked her tongue, shaking her head ruefully. 'You don't know anything about family.'

'That's true,' Manu murmured and groped for her glass, downing the shot with a grimace and beckoning for Nòna to refill.

Nòna's gaze was sharp, pinning Manu to the spot. But Gianluca recognised that gaze. It was the look that had accompanied many of the mistakes of his youth and it was a kind of love. Perhaps it was the alcohol reaching his veins, but he felt hot in the face, watching their relationship shift unexpectedly.

'You never had to be alone. Ever,' Nòna snapped.

Manu looked up, meeting Nòna's formidable gaze with the courage of sorrow. 'Even now?' They turned to Gianluca in concert. 'Norah said you wouldn't stay angry with me,' Manu said softly, 'even if I deserve it. She knows you well, doesn't she?'

He had the urge to laugh. Yes, Norah knew him very well. And so did Manu, if she realised that mentioning Norah now would soften him. 'What does it matter? Look, Manu, if you hang around long enough, I'm sure I'll forgive you.'

She took his hand and he stared. 'Fernanda and I have been talking.'

'And drinking,' he muttered.

'I want to help you – and Norah. It's not too late for you.'

'You want to help to ease your own conscience,' he accused.

Nòna grasped his ear and tugged, just hard enough to make her point. 'And *you* are making cowardly excuses!'

'What do you think I should do? Go to the Arctic and fall on my knees begging her to let me stay with her?' he asked, filled with bitter sarcasm that also pinched, because sarcasm reminded him of Norah when they'd first met.

Manu and Nòna were shocked into silence – although it wasn't shock, because a moment later they shared a nodding look and then smiled at him. 'You are smarter than I thought,' Nòna said, beaming.

'What?' he said, looking between them.

'Did you even ask her to stay? Norah is afraid – just like me,' Manu said gently.

'Did she tell you this?'

'No, of course she didn't confide in me. But I do know she loves you and I hate to think... that something I did will stop you from accepting that. Norah's not me.'

'I know that,' he insisted, but he was unable to ignore the truth in Manu's statement. That fragility in him, the bitterness – it was unproductive fatalism, a belief that everyone would leave him. And that was his problem, not Norah's.

He'd started things with Norah under the assumption that they could never be together and he'd fulfilled his own prophecy. But what if he could start again, knowing what he knew now about how much they meant to each other? She'd admitted she loved him and a part of him had dismissed it, but what if she'd meant it as deeply as he had? What if he truly meant as much to her as she did to him?

He suspected Manu was at least partly right: Norah hadn't left because she'd chosen her career over him. She'd left because he hadn't given her another option that she could trust. And he knew how many people in her life had let her down before.

The realisation that *he* might have let her down spurred a

sudden determination to put things right. He didn't know where or how, but he would think of something. He had to think. And his thinking had been significantly impaired by God knew how many shots of Nòna's grappa.

He needed to talk this over with Pino and Chiara – and maybe Didi, if he could work out how to contact her. Gianluca stood, which turned out to be a bad idea. 'Maria vergine!' he cursed as he teetered, earning another scowl from Nòna.

'Ài, fio!' Nòna exclaimed. 'What did the holy mother of God ever do to you?' She punctuated her question with a furious hand gesture.

'Nothing, but the mother of my father got me drunk,' he mumbled. 'I'm... going to go and work this all out.' He took a step and the room didn't spin too much, so he figured he was all right to leave. He managed to lean down to kiss both of their cheeks in farewell. 'Are you all right?' he asked Manu, hoping she hadn't drunk as much as he had.

'Go, go!' She waved her hand a little wildly. 'I'm okay, now. Fernanda! More grappa!'

Gianluca stared, his hazy thoughts not questioning this development as much as they should have. Instead he lifted a heavy hand. 'Be good, you two.'

* * *

Gianluca's tongue felt distinctly hairy and when he blinked his grainy eyes open, the world was fuzzy. As his surroundings gradually came into focus, he realised he was sprawled on a sofa in an unfamiliar room.

He remembered phoning Pino the night before and stumbling to the boatshed. His friends had bundled him into a boat and plied him with more alcohol, for a reason which had made sense last night, but escaped him now. If he'd found some clarity in drunkenness, he didn't remember what it was.

He rolled over and groaned.

'Haven't slept it off, yet, then?' came an unfamiliar voice. 'You've beaten your own head with wood, fio.'

It felt as though he were still beating his head with wood. 'Where am I?' he mumbled.

The unknown man clucked his tongue. 'Even I know your nòna's grappa is deadly. You were out as a balcony when your boys brought you here last night. And now you must regret it.'

'Can I regret it when I've had a glass of water?'

'I'm not going to nurse you like a child.' The voice was much closer now, so Gianluca forced his eyes open again. Salvatore Zanetti stood before him – Piero's father. What the devil?

He held out a glass of water, which Gianluca took with a muttered, 'Grasie.' He looked around for his phone out of habit; Norah often texted late at night. He found it, only to see he had 1 per cent of his battery charge remaining. The screen lit up for long enough to show him that he had several messages from Norah, before shutting down.

'Can del porco eso! To mare vaca!' he muttered at his phone. God, hadn't he decided yesterday that he was going to do something to make things right with Norah? Why was he lying on Salvatore's sofa with a blinding hangover when he should be doing... something? He was going to kill Pino.

'Are you insulting my mother?' Salvatore said as he emerged with a plate of bread and a steaming cup.

'El me scuxa, sior Zanetti,' he said.

To his surprise, Salvatore snorted with laughter. 'Your friend was right. You are hungover not only from grappa.'

Gianluca blinked, his sluggish brain struggling to follow. 'Hmm?'

Salvatore clapped him on the shoulder, which nearly made Gianluca spill his coffee. 'Love, boy. You are hungover from amore!' Gianluca eyed him, but slurped the coffee gratefully. Salvatore continued to study him with an amused grin. 'You don't remember why you're here,' he commented. Gianluca shook his head, heat stealing up his neck. 'You will find out in a minute.'

On that ominous note, Salvatore disappeared again, through a door Gianluca assumed led to the kitchen, and then emerged with his phone, tapping it absently. It rang and Salvatore connected the call with a smile, holding it in Gianluca's face. On the screen was Piero, a grim expression on his face.

Piero called Gianluca a devil pig and insulted his parents quite thoroughly, before getting to his point. 'Why has she escaped to the fucking Arctic? What the devil did you do?'

Gianluca was glad he still remembered the answer to that question. 'I didn't ask her to stay. And I didn't offer to go with her,' he admitted quietly.

That shut Piero up. He was visibly taken aback. 'Col casso, why didn't you? She finally found someone she really loves! Chel insemenìo del tóso!' he muttered. 'The boy is a fool.'

'I'm done being a fool,' Gianluca said. 'In fact, I think that's why I'm here?' He glanced at Salvatore as vague memories from the night before returned to him. 'If you're done insulting my dead father, I could use your help.'

'Give me the phone, Piero,' he heard Didi say in English in the background. 'You've had your fun.'

Piero shot an innocent look to someone off-screen. 'Wasn't that the plan? Good cop, bad cop?'

'You're a very bad cop,' Didi said drily. She appeared on the screen, frowning when she saw him. 'Are you still drunk?'

'I don't think so.'

'Just don't let Salvatore give you any hair of the dog,' she advised. 'Good. Pino said you needed our help. What are you going to do?'

Piero interrupted. 'Pino said he needed a kick up the—'

'I think he's had the kick up the backside, don't you?' Didi said.

'But if he's hurt Norah...'

'I know. It makes me happy to see you so protective of her,' Didi said, giving Piero a quick kiss, as though she'd forgotten Gianluca was watching.

'I'm not going to hurt Norah!' Gianluca insisted. He remembered with a flash the realisation he'd come to the night before, propped up on Pino's shoulder while his friend tried to stop him falling drunk into the lagoon. Pino had asked him if he'd given up on Norah because of what had happened the last time he'd got involved with someone who was only visiting.

The question had struck him as all wrong. He'd let Anna go because his place at home in Venice was more important to him. This time... Venice was still home, still important, but he would leave in an instant if Norah asked him to.

The only remaining problem was that Norah wouldn't ask.

'I should have talked to her properly before she left,' he muttered.

Didi glanced off-screen. 'Sometimes we don't realise what we've got until we've lost it. But it's not too late. I'm sure it's not.'

'I hope not. She's been sending me a lot of bird photos, so I think that's a good sign.'

'From Norah? That sounds like a declaration of love.'

Gianluca grinned, thinking of his dear friend, how prickly she'd been at the beginning, how stubborn and intense.

'"Hope is the altar of fools,"' Salvatore called out from the corner of the room. Gianluca saw a sudden image of Christmases to come, with Salvatore and Nòna sitting across the table from each other, quoting proverbs and sipping grappa in a competitive manner that would become increasingly slurred as the night wore on. 'Have confidence, or give up!'

'That's not very helpful, Salvatore!' Didi called back, muttering something about the men in that family.

'I suppose I'm going to have confidence, then,' Gianluca said, glancing at Salvatore.

'Good man. Does that mean I've done my job? I'm sick of stupid young people and their love disorders!'

Gianluca chuckled, sharing a smile with Didi. 'Don't worry. I'll work things out with her. I have to.'

'What are you going to do?' Didi asked. 'She'll be in Svalbard until September and then God knows where, if she gets a PhD position. You have to convince her somehow to come back to Venice!'

Gianluca smiled to himself. That was what Didi thought, but it was now clear to him what he truly needed to do.

34

Norah buried her face in her hands and took a deep breath. It had been a nightmare day of phone calls, after she'd had to beg a day off from sampling. She needed to pop back to the lab to check her propagators at least, but she'd had nothing but discouragement and far too many terse Italians yelling, 'Pronto!' at her instead of answering the phone like normal people. She was sick of explaining herself over and over and receiving the same answer: no.

She was frustrated and, if she was honest, panicking a little. But now she knew what she wanted, she would fight to get it. She had a few more departments on her list.

Her call connected to the department at the University of Padua with a 'pronto'. She still wasn't sure what she was supposed to say in return, so she launched into her spiel, wondering if it even made sense any more, or if she was just babbling.

'So, I'm just asking if you have had anyone pull out of their PhD or, um, if you're looking for someone. I have experience in the Venice lagoon and am entirely flexible about the project. I can write an appropriate proposal to any timeframe, if there might be...

something...' She trailed off and winced. *Great, Norah. Super professional.*

'We have no cancellations from our new PhDs,' came the expected answer and Norah dropped her forehead to her desk, glad the woman on the phone couldn't see her. 'But one of our teams has recently received some funding for a new project and I believe the group leader is considering taking on someone else. It could become a PhD position, when it's finalised.'

Norah's head shot up again. 'I'd love to apply!'

A little laugh on the other end revealed she'd come on a little strong, but she was a damn good scientist – at least she had stopped worrying that the opposite was true. 'The group leader is in the office today. If you will hold the line, I will ask her to speak to you, if she has time.'

'Thank you!'

An hour later, she put down the phone with a pervading sense of disbelief. She'd done it. Well, she still had to write a proposal in a hurry – a proposal that was so good, no other candidate would get a look-in. But she'd taken a step – a big one – and found a path she wanted to follow. This was a chance she was going to take with both hands, even if it meant she had one more phone call to make that day – one she wasn't looking forward to. She dialled the number and tapped her fingers on the desk as she listened to the tones.

Her phone flashed up and she glanced at it to see that Gianluca had sent her a photo. She was about to tap on it when the phone call connected.

'Pronto.'

'Uh... hi, Manu.'

'Norah? Cara! I am so happy to hear from you!' Manu exclaimed. Norah hesitated. That had not been the response she'd expected. 'How *are* you? Is it freezing cold there? What species do they have?'

Norah took the easiest question first, explaining her work and the Arctic algal bloom that was just beginning. With anyone else, she would have cut herself off well before she got to the bits about quantitative sampling, but Manu kept asking follow-up questions.

'Perhaps we can arrange for the transport of some samples to our labs here. Could you ask?' Manu said.

'Sure,' Norah said. 'I'd be glad to help,' she said with some uncertainty.

'But I imagine... this wasn't why you called,' Manu responded. Norah thought she heard the older woman swallow but this didn't need to get personal. Norah only wanted a recommendation – a strong one – and someone to look over her proposal. She was about to explain herself when Manu continued. 'I owe you an apology – many apologies.'

'It's okay—'

'It's *not*, Norah. I was neither a good mentor to you *or* a good friend. I should have explained I wanted to pitch the project to Neal. I was afraid you'd refuse or that it would cause a conflict of interest while you were working for me. It was unprofessional and a mistake I won't repeat.'

'Okay,' Norah said slowly. Manu's tone indicated she wasn't finished.

'And... when it was clear Gianluca meant a lot to you, I panicked. If you... chose him instead of your career, what would that say about me? What would happen to my relationship with Gianluca? I had no right to involve my own feelings. I do believe the Biotechnology Centre will be lucky to have you. You could still go. And it wouldn't have to mean... People have long-distance relationships all the time. It's not so far from Venice, you know.'

'It's over four hundred miles!'

Manu's sigh was long and eloquent, as though she was disappointed by the fact. What was going on? 'Something would work out,' she said firmly. 'If you love him, it would work out.'

'That's... unexpected, coming from you,' Norah replied as her mind raced to process Manu's words. She could feel a subtext she didn't understand. 'But I didn't... that's not why I called. I need a favour – a professional favour.'

'Of course, of course, but... Just don't do what I did, cara. Don't give up. I don't want to have to sit you down in thirty years and force-feed you grappa until you are numb enough to be able to express your true emotions. Who am I kidding? I will never be as fierce and... wonderful as Fernanda.'

Norah coughed, choking on a response. 'Please, don't worry, Manu. I've already made a different choice. You can save the grappa.'

'Good, because I think I'll be happy if I never see a glass in my entire life,' she muttered.

Norah frowned, perplexed, but carried on to put Manu out of her misery. 'That's why I was calling. I was way too late for most programmes, but there might be a last-minute opening for a PhD student at the University of Padua. I wanted to ask for a letter of recommendation and whether you could help me with the proposal.'

'Padua, Illinois?' she asked haltingly.

'No! Padova, Veneto. Why would I go to Illinois when everything I... love is in Veneto?'

Her gasp was so loud that Norah had to pull the phone from her ear. 'Oddio! This is true?'

'I just got off the phone with Dr Rossi. They have some funding and I can apply.'

'Grazie al cielo, you really love him! I must tell Fernanda!' Manu cried. 'The job will be yours!'

'Hang on,' Norah said. 'I still have to believe I've earned it.'

'I will give you some advice: you will have times when you feel like a fake no matter what. But don't think that way. It's not true. I will give you the recommendation you deserve. I don't know Dr Rossi well, but I know your experience with me will mean a lot to the project. All of that you have earned. And you will be back with us! Everything will be right again.'

'Uh,' Norah huffed, 'that's all very starry-eyed. But you can't tell Gianluca yet.' She bit her lip as she considered her next words. 'What if it doesn't work out? And I have to find a way to tell him where he doesn't feel like he's responsible for me. I'm coming back on my own terms so he... shouldn't feel pressured... into anything. I know he's had a bad experience, so I don't want him worrying that history is repeating itself.'

'Oh, don't worry about that. You brilliant, wonderful woman!'

Well, she could say for certain that she felt valued for herself just then.

While she waited for Manu to stop her gushing, she picked up her phone to look at the picture Gianluca had sent. It was a bird. She'd started the tradition so she supposed she shouldn't be disappointed it wasn't a selfie. It was an odd-looking black-and-white water bird with a fine beak. His caption read:

Any idea what species this is? Some kind of duck, I think.

'Well, thank you, Manu,' Norah mumbled, distracted. 'I'll see you, hopefully, in October for the start of term. I'll send you over my draft proposal in a few days.'

'And in the meantime, I will phone Dr Rossi.' Manu sighed audibly. 'October is so long to wait.'

'You're telling me,' Norah said with a sigh.

'It will all work out. Now, I have a phone call to make. Fernanda sends her greetings, too.'

'You never said why you—'

'We'll talk soon!' Manu said, cutting her off. 'And don't forget the samples for me.'

'I won't,' Norah said warily and then Manu hung up. What an odd phone call. Norah shrugged and opened up her messaging app again. She typed out a response to Gianluca, glad she was connected to the Wi-Fi during the day for once.

Send me a selfie with the bird and I'll tell you what species it is.

A few minutes later, another photo popped in and she tapped on it with far more excitement than the occasion warranted. There he was, his hair blowing in the wind, a wild swirl over his forehead. His chin was cut off, but she could see the little smile on his face. Looking at him was everything – and not enough.

The caption read:

Eccomi. Now can you tell me what kind of duck this is?

She regretted offering, when she remembered that her bird book didn't cover the species of the Venice lagoon or the Adriatic. There might be some Arctic birds in the lagoon over winter, but the birds that migrated south did not do so in the summer.

Before she spent too long sifting through pictures on the Internet, she downloaded an app, feeling as though she was cheating, but not minding if he teased her about it. The app made a clear identification, with 90 per cent certainty. But when Norah clicked on the bird, she frowned. It couldn't be right. She picked up her book, locating the entry.

It was a male common eider, an Arctic breeder. She typed a reply carefully.

He's a long way from home...

She stared at the picture again as she waited for his reply. She couldn't see anything except water in the background. He was either a terrible photographer or...

No, what she was thinking was crazy. Gianluca's reply dropped in – four words that did nothing to allay or confirm her suspicions.

For sure he is...

Norah didn't know what to think. All she knew was that she was incapable of resisting the hope. He couldn't be on his way, not to Svalbard, the most remote posting she'd been able to find to escape her feelings. Andrej hadn't even followed her to London when she'd needed him most.

Gianluca just couldn't be that wonderful. Her phone pinged with another message.

You're not out on the ship today?

She typed back immediately.

Nope. In the lab now. I won't bore you with algae pics.

I'll accept a selfie with algae, if you don't have access to birds.

She chuckled, the smile spreading across her face. She arranged her lab coat until it billowed all around her and found a pair of protective glasses to complete the look before snapping a selfie and sending it.

Here you go: science is such a hot look.

His immediate reply made her choke.

God, I miss you. You're so beautiful to me.

Her fingers shook, hovering over the keypad. She bit her lip, wondering if he knew the effect his words had on her. She wrote back quickly.

You're so full of shit *kiss emoji*

35

Casso, he was freezing. He shouldn't have been surprised. It was the *Arctic* after all. It was five degrees – colder than many winter days in Venice – and there were ice floes everywhere. Trust Norah to run off to the most godforsaken place. She didn't make herself easy to catch.

Gianluca stood out on the deck of the *Polar Explorer*, the only ship that took paying passengers – usually tourists – around Svalbard, as they inched along the dramatic coastline. He pulled his scarf tighter and marvelled at the odd quality of the light that made the landscape entirely surreal, as though he'd followed Norah into another realm.

They'd left Longyearbyen, what Svalbard optimistically called its capital, the day before yesterday and hadn't seen a settlement since. This afternoon they'd finally reach the British research station, where the captain had reluctantly agreed to drop him off although no one seemed quite sure whether it was allowed.

Apparently no one had ever been crazy enough to follow the woman they loved to this remote Arctic research station.

After a morning stop at a slippery glacier – which he felt a certain affinity for, coming, as he did, from another place threatened by climate change – the *Polar Explorer* finally made its way into the inlet where the drab research station stood at the top of a rocky incline by a makeshift stone spit.

Gianluca's heart pounded as he finally saw his destination, but he was grinning. It was an ugly structure from the 1970s on a pile of dirt with patches of snow, but it looked strangely like home.

A chunky ship with a crane on the back was moored at the spit, so the *Polar Explorer* came to a stop a hundred metres away. The captain approached him with the perplexed expression Gianluca had grown to expect.

He stroked his beard. 'Ready to go? We can't moor, so Kore will take you ashore.'

'Thank you.' Gianluca held out his hand to shake the captain's.

He shrugged. 'You might not thank me if you can't get off this rock again.'

Gianluca climbed into the dinghy and the captain passed down his beat-up backpack. A moment later, they were motoring towards the shore. As they approached, he saw figures moving along the spit, carrying equipment from the ship in the direction of the research station. They looked up and stilled as they realised the dinghy was coming towards them. Someone waved and the crew member, Kore, waved back.

They pulled up to the spit, the dinghy rocking in the gentle waves and knocking on the stones.

'Got a visitor for you!' Kore called out.

'A visitor?' a tall man with a dishevelled beard called back in disbelief. Kore prompted Gianluca with a look.

'Eh... I'm looking for Norah. Norah York.' More members of the rugged crew of windblown scientists gathered to watch.

The first man called out, 'Norah, some boyfriend of yours is here!' without taking his perplexed gaze off Gianluca.

Even then, he didn't question his decision. He heard stones crunching in the unmistakable, slightly uneven cadence of her steps and she stepped out from behind her colleagues. The otherworldly sunlight glinted behind her. Her hair had grown so long that it poked out from beneath her beanie on one side. She was wrapped up in a puffy jacket and a scarf that covered her chin and she carried a rifle casually over one shoulder.

He grinned, flooded with relief to see her again, dazzled and so certain of his feelings that he couldn't hold it all in.

The words tumbled out. 'Norah, ti amo tantissimo,' he murmured.

'Gianluca! What are you doing here?' She dropped the gun and rushed towards him in a blur. She grabbed a fistful of his coat and tugged. 'Gianluca,' she said again, her voice wavering and her eyes shining with gathering tears.

He couldn't get up onto the spit fast enough. His foot slipped, but she had an iron grip on his coat and he realised how much he liked the role reversal. She'd arrived in Venice out of her depth and a little fragile and he'd helped her in and out of boats many times. But today, she was the one helping him out of the boat, bringing him into her world.

'You left Venice and you haven't disintegrated,' she said, studying him. She loosened her grip on his coat and opened her palm on his chest.

'Still whole,' he confirmed. *Better now.* 'Just cold.'

'Why did you come all this way?'

'Why do you think?' he said, forcing himself to take a much-needed breath. Norah's face was close and everything inside him settled into place. He reached a clumsy, semi-numb hand to her cheek.

She flinched, pulling back. 'Your hand is *freezing!*' she grumbled, but her mouth twitched in the beginnings of a smile.

'Of course, it is. You went to the damned Arctic!'

'You didn't have to follow me,' she said, crossing her arms.

Gianluca stifled a smile with some difficulty. 'Yes, I did,' he insisted. 'I had to come.'

She blinked. 'Because you wanted to see the midnight sun?'

He smiled at her, marvelling again at the way they slipped naturally into easy banter. But he wasn't going to let her get away with using jokes to deflect her fears – her feelings. Not this time. 'Because I wanted to see *you*.'

'But you hate leaving Venice.'

'Here I am,' he said simply, knowing any number of words would not make the point better than that.

She tugged off one glove with her teeth, shoved it into her pocket and raised one hesitant hand to his face. When her warm fingertips settled against his skin, she exhaled heavily and her eyes drifted closed. 'Here you are,' she repeated in a whisper.

* * *

Norah decided Gianluca had no idea how rough he looked. His face was pale and his jaw clenched against the cold. His forehead had a permanent wrinkle. His shoulders were hunched. He was wrapped up in an old jacket that wasn't fit for purpose out here and his ears were red from cold.

He was a Venetian out of water and she'd never seen him look so uncomfortable. But, damn, he was gorgeous. The warmth in his eyes, the way he cocked his head and smiled at her – she'd missed him even more than she'd realised. She couldn't believe she'd nearly given up on this – on them. And had he really muttered, 'Ti amo,' a moment ago or had she wished it?

She curled her hand around his neck and tugged. He sighed,

shaky with relief, and Norah slowly unravelled. Their lips met, parted and aching.

One kiss became several, punctuated by amused laughs and cheers from Norah's colleagues and the clatter of her cane when Gianluca lifted her with his arms tight around her waist. She knocked his beanie off and ran her fingers through his thick hair, cupping his cheeks as she pressed more kisses to his mouth.

'I missed you,' she hummed between kisses.

'I missed you, too.'

'I'm sorry I left.'

'I'm sorry I didn't leave with you. I—'

He tried to say something, but she kept kissing him. Eventually he laughed, and she reluctantly drew back.

When her feet touched the ground again, she pressed her cheek to his chest and squeezed tight until he made a little 'oof' and stroked a hand down her back.

'I love you,' she whispered. 'I'm sorry I didn't say it at Treviso. I wanted to.'

'I'm sorry I said it but I didn't reinforce it with actions.'

She shook her head. 'I should have believed you – I kind of believe you now. No one else would be mad enough to visit me here.'

He pressed a kiss to the top of her head. 'You need to believe me. There isn't anywhere worse I could follow you. Apparently, I'm stuck here, too. That tourist boat could bring me here, but they're not allowed to pick me up again.'

Norah lifted her head. 'What?' Any final protests that it was too good to be true began to crumble at his words.

He grinned. 'I'm not visiting. I'm staying – here, and wherever you go after that.'

She stared up at him, barely registering the tears rapidly cooling on her cheeks. She'd decided to give this love a chance by staying in

Venice as long as she could, but he was two steps ahead of her. He was giving them more than a chance, he was giving her everything. He didn't even know she'd decided to stay.

His thumbs brushed at her tears and he stroked her face. 'We belong, nanarèła. Friends, partners and lovers – family.'

'But... your workshop.'

He shrugged. 'It'll keep. Maybe I can rent out the space for a few years. I can... make other stuff.'

Norah's breath whooshed out. She couldn't doubt him when he'd stranded himself here – or when her own heart said the same thing.

What Andrej had done – what *Manu* had done – were not reflections on her. No matter what crap she'd believed about her self-worth, the truth was staring her in the face, now – from up close, where he rested his forehead against hers.

His arms tightened around her waist. 'Maybe we can talk about going back... one day. But I want this... you... enough that I'll live anywhere if it means we're together. I'll miss Venice, but, these past few weeks, I missed you.'

Her tears came in earnest then. 'Stop making me cry. I have something to tell you, too.'

'Please don't say you're doing your PhD up here.'

She gave him a wobbly smile. 'It is about my PhD,' she said. 'It's not confirmed yet, but... I might have a chance to do it at the University of Padua. The lab is in Chioggia. I'm writing the proposal now and Manu will vouch for me.'

His mouth dropped open. 'When did you...? Why...? You don't have to... for me.'

'I had to,' she echoed his words from earlier. 'For you – for us. I'll probably have to leave Venice at some stage, but... maybe I can make it... my home, first?'

He gathered her close again, his expression unbearably touched. 'It's your home already,' he murmured.

She tucked herself against him and smiled. 'I think you might be right.'

* * *

The weeks on Svalbard passed slowly. Norah earned another glowing recommendation from the team leader and spent her spare time designing a tattoo, which would resemble a chain of phytoplankton winding around her arm, with a little boat and a few ducks hidden in the chain.

Gianluca haunted the research station, willingly becoming the butt of jokes. He played an awful lot of table tennis, with anyone who so much as looked at the table. He wanted to try jogging, but he wasn't allowed to go far and even laps around the station would have required him to carry a rifle. A Swedish research assistant convinced him to take a dip in the frigid water for a bet and he only proved that his vocabulary of curse words was extensive and he had no tolerance for the cold.

He was the first to volunteer to fix anything that was broken and even took apart an old motor, although he grumbled about the fossil fuels and insisted the station should invest in row boats.

By the end of Norah's placement, everyone on the team could sing along with at least three punk-rock songs in Italian and had received something useful or symbolic carved out of the bits of wood Gianluca scrounged from the storeroom. Considering there were no trees on the islands, he'd made do with what he could find and been generally dissatisfied with his work.

Norah and Gianluca's relationship continued as it had begun: squashed together in a single bed and full of laughter.

When the day came for them to finally leave, in late September,

Norah was almost fond of the frigid islands. They couldn't compare to her favourite lagoon, but apparently any place could be magical as long as she went there with Gianluca.

They returned to London in time to help Didi pack up the last of her things. And after a final visit to her friends in Portsmouth, who were very keen to meet Gianluca and hear about the lagoon, they took their one-way flight back to Venice.

Norah clung to Gianluca's hand when they were met at the airport by Pino and Chiara, Manu, Nòna, Didi, Piero and even Saffron and Neal, who were helping Didi and Piero settle into their new house. It was overwhelming to have so much family all of a sudden. She was going to have to get used to it – and get used to how much they loved and supported her.

After a raucous, celebratory meal – something else Norah felt certain she was going to have to get used to – she escaped to Pellestrina with Gianluca, where she would live during the week, to be in easier reach of the lab in Chioggia.

The house was a mess, with workmen halfway through installing a heating system so the house would be liveable in winter. A kitchen was stacked in boxes in the downstairs room, ready for Gianluca to build it.

'Welcome to Venice, eh?' Gianluca said with a rueful smile. 'I would have got it ready for you, but...'

She slung her arms around his neck. 'But you stranded yourself on Svalbard with me.' She gave him a smacking kiss. 'I approve of your priorities.'

'I love having... priorities. Welcome home, nanarèla,' he whispered, pressing a kiss just below her ear.

'Thanks for bringing me home,' she whispered back. 'Bigfoot,' she added with a grin.

EPILOGUE
FIVE YEARS LATER...

'Pina! Get off the wall! It's not for climbing on!' Didi picked up her long skirt and set off after her adventurous three-year-old in the heels that no longer seemed like a good idea. Piero laid a hand on her arm to still her and went after their daughter himself, plucking her off the stone wall and lifting her high in the air until she giggled.

The lagoon shimmered in the afternoon heat, crickets singing their own serenades as the water lapped at the rocks on the other side of the wall. Scrubby islands dotted the still water and the sky stretched, wide and bright, over Burano in the distance.

There were grass stains on Pina's bright blue dress and the bow in her hair was askew. Norah loved her niece to bits, even though she hadn't seen as much of her as she would have liked during her post-doc placement in the Caribbean. Pina had made life... interesting for Didi and Piero, but for an aunt, she was a wonderful, stubborn delight – a reminder that family existed to smooth over faults.

Pina's sister, Giorgia, lay in her Zio Lulu's arms, dropping off to sleep peacefully with her knuckle in her mouth. Giorgia was as contented as Pina was curious, laughing at everything with her gummy smile. She had a single tooth now, breaking hearts every time she opened her mouth to coo or grin.

Norah shooed away Manu, who was trying to adjust Norah's wide skirt. The stupid thing had caused too many problems already, making it difficult to walk with her cane and keeping her too far away from the people she loved. Perhaps she and Gianluca should have sneaked here alone and avoided all of the fanfare, but their family would never have forgiven them.

She wouldn't do that to Nòna, who had spent the day clasping her hands together and sighing and saying she'd always known they were meant to be together forever. Then she'd grumble that they'd waited five years, when it had been perfectly obvious to everyone that they were already family. Then Manu would gently remind her that they should be thankful that they hadn't eloped during their time in the Caribbean.

Norah came up behind Gianluca and slung her arm around his waist, leaning her head on his arm to gaze at her niece with a sigh. He met her gaze with an amused smile.

'I know, I know!' she said before he could get the words out. 'Someone's about to ask me if I'm broody and I'm going to bite their heads off!' She fiddled with Giorgia's tiny foot, her smile belying her words. 'I like nieces, though.'

'I like you,' he quipped, giving her a kiss on the forehead.

'Good thing, too, bigfoot, since you just married me.' He grinned, a smile that sizzled down her spine, even through the wonky bits that had healed around the pins. 'And you got nieces in the deal.'

'They were my nieces as soon as they were born,' he said softly. 'Like you were my family even before Brother Giuseppe declared it today.'

'Then why did I have to put on this stupid dress? Although,' she continued, cutting off any answer he might have given, 'I could get used to the suit.' She tugged playfully on his collar.

'Allora, you two?' came a voice and Pino pushed between them, his arms over both of their shoulders. 'He's officially your Italian stallion now, eh?'

Norah snorted and Gianluca wrinkled his nose. 'Do you have any idea how many people made that joke while we were on Guadeloupe?' he groaned.

'I know, I know!' Pino laughed. 'And they all wanted you to row them around singing "That's Amore".'

'But we're home now,' Norah said, looking around at the peaceful gardens, the rows of cypress trees and the friends and family in colourful dresses and formal suits that dotted the lawn. The Caribbean had been nice, but things were... normal, here, in this waterlogged city of ancient wood and crumbling stone.

Chiara approached and kissed them both on the cheek. 'I hope you're not taking too long for a honeymoon. I told some people at the rowing club that you'd be back in the summer and Gianluca's order book is going to explode.'

'And I have a bunch of hotels asking me all the time if you're going to take tourist charters again,' Pino added.

'Piano, piano, fioi.' Gianluca dipped his head in what would have been a sweeping hand gesture if he hadn't been holding baby Giorgia. 'I'm still on Caribbean time.'

'Which is even slower than Sunday time in Venice,' Norah said with a grimace. 'But I reckon *Dafne* has been raring to get out again.'

'She might need a refit and a polish,' Gianluca said with a mock frown.

Norah smiled up at him. 'I'm sure she missed you, too.'

The loud snap of a camera distracted her. 'Wow, what a great photo. Feeling broody, Norah?'

Gianluca laughed, juggling Giorgia so he could take Norah's elbow and turn her away before the steam coming out of her ears became visible to the photographer. 'Can we get a group photo?' he asked over his shoulder.

Pino ended up with the baby, fussing over her as his boyfriend entertained her with peek-a-boo. The newly-weds gathered all of their guests around in front of the crumbling wall of the monastery. Saffron and Neal had to stand at the side. They'd just got back from a safari and Saffron's enormous yellow headwrap would have obscured too many other guests. Neal's tie was in matching fabric. Salvatore waved a lollipop in front of Pina in an attempt to keep her still, but, in the end, she had to go up on her popà's shoulders.

The photographer snapped away and it was these candid shots that Norah enjoyed looking at in the years that followed. There was Didi, smiling up at Piero with that wry sense of humour that life had given her – which she now needed more than ever. Saffron looked between Neal and her daughters and, in one shot, was dabbing at her eye. One photo caught Manu staring at Giorgia with a perplexed kind of longing that broke Norah's heart and reminded her that, although anything could be repaired, nothing could be relived.

In all of the pictures, Gianluca's arm was tight around her. And in Norah's favourite photo, he gazed down at her with a grin, his thumb gently tracing the chain of algae tattooed on her arm, while chaos erupted around them, in the form of their family.

Norah got changed after the photos and they finally made their way down the gravel path to the pier, where Gianluca surprised her by revealing *Dafne* there, already packed for their honeymoon. After lengthy farewells, Brother Giuseppe walked them to the boat to see them off the island of San Francesco del Deserto.

'Grasie, Fra Giuseppe,' Gianluca said, shaking his hand warmly.

The older man nodded. 'I'm just glad you finally made it to the altar.' And with a smile and a wink, he stepped back to allow them to board the boat.

Gianluca blushed and Norah stifled a snort of laughter against his shoulder. 'We'd better go before Brother Marco comes out and tells everyone we slept together in a monastery!'

Gianluca gave her a tolerant smile. 'You told me my feet stank.'

'You called me a duckling.'

'It was affectionate.'

'So was the stinky feet comment.'

Norah grinned and gave him a playful shove towards the boat. They stepped into *Dafne*, Norah now grasping her own oar and settling it into the fórcola at the front.

'Pronto?' he asked.

She grinned at him. 'Andemo, amìgo!'

'Ah, look at those lovebirds.' Saffron sighed, loudly enough that everyone looked at her and laughed.

'You know what "lovebirds" is in Italian?' Gianluca asked.

'I haven't learned that one,' Norah replied.

'Piccioncini,' he told her, his grin widening.

'Pigeons!' she cried. 'No wonder there are so many in Venice!'

When she looked back at Saffron and Didi, so happy in love, and even at Manu and Nòna and Salvatore, who'd known love, she knew it was true. Hers was a city of lovers.

ACKNOWLEDGMENTS

This book was inspired in large part by my amazing sister, Dr Jillian Petersen, who patiently listened to my ideas and answered my questions. But any errors or mistakes in the science aspect are entirely my own, because she is a kick-ass scientist and I am just a sappy storyteller.

The inspiration for the other part of this story comes from another real person, who I have nonetheless very much fictionalised. So, thank you to Piero Dri of the Forcolaio Matto for sharing your passion for an amazing city and a unique craft. You can visit his real workshop in Cannaregio when you head to Venice!

My crew of friends/beta readers have done an amazing job as usual, keeping me sane during this process by being on the other end of the email and giving their invaluable feedback. Lucy Morris and Lucy Keeling – I love you guys as always. Jenna Lo Bianco – I'm sorry I keep wasting your precious time with my messages, but THANK YOU for answering my questions and sharing your enthusiasm for all things Italian.

And lastly, I want to thank everyone who's picked up a copy of this book, or the first in the series, *A Match Made in Venice*. I'm so grateful to every one of you and I hope you've enjoyed your trips to Venice. I also hope it's brought to life this amazing place in your minds and that we can all find a way to protect and respect the endangered city and its lagoon.

MORE FROM LEONIE MACK

We hope you enjoyed reading *We'll Always Have Venice*. If you did, please leave a review.

If you'd like to gift a copy, this book is also available as an ebook, digital audio download and audiobook CD.

Sign up to Leonie Mack's mailing list for news, competitions and updates on future books.

https://bit.ly/LeonieMackNewsletter

A Match Made in Venice, another wonderful read from Leonie Mack is available to order now.

ABOUT THE AUTHOR

Leonie Mack is a bestselling romantic novelist. Having lived in London for many years her home is now in Germany with her husband and three children. Leonie loves train travel, medieval towns, hiking and happy endings!

Visit Leonie's website: https://leoniemack.com/

Follow Leonie on social media:

 twitter.com/LeonieMAuthor
 instagram.com/leoniejmack
 facebook.com/LeonieJMack

ABOUT BOLDWOOD BOOKS

Boldwood Books is a fiction publishing company seeking out the best stories from around the world.

Find out more at www.boldwoodbooks.com

Sign up to the Book and Tonic newsletter for news, offers and competitions from Boldwood Books!

http://www.bit.ly/bookandtonic

We'd love to hear from you, follow us on social media:

facebook.com/BookandTonic

twitter.com/BoldwoodBooks

instagram.com/BookandTonic

9 781801 623957